ALSO BY RANDOLPH LALONDE

THE CHAOS CORE SERIES

Trapped

Cool Pursuit

Savage Stars

THE SPINWARD FRINGE SERIES

Spinward Fringe Broadcast 0: Origins

Spinward Fringe Broadcast 1 and 2: Resurrection and Awakening

Spinward Fringe Broadcast 3: Triton

Spinward Fringe Broadcast 4: Frontline

Spinward Fringe Broadcast 5: Fracture

Spinward Fringe Broadcast 6: Fragments

The Expendable Few: A Spinward Fringe Novel

Spinward Fringe Broadcast 7: Framework

Spinward Fringe Broadcast 8: Renegades

Spinward Fringe Broadcast 9: Warpath

Spinward Fringe Broadcast 10: Freeground

Spinward Fringe Broadcast 10.5: Carnie's Tale

Spinward Fringe Broadcast 11: Revenge

Spinward Fringe Broadcast 12: Invasion

Spinward Fringe Broadcast 13: Warriors

Spinward Fringe Broadcast 14: Rebel

FANTASY

Highshield

Brightwill

HORROR

Dark Arts

www.RandolphLalonde.com

Spinward Fringe Broadcast 0:
ORIGINS
A Collected Trilogy

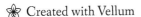 Created with Vellum

SPINWARD FRINGE BROADCAST 0: ORIGINS - A COLLECTED TRILOGY

RANDOLPH LALONDE

BOOK 1: FREEGROUND

PROLOGUE

The Last Mission

THE ODDS WEREN'T in our favour. They rarely were, but this time it was different. The stakes were higher.

As I drifted through the silence of space in my Raze Starfighter, I watched the shadows of the debris around my ship pass overhead. Our wing was hiding amongst thousands of meteors that we'd stirred up and directed at a nearby gas giant. All systems were deactivated, including life support.

There were one hundred of us this time; all set up in fighters, bombers and shuttles. In times like these, everyone's performance was critical. Signal silence had to be observed. Only my low-power personal computer was on, and it was set to passive mode, only receiving signals. My suit's shielding prevented it, and my life signs from being detected at a distance.

People were watching, machines were scanning for

anything in the field that could be something other than rock. It was hard to stir up so much mass and send it close to the munitions station. If one of us were scanned because we were just a little out of place, all that work would be for nothing.

I looked towards our target through the cockpit and barely caught a glimpse. It was massive, two wheels surrounding a tall centrepiece hanging in orbit around a gargantuan blue and purple gas giant. The station looked small even though it was over a hundred kilometres across with fighter bays, drone launch tubes, dozens of point defence turrets, and missile launchers. No one had ever gotten anywhere near it. Beyond it were small silhouettes against the sun. One of the All-Con Fleet Battle Groups had stopped in to rearm and would be there for several days. They suspected someone would attack the station.

The command and control display on my wrist, counting down the distance between us and the station, showed 43,477 kilometres and I knew that in less than four thousand we would know whether or not the station saw us as a threat. It would come quick, just a flash of light and it would all be over. Modern super nukes were like that, no harmful residual radiation, just a massive flash and over four hundred kilometres worth of matter would be gone.

I caught myself holding my breath and shook my head. Breathe normally, I thought. If we get a chance to see the nuke coming, we might have a chance to turn and run.

I checked my counter again. We'd passed the safe range for a nuclear explosion. If the base hit us with one they would risk shorting out its own perimeter sensors with the electromagnetic pulse and taking damage. That brought us to our next challenge.

The perimeter sensors were finely tuned, and would scan

all passing objects. Thankfully they wouldn't be able to pene-trate our hulls and discover our body heat, but it would trace the outside of all the objects, creating profiles it would look up in the base's database.

We had attached all kinds of random objects to our hulls, making our ships look like floating trash or strangely shaped meteors made of compressed garbage jettisoned by some unknown interstellar vessel. If it worked, we'd be past the perimeter sensors, but if someone didn't disguise their ship well enough or activated any kind of system, we'd be finished. Once one of us was found out, the station would send a squadron of fighters to check it out or they'd just start shooting at the meteors and we'd get ground up in a blender of colliding rock and debris.

I looked back to the counter on my arm display and watched the kilometres tick away. We were closing on 20,000km and fast. The gravity of the massive gas giant below was tightening its grip. An All-Con Fleet destroyer was moving towards the station, and I found myself wondering if we'd have to use it for cover later.

Two years ago, when I joined up with this crew, I would have thought the strategy of using a kilometre long fully armed destroyer for cover was absolutely crazy. As I double checked my fighter's thermal silhouette, I found myself acknowledging that it was just another checkpoint on the list we call 'they'll never see it coming'.

My command and control display beeped once quietly and I saw that we were a couple of seconds away from our destina-tion, the closest point we could reach under inertial drift. I watched and waited as it counted down to 937 kilometres. Just as it reached that magic number and started counting up again, I covered my eyes and flipped a switch.

Hundreds of thermal charges planted in the meteors all around us went off with a blinding flash. They weren't hot or explosive enough to change the meteor shower's course, but it would create an intense visible wave of light for hundreds of kilometres that would make it impossible for the station to pick out our fighters until we were close. Real close. They'd need to use visual scans, which wouldn't work well for their computers since our shapes were irregular. That would leave manual targeting until they figured out what we'd done to our ship profiles. "Let's go! Everyone knows what to do!" I yelled into my communicator.

"Yeeeehaw! Seven hundred kilometres and closing! Let's do some damage!" Oz replied.

"Cover the boarding shuttles, if we don't get our people inside this'll be for nothing,"

"Bombers on first run! Don't launch your shells until you can read their serial numbers!" Ronin shouted. I could see him and his thirteen bombers heading off towards the fighter launch bays and drone tubes. There was some activity out there, but not as much as I would have expected. The station computers and personnel weren't sure what was happening yet.

My targeting scanner picked up the first group of fighters coming in from the far side of the station. I turned my ship towards them while floating past the outer ring of the station and started firing. The loaders for my three rail guns vibrated the entire craft as they propelled hundreds of rounds towards the group of fighters. "Marking alpha group," I said as I selected them on my targeting computer. "They're after the bombers."

"It's their funeral!" Ronin called out.

I watched the tactical screen as most of my shots went flying harmlessly through the enemy fighter formation. Then the enemy fighter group started to show some real damage, explosively decompressing and flying to pieces. I looked to where I knew Ronin's fighter group was moving towards the station to see that they were drifting backwards at speed while firing at the incoming fighter group. "Show off."

"All right, let's drop our shells and close the doors," Ronin ordered.

"Boarding shuttles under fire!" I heard Sunspot, the commander of shuttle two, call out.

"Could use your help here, whenever it's convenient. You know, drop by sometime," Oz said over the sound of his turret firing. He was in command of the first shuttle and shouldn't have been in the gunner position, but telling him that was a waste of time.

"On our way," I said. "All interceptors, keep those shuttles clear. Let's make a hole." I spun my ship towards their flight path and hit the thrusters.

"More resistance than we expected, about thirty drones and a dozen fighters," Zanger replied. His fighter group was the primary cover for the shuttles, and I could see that he had lost four out of fourteen.

I caught a glimpse of the fighter bay and saw that the shells Ronin's group dropped had exploded, causing massive damage. That left one launch bay and only a few drone tubes open for business. The station was already hamstrung. I brought his fighter group up on my display to see that they had only lost two and were skimming the hull of the station's inner ring to avoid weapons fire. I had to admit, he was always the better pilot. "Be careful out there, Ronin. There's close then there's too close."

"If what you see frightens you, then stop looking," he replied.

"Old Chinese proverb?"

"No, crazy pilot's advice."

My fighter finished coming around the middle ring of the station as the drones en route to intercept our shuttles came within firing range. I opened up with all three rail guns and scored disabling hits right away. My wing tore through them in no time and had several seconds to get ready before engaging the incoming enemy fighters.

The manned station defence fighters were a different story; they took three of my fighters out right away and I was under heavy fire. One shot struck the loading mechanism for my port rail gun and I had to shut it down.

We scattered, marked our targets, and re-engaged. I sent my fighter hurtling towards the inner ring of the station and spun using manoeuvring thrusters so I faced three of the enemy defenders, all of which were after me. "You see this, Oz?" I asked.

"I see it. Firing right over your head."

My path took me right below his shuttle and he laid down a barrage of cover fire with the rail turret mounted on the back of his ship. I opened fire as well and took out one while Oz took care of the other two. The station was starting to see through the fading distortion of the thermal bombs I had detonated earlier and their defensive batteries started firing. "Get close! We have to stay between the station batteries or this ends now," I shouted

as I watched one of my fighters take several pulse beam hits and
fly apart in super heated pieces.

The boarding shuttles had reached the hull of the station
and docked hard. "Shuttle two docked and popping the cork. I
beat ya here, you owe me fifty, Oz!" I heard Sunspot say over
the comm.

"Shuttle one docked, popping the cork. Oh, and Sunspot?"

"Yeah?"

"Be quiet or I'll tell everyone," Oz replied.

"You wouldn't dare."

"Oh, I would, Sugar, trust me."

I didn't know what they were talking about, but judging
from the tone it was some kind of inside joke. I shrugged and
decided to ask later.

My attention was called back to the moment as a beam
pulse nearly caught my port side. I was almost close enough to
the inner ring to be out of the larger point defence weapons'
lines of sight, but I was nowhere near safe. The hull of the inner
ring loomed larger and larger until I was finally clear of the
beam weapons' firing arc. My wing was down nine fighters;
there were only five of us left, we had lost half of beta wing, and
theta wing was down to only two. "How are you doing, Ronin?
Gamma wing holding together?"

"Just waiting for our shells to go off."

I manoeuvred my fighter so I skimmed along the hull of the
station, trying to stay as close as possible while firing at targets of
opportunity. "Well? Is that second fighter bay out of
commission?"

"They destroyed the shells before they hit. Heading into the bay, take the rest of the wing to the docking site, Mira. Cover them."

"What the hell are you doing, Ronin?"

"I'm setting my reactor to overload and ejecting into the fighter bay. What do you think I'm doing?"

"Bad idea! Just get out of there and we'll try to deal with whatever they launch."

"Good idea, bad idea, what does it matter when everyone already thinks you're crazy? Say hi to my sisters for me." I could hear the sound of his ejection and tried to track him. I was on the other side of the station and there was too much interference between us for me to get a lock.

"Can anyone see him?"

"I did for a second, but then his fighter exploded. I don't think he made it," Mira said. "That bay is a mess, though. I don't think they'll be launching anything today."

As I came around another section of hull, two wings of enemy fighters came into view. "Good, hurry up and get over here, we need help. How is it going, boarding crew?"

"Never saw us coming," Oz reported. I could hear weapons fire over the communicator.

"Oz is down, but his team got the explosives in place. Planting ours now," said Sunspot.

"It's a flesh wound. Just get your little behind back to the shuttle."

I called his status up on my secondary display and saw that he and one other member of his team were the only ones left. They were both badly injured.

"Heading back to the shuttle now. We'll be out in a few seconds," Sunspot said in a rush. I could hear her running.

One of the enemy fighters clipped my starboard side and sent me spinning. I barely had time to figure out where I was before I skipped off the hull of the station and into open space. I struggled with the controls and tried to stabilize the ship.

Just as I was starting to bring it under control, I saw the enemy fighter firing on me. I tried to get a manual missile lock as he whipped past my view. He scored another hit on my hull and flashed past me again. As he came around a third time I hit my secondary trigger and got a lock on him. I fired three missiles as fast as I could and worked to continue stabilizing my ship. "Come on, pick a direction, god dammit!" I growled through clenched teeth to the controls.

I finally got my ship under control just in time to see the enemy fighter explode a hundred meters in front of me. "Collision warning!" my computer warned.

"Smart ass!" I replied as small pieces of my opponent's ship impacted against my hull. My cockpit started to decompress through a leak in the canopy and I was thankful that I wasn't relying on the fighter's environment. My vacuum suit could keep me breathing for days.

Cannon fire from the station streaked across my cockpit canopy. I turned my fighter away from the weapon bank and hit the thrusters. I kept moving back and forth laterally and vertically while I made my way out of the range of the station's weapons. "My fighter's full of holes, I'm on my way out."

"Detonating our charges. The implosions should start in a few seconds. Do you think you can make it to the rendezvous?" Sunspot asked.

I checked the status of my engines. "I only have one ion array left, but I can make it." The energy readings behind me spiked wildly, indicating that the explosives had gone off and the station's core had begun a cascading decompression. "I love your handiwork, Sunspot."

"Why thank you, you're not so bad yourself."

"Make your best speed to the rendezvous point so we can open a worm hole home. I think we've worn out our welcome," Marauder said. He was the pilot and navigator for boarding shuttle two.

The station was no longer firing and I could see lights going out all around the rings through the rear view on my console. I made it to the jump point and counted what remained of our raid fleet. Four fighters, two bombers and the boarding shuttles. Seventy eight casualties out of a crew of one hundred. A flash of light appeared in front of the boarding shuttle. My computer marked the coordinates as the opening point of the wormhole home. We all made the jump. Shuttle one, which held the point open, jumped last.

The simulation ended. "Scenario complete, all win conditions met. Congratulations! Your Academy rank is increased to Brigadier General," the computer said cheerily. "Entering social mode."

Another screen came up on my display, replacing the fighter cockpit and field of stars. It listed all the participants of the scene we had just completed. "Too bad I'm not in the Academy," I said quietly.

"None of us are. Think they'll ever find out who's setting new records in their hardest simulations?" Oz asked.

"I'm sure a few of us would be re-enlisted if they ever did. I wouldn't mind the chance to get in a real cockpit again," Ronin added.

"Some of us are already enlisted, so we already have clearance for these scenarios. I'm sure my C.O. would still have some choice words for me for participating along with uncleared civilians, though. With Marauder's hacks in place, it'll be a while before we have to worry about it. Wish I could stay but I have a duty shift in ten minutes. See you all later. Bye, Horus, I'll see you soon," Sunspot said before she dropped her connection. Her accent always set her apart in simulations. Her speech had a light British manner, and I had to admit I never tired of listening to her.

"I think she likes you, Horus," Oz whispered.

"Yeah, seriously, you two have been flirting for months whenever she's in a scene with you. I can't count how many times I've stepped into the Nessa Club and run into your avatars chatting into the wee hours. When are you two just going to meet and get it started for real?" Ronin asked.

"She told me she's with a ship that's on assignment somewhere out there, I don't see that happening."

"Oh, come on, you've gotta get together with her some time. Living vicariously through you has been seriously dull lately."

"Well then, go find your own squeeze," I replied.

"Bah! With a restaurant to run while living with three sisters? I'll be single forever."

"Seriously, Horus, she's got to make it back to Freeground sometime. No harm in meeting face to face."

"Sure there is, it changes everything. I have a really bad record with meeting people from scenarios. Remember the last one, Ronin?"

"Oh, the Issyrian?"

"Yup. Looked human on the outside, was anything but on the inside."

"Issyrians can't be that bad, can they? They can change their appearance to pretty much anything, I thought."

"They can breathe out of the back of their heads if they want to. I won't go into the unchangeable differences."

"Well, I met Sunspot while I was at the Academy and we've been in touch since. She's as much fun in person as she is in scenes, trust me," Oz interjected. "Oh, and she's a real human. She has this whole cheeky redhead thing going, actually."

"All the more reason not to ruin a good thing, I say. Well, I'd love to stick around and get more love advice from a lonely restaurant owner and a career infantryman, but I've got a shift starting up in a few minutes. Thanks for running that scenario, I can't believe we pulled it off," I said. I took off the virtual visor while the team members said their goodbyes.

ONE

JUST ANOTHER DAY IN THE DARK

There are sectors so dark, so barren, that starliners chart their courses along the fringes. Breaking down in dead space, having to drift for years without any hope of assistance, dissuades the big transportation companies from putting their passengers at risk. Other crews, especially freighter crews and more dubious folk, take the risk, going to sleep for weeks as their vessels make the crossing.

Some visionary decided to build a state of the art repair and resupply station right in the middle of nowhere, where there's literally nothing. For three hundred years, Freeground has been the only beacon of light for travellers, refugees, and those seeking out the darkest spot in our galaxy, right on the fringe downward from the old Sol system.

Once Freeground Station was a massive clover leaf complex with habitat, control, mechanical, and hydroponic sections. By the time I was born here thirty three years ago, it had grown exponentially with kilometre after kilometre of structures including factories, research facilities, ship yards, forests, malls, housing, entertainment centres, and its own military and government based on the ideals of democracy and freedom.

The walking surface area of Freeground is just over half that of Earth, that forbidden blue ball in the distant Sol system. My home looks like thousands of plates connected by circular frames, all spinning, surrounded by skeletal frameworks that stretch out into the dark like long arms and fingers grasping for light that's so far away that it's just a faint glimmer.

I served during the last great war, when the All-Con Corporation spent twenty years trying to take control of the station. They sent fleets and spies, blocked trade, and used misinformation to turn our allies away from us, but we resisted. In the end the Freeground Fleet pushed them back all the way to their home world and destroyed their factories, once again proving that Freeground could not be owned by any corporation or governed by any external body.

I remember those days, setting foot on solid ground for the first time in my life, looking over manufacturing facilities as they went up in smoke. All-Con Prime was already a grey, scorched ruin of a planet before we arrived. They had mined it to the core and covered the surface with thousands of manufacturing complexes. I was shipped planet side to repair a communications array on a troop carrier. I wouldn't have had the opportunity to stand on the surface of the planet if I weren't a fleet technician.

Even through the grey blue sky, the free blowing wind and distant horizon were impressive. I still didn't feel that I had been missing much growing up on Freeground station. Watching the fighter and bomber squadrons fly overhead, I remember wishing

I had served with them instead, seen more fighting. What I didn't know then was that while I was away doing my duty at the front with the last wave, Freeground had suffered a massive coordinated terrorist attack.

Three habitat sections had been destroyed in the blink of an eye; my entire family was gone. Everyone lost someone in the war. No one was untouched. The people who were responsible for the bombings had been living with us for years. These days, Freeground does not favour a stranger.

The Freeground Fleet is filled with people who crave excitement and pursue our enemies on a fraction of a second's notice. I wasn't one of those daring few, however.

When I arrived back home twelve years ago and discovered what had happened to my family, I reported for duty with the engineering and construction crews. We rebuilt the habitats that were destroyed and when that was finished five years later, I became a communications and priority assessment officer in the operations and port control centre.

For four days out of a five day galactic standard week, I discussed the needs and requests for supplies, repairs, and anything else an arriving ship either required or desired. They circled the station slowly, sometimes dozens of them, sometimes hundreds. Military, corporate, and civilian alike, all calmly waiting to be directed by the port artificial intelligence to someone with a beating heart. There was a one-in-fifty chance they would get me. Their requests ranged from the mundane to the unreal. The traders mostly offered more than they requested, some of them willing to do anything to sell their cargo, especially when they knew it wouldn't survive the trip to another port. There were days when I wished I was back between decks, alone, repairing some tertiary system in a neglected section of the station no one visited rather than speaking to one more trader who had already tried peddling his perishable wares to everyone else. Sometimes the sense of entitlement and self-importance travellers carried like rotting baggage was so infuriating it took everything I had to return to work the next day.

I couldn't spend more time than I had to in my quarters, either. I may have helped build the replacement habitation sections but that didn't get me my pick from the hundreds of new homes. What I had was smaller than the bathrooms in the deluxe sections,and it had that easy to disinfect and reassign prefabricated look. However, two rooms were more than some people got; in the hive levels, units are one point two metres tall, one and a half metres wide and three metres deep. So I didn't complain. Much.

That day, like almost every other day, I made my way out of my small home and through the catacombs of hallways until I reached the causeway. The habitation we built years ago was so large that its centre housed a forest. Rows of shops and entertainment centres featuring everything one would expect on a core world, or so I was told, lined the walkway. Awnings shielded their open and closed fronts and seating areas. The perfect circle of streets was filled with people, and many of them wore loose clothing over their reshaped vacsuits. If they sealed them up, they'd be protected from the rain - from anything, really - but there was something undeniably fashionable, visibly human about letting the drizzle wet your hair, or hiding under an extra layer of clothing. The clothes told as much about what people did for a living, about their place, as they did about their income. Some wore square-cut business suits, others were attired in a myriad of garments that provided scant coverage and high style, all the way up to the practical and overly modest.

We Freegrounders are a melting pot of travellers, founder descendants, transients, and lost souls.

I glanced up at the overcast holographic sky and cursed the rain as I stepped out into the open concourse. In half an hour, civil servants would change shifts; the foot traffic was melee thick.

By reflex I closed my black and grey engineer's coat. There was really no need since the Freeground uniform of white and blue I wore underneath was completely sealed all the way up to my jawline. It sustained its own environment, protected from most stellar elements and even sharp objects all in a skin tight shell that was as thin and flexible as common cloth. It was a little too skin tight for my tastes to be honest, so I wore my old engineer's coat, which protected from almost everything the uniform didn't, and held every old tool that survived my career as a field repair technician. Most people looked and wondered where I found one, since it looked like an old trench coat used by ground militia on ancient Earth when impact reactive armour was invented.

Nodding at a passerby, I pulled up the collar and made my way down the sidewalk to Minh-Chu's, a small restaurant that was little more than a booth with a few stools and tables on a widened area of the walkway. Minh, Ronin in the simulations, waved as I approached and started heating some lo mein. He shook some black sauce on it and added vishri, a water vegetable that I had heard tasted just like shrimp, a fish from Earth I had never seen.

"Your mood matches the weather, Jonas."

I poured myself a cup of coffee and nodded. "You'd think they would have planted vegetation that didn't need so much rain. If I had the rank to know what this habitat would be like, I would've found other housing."

"Ha! Watch what you wish for! Someone from Fleet Operations was in here just the other day and she couldn't help talking about Core Port Operational personnel being promoted. The team on your shift is doing such a good job they're looking at promoting the leads. I'd bet you a year of dinner you're on your way up," Minh said as he handed me my bowl of noodles and chopsticks.

"Oh, just what I wanted."

"Don't put down rank, friend. This was my reward for retiring early from Infantry Command; a Kingdom built on noodles and rice. Well, I had to sell that fighter I stole from All-Con Prime too, but it's still my Kingdom."

"I'm your loyal subject, as always. Best lo mein I've ever had," I managed around a mouthful.

"Probably the only lo mein you've ever had. You should get back into Fleet, see some solid ground somewhere. Maybe spend some time at another restaurant. I won't mind as long as you come back with friends."

"One year on All-Con Prime was plenty."

"Not much of a world, especially after we set most of it on fire at the end of the war. You really should get out there, find a nice home world to make landfall on. Just make sure there's a beach and plenty of women around so I'll have something to do when I get there!"

"And leave your Kingdom?"

"Nothing is a constant but change, I've heard someone say."

"Ah, we'll both be here until they rebuild, and even during reconstruction you'll probably be on crowd control duty while I put the roof up. Then we'll just settle again. This is our home world, as intentionally wet and miserable as it can be."

"Who let an old man sit on my friend's favourite stool? Move on, old timer! My friend will be along any minute."

"Ha, very funny."

"You shouldn't be settled so young, people are living to four hundred these days, and they still look fifty!"

"Look who's talking, Mister Restauranteur."

"Oh, I'm not settled! This place breaks even in just under three months, then I start making credits I can keep. Maybe hire someone who can do my job and then I'm free. I could even qualify for Freeground Fleet and join a Reserve Fighter Squad."

"First Infantry, now Fleet."

"Reserve Fleet, my friend. Missions on a mostly volunteer basis, with mandatory patrols twice a week close to home in a Black Hand Interceptor. The only way I'll see combat is if someone attacks the station."

"Unless they promote me to Command and I send your ass out to Kamshi. I hear the Tertiary Battle Group is having a blast maintaining the territorial lines out there."

"You wouldn't take me away from my noodles."

"If they make the mistake of promoting me, there's no telling what they'll let me do."

"Well, then I suppose I'll have to make the best of things out in Kamshi. After they saw our squad simulation replays they didn't have much of a choice."

I couldn't believe he set me up for a promotion. I knew that Minh's days got a little long, and his kitchen staff of four wasn't exactly the most thrilling bunch - especially since three of them were his sisters - but this was beyond beating the boredom. "Which replay? Who did you send it to?"

"The Lost Wing sim. You remember, when you took command of three wings, took us through the asteroid belt, and jumped the Anterans from behind?"

"That was on the secure Academy network! No one is allowed to take on level eight training simulations without clearance, especially since the opponents are trainees and officers!"

"You're a Lieutenant Commander, you have clearance. That's how we were able to play."

"An inactive Lieutenant Commander, deactivated! Civilian of rank, and you're not even in the service anymore!"

"Ah, but someone knows Admiral Ferrah's favourite recipe for Dim Sum. It's amazing how many people in Fleet just love my cooking. You should have heard her go on about our near zero thermal manoeuvres. If that were a real operation, it would take the best scanners in the galaxy to pick us up. I'm telling you she was-"

"She's a former pilot. But of course, you knew that."

"Of course. And you're in her command chain. She was equally unhappy when she heard that you were still filling requisition orders and providing commercial traffic control."

"Well, there goes the simple life. At this rate she'll hand me a command on a starship somewhere, maybe set me up as a trainer. All because I can give orders from a simulated cockpit."

"You can also make fifth on the kill leader board while doing it. Not the best, but then, we can't all have the reflexes of an android that can look three seconds into the future," Minh said as he pretended he was back at the controls of a starfighter, firing at some unseen ship.

A thought occurred to me and I couldn't help but grin. I put down my bowl and slapped the chopsticks on the counter. "Oh, well, sounds like you're a necessary asset!"

"But my restaurant!"

"I'm sure you'll be able to hire someone to take your place with the Fleet pay you'll be drawing. If I'm getting promoted back into a career position I may as well have someone I trust working to keep the fighter jockeys in line," I said as I stood up. I started walking towards the tube shuttle that would carry me to the Operations Deck, where I'd start another uneventful shift.

"You're a mean spirited man, Jonas! My customers will miss me! I'll put a picture of you up right here on the counter and it will say 'Jonas Valent: Noodle Master Kidnapper!'"

"May your life be interesting!" I called over my shoulder as I walked through the tube entryway.

TWO

WALKING TO THE CROSSROADS

During the war I was assigned to the engineering staff of a Destroyer named the Loki. It wasn't as interesting as it sounds. There were one hundred and twelve of us engineers there just to keep the systems running while we were on our way to the front. Only half remained on board when we reached All-Con Prime. That's when the excitement started.

The low grade engineering crew was set up with infantry units and sent out to blow up and burn every factory they had. Originally, I was sent down to repair the shuttle that Minh-Chu's unit had dropped in on, and then I was assigned to them as their engineer. Our objective on the ground was to put a stop to the All-Con Corporation's primary production lines. Minh-Chu saved my hide more times than I could count during that year. He taught me how to stay alive in a firefight, even tried to teach me how to shoot. I qualified easily in basic training, but I was never a great shot, definitely not what one would consider a marksman. Minh took me on as his pet project, and after a year I was actually a very good shot. I scored in the upper ranks after we got back home some time later.

The fighter pilot stint came later, when our units had to use stolen Raze starfighters to get off world and break through what remained of the All-Con fleet to get home. We never saw combat, but there was something about being at the controls of a one point five million credit Raze Starfighter that made it hard to give up the cockpit when we got home.

Don't get me wrong; there's no glamour in spending three days in a cockpit, speeding away from the stars into the darkness. We infantry, engineering, and other support crew set on our own with simple orders: get your butt back home using stolen fighters and supplies. It was an exciting challenge - if you weren't so terrified that you couldn't enjoy it.

Most of us only had the most basic pilot training. Min-Chu and I were two out of a handful who had taken the time to be fully certified. All together, five of us had piloted craft outside of a simulator and we had to lead everyone else, over a hundred ninety untried factory fresh ships flown by green pilots all the way back home. When one hundred eighty seven of us arrived in mostly good condition, there was a welcome party the likes of which we had never seen.

After getting back, I transferred to the reserves and signed up for the volunteer patrols. Since I was already enlisted, they were nice enough to let me keep the fighter. It didn't take me long to realize that the reserves were filled with rich kids who bought their own fighters, or cadets looking to go career-military but who hadn't finished their turn at the Academy or weren't old enough to be in the field. There weren't many so called veterans like myself out there. Minh had sold his fighter to start up his restaurant and didn't have time to volunteer.

I eventually took a non-advancement position in the Freeground Fleet. My rank of Lieutenant Commander guaranteed me a reasonable pay grade even though I was deactivated, and I chose communications. There weren't many positions available, so I thought it would be a good post. I was wrong.

Being a part of port administration wasn't as empowering as I thought it might be. We were forced to adhere to strict policy and had very little deciding power. Speaking to travellers from across the stars wasn't a good place to learn about the galaxy. We were inundated with unreasonable requests, strange pleas, and lonely, chatty captains who just wanted someone to talk to and would keep the comm open no matter what it took.

It was irritating but as I finished directing my first ship of the day, a hauler called the Queen Virgo, I found myself glad I wasn't assigned to a Freeground Fleet vessel in the middle of nowhere. The only thing more boring than port control was a maintenance post on a military non-combat vessel. I was perfectly qualified to keep a vessel like that together, but I couldn't help but appreciate sitting behind a desk in a comfortable seat. It was better than a cramped maintenance crawlway.

I hoped I wouldn't be in for serious trouble from accessing the restricted simulations. Minh's heart was in the right place, but there was a chance his good intentions would land me in a military punishment post. Forced enlistment wasn't uncommon, and my civilian friends would be in for equivalent punishment. Professional demotions, hefty fines, even imprisonment. If we were discovered and Fleet Command wanted to make an example of us, things could get bad.

I would never have guessed that the true-to-life sensory simulations would lead to so much trouble, but as the civilian encounters became over practised and mundane, we couldn't help but delve into the secure military scenarios. The challenge was thrilling, but what kept me going back day after day, month after month, were the people. Ayan, Oz, and Minh were the closest friends I had and I had never met two of them in person, seen their real faces, or heard their real voices.

The people at work were kind, but most of them were much older. Among semi-retired military officers and career communications personnel, I was the odd man out. Someone who had seen military service, been in the highly regarded Fleet Engineer Corps, and walked away.

Being an engineer was my father's dream. He was a deep thinker, always had a simple solution that had everyone in the room saying "why didn't I think of that?"

When I was very young I headed straight to the academy with the intention of getting as far away from Freeground as possible. I got just enough training to qualify for the engineering staff of a ship and found out that I was dead wrong about that choice, too. I excelled at the academic challenges but I didn't enjoy the work once I was in the service.

My heart jumped into my throat when the staff sergeant, a tall fellow with a narrow face and greying hair, tapped me on the shoulder. "You're relieved, Lieutenant Commander. Admiral Rice wants you in her office in twenty-two minutes."

I nodded, collected my coffee mug, and stood up. My sergeant cracked a smile and shook my hand. "Don't take this the wrong way, Sir, but I hope the next time I see you back in this room you're the one giving me orders."

"Don't call me sir yet, Carl, my rank is still deactivated as far as I know."

"Not as of five minutes ago, Sir. You're active now, and that's all I know. The Admiral will tell you more, I'm sure."

I smiled back at him, though I don't know how convincing I was. "Just enough time to refill my mug before meeting her."

I put my coat on and made for the cafeteria, where I tossed my mug into the recycler instead of getting more coffee. The last thing I needed was more caffeine. I stepped into the transport tube and tapped the activation point on my wrist to turn on the screen built into the arm of my uniform. Alice, my personal digital assistant, came on. "Hello, Jonas. I hear you have an appointment with Admiral Rice," she chirped cheerily. I could practically see the curiosity of the other five or so passengers in the tube car pique. The doors closed and the express car began to speed around the station to drop off everyone who had already stated their destination.

"Why am I the last to know?"

"Only the Admiral, her assistant, and your former sergeant know about it, actually."

"So I'm fired. Great."

"In a manner of speaking, but I'm sure that if you present yourself as an incompetent baboon the Admiral will be happy to put you back where she found you. I'd advise against it."

"I'm going to have to look into where I went wrong with your sense of humour sometime, Alice."

"You would regret the results. Simplifying my programming would make me a very dull girl."

I sighed and shook my head. "Where am I supposed to meet her?"

"In the Officer's Forward Observation Room."

"Forward that to the tube system."

"Done. We'll be on our way after we drop everyone else off. You're the only one in this car with clearance to visit that section."

"I'm sure everyone appreciates you mentioning that, Alice," I whispered in response.

"When the Admiral makes your promotion official, will I have to start calling you sir?"

I should have expected that kind of behaviour from her. I had kept the same personal assistant program since I was a teenager, and she had grown to love embarrassing me when she found the opportunity. I suppose it's the price I paid for having the most sophisticated AI allowed as a personal assistant program. I saved up for two years so I could afford her software package. "No, but would you mind looking up what my current rank is and whispering it to me?" I asked quietly.

A moment later I heard Alice's response in my left ear. "That information is currently restricted, I can't find my way to it presently. It only tells me that your former rank was reactivated and has been changed since. I can keep digging."

"Okay, you can stop trying."

"Are you sure? There are a couple things I could try for you. They might not be entirely legal, but-"

"I'm sure. Let's not get into trouble."

"All right. Good luck, Sir."

Sometimes I thought witnessing all my experiences and learning from every decision I had made since I turned seventeen had made Alice a little smarter than the programmers intended, and other times I thought it just made her more eccentric. I was never quite sure.

The tube car arrived at my destination two minutes early. Admiral Rice's assistant, a short, dark haired man who sat manipulating a holographic representation of crew schedules beside the door leading into the Officer's Observation Lounge, looked up at me for half a second before going back to his work. "For future reference, the Admiral prefers all her officers to be fifteen minutes early. She's inside, don't keep her waiting."

"Thank you," I replied stiffly before walking towards the doors. There was a two second delay while the computer scanned me and I heard the locking mechanisms decouple. The security systems were old, but reliable and near indestructible.

I didn't know what to expect as I stepped inside, and I definitely wasn't prepared for what I saw. The room was arranged like a clover leaf, with a main platform featuring seating and tables near the entrance. Three sets of stairs lead down into the separate multi-level sections. There were command and control consoles in each area, holographic representations of ship deployments and advanced record keeping interfaces surrounding some officers, while others wore visors that provided advanced visual interfaces privately. Catwalks above and around the command centres provided space for many more operational and intelligence officers.

White noise generators kept the specific images and sounds on the command sections hidden, but it was obvious to me what I was seeing was a large part of Fleet Command. My best guess was that there were at least twenty high ranking officers in each of the three sections, and room for a lot more.

The section I stood in, nearest to the entrance, was a

contrast to the command sections. The lights were dim, more like a classy dining club, and a few Captains, Majors, Generals and Admirals sat quietly and sparsely at the thirty or more tables. A woman in her middle years with short red hair and sharp features smiled at me and stood. "Mister Valent, I presume?" she asked with a British accent.

"Yes, Ma'am," I said with a salute, noticing the nine platinum slashes on the neck of her uniform, marking her as an Admiral.

"I'm Admiral Rice," she said, shaking my hand firmly. "Impressive, isn't it?"

"Just a bit, when I was told to meet you in the Officer's Observation Deck, I expected something else."

"That's the point, as I'm sure you realize. We value our privacy and misdirection is an important tool for protecting the senior staff."

"This is almost as large as the official Fleet Command Deck. I didn't know Fleet was this active," I muttered.

"Well, let's get started. Follow me please." She led me across the section closest to the entrance, down the right-hand steps, then into a side office. The door closed and the din of sound, muffled and clear alike, was gone. One wall of the office was transparent and looked over the military dry dock. Few civilians had ever seen the inside of it, a massive open space that was set stationary and without a gravitational generator so there was no measurable force exerted on the ships inside. It was over twenty kilometres at the far, narrow end, and to hazard a guess it had to be at least fifty kilometres wide below where I stood, which was roughly in the centre. I could see dozens of ships in for repair. Many had taken extensive damage and one, a massive three kilometre long Abolisher Class Carrier, was missing most of its middle. Ragged beams and a scrap of hull was all that held it together. The edges of the damage looked melted.

The Admiral had obviously followed my gaze to it. "The Lockheed, sister ship to my old command when I last captained a ship. She was hit by a high-rad dirty nuke in the field. From what the logs say, the enemy left her adrift and a few members of the crew managed to get her drives online before dying of radiation poisoning. By the time it got here it was a ghost ship. I knew her captain, he was a friend of mine for over twenty years."

"I'm sorry, Admiral. I know what it's like to lose someone."

"Your family, I know. We're looking to prevent that kind of loss from ever happening again, even though the likelihood of it increases by the day. We need to change our manner of thinking and fast. The Lockheed is a morality tale. Her captain directed his battle group around to the dark side of the fourth moon orbiting the planet Rindega in a Colthis Corporation system and was ambushed by an AI fleet. They had dug into the moon and were protecting something. We're not sure what exactly. When the Lockheed's battle group came into range, they sent out dozens of drone fighters, each armed with a dirty nuke.

"Captain McKay's battle group nearly destroyed all of them before they were within range, but a few got through. The fact that corporations like Colthis Intergalactic are using illegal AI fleets, breaking nuclear conventions that have stood for four hundred years, and throwing away millions of credits on defences like this tells us two things. Firstly, they are doing something — or have something — that is worth protecting at any cost. Secondly, we have to look beyond conventional thinking. All of Captain McKay's precautions and countermeasures were by the book, but even with an experienced crew, it didn't mean a thing. He was overpowered by a more reckless, forward thinking enemy with no moral restraint.

"We're big enough to draw a lot of attention but not powerful enough to make claims on areas with the resources we need to grow, so we have to think outside the realm of conventional methods."

Admiral Rice looked from the Lockheed to me. I felt like I was being inspected from the inside out as her eyes locked with mine. "Being in command has taught me that solutions sometimes come in surprising ways, in strange packages," she said quietly. "Your friend, mister Minh-Chu, did us all a favour when he showed my colleague your replays. We've been trying to find out who has been raking trainees over the coals the last few months. You and your friends, some of whom are actually ranking members of the Fleet, don't just out-shoot our trainees, you have been embarrassing them. At first we thought one of the basic opposing team AI's had gone rogue, learning too much and performing past its normal abilities, but then we managed to get into the simulated communications chatter and heard the disguised voices of you and your team. Not simulated chatter at all, and heavily encrypted. Ever since then we've been watching and trying to find out exactly who you and your friends are, but the trail never led back to the right place. Your programmer friend, Jason Everin, has done such a good job at hiding your transmission trails that at one point we were led to a door control module in a waste reclamation plant as the source. We were able to determine something interesting from our findings, however. Your entire team uses direct neural interfacing for simulations. The same kind of nodal interface our cadets use, so you people have some kind of need to make the simulations feel as real as possible. I'm surprised some of you aren't suffering from link disorders. The simulations you were running were so real that they're part of the encounter hours debate."

The encounter hours debate. I had heard about it all through my academy days and into my early military career. Some instructors argued that the stress and conditions of higher level training simulations were so real that they should be counted as actual combat in personnel records. I didn't take their side. No matter how real the simulations were, and some of them were so real that they left trainees shaking and mildly traumatized by the end, there was a safety feature in the neural link node that subconsciously reminded us that it wasn't real, like we were dreaming awake. She was right. Everyone who I counted as friends craved the experiences. They were so exciting, such a complete escape, and every little victory came with a rush that could only have been surpassed by the real thing.

"If I were to meet this Jason Everin, I would have to congratulate him on his ability to maintain the fidelity of the transmissions while keeping you perfectly hidden. Accomplishing both is difficult. Normally I'd have every opportunity to meet him while he spent three to ten years in prison for violating a secure network." The Admiral's accent seemed to slip. Her perfect diction failed for a moment to reveal a hint of an aristocratic bend to her words. I had heard it before but I couldn't be sure where.

My heart was sinking, but I kept a stiff upper lip and tried not to show it. "I've never met him, Ma'am."

"I'm not surprised, but you will."

"I would like to take this opportunity to apologize for any inconvenience I may have caused and take full responsibility for the actions of all my teammates. They followed me in and we initially used my access codes to gain entry into the training simulations."

"We realize that now, and it's too late. We've already singled out who we can, and are acting accordingly. You, along with three others, are being dealt with presently. Just so you know, we were on the verge of finding out exactly who you all were. The last simulation you ran was one of the most difficult we have to offer. As you well know, it is among a chosen few that are reserved for optional study among trainees. When we realized that you and your people had started it, our cadets were removed and replaced with a group of seasoned commanders and pilots we had in place to test you. They were beaten. Not impossible, but bloody unlikely.

"You managed to embarrass a number of the senior staff, and they think you've been brought in so I can administer your punishment personally."

I wanted to say something, but didn't know what, so I kept my mouth shut and clenched my teeth.

She shook her head and continued. "Computer, display full career path of Jonas S. Valent." A holographic tree of everything I had done appeared over her desk, starting at age seventeen. She pointed at the first one. "You purchased a top of the line personal organizer program, called it Alice, and started modifying it. By the time you joined the service at the age of twenty, Alice had grown into the most sophisticated level of AI we allowed by law, and her limiters have been in place ever since. There have been three attempts at copying her, which failed since her AI is complex enough to warrant severe usage limitations, and she was moved twice.

You joined the Fleet, spent two years training as an engineer, four as a cadet, received basic engineering, infantry, and combat pilot certifications. You then went on to complete a year of officers's training and entered the service proper as an Ensign. During the voyage to All-Con Prime, you received field promotions more than once because they saw great underutilized potential and they were short on leaders.

Your commanding officer noted that you had no difficulty meeting and sometimes exceeding expectations as an Ensign, but as a Second Lieutenant Commander you only did as much as was required and no more as an engineer. But where it came to the staff under you, there was no limit to the time and effort you would expend on them. People under your command flourished, the few that didn't meet your standards were routinely written up. The discipline and professionalism with which you conducted yourself while in that position earned you the respect of the senior staff. Final reports entered by those under you generally noted that you were fair, personable, and a few even claimed it was a pleasure to have you in charge. Two years later you arrived back here with a stolen fighter group that you helped command safely back home and were promoted to Lieutenant Commander. You requested a non-career position shortly thereafter, joined the reserves, served for a while as pilot on patrol, and then had your rank fully deactivated when you left."

Admiral Rice sighed and walked to the window, folding her hands behind her back. "Years later, you're back on our sensors but as a Command maverick on our simulator network. From what I understand you joined with a group of hobby pilots and infantry who you then led to the top of the leader board using the call sign Horus. Then you got bored and used your clearance to gain access to actual training scenarios, where you've gotten everyone into a great deal of trouble by disrupting our curriculum, exposing civilians to high level military training materials, and making a mockery of our standards and war game grading. Do you know what the officers just outside that door are calling you?"

"No I do not, Admiral," I replied stiffly, bracing myself for the inevitable conclusion to her lecture.

"They're calling you an asset. Anyone who hasn't seen your full record thinks that you've lacked the opportunities to make your skills known and find your place." She turned her head and looked at me out of the corner of her eye. "You and I know better, don't we?"

Officer training and common sense made it clear that any response I offered would only make things worse. I kept my mouth shut and eyes staring forward. The ruined husk of the Lockheed was being towed directly into my line of sight.

Her words were enunciated sharply as she continued. "You're bored, but lack the direction and ambition to step forward and make a place for yourself. You've grown complacent and lazy. Sure, you're exceptional at directing traders, resupplying incoming ships, and arranging for repairs, but Alice, that AI you keep strapped to your arm, could do the job just as well while working on eight other tasks. You're wasted, Mister Jonas. How does that make you feel?"

My face was red, my palms were wet, but my nervousness had gone. That little voice in the back of my head — the one always telling me to stay out of the fight, that it was a good idea to step away from the military and that I had found a peaceful, leisurely life that was worth keeping — was gone. I knew everything she was saying was true, that I had convinced myself otherwise over time, making little compromises, small, short-sighted retreats away from what I wanted. No wonder I dove right in when the opportunity to do it in a game came along. To feel the warmth of camaraderie, the rush of command.

She was right, and I realized that the anger that filled me had nothing to do with her. My admission came out quietly. "I am wasted."

She walked softly, calmly to her desk. I couldn't believe how calm and clear she was as the anger within me clouded my judgement and rendered me speechless. The admiral picked up a small data chip and turned it on. I recognized the holographic icons that sprang up above it immediately. "Well, there is something we sometimes do for people like you. We challenge them, only you've gone too far for us to make it a simple matter of reactivating your rank and putting you back into the service. You're a passable engineer, but from what we've seen, that's not your true calling. Few people on this station know it, but we're fighting to maintain what little territory we have and the opposition has become more fierce than ever. We can not afford to have trained, qualified personnel sitting around directing traffic. Having said that, I'm not going to hand equipment and responsibility over to a man who hasn't been properly tested. Let alone a crew who, for the most part, share the same problem.

"I'm giving you and everyone who is involved in this fiasco a choice." She turned the data chip off and tossed it at me. I caught it by reflex, but barely. "You can pay fines and be permanently barred from any ranking Fleet position, or participate in one more high-stakes simulation. For the purpose of this simulation, I'm promoting you to the rank of Trainee Captain, and everyone else is being assigned a trainee rank befitting their position in your crew. Anyone who accepts this challenge will have six days to prepare for the simulation, which will be conducted on an actual ship.

"The scenario will be at my discretion, and chosen five minutes before it begins from a list of historic scenarios in which the casualty rate was seventy percent or higher. To ensure that everyone has the proper motivation, death in the simulation will have real consequences. Anyone whose avatar dies will be charged with violating military digital security which carries a prison sentence of one to ten years as determined by the sensitivity of the accessed materials. If our officials determine that damage was done to our systems, morale, or procedures, more fines and prison time could be brought down on people who lose their simulated lives."

I don't remember what went on in my head exactly, but I wasn't willing to back down. "I can only speak for myself, Admiral, but I accept your challenge."

Admiral Rice smiled at me and nodded. "Good, a number of your team mates made it clear that they would not participate unless you were put in command. We've had a chance to meet with everyone, and though most are choosing to become permanent civilians, twenty one of you are going to be participating in this exercise. All but you and three others have already reported aboard ship and I've had your things sent to your quarters there," the Admiral walked to the window and pointed. "You'll be using a Combat Carrier that's been converted into a Strikerclass Destroyer that's undergoing a refit. Her name is the Sunspire, and we're in the process of replacing her primary systems starting with the power plants. Her age comes with a distinguished history."

I stepped up beside the Admiral and looked down. The entire lower half of the hull was opened to accommodate the replacement of the ship's old reactors. The ship once had a reflective surface to minimize beam weapon damage but it had been tarnished by weapons fire and it looked mismatched where hull plating had been replaced with different materials. I could see why they would refit the ship instead of decommissioning it, however.

Even from where I was standing I could see the hull was made of ergranian steel, a rare regenerative, incredibly dense metal that was difficult to mine and next to impossible to find. Looking at the exposed portions I could also see that the hull was well over a meter thick, more in some places. Tethered just behind the ship were two dozen starfighter training pods ready to be loaded into some part of the ship. Judging from the ongoing work, I couldn't begin to guess where they'd be putting them.

"The old reactors they're pulling out of her are huge, they've got to be almost a hundred fifty years old. What are they going to do with all the space left over after the new ones are installed? They'll be an eighth the size and generate the same amount of energy," I found myself asking.

"There won't be much space left over. We're quintupling her power generation capabilities and outfitting her for long range missions. Her new fuel manufacturing systems will be able to make energy out of almost anything. We're putting those huge ram scoops to good use with the new design. They'll also be installing new automation systems so she'll require one twentieth the crew."

"That'll give her the power generation capabilities of a juggernaut and the ability to turn anything into energy."

"Exactly."

"So, I suppose I'll be commanding the ship in its original configuration during the simulation?"

"No, part of the test is to find out how you and your team mates deal with new technology. The Sunspire may look like a ship ready for retirement on the outside, but we're updating her with all our best technology on the inside and reshaping whole sections of the hull. The regenerative qualities of the metal allow us to do a great deal with this ship that we couldn't with any modern vessel. One of the unique things about the challenge I'm setting you and your friends on is that no one really knows all the details of this ship from stem to stern except for the lead engineers who redesigned her.

"The specifications, real life profiles, and everything other than the scenario are on the data chip I gave you. As of this moment you're in full command. Crew assignments, drills, and even who you might want to excuse are completely up to you. I'll also allow you to request a number of qualified, low ranking officers to fill in for missing crew members. You'll be restricted to three decks, one of which is being temporarily fitted as a training area with simulation pods but that should be more than enough room. Everyone has been instructed to stay clear of anything that involves the refit. Do you have any questions before you ship out, Trainee Captain?"

"What happens to anyone I excuse?"

"Civilians will be banned from serving in the Freeground Fleet and career military will be demoted or imprisoned depending on what the courts decide on the charge of conspiring to violate security protocols. If they're not good enough for your crew then they're certainly not good enough for Fleet. Any other questions?"

"No. Thank you, Admiral."

"Good. Then Godspeed, I'll see you after the simulation. Security will see you to the Sunspire."

I started walking out of the room when the Admiral stopped me. "One more thing, Jonas. One of your team mates, Sunspot was her handle, is the new Chief Engineer aboard the Sunspire. She was overseeing the refit until today and her rank is still effective. The charges of conspiracy were waived in her case since we couldn't prove that she knew some of her team mates were illegally participating in simulations. Despite this, she's convinced me that she should be treated like anyone else in the team, and will face charges if she is killed in the scenario. I like this officer. She's a bright, dedicated engineer and a better commander than most with a long history in the military despite her age. If she goes down with your team, I'll hold you personally responsible. Dismissed."

THREE

CONSPIRATORS

The meeting with Admiral Rice had changed my world. I felt numb as security led me up the Sunspire's broad boarding tunnel. The battered destroyer stretched on forever to the left and right. Her curves made her thick and heavy at the front. The armoured ram scoops flared out like great metal shoulders. Massive intake control fins gave the front of the open scoops a sharp, toothy look. From there the hull tapered inward, only to flare back out at the rear where three main articulated thruster pods waited to be rebuilt. Two of the pods were placed high on the aft end, pointing upwards at forty five degree angles, while the third and largest hung straight down.

The grace of the ship's design was evident despite the open sections of hull. It was more like something that had been born than built. Her main beam was the better part of a kilometre long and I found myself wishing I could see a holo of the ship in her heyday.

The size of the ship up close only reminded me of the enormity of my situation. Twenty one lives were in my hands, each one of them taking their chances with me and their fellows instead of taking the easy way out: civilian life.

The busy boarding tunnel was filled with personnel involved in the refit. When I arrived at the end, I was met by a security officer in a green and blue trainee vacsuit. "Welcome, Captain Valent, your quarters are ready. Follow me please," the Officer stated pleasantly.

"Decks four to seven are at the disposal of you and your crew. You'll be using a temporary bridge on deck five for the simulation, and most of your crew are settling in to their quarters or will be arriving soon." The security officer was a thickly muscled fellow who stood at least two metres tall. He seemed very happy to see me which was a bit surprising and unnerving at the same time.

The halls were two meters across and unpainted, leaving the blue sheen of the ergranian steel plain to see. It struck me then that it was the perfect bare material for the interior since it would absorb massive amounts of energy instead of conducting it freely. The cables, wiring, and pipes that ran along the sides of the corridors were perfectly arranged, neatly clipped against the bulkheads so they were out of the way. There were pressure doors every fifteen meters that decoupled, moved outward, and separated at our approach. "Are these doors always closed when the ship is in operation?" I asked.

"Only during yellow or red alert status. Normally they're only closed at major junctions. During the refit we're keeping everything bottled up just in case we blow a seal somewhere."

We had to traverse the ship vertically by using an empty lift shaft since the elevator cars were being replaced. Aside from a safety tether, we were floating free in a shaft that ran the full height of the hull, eight decks above me and thirteen below. The size of the vessel couldn't have been more apparent as we drifted up several decks to the third. "This is huge! How big is her normal compliment?"

"As far as I know it depends on how she's tasked. During a drop mission she can carry eighteen hundred infantry, sixty drop ships, forty fighters, and requires a main crew of over a thousand. For long mission configuration I hear you can run the ship with automation and one hundred crew. That's how she's being fitted. What it was like when she was a Combat Carrier, I couldn't tell ya. She's been off that duty for a century or so."

"Sounds like you know a lot about this ship. Have you served on her before?"

"No, Sir, I just like to read."

Whereas the busy decks below were filled with people, equipment, had open compartments everywhere and noise all around, the officer quarters and mess hall on the third deck were deathly silent. Our footsteps echoed as we came out of the shaft slowly and let the artificial gravity — which was fairly light and not fully operational either — draw our feet down onto the floor.

The narrower halls were surfaced with padded panels and the lighting was subdued. It already looked better than my apartment, which may not be saying much by normal standards, but it was enough to make me grin.

I didn't realize that we had arrived at my quarters even as we stood in front of the pressure doors that were clearly labelled Captain with space for a name to be posted below. I cheerily stood there, looking around with the doors closed.

The guard smiled and announced, "Here we are, Sir."

I nodded as though I was perfectly aware of the fact that we were standing quietly in front of my quarters and stepped forward to trigger the doors. As they opened I looked inside to find a main room that had a table with four chairs on one side, a sofa, a thickly cushioned armchair, and archways on either side leading to additional rooms. "You could fit four of my apartment in just what I've seen so far and have room for a walk in closet."

"The privilege of command, Sir," the guard said with a big toothy grin.

It was then that I recognized his voice from the simulations. "Oz?" I asked with a smile.

"About time! I was starting to wonder if they got the right man!" he said, shaking my hand firmly. "Warrant Officer Terry Ozark McPatrick, at your service. Most of my friends call me Oz."

"Just like in the scenarios, that's something I can get used to." I stepped into my quarters and he followed. "So you're actually a security officer? Not infantry?"

"Well, I started in infantry and got poached into Fleet by my uncle before he retired. I told him I made a mistake joining infantry and he agreed. I've served for eight years in different security roles, just got my flight and gunner certifications last year, and I'm almost finished with my bridge command training. Can't get promoted until I finish that. Unless you have other plans for me, I'll be on security detail while we're aboard."

"You're welcome to it. Have you met anyone else yet?" I asked as I sat at the table.

"Just Ayan, turns out she's changed a bit since the Academy. When I first met her she was in advanced engineer training. I was in first year trying to figure out what I wanted to do. Now she's used to commanding an engineering crew of about a hundred and fifty and, well, let's just say she grew out of her awkward stage."

"Well, that's not intimidating at all."

Oz laughed and put a big hand on my shoulder. "She's just as nice as I remember, got a smile that can light up the main cargo hold. I don't know why, but she's glad to be here, all excited about this challenge. Don't get me wrong, I'm looking forward to it too, but she already has a career that would make any cadet envious - she made Commander before thirty and could have Captain by thirty five. She doesn't need something like this making her life all complicated. Doesn't matter though, she's trying to flip her rank over into training status like us, but Fleet won't let her just yet."

"I know, she's taking a huge risk by signing on for this challenge. I really don't know what's behind it either."

"Her mother is less than pleased, I'm sure you've heard."

"I had no idea. Her family lives on the station?"

Oz's jaw dropped and he sat down on the sofa. "You really don't know, do you?"

"Know what?"

He shook his head and ran a big hand down his face. "Okay, there's something you have to know about our Chief Engineer. Her full name is Ayan Rice. Her mother is-"

"Rear Admiral Rice." I felt as though all the air had just left the room. Suddenly I couldn't breathe, the room was spinning. I reached out to put my hand down on the table and missed. I was falling and then everything went black.

When I opened my eyes, I was looking up at the faces of Oz and Minh-Chu.

"He just started hyperventilating and passed out. I think he's coming around though," Oz said as he propped my head up in one of his hands.

"Some fearless leader," Minh added with a smirk.

"I heard that." I tried to blink the white spots out of my eyes. Oz helped me up and we all sat at the table. "How long was I out?"

"Just a few seconds. Long enough to scare the hell out of me. Don't do that on the bridge," Oz replied.

"I came in and this big guy was standing over you. I was just about to run for the nearest exit," said Minh.

"Well, I'm glad you're not going to be involved with security," I told Minh, to Oz's amusement. "So, I have a Fleet Admiral's daughter on board. That's going to be a little awkward."

"Only if you give her any special treatment. I think she might be participating in this thing because she wants to prove that she gets the same treatment as everyone else," Minh said in more of a serious tone than I'd heard from him in a while. "That, and rumour has it she was assigned to the Sunspire's refit as some kind of rehabilitation. No one knows what from."

"Well, she can demand as much respect as she wants as long as she keeps our simulated ship together. From what the Admiral told me, we're in for a rough ride."

"You mean the Admiral briefed you herself?" Oz asked, agape.

"She did. And thanks for that, by the way." I half bowed to Minh from my seat. "Didn't turn out the way you expected it, did it?"

He looked almost panicked, and I realized that until that moment only he and I knew he was the one who informed command of my identity and got the ball rolling. "I knew you were good, but not good enough for this kind of effort. I thought they'd promote you and put you to work somewhere you'd feel useful again."

"You're the one who popped the lid off our little covert fun?" Oz asked, wide eyed. "Did you tell command about me, too?"

"No! Just Jonas and myself, I swear! I had no idea they were already tracking us down or that we were doing so much better against the cadets in training than the AI or training staff. I thought we were just bumping in and messing around, embarrassing a few trainees, especially since no one cancelled the exercises once they started. How was I supposed to know that they were watching and throwing their advanced trainees against us once they realized the AI we were replacing was deactivated?"

"Well, since we're getting our asses kicked out there, Fleet is interested in new solutions," Oz said, pointing to the large view port. "That's why the Sunspire is here. It's not just a refit, she was so badly damaged that the primary generators weren't salvageable and they had to force the hull to regenerate by energizing it as soon as it got here. Ayan couldn't talk about what happened, but I could tell it was worse than bad and it wouldn't be long before everyone on Freeground would know about it."

"The Admiral told me there was a lot more going on out there than Fleet was telling the public about. I think, in the bigger scheme of things, who told who what is pretty insignificant. When it's all said and done, I'd rather be in a position to do something about the problems facing Freeground than be directing trade traffic and resupplying ships. I was born here. The only people I've known are all here."

"I was born here, too and have three sisters who wouldn't leave if their lives depended on it. They might drive me crazy, but I know I always have a bunk waiting," Oz said, nodding.

"Someone's got to protect my restaurant. It may as well be me," Minh added with a shrug. "My sisters can take care of things while I'm gone, and it's hard for them to scream at me while I'm light years away in a fighter cockpit, if that's where I end up."

"Well, let's get to work then. I have a lot of catching up to do. I have to learn about the ship systems, find out who I have and who I need to bring aboard, set out the crew assignments, then we have to start drills. Then there's everything I'm not thinking of." I turned to Minh then. "Can you get everyone set up with quarters tonight? Make sure they're settled in and tell them there will be a meeting at ten tomorrow morning in the Mess Hall."

"Sure, but the main mess hall is open to space right now. Won't be very comfortable."

"Do we have another space available?"

"We have the common room at the rear of this deck. That should be big enough."

"Good, that's where we'll meet tomorrow." I turned to Oz and smiled. "Do you think you could talk to Ayan and review the roster with her? She'll need an engineering staff, a repair team, you'll need pilots, I'll need a bridge crew, and you'll need security personnel."

"All right, and what will you be doing?"

"Everything else. I'm hoping to have all the essentials ironed out tomorrow afternoon so we can have our first drill before the day's out."

"Well then, we should get going. I have crew members to track down," Minh said, standing up and heading for the door.

"I have an Engineer to find. From her reputation I'll probably find her half way inside one of the main systems." Oz shrugged with an amused smile.

"One more thing. We shouldn't tell anyone that Minh here was the one who helped Fleet Command put two and two together. I know I'm past it, but we don't need the extra trouble."

After they left, I walked to the view port. It stretched the length of the main room in my quarters and was a meter and a half tall. I looked out at the work crews, all so efficient, getting the Sunspire ready for God knew what. Was I going to be her next Captain? First Officer? Or would I be a footnote in the Fleet's history as the man who could handle a virtual command but cracked when there were real consequences? I shook my head and called out to the ship's computer system. "Sunspire control, this is Trainee Captain Jonas Scott Valent. Am I clear to enter operational data?"

"You are clear, Captain Valent. Please upload critical mission data," a strong male voice replied.

I held the data chip I was given by the Admiral in front of me. "Scan and record all operational data from this storage unit."

"Scan complete. Do you have further orders, Captain?" the computer asked after a moment.

"Forward roster to Terry McPatrick, Minh-Chu Buu, and Ayan Rice. Leave general instructions that I am not to be disturbed until five AM tomorrow morning, set ship wide wake alarms for the same time."

"Acknowledged and completed as ordered."

"Thank you, computer. Now could you give my personal assistant AI, Alice, access to your database, display controls, and communications system?"

"Processing," the computer replied, and as I expected, Alice giggled through my ear piece. "It tickles!" she said as the ship computer came on once again. "Complete. Command and control circuitry remains isolated from Alice AI."

"I never have any fun," Alice pouted.

"Thanks again, computer, that will be all," I said, dismissing the voice interface. A holographic representation of Alice's head and shoulders appeared suddenly in front of the sofa. I jumped back so fast that I nearly knocked the table over. The representation of her was a black haired, blue eyed woman about twenty and her head was two meters tall. "Don't do that! My day's had enough surprises without you popping out of the floor as a huge floating head."

"So I've noticed," she said with a grin. "I suppose we should get to work."

"You know me too well. Let's take a look at those systems."

FOUR

EVEN THE SUNSPIRE CASTS A SHADOW

With Alice's help I pored through most of the details I needed to assume command. I knew there was no chance I could retain all of it. I didn't think anyone could after having such little time to commit it all to memory but Alice learned how to prioritize the information. I was sure she'd be whispering in my ear in moments of hesitation while I tried to remember a name or other detail.

I wasn't the first captain aboard the Sunspire to have a personal AI, either. Captain Grace Cameron, the last person to command the Sunspire, carried an AI much like mine but that's where the similarities ended. She was a career officer, worked her way up through the ranks the hard way through nearly thirty years of service, and had commanded the Sunspire for six years before being killed with most of her crew. Before I knew it, I fell back into my chair, reading the report detailing how six hundred and five crew members and the captain were killed.

The Sunspire was in the Ukonis system, some three weeks'

hyperspace travel away from the station, with the fifth battle group. They were on the run from Triad Consortium ships and after several days of trying to win free from gravity traps and scrambling posts that kept them from entering hyperspace or generating a wormhole entry point back to the station, they found themselves separated from the battle group and trapped. To Captain Cameron's credit, she tried everything before making a last ditch effort to break through by openly attacking the smallest group, blocking the path of two destroyers and a gravity generator. I was absolutely astounded as I watched the tactical replay.

Looking at the Sunspire, I would have never guessed it could be so quick and agile in space. It managed to use one destroyer as cover and survive its barrage of beam weapon fire while hammering at a section of the ship that must have seemed non-essential at first to the enemy crew. After several minutes of close fighting, taking a lot of damage and sacrificing most of her fighters, the Sunspire broke through the closest destroyer's heavy shielding, disabled its main stabilizers and overloaded its port side engines. Without full control, the destroyer couldn't stop itself from colliding with the gravity generator ship it protected.

It was daring, requiring sacrifices I didn't know I could have made in her place. The Sunspire was just about to make her escape when the remaining destroyer, Enforcer 2117, launched several dozen missiles. The Sunspire's fighter screen was down to two ships and most of her gun emplacements were either damaged or destroyed. There was nothing they could do to stop the attack, and as the Enforcer 2117 turned away and jumped out of the system, I realized what was about to happen. The missiles they couldn't stop were never meant to hit the Sunspire, but rather, surround it and emit a massive electromagnetic pulse.

Anyone not already within the field surrounding the Sunspire's main generator was killed instantly and most of the ship's systems were devastated. Ayan and four of her engineering staff survived because Captain Cameron had just enough time to command them to climb into the centre of the ship's main generator while it was still running.

According to Ayan's report they were adrift for a week while they got basic propulsion back online. They hid the ship in a stagnant asteroid field for five more weeks while they repaired the secondary wormhole generator. I thought about Ayan and her remaining staff for a long time after I finished reading her report. I couldn't imagine being defenceless, left for dead on a ship filled with the corpses of my crew mates for weeks, knowing that any moment we could be discovered and killed or captured.

I went to bed late that night thinking about the good humoured, fun loving Ayan I had grown to know in simulations as Sunspot, and what she must have gone through. Weeks relying on just her vacsuit for life support with no gravity, little light. By the time I was asleep I saw nothing but dark hallways and corpses drifting in and out of some faint unseen luminescence. I woke up and looked at the time. I had drifted off for less than an hour then tossed and turned for the rest of the night, sitting up occasionally to dictate more details for Alice to add to my action plan. "So noted, now go to sleep or I'll convince the ship computer to flood your quarters with sleeping gas," she scolded after the fourth or fifth time.

The humour helped lighten my mood a little and I tried to stop going through all the past events of the day, reports, and plans I was in the middle of making.

It must have worked, because when Alice woke me up it was a few minutes before five in the morning. "There is someone at the door for you, I think it's urgent."

I sat up groggily and tried to clear my heavy grogginess. "I'll take more sleep at any price."

"They brought coffee."

"Thank you, Alice," I said with a dry mouth. I reached for my command and control unit and snapped it on my wrist. The status lights came on and I dragged myself out of bed to stand in the middle of the bedroom. "Cleaning cycle, then apply uniform for Trainee Captain, vacuum suit version, two millimetre thickness, with extra material in sensitive areas," I commanded. The small projectors in the wristband vibrated the air over my body, shaking off dirt and dead skin, reducing all the matter to particles finer than visible dust. Then I passed it around my body so it could spray on the uniform with blue extremities, shoulders, legs and a green coloured core. I always hated the colour of the trainee uniforms. It only took a few seconds for the material to finish bonding to itself and I stretched to loosen it from my skin.

"Please let them in Alice," I said, then realized that I hadn't even asked who was at the door.

The pressure doors decoupled and parted to reveal Ayan who patiently waited with a tall, sealed silver coffee mug in each hand. Her roster image didn't do her justice. She was diminutive in stature, and her face was heart shaped with wide cheekbones and bright blue eyes. She had changed into a trainee's uniform like my own, which made it plain that she had been relieved of overseeing the refit while she was on my roster. Her engineering kit was slung around her waist, filled with all the tools and advanced devices of her trade, some of which I didn't even recognize.

She smiled and looked at me for a moment before flinching and avoiding my eyes, smiling even wider. Offering me a coffee she said, "I think you need this more than I do. Can I come in?"

"Only if you tell me what's so funny."

"I'm sorry, I must have caught you sleeping, Sir. Your hair is a little out of place," she replied, trying to keep from laughing. She was obviously trying to ignore my crow's nest with great difficulty.

"If you'll excuse me," I expressed with exaggerated polite-ness before stepping into the bathroom. "There are days I think it would be just as well to go bald," I said to myself as I did a serviceable job of fixing the mess. I chewed an oral cleaning tablet and stepped back out.

Ayan was sitting in the recliner, thumbing her way through a report she was viewing on her personal holographic projector. "Feel better?" she asked.

I nodded. "Sorry about that."

She smiled up at me and turned off the mini-projector. "No worries, you should see me in the morning. It takes a good twenty minutes for me to look even close to human."

I sat down on the sofa and took a sip of coffee. An uncom-fortable silence settled in almost immediately. She stared at me over the rim of her mug for several more protracted moments before saying, "You're different. From what I expected, I mean." Even though she was being very quiet, even shy, there was still a lightness to her. As if even though she was dealing with the unexpected, she was right where she wanted to be.

I didn't know what to say and before I could come up with anything she put her mug down and went on. "I'm not what you expected, either."

"It's not that. I just read the reports on the Ukonis System last night." From the fallen expression on her face, I realized I had said exactly the wrong thing.

"Not you, too," she said quietly.

"We're lucky to have you back. Very lucky."

"Luck had nothing to do with it. Ensign Richards recognized what those missiles were and before we knew what was going on the Captain ordered the engineering staff to take cover because she knew we were the only ones that could. A moment later, there was a flash and everyone was dead, the entire ship shut down and just a few of us were left, huddled into the heart of the ship in the dark. What isn't in the report is how it's been almost four months since then, and even though most of us lost everyone we knew, all our friends, some of us are almost over it."

"Anyone who's gone through that has to have a lot to deal with. It can't be easy, everyone knows that."

"But do they have to treat me like I'm made of glass?"

I didn't know how to ask her how I was supposed to treat her without making things worse, so I didn't say anything as she stood up and started pacing the length of the room.

"That's why, when I came back, I jumped into the first simulation that I saw Oz, Mira, Ronin, and you in. You were friends that didn't know what I'd just been through. To you, I had only been away for awhile. On duty, nothing out of the ordinary. I could try to be myself for a while and if I felt low I could just hide it behind my avatar or take off the simulation node. My one candle in the dark, and now you're all here and you know who I am. What I've been through."

I started to say something, but she wasn't finished. She turned towards me with tears in her eyes.

"I went to the common room last night and looked for someone I could recognize. Oz was there and he was talking to Ronin, who I never met before, but there was something about him. The way he was joking around, how everyone within five feet of him couldn't stop laughing. I recognized that crazy voice I knew so well in the scenes even with the disguiser, and when I went over to meet him, Oz whispered something in his ear and all the laughter was just gone. Instead of meeting Ronin, the crazy pilot, I met Minh-Chu, who had been told all about poor little damaged me and was very concerned. Everyone was staring and trying not to stare at the same time. No one knew what to say and all I wanted was to be myself with the only friends I had left," she yelled.

I stood and started crossing the room towards her. I remembered what it was like when everyone thought you would break if they looked at you wrong, or said the wrong thing. Even Minh was overly cautious when my family was killed. The therapists didn't have the answer for my grief. "Time and patience. Be with positive people," they would say. What I needed was to break down and have someone show me it was all right to have a moment to feel, to be human. I needed someone to show me I still had someone. For me it was Minh and his eldest sister, Kim-An. I didn't know if Ayan needed what I did years before, but I took a chance and duplicated Kim's solution.

"No, don't you dare try to fix me! I couldn't take it from you," she said, backing away.

I stepped forward and pulled her into my arms, crushing her to me. She was stiff at first but accepted the embrace before long. Her tears came quietly, her hands gripped my back and I felt a little selfish deriving some satisfaction at being there for her. We'd spoken through avatars for hours numbering in the hundreds, late into the night after simulations had concluded. I'd show up for my shift tired the next day, but it was worth it. As we stood there after her tears had gone, swaying slightly, I knew every sleep-deprived day after was well worth it. "Now who's a big mess?" I asked her when her grip had loosened and the silence threatened to thicken.

She couldn't help but laugh. "No one other than my therapist has done that since I got back, thank you." She squeezed before we both let go.

I sat back down on the sofa, she on the chair. When we both had our coffee in hand, I smiled at her. "I'll make you a deal. I'll treat you like my Chief Engineer and friend if you help me get the crew through this scenario so we might have the chance to sign up with the military officially."

She smiled brightly and nodded. "Deal."

Before long we were hard at work, going through the post-refit ship configuration, reviewing the five staff members she had selected, and passing ideas back and forth about modifications we would be making to many of this ship's systems before the simulation started. Some of the changes she'd be making would be minor tweaks, but there were some very forward-thinking ideas that came from her side of the table, and a couple more obvious ones from mine.

Her imprint was already all over the redesign. She had added seals and housings that would make the ship completely impenetrable to any electromagnetic weapon while the inner hull was intact. She knew the ship like no one else, and I recognized that I couldn't possibly have a better engineer aboard. She was very easy to work with as well, willing to explain the new, and allowing me to ask all my questions without worrying about looking like I had just spent years on basic communications detail. My experience kept me from looking foolish, but I had gotten a little behind on a few important systems.

At about nine thirty, we knew we were out of time but with all the work out on the table, we were glad we were only preparing for a scenario. Some of our ideas would require much more time or manpower than we had to prepare if we were really applying them to the ship, while in the scenario we could spend several hours and have them all done with competent help. Everyone would be busy, especially considering there were to be two drills a day using completely different scenes each time.

When it was time for her to finish getting ready for the assembly. we embraced for a little longer than two people who were just friends would. "I'm glad I signed on," she said quietly.

"I couldn't do this without you."

She looked up to me and smiled before we moved apart. She was out the door in a few steps and that was the last time I saw that side of her.

FIVE

TRAINING

The common room was different from the rest of the ship. There were one-by-one meter port holes spread out along the front and sides, but that's where the extravagance ended. The tables and chairs were synthetic wood and at least forty years old, some even older by the looks of it. There was an old dartboard and space in the centre was cleared for holoprojections.

The floors were covered with a scarred, short ended, spray on shag application that was peeling in some places and the walls were unpainted. To the left there was an archway with its emergency doors shut, and to the right another archway with one of its emergency doors detached completely and propped up beside the opening. I knew this room was considered non-essential, but I had never seen such disrepair anywhere in a starship.

Some effort had been made to tidy up, I could tell, but no one had time to actually repair anything.

"Captain on deck!" Oz yelled as soon as the main doors

opened. In a matter of seconds, commissioned and non-commissioned officers alike were in a line along the back wall. All of them were in uniform, arranged by rank, at attention with their eyes to the front and hands at their sides. I knew that I had met each one of them in the simulations we ran, spoken to many of them for an hour or more while we waited for the scenarios to load up with opponents. I had discussed strategy with a good number of them for hours, talked about details of our lives, our jobs. I didn't recognize the majority of them, since I had never seen their faces and we didn't use real names.

I stood up straight and ran my eyes from highest ranking at the left where Ayan stood, to the lowest on the right. I didn't recognize the dark haired woman I saw there. "As you all know, I am Trainee Captain Jonas S Valent, your commanding officer. My call sign in the simulations was Horus. We've been given an opportunity to demonstrate our skills in an exercise that will determine whether or not we can take a real rank in the Freeground Fleet. This is a unique opportunity for two reasons. One, we avoid criminal charges or fines; and two, we can all become a part of a crew together in defence of our home. I've never heard of anyone getting this kind of opportunity. That being said, I don't expect everyone to take advantage of it. Many have already decided against the risks, chosen to become permanent civilians, and I can't blame them. I will still call them friends when this is over.

"Since we were able to engage in simulated combat with not only trainees but some of the best Freeground's Fleet had to offer and we kicked their asses, they want to see what we can do when the stakes are much higher. Each one of us will enter into this simulation knowing that if we are killed we will individually be tried in court for our roles in violating military security laws." I waited a moment for the stakes to sink in and watched as a few of them started to look nervous. To my surprise, they waited patiently for me to go on. "Now that I've made sure that you understand all the conditions of the Fleet's offer, here's what I have to say about it. Everyone here is aware that in most scenes, someone's avatar dies. Whether it's by rare accident, a conscious sacrifice to ensure win conditions are met, or because for just an instant someone else was better than you, someone's avatar almost always dies. I expect the projected casualties for whatever simulation we're dropped into to be very high, and that some of our avatars will be killed. That is simply a reality and the Admiral made me aware of it herself.

"If your avatar dies I will stand beside you and the rest of our fallen and do absolutely everything I can to ensure that the consequences are lenient whether we win the scenario or not. If there is a way for me to get you out of having to stand in court, I will find it for you. If we fail as a crew to meet the win conditions of whatever scenario we find ourselves in, however, I don't expect I'll have much influence with the administrative staff. We have to work as a crew united, just like we were in the scenarios, putting the group ahead of ourselves and working for success as a team. That is why, despite our eclectic make up, I believe we were able to lick trainees and experienced personnel at their own scenes. Individual skill is one thing, and we all have it, but it means so much more when you apply those skills as an organized crew. We'll be working drills every day leading up to the final scenario so we can tighten up our teamwork.

"That brings me to what I see in front of me now. Once, we were a team in a simulated environment, and though our challenge now will take place in a scenario, the Fleet has been kind enough to bring us all together on this fine ship. I'm assuming that it's another part of the test. They want to see if we can get along as well in person as we did in the sims. I'd like you to take a moment to quietly look at the faces in this room, think of the relationships you have with them, how good it felt to meet them in person for the first time."

I mentally counted to thirty, watching as my crew calmly looked at each other. At first there were some quiet nods, then a few smiles were exchanged and by the time I finished counting a few were just starting to quietly whisper to each other. "There's no doubt in my mind that this crew is good together. It's too bad some couldn't follow us on this particular adventure, but we can't blame them, can we? Could you imagine entering this simulation, doing your best, and getting your avatar killed? After a few moments to say goodbye to everyone you'd be brought to a cell, then a few quiet days would pass as friends and family visited, before you stood before the Military Judiciary Council. Some of us have a great deal to lose. We have family, property, responsibilities. But I'm going to ask you to forget all that for a moment.

"Instead, imagine yourself coming through this thing as one of the virtual survivors. Take a moment to visualize all those win conditions met, and when the simulation is over, a select few of us are in the winner's circle and awarded with a career rank in the Freeground Fleet." I paused for a few moments then, and noticed that only the previously commissioned officers were staring straight ahead; the rest were looking right at me. "Now, like I said, it is a dead certainty that some avatars will be killed, there is no way to victory in this scenario without sacrifice. As you stand in that winner's circle with a few crew members, you're watching as others say their goodbyes. Some of them are angry, others are disappointed. A few may be able to keep a stiff upper lip as they congratulate you, and I'm sure still more are in tears because they know they'll be headed straight into the court system, about to be processed and deposited straight into the stockade.

"What would you want to do? I'm sure that every single one of you would want to step forward and do everything you can to share the victory they worked as hard as you did to accomplish. That is a very special thing, to have the opportunity to stand up and honour those that sacrificed so you could go on and lead your life. Every one of us is just one candle held up against the darkness that surrounds us. We aren't much in our singularity. Bring those points of light together, into a crew who works for the good of the whole, who can make good decisions for them-selves and others, who can trust the men and woman at their sides, and suddenly that one candle grows with the light of many and we are an inferno that presses anything that would violate us back into the darkness.

"I say we'll win this because I know you, and I trust you all to do what you have to and more to keep our fires burning through to the end. When some of us stand in that winners circle, I say we all step forward and tell Admiral Rice and the administrative staff that they take all of us or none and anyone who doesn't agree with that should leave now, because it's your last chance to drag yourself and your kit down that ramp with your dignity intact!"

Oz stepped forward, and started shouting, "All or none! All or none!" and all but one man who stepped forward joined in.

He walked right up and fixed me with a sad smile, then shook my hand. The chant was beginning to falter at the sight of one fellow quitting, so I quickly said, "I understand. Good luck."

As he departed I joined in on the chant and it rose to a deafening roar before we were finished.

When the chanting abated and people had started talking amongst themselves, I got Oz and Ayan's attention. When they came closer, I told them that we'd break so we could continue to get acquainted and then continue with the agenda after lunch. During that break, I met everyone and managed to connect everyone's face with their voice in the scenes and what role they played. I was starting to feel pretty lucky about who had stayed on. So far it was a selection of the best, with few exceptions, and even then the lacklustre members of my new crew had practical experience that would come in handy.

Before long I realized we only had three fighter pilots. Minh-Chu was the only one with any experience in the military, and he'd never really been outside the infantry. Oz came over to the table I was sitting at with a couple of other crewmen. I was nursing another coffee and had become lost in my thoughts, mentally reviewing the roster and what was missing. He tapped me on the shoulder and we moved to a table in the corner.

"You look like you're doing that deep thinking thing again."

I looked at the nineteen crew members left in the room. Including Oz and me, there were twenty one. "We're seriously short. Our finest are sticking around, but we need eleven more fighter pilots, at least fifteen more engineering personnel, thirteen more security people, and at least twenty eight specialized crew, including fighter mechanics, general maintenance, computer specialists, and a few others. We're also missing communications officers, a second shift on the bridge staff, our legal officer, and I'm sure I'm missing something."

"Your second officer."

"Right, and there's no one other than Ayan with a rank that would put them up there and I need her to run Engineering." I watched as some of the non-military put trays out. As directed by Ayan, all the non-military joiners from our team wore the uniform and rank of private or ensign, putting them at the bottom. "These people are good in a simulation, but even in a scenario with automation we're really low and that's going to hurt us. The Admiral is allowing me to choose some trained officers. I thought that would help but now that I've got a head count I'm not sure what kind of scenario we can win."

"Well, we can assume that we won't need the second shift so that's a lot fewer right there, bringing us down to sixty six, then there are the officers which makes us fifty eight short." Oz smiled nervously. "So what you're saying is this is going to be interesting."

"Without knowing how long the simulation will be, what kind of situations we'll run into, or what the win conditions are, it's hard to cut corners, but we don't have much of a choice. How many security personnel can you manage with?"

"Minimally? Five would be the smallest effective counter-incursion team, but if we're boarded in two places we can only secure one location."

"Okay, then we arm everyone who isn't liable to shoot themselves and you're going to have to train them. I'll set you up with a primary team of five and they'll have to do. If we're boarded in two or more places, you go for the nearest incursion and everyone else will have to keep the boarders bottled up until your team can get to them."

"It makes sense, but we'll lose some specialists that way."

Ayan set down her tray and motioned for an ensign to bring two more as she sat down. "I joined the Junior Military Academy when I was fourteen. Graduated right before my eighteenth and celebrated my birthday in Fleet Academy boot."

Oz laughed in surprise and looked her up and down. "Really? No offence, but I wouldn't have guessed."

She shrugged and smiled. "I was a bored military brat looking to rebel against my stuck up Fleet mother, so as soon as I reached the qualifying age for infantry cadet training at fourteen, I signed up. I was a tall girl at five foot one then, but I stopped growing at five three. So I just got stronger than everyone else. My mother was out captaining a ship somewhere and I was able to convince my aunt to sign for my enrolment. I finished my first semester before my mother got back.

"You should have seen her face when she got home and found her muscular daughter in her infantry gear. There's nothing like the daughter of a high ranking Fleet officer signing up for Infantry and beating her mum's entrance marks." Ayan smiled and shook her head at the memory before going on. "She realized that it was better than me running off and breeding with some high school boy, so she let it happen. I finished three more years in cadets and slid right into the Fleet Engineering and Officer's program. I don't know if I could bench press my own body weight anymore, but these days I prefer yoga anyway," she said with a grin.

"Well, there goes that myth. It seems half of Fleet still thinks that the Admiral had a hand in getting you into the

Academy right after your eighteenth birthday in both of the hardest programs they have at the same time," Oz said.

"So you've been checking my file and asking about me, Oz?" she said, looking at him with a raised eyebrow and a hand on her hip. "Do we have a personal issue to discuss here, Warrant Officer?"

Watching her make a man easily twice her size so completely uncomfortable made my day. I don't think I've ever made Oz squirm as much as she did just then. "I've been looking everyone up, you know, to make sure I know what they can do," he said quickly before digging into his salad. I don't think he even looked at it before assaulting it with his fork.

I couldn't help but laugh and shake my head. "Okay, so you can lead your staff in an incursion. Oz will train them with everyone else and engineering won't be a soft target."

Ayan said, "I have an idea that might help us with our security situation, too. During the scene, let's all keep our vacsuits sealed up, hood and all. We'll clear all the unnecessary decks and if we get an incursion, we'll blow the seals in that section. They might be boarding in vacsuits or armour, but I'm sure if we time it right it'll slow them down, maybe even blow them right out into space. Sealed suit or not, it will probably take them some time to boost back to an airlock."

"That could work. It's a really old strategy, but it could work," Oz said around a mouth full of lettuce.

"It's an old ship. There's enough metal in five feet of deck plating to build a modern Raze fighter. The Fleet built her before the form fit adaptable vacsuit was invented, so decompression was an even bigger issue then and people couldn't run around in a suit they could seal in under three seconds with their hands free. They also had more ergranian steel than they knew what to do with from the Blue Belt. Too bad they lost it ages ago."

"If we keep this up we might only need the officers the Admiral offered. The only problem is, we have no wing commander."

"What about Minh-Chu?"

"He works alone better than anyone I've seen, but he takes a lot of risks and doesn't always track what everyone else is doing," I replied, though it stung to admit it. "He's our best pilot, and he's had actual time in the cockpit, but I'm not sure of him."

"I think he's going on the understanding that he's your wing commander. I've heard him talk about it a few times now, and he's not thinking like a soloist anymore, for the most part. I'd give him a shot," Oz said quietly.

"'Balance against uncertainty with sure things and reliable people.' Officer training 101. He might be good, probably has the mind for it, and I know he can command people on the ground. I saw it in the war, but I've never seen him do it in the cockpit," I replied.

Ayan fixed me with a serious look. "So set him up as your wing commander in the drills, and request a qualified commander from the Admiral. That way you're giving him a chance and providing for the possibility of him going off on his own when it counts. He'll have a second in command who can pick up the slack. I'm surprised this is something you haven't thought your way through. Excuse me, I have to get my staff together, it's almost time to resume the briefing."

Oz and I watched her walk away. "She runs hot and cold on

a millisecond's notice. Keeps us guessing, that's for sure," he muttered.

"She's under a lot of pressure, and the few of us who are officers are trying to balance the friendships we have here with our professional responsibilities. We're trained for it, but these are unusual circumstances. A lot of these people aren't used to taking orders from a superior officer."

"Guess that's how she deals: one face for friends, another for command."

"That's what they teach us in officers training, and she's right about the situation with Minh. I should have had that figured out as soon as I saw the roster. I'm getting distracted by worrying when I should be thinking my way through these problems."

"Sometimes it takes a few heads to come up with the best solutions. You're also taking on a lot more without as much experience. I trust you as our captain. I've seen you work in a lot of scenes, but there's a hell of a lot here you're not used to dealing with, like keeping a ship together when it's not in combat, managing a crew, setting up training, and dealing with shortfalls. Without a first officer to share some of that, it's twice as bad. But there's hope. You've got me here, Skipper." Oz grinned, gripping my shoulder. "I'll keep the crew in line, make sure people are where they are supposed to be, and you have a Chief Engineer with years served on this ship. Not just any ship, but the one we're on right now. Oh, and you just handed the wing command position over to a hyperactive pilot with something to prove, so I'd say let him take charge and watch him go."

"You're right, Oz, that's a lot off my shoulders. Consider it done. You're in charge of crew and all that comes with it, and I'll hand Minh-Chu his orders after the briefing."

The rest of the briefing went well. Ayan's part was quick and professional. She marked the areas of the ship that would be off limits in our drill simulations and the final scenario, went through emergency procedures and our virtual weaponry inventory. The Sunspire was equipped with eight rail cannon turrets firing any of six different kinds of ammunition, one heavy beam emplacement, two multi-purpose torpedo launchers, and one fighter bay that could launch seven fighters from small chambers located lengthwise along the underside of the hull. All the weapons could be secured and hidden away while not in combat.

The final refit of the Sunspire would include low energy shielding, multi-purpose materializers distributed evenly across the hull, multi layered refractive energy shields for redirecting incoming beam weapon fire away from the ship, and a regenerative reflective hull. Using the emitters, the Sunspire would be able to create its own wormholes. It also had hyperspace systems for travelling to other destinations at a much slower rate.

She assigned everyone to review some of the schematics so they would know more about the areas of the ship they would be working in, and referred the crew to some short documents that would help them understand some of the technology the ship depended on before ending her part of the briefing.

After she was finished, Oz gave his part of the briefing and informed everyone that there would be weapons training, that anyone with some proficiency would have to carry a sidearm during any and all drills and simulations, and introduced the four members of his security team. The crew seemed comfortable with him and his team being in charge of keeping order on the ship. He was personable, and as I watched him give his briefing at the head of the room, I realized that he looked the part as well.

After the briefing was concluded, I announced that the first drill would be in fifteen minutes. I hadn't warned anyone our first drill would be so soon, but Ayan, Oz, and even Minh-Chu had the crew organized and on their way to their stations in no time. As he rushed by, I caught Minh's arm and activated his trainee wing commander rank. Seven gold wings appeared on his collar and shoulder. "It's official, you're my wing commander. Congratulations, Commander Buu. I'll get you a real rank pin when this is all over," I said quietly.

He grinned broadly and pinned the wings to his collar. "Your best decision yet, Captain!" he said, before snapping me a salute and rushing his two pilots down the hall towards their simulation pods.

It was time to find out how much work we had ahead of us as a crew. The scenario hadn't been running more than two minutes before it became obvious that we had a long way to go. The new conditions had shaken us up, broken us out of our familiar routines, and we were missing so many people, filling so many gaps. Once again, we were talented individuals; the challenge we faced was becoming a team all over again.

The next day, my requests for personnel were sent and Fleet Command had new crew members on their way by early afternoon. They were all young men and women with spotless records. Several pilots came with more than a year's experience and a mission success rate higher than our simulation win rate. There were deck crewmen who were just coming off leave, and a few computer systems and general systems maintenance personnel with medical and basic combat training. I couldn't have been more pleased, especially since they all seemed very happy to come aboard, had their gear stowed and were at work within twenty minutes. They were in the next drill and boosted morale by helping us meet all the win conditions.

Over the next three days, anyone was lucky to get eight hours of rest and relaxation time - officers were fortunate if they got six. Drills, system reconfigurations, customizations, combat, flight systems, and general training filled every hour of our waking days. By the last day only two of us were unarmed in the drills, we were getting comfortable with the new systems, and the response time of the entire crew was better than I had ever seen when we were running scenes in our spare time.

It took over a dozen drills and hours of training over the course of three and a half days, but as I sat on the makeshift bridge in the middle of a semi transparent command hologram, I realized how far we had come using only a fifth of our original team. I listened to the chatter and watched the tight precision with which everyone performed. The small squad of seven fighters, six two man gunnery crews, engine efficiency, and bridge crew all worked the plan moment by moment as one unit. The scenario that I was putting them through was famous for being difficult to coordinate and harder to win. It was called Three Stations and the objective was to wipe out three enemy fighter squadrons and deploy a worm hole point generator so boarding parties could come in shuttles and begin boarding operations.

The Sunspire and its seven fighters had little if any chance of even finishing this scenario, let alone surviving for more than twenty minutes. But with everyone doing their best, working a good plan that changed as needed and reacting faster than I'd ever seen, we were over forty minutes in, had three fighters left and had collectively killed or disabled more than half of the forty eight enemy fighters.

Just as we lost one rail cannon turret and the crew — who had abandoned just in time — were running to another, Oz tapped me on the shoulder.

"There's a command level communication coming in, Sir. Your eyes only," he whispered.

"All right, scrub this drill in five minutes. We've already gone much further than expected with the people we have. I'll take the communiqué in one of the storage rooms."

"Yes, Sir."

I turned the command hologram off and got my bearings for a moment. After staring at a hologram that surrounded my command chair for so long, it took a moment to regain my balance.

The temporary bridge, which was set up just for simulations, was in the forward section of the main engineering level. Everything behind was still open to vacuum since they were just about to bring in the four new power plants. There was a storage room just a few meters down the hall, and after I stepped in and the door was closed, I called up a screen on the command and control unit on my left forearm. "You were doing very well in that last scenario, Jonas. It is too bad you could not complete it. Your chance of success was up to twelve point nineteen percent, rounding up of course."

"Of course. Thank you, Alice, I don't think we would have made it, but the crew is getting used to the odds. Do you think you could bring up that Command level transmission? I don't want to keep them waiting."

"I'll put Admiral Rice on right away."

With less than a second's delay, the admiral's holographic visage was in front of me smiling. "Hello, Captain, how are things going in dry dock?"

"Good afternoon, Admiral. Better than I expected. Those crew members you sent us fit right in."

"I'm glad to hear it, but not surprised. When we put your ship on the internal board as a volunteer posting we had over two hundred applicants. We let our psychologists pick for you. However, that's not why I'm on the line with you, Trainee Captain. I've been watching your drills, and quite frankly I'm impressed. Everyone is holding together well and even the crew members that didn't start out as military are holding up to our standards."

"Thank you, Admiral, I'll pass that on to the crew when it's appropriate."

Admiral Rice smiled, an expression I hadn't seen from her before. It was unnerving. "That doesn't sound like the young man who stood in my office a week ago, I hope there's some of him left under that uniform. You've come a long way, you deserve some credit."

"Thank you, Admiral. I have a good crew."

"I'm aware of that. Now, let's get to the root of the matter. I'm making your rank official and drafting everyone on the Sunspire. Her refit is getting a rush and she's to be ready in four days. Congratulations, Captain."

I was startled but managed to lamely blurt out, "thank you, Admiral," and she went on.

"The Paladin is on her way back with a Triad Consortium fleet on its heels."

"Isn't the Paladin a twelve kilometre long super-carrier?"

"It is, but she's no match for what's behind her. The transmission they were able to relay to us indicated that they were searching for activity at the edge of our coreward territory when they intercepted a burst transmission. The decoded message detailed a Triad invasion headed our way. I can only assume that The Paladin was discovered and had to make a break for it. With two of our battle groups too far out to be of assistance, they have no choice but to regroup in another sector and see what happens here. Meanwhile, our third battle group will arrive ahead of the enemy. The fourth battle group will be on station at approximately the same time as The Paladin and her pursuers. We need every ship, and since your crew is looking better than any of our fresh graduates and they already know the Sunspire, we're activating you, promoting one of your officers, and filling the empty spots on your roster. Your new crew should begin arriving in one hour. Until combat orders are issued, any qualified personnel should assist with the refit while others continue your training regimen. After all, your training is harder than the simulation testing we're putting our cadets through. Do you understand our situation and your orders, Captain Valent?"

"Yes, Admiral, I understand and will carry them out," I said officially.

"Good luck. Admiral Rice out."

I took a moment to look at our orders and the conditions of our commission and I was surprised. The Sunspire was to be renamed at my leisure and assigned to a blind battle group that would only be aware of the other ships in the group if necessary. There was another detail that made me grin and chuckle to myself.

I turned off the screen and projector on the arm of my uniform and heard Alice whisper in my ear. "So, since you're a real captain now, do I get to live in one of those big, powerful, and oh so pretty officer class forearm command consoles? I've always wanted to see what it was like to operate on eight trillion nano processors," my AI cooed.

"I suppose you will, as soon as I figure out where I pick it up."

"I believe it should be brought aboard by one of the new maintenance staff. It's in the roster you didn't have time to look through."

"Right, no time. Broadcast a shipwide message, all Sunspire crew must report to the common room immediately."

"Transmitting shipwide, Jonas."

"Can you do me a favour, Alice?" I asked as I walked out into the hall.

"That depends on the favour."

"Call me Captain." I grinned.

I was one of the last to enter the common room. "Captain on deck!" Oz called out in a thunderous voice. Everyone lined up according to rank and I waited quietly as the last of the crew filed in. Their expressions ranged from the passive readiness that came with training all the way to outright nervous.

"Sunspire computer, change all crew uniforms from trainee to current profile rank and colour," I called out. A moment later, everyone's uniform turned from green and blue to blue and black and the rank insignias on everyone's collar changed. The circular pips of the trainee reformed into slashes on their collars. A silent notification appeared on small screens on everyone's wrists, informing them of their new rank and that they had new orders to review.

The members of the crew that had military training stood still and at attention, trying to suppress whatever reaction they would normally have but with varied success. Everyone else celebrated. Oz looked to me and raised an eyebrow as I nodded in response. "Settle, people!" he called out.

Everyone was back in a quiet line within seconds. "The Admiral and her staff have been watching us. Our progress was so impressive that she didn't see fit to enter us into an official test. Our progress and current Fleet conditions made an early decision necessary, and we're all being pressed into service. As soon as the refit is complete we will join a blind battle group." I could see Ayan trying to suppress a big smile and until that moment I hadn't realized how low my spirits had fallen. Seeing her so happy was all I needed.

I went on. "The bad news in all this is that we are about to go to war. The Triad Consortium is on their way, right on the heels of the Paladin and we have to be ready. We'll be receiving new crew members over the next five hours, so make them feel welcome. All qualified personnel are to aid in the final refit as directed by our Chief Engineer, and we are all on orders of silence with concern to the details of our ship's role. I can give you all two hours before we get to work, so get something to eat and relax. Oh, and one more thing : welcome to the Freeground Fleet."

I couldn't help but notice Oz look down at his wrist for the first time since the uniform shift. A big grin spread across his face before he looked up at me. "Commander?" he mouthed silently.

I nodded and made the hand signal for first officer and his grin got a little toothier. I was so distracted I didn't see Ayan, who came to stand right beside me.

"Congratulations, Captain." She smiled.

"Thank you. Congratulations on your reactivation as Commander. Are you staying with us?"

"Those are my orders."

The joviality drained from me and was replaced with concern. "Do you want to stay with us?" I asked in a whisper.

"Nowhere I'd rather be," she said with a tired looking smile. She took my hand and shook it, one officer to another. "Congratulations again. I'll be in Engineering."

She was out the door before I could think of anything to do or say that wouldn't draw attention. One of her engineering staff did notice what went on, and was looking at me. I called her over. She was one of the original simulation team members. Mira was her name in the simulations, but her real name was Laura. From what I could remember, she held two Masters Degrees: one in advanced field mechanics and the other in hyperspace theory, which earned her a higher entry rank than most of the team. "Can you do me a favour, Sergeant?" I asked.

"Yes, Sir." She smiled as soon as she heard her rank aloud for the first time.

"Take a few minutes to say congratulations to any friends you have here, then get a few sandwiches for yourself and Commander Rice and join her in Engineering. Learn as much as you can about the systems down there while you have the chance, but refit or not, everyone has to eat sometime. Make sure you eat together."

"I'll bring her favourite tea while I'm at it, Sir," she said with a salute and a smile. "You're good at this, you know," she whispered.

I really didn't know what to say, and it must have shown.

"Taking care of us, I mean. I can't see anyone else with these slashes, not on this ship, anyway," she said, pulling at the rank insignia on my collar and for the first time I think it finally sunk in. I was really a captain, with all the responsibilities and respect that came with it.

"Thank you," I managed to say before she ran off to talk to a few friends.

I was just thinking how hard it would be to get used to being saluted, when Oz tapped me on the shoulder. Minh-Chu was standing beside him, polishing his new rank insignia of lieutenant. "So, I'll be your First Officer for this trip," Oz said.

"Better you than me. He's a handful. You should have seen him as a civilian, always coming around my restaurant, drowning his sorrows with lo mein and sweet and sour pork," Minh said.

"I never heard you complaining, and come to think of it, I didn't see many other customers, either."

Oz put one hand on each of our shoulders and shook his head. "You two are going to have to cease fire otherwise I'll just have to take charge. Captain Terry Ozark McPatrick. Has a pretty good ring to it if, I say so myself. Maybe I'll have the crew call me Skipper."

The next day seemed to go by in a flash of minutes. Single

tasks seemed to take too long and there was never enough time for me to get other things completed as well as I liked.

I was finally starting to get used to delegating, but people still had to remind me that there was always someone else who would be happy to finish most jobs I started. The second day went much more smoothly. My officer training had never been fully put to use before then and I found that as time went on it was all coming back to me. My own duties started falling into a specific order, and with no time to spare.

My job was to ensure the well-being and success of the crew and ship. When I wasn't making general decisions, my central task was to make sure that all the different sections were doing what I needed them to do. Micromanagement was left to all the officers below me and there were long moments of quiet between the busy times where I could watch them sealing up the lower hull after finishing the implementation of our new power plants, or load our twenty one fighters and two combat shuttles. These were the times when my officers had everything well in hand and it was up to me to consider the big picture, tactics, strategy, and the strengths and weaknesses of the ship and crew.

I found I was always researching the crew members, ship systems, our capabilities, and every few hours I had questions for one of my officers. As a former technician, I had a place to start, some idea of what I was talking about. As an officer, I knew how to point my questions to get the answer as quickly as possible and not distract my crew from the variety of tasks they had to perform.

The new arrivals were all there because they wanted to be. I could see it, walking the ship as Alice whispered all the crew requests and details that needed to be ironed out. I may have looked like I was inspecting the ship, but I was more interested in seeing how everyone worked together. The trained staff who had just come aboard were more interested in helping the newly enlisted than turning their noses up at them, and I even saw one of our original team show one of the new arrivals a few improvements she had made. The crewman looked pretty surprised and even more impressed.

When I arrived on the flight deck, where a great deal of fine tuning was being done on the fighters we had been given — three groups of used but well repaired Valkyrie Interceptors — Minh-Chu pulled me aside. "Do you know that all these pilots and mechanics are volunteers?" he asked, obviously surprised.

"From what I understand, everyone volunteered. Playbacks of our last few scenarios leaked out while we were busy training here. I think the Admiral actually expected us to pass their test."

"Most of these pilots have more flight time than I do, but they listen to everything I say. One is even modifying his ship so it's more like the mods I flew with in the scenes."

"Well, that's what happens when you log a few thousand hours in simulations then wipe the floor with the academy instructors on a hacked connection. We're the Fleet's new bad boys. Don't let it go to your head. We have to be better than ever to live through whatever the Admiral has planned for us. Something tells me that she won't be pulling punches just because her daughter is on board."

"What do you think she has planned?"

"Well, we're in a separate battle group in a newly refitted ship. They haven't resurfaced her either, so I'm assuming that our ship looking a lot older than its systems might play into our strategic placement. Whatever it is, I'm thinking it'll lead us into a very dangerous situation pretty early on."

"Is it true that we've been refitted as a gunship? The gun crews have been loading ammunition materializers bigger than I saw in the infantry. They got that technology to work just in the last few years. Our cannons will never run out of ammunition as long as there's power and liquid or scrap for the materializers. How many turrets do we have anyway? I counted at least ten."

"The final refit has us loaded with twenty eight rail turrets, and all of them are retractable and hidden. We only have one beam weapon, though."

"Why did we only run our drills with eight?"

"It's the original compliment of cannons for the ship. There were some things we couldn't modify. I also don't think they wanted us to know about it in case we failed the final scenario."

"Good point. Well, I know which direction to go if I need cover." Minh chuckled. "Twenty eight variable-load rail cannons on turrets that never run out of ammunition. I thought these Valkyries were heavily armed for their size. A pair of rail guns, two particle cannons, and a rocket launcher with enough room for forty eight missiles. There's even retractable exterior clamps for extra heavy weaponry. I don't think they're outfitting us for espionage."

"I know you'll find a way to hide when you have to. Knowing Fleet Command, they'll find a way to use that, too."

"Well, a small cloaking field on each ship may help. Think you could ask for me?"

"Put in a requisition. I'll forward it on," I replied with a grin.

"Oh, put an extra couple slashes on your collar and you're Fleet's man now. I see how it is."

"I'll see what I can do, but a requisition would still help."

"Sure, as soon as we get back from whatever Fleet has us doing. I'll ask for energy shields and a cup holder, while I'm at it. That way I might get the cup holder."

"There's a transmission from Fleet Command, Captain and they need you on the bridge," Alice chimed in so both Minh and I could hear.

"Looks like things are about to get started," I said. "Are you ready?"

"We're fully loaded and just fine tuning. Good luck, Captain," Minh said with a sidelong smile.

"Good luck, Commander." I stopped at the main hatchway for a moment. "Commander Buu," I called out.

"Yes, Sir," he shouted in response. It was an image that is still so clear in my mind, him standing there with one hand on the hull of his Valkyrie fighter.

"May your life be interesting!" I shouted before continuing on to the bridge.

When I arrived on the bridge, I checked the transmission from Fleet Command. Our orders were in and we were out of time. After reviewing them as quickly as possible, I forwarded them on to the officers. I knew that within minutes, briefings would begin all over the ship. And I knew we would be greeting the Triad Consortium fleet in our own very special way soon after.

SIX

THE DEFENCE

The ship was adrift amidst a field of compressed waste and old hulls that were in queue to be recycled. There was always a heavy trash drift near the station, forever changing shape as different materials were added. With our power plants idle and our systems running on cold capacitors, we looked like just another piece of flotsam.

Hiding in plain sight was a tactic the original team used all the time, one of our specialities, and it made all the new members of Fleet aboard feel like this was somehow familiar. It was no mistake. Fleet Command knew exactly how to put us to good use.

Minh-Chu and his entire wing of twenty one fighters were individually hidden as well. Looking to the thermal, electromagnetic, and visual scanner results projected in the middle of the bridge, I could see that none of us were emitting detectable levels of energy. There was no way to separate us from the trash.

I set my command hologram to view the field and it

appeared on the main holodisplay. My personal display contained two visual representations of the ship's position, another broader view of the entire combat area, ship system details, communication summaries, and the command controls, but everything was much more streamlined. With Alice controlling its functions, she could assist in carrying out my decisions and prioritizing information.

"Set the main display to the expected arrival coordinates and encompass the starboard side of the station," I commanded. The ship computer rotated the main holographic image so my viewpoint started at the station's centre and looked out towards the core of the galaxy to the point in space we expected the Paladin to drop out of hyperspace.

Oz stood beside me, and I looked over the rest of the bridge staff who were reviewing the status of their systems, glancing up at the main hologram in the middle of the bridge occasionally and collectively holding their breath.

Without thinking, I squeezed Jason Everin's shoulder. He was one of the people I knew from the simulation team who was qualified as a Communications and Intelligence Officer. "Deep breaths, just keep your mind clear until there's an enemy transmission to decode," I said quietly.

"Yes, Sir," he replied, trying to disguise his tension with a half smile.

In the space of a heartbeat our circumstances became very real. The Paladin decelerated out of hyperspace, dispersing the white and red particles that covered the ship during faster than light travel, and appeared in front of the Third Fleet. The Fleet made a hole in its centre for the allied ship to move through. After a few seconds, I realized my hands were balled into white-knuckled fists. I shook them open and sat down in the Captain's chair. "Easy, the Triad Fleet should be right behind. Silent running."

Seconds passed, then minutes. Hearing Sergeant Everin's console come alive with incoming enemy transmissions was a temporary relief to the tension on the bridge. Too temporary. The digital noise was from the Paladin, the signal that preceded a ship's arrival. I always thought I could hear hints of voices under the signal, but it was a trick of the ear, ghosts our imaginations conjured while trying to make sense of the noise. "Enemy comm noise," Jason said as he started working his holographic and key command console with blinding speed. "Decoding. Looks like ninety four layer ten twenty four bit encryption. We'll be unscrambling their transmissions over five minutes behind using the codes we already have to start from."

"Just keep working and remember to patch into the station's cypher database as soon as we can start communicating with Fleet again. They might be able to provide us with more up-to-date codes."

"Yes, Sir."

"Computer, start a countdown on all ship displays coordinated with the arrival counter on my command console and label it 'Triad Arrival.' Base the counter's value on when we first started receiving transmissions." The count-down started on everyone's display at seventeen seconds, floating just off to the side of whatever task they were doing.

On the main display, I could see the Paladin forming up with the rest of the Third Fleet alongside several other carriers half the size, fifteen destroyers, a five kilometre long command ship, and over a hundred smaller ships. The Paladin began launching wings of fighters and small gunships.

My eye wandered to the half of Freeground Station I could see on the display represented semi-transparently. At the current magnification I couldn't see specifics, only the general shapes of habitat rings, platforms, extensions, and construction frames. Even though it was my home and I'd grown up seeing its image, it had never looked so beautiful or so fragile. It hung in the darkness like a luminescent metal flower.

The seconds counted down to zero and the digits disappeared. The Triad Consortium attack fleet appeared right in front of the Freeground Third Battle Group. Both sides opened fire immediately, and even from where we sat we could see flashes of light through the window. The main holographic projection switched to tactical mode and Sergeant Everin looked up from his display.

The Triad fleet was easily twice the size of our forward defences, and the Third Fleet began a planned retreat to draw them towards the station. The immediate combat status appeared on my personal command screen and I made it too small for anyone else to see. The cost of the engagement was mounting by the second.

"Wormhole distortion detected! A second enemy fleet is about to arrive!" Sergeant Everin marked the projected arrival point on the main display and returned to deciphering enemy communications.

"Command expected this. It's why we're here," I said just as much to myself as to everyone else.

"The communications we can understand indicate they're

pre-plotting fighter launch sequences. There must be more than one carrier coming in."

"Nice decrypting, Sergeant."

The marked point was right between where we were hidden and the station. I stood up, looking at nothing else. Five Triad carriers came out of hyperspace just outside the engagement area. "They don't come light, do they?" I said. "Continue holding, we need to give them time to launch fighters. Recheck the loads on our rail cannons. We'll only get one good shot at this dirty little trick."

"Gunners all report one hundred twenty rounds of munition seven loaded. They're ready to switch to piercing and explosive shells after their initial barrage."

"Good. Get ready to fire everything on my command." I could see the first waves of fighters and smaller gunships launching from the Triad carriers and waited for the second group. It came seconds later.

"Their launch crews certainly are efficient," Oz said from just behind me.

"With the credits the Triad has, they're probably all automated," I said as I watched the third wave launch. "They can probably afford combat androids."

"Or they're mass produced genetically altered clones. Messy, but effective."

I nodded at Oz's supposition. "Just one more wave." I didn't have to wait long before I saw another mass of fighters and other small ships appear on the main display. "Ahead full! Begin firing sequence and get me a firing solution on the nearest carrier. Prioritize her sensors with the beam weapon, and launch bays with both torpedoes," I commanded.

The dead silence that had threatened to smother us was gone. The hum of the ship's systems and burning of the massive ion engines thrusting harder than ever added to my enthusiasm. The bridge crew of fourteen officers was hard at work. "Bring refractive shielding online, and focus our energy shield on the bridge. Be ready to counter-charge the ablative layer of the hull."

"We've got to look like a flare on their sensors," Oz said with a chuckle.

"If we're lucky it'll be the last thing all those fighter pilots see," I commented as I watched the orientation of the ship shift as the rail guns pointed towards the groups of enemy fighters, bombers, and gunships. We fired our specialized railgun rounds. Munition seven was restricted for a reason; they were micro nukes made to detonate in a long dispersal pattern. In less time than predicted - nine seconds - all the rail guns had fired their one hundred twenty rounds. The deadly projectiles drifted towards the multitude of enemy ships, emitting no detectable radiological, magnetic, or thermal signal, and too small to track individually on most sensors. They wouldn't do anything against the hull of a carrier, but it would be a different story with fighters and gunships.

I held my breath as the shells closed the distance between the hundreds of fighters headed towards the station and our fleet.

The carriers began firing beam weapons at our ship, but our refractive shielding redirected the energy and light components of the beams while our thick ablative hull absorbed the impacts of the tiny charged particles.

I kept watching the progress of our nuclear shells; I couldn't look away. The enemy ships began turning suddenly. They realized what we had fired, but too late. I couldn't help but bring my fist down on the arm of my chair as I saw thousands of points of light wipe out or disable all the fighters, bombers, and shuttles the carriers had launched. Six waves by the time the shells went off, their entire offensive compliment. I wasn't the only one. Most of the bridge crew couldn't help but cheer momentarily as the bulk of the Triad fighter cover for the engagement was destroyed. All that read on our sensors was a mass of ruined hulls where the small crafts had been. The smallest of the craft had been vaporized.

The fight was far from over. The Sunspire was headed towards the carrier group, still rotating slowly, giving our rail cannon turrets even access to targets and preventing any overheating. "Prioritize rail cannon fire on any incoming torpedoes or other projectiles. Don't let anything through. Fire the beam weapon at any sensors you can lock onto, we just need to keep them blind long enough to use the nearest carrier as cover."

"First torpedoes are away, Sir," Tactical reported.

"Target their weapon emplacements and fire both tubes until we get to one thousand kilometres, then load tube two with a high-focus nuke and hold it. We can deal with any beam weaponry they've got, and maybe redirect their fire back at them once we're close enough."

The first of the defensive screen of fighters began heading towards us from the nearest carrier and I smiled, flicking a switch on my chair. "Are you still awake out there, old friend?"

"Barely. Need some cover?" replied Minh-Chu. A second later, the field of debris behind us lit up as our screen of twenty one fighters came to life and fired their engines to close the short distance between them and the enemy.

The first wave of enemy fighters was destroyed in seconds thanks to our own squadron and the assistance of our railguns. They had come at us straight on, leaving themselves in the open. It was unlikely the next enemy squad would make the same mistake. Our fighters took up position behind the Sunspire to keep pace and stay out of the way until we needed them.

As we drew closer to the nearest carrier, its size was becoming apparent. It seemed to stretch on forever to the right and left, over eighteen kilometres long with dozens of beam emplacements and large rail cannons. We were closing on the four hundred kilometre range, and all the beam weapons on our side of the destroyer were firing. Most of them didn't carry any particles, and our twelve layer refractive shielding was redirecting all of it away from the ship.

There were only two rail cannons left that were large enough to damage us, but that was two too many. "I need those rail guns destroyed." We were close enough for our next torpedoes to travel so fast that the chance of hitting before the enemy perimeter defences could destroy them were very high, but I had other plans for our torpedo bays at this range, so I opened communications with Minh once more. "Take out those rail cannons," I commanded, knowing I was sending his wing into the most dangerous zone on that side of the enemy ship.

I turned to Oz then. "Fire the nuclear torpedo right into their launch bay, set it off deep." He knew there was no time to argue, we were closing on three hundred kilometres. "Helm, reverse thrust and turn us sideways as soon as the torpedo is away. Take us along her starboard side." I opened a line to Engineering. "How are our power systems holding out?"

"Generating forty percent of capacity, storage cells are all holding at ninety seven percent. We have enough to run another ship our size," Ayan replied.

I was more than a little surprised. "Hull integrity?"

"No serious damage yet, seems the Triad didn't expect anyone to use refractive shielding since it was phased out a century ago by most corporate outfits."

"Can you give me another eight layers? I think it's time we cause some real damage."

"Yes, Sir!"

I looked to Ensign Fielding and she nodded. "We have enough refractive layers to redirect their beam weapons right back at them, Sir."

"Let's cut them up a bit," I ordered with a grin.

Just as I gave the order, the nuclear torpedo that had targeted their exposed launch bays went off, and I double checked the status of our fighters. Only two had been destroyed so far, and none had been caught in the nuclear blast. I couldn't help but look at the damage we had done to the launch bays as the area became visible through the bridge windows. It was a glowing pit of a wound, outlined by molten metal and sections explosively decompressing.

"Commander Buu reports both rail cannons have been disabled," Oz reported from behind me.

"So Minh made it out of there?" I realized how unprofessional the question was as soon as it was asked. Oz didn't seem to fault me for it.

"He made it out fine."

"Good, get him out of the high risk zone and tell him to use the Sunspire as cover. We'll need them for more important tasks."

We had crippled the carrier, but as we moved past the rear section and ruined launch bay, it became obvious that we hadn't disabled her. All the beam emplacements fired at once, along with her much smaller remaining rail gun turrets. The beams were reflected straight back at the carrier's hull, cutting into and opening entire sections.

"Sir, we're not taking any direct damage from weapon's fire, but our hull is heating up fast from the near misses and their rail guns are all targeting the bridge. The energy shield won't last more than ninety seconds at this rate."

I didn't have to think about it, the words just came out. "Abandon the bridge. Head for the emergency command centre." I opened communications with Ayan as everyone stopped what they were doing and made for the pair of lifts at the rear of the bridge. "Reinforce the shields on the bridge for two minutes and take command. We're headed down to the emergency controls."

"Yes, Sir," she replied. I felt the deck shake violently and heard an impact that made my ears ring. As the lift closed I remember thinking that wasn't a small rail gun impact.

SEVEN

DAWN

There was no warning, only bright lights and doctors. I was out of bed and on my feet in what felt like the blink of an eye. I glanced around the room and saw the bed, restraints, two medical technicians who were in an absolute panic, an emergency cart, and a neural interface cart with the cable ripped out.

The technicians were on their way out the door and I grabbed one by the elbow. "It was simulated?" He looked at me nervously and nodded.

Security came running and stopped at the door. The technician freed his arm and waved them off. "He just came out of it a bit too suddenly and ripped the cable out of the neural interface circlet. Other than a really sore neck, he'll be fine."

I reached up to find the headpiece still firmly seated on my head and the cable leading from it. My neck was already aching and getting worse by the second. Oz and Ayan were in the doorway a moment later. "Some scenario, wasn't it, Captain?" he asked, flicking his rank insignia with a finger, looking a little disappointed. Suddenly I felt very foolish and took the head piece off properly, put it on an instrument tray and nodded. "I wonder why they felt they had to trick us into it?"

Ayan stepped into the room with a crooked grin. "At least you didn't actually get crushed in the remains of the bridge. They put us all under the night after you met with the Admiral. None of us were told."

"The Admiral. Your mother."

"Yes, my mother," she affirmed, looking so irritated I wished I hadn't brought it up. "This has got to be the most twisted thing she's ever put me through." She looked up at me for a silent moment. "Anyone through," she added.

I fixed the security officer with a level gaze. "Lead the way, Private." I meant to say it cordially, but realized after I sounded forceful. I knew there was a debriefing coming, and soon. He'd know where to take us so we could get on with it.

He led us to a large briefing room furnished with a long table and chairs. I felt betrayed, deceived, and even a little stupid at being fooled into thinking that all that had happened over the past few days was true. I tried massaging my sore neck while wrapping my head around the idea of just lying in bed for however many days had passed instead of living through the challenges we had faced.

After a few minutes Ayan got up from where she sat and took a seat beside me at one end of the table and Oz sat on my other side. She rubbed my shoulders and neck. "I shouldn't be this angry," I said quietly. "If that were real, I would have gotten us all killed."

"No, most of us survived until the next allied battle group came out of hyperspace behind the Triad carriers. I was leading a rescue party into the lift shaft when they shut the scenario down."

"Even I managed to survive," Minh-Chu said as he walked in. He dropped himself into a chair. "I was about to take out a fighter as they woke me up." His mood was equally dark but somehow casual, relaxed. "Going back to making ramen and egg rolls is going to be difficult."

Others were coming in, their moods unsure; no one was talking.

"I can't call it. Did we meet the win conditions?" Oz asked no one in particular. "First Officer felt good. Real good."

"That's the question, after all this, living days in a simulation without even knowing it. Did we pass their test? Did they like what they saw?" I agreed.

"I suppose they did see everything," I heard Ayan say to herself quietly. There was a sedate sadness in her voice. I took her hand.

"About time we met for real," I said to her with a smile. It took a moment for her to realize that it actually was the first time we had met in person. She smiled back as she put her chin on my shoulder and took Minh's hand. He took Laura's, Laura took Jason Everin's and so forth until the circle led back to Oz and I. It took me that long to figure out what I had to say. "No matter what happens here, we were a damn good crew in there."

"All or none," Oz said quietly.

"All or none," several people in the room replied. The twenty one crew members that had started in our regular simulations were all there, and I couldn't have been more proud of them. The chant began, and by the time a sergeant entered the room I'm sure half the station could hear us.

"Attention! Admiral on deck!" the sergeant called out, silencing the room. We all stood at attention, most of us doing so from reflexes learned in Academy, the rest by example.

Rear Admiral Rice and another officer with the rank of Vice Admiral, a woman in her fifties with long blond hair, walked into the room and sat down at the table opposite me. "Be seated, everyone. At ease," she said in a raspy voice. When we were all seated, she went on. "I am Vice Admiral McKinley. Before I begin, Rear Admiral Rice has a few things to formalize."

"Thank you, Vice Admiral. The decision to insert you into a surprise scenario came from Fleet Intelligence. After reviewing my reports on you, they thought that we had to increase the perceived risk factor. After reviewing the preliminary results, I can see that we satisfied their requirements and passed their psych evaluations.

"Having said that, it is my distinct pleasure to inform you that all charges have been dropped. As a crew, and as individuals, you have surpassed the expectations of Fleet Command and met all win conditions of the simulation in which you have participated in for the last six days."

The last sentence was more a matter of record. Everyone was so busy sighing with relief her words went practically unheard. It took at least a few minutes for us to get it out of our system. When we had, Admiral Rice went on. "The results of the exercise are being studied. You had many unconventional solutions for the problems we put in front of you. There were also signs that members of the crew who didn't complete an Academy program are in need of instructions where the chain of command and basic procedures are concerned. You will all receive a report on your performance as well as instructions on how to operate within the structure required while you're aboard. It is important you put this into practice as soon as possible, so your department heads don't have to waste their time holding your hand while you learn the ropes.

"Service men and women should see a report from your former commanding officers tomorrow morning. It is our expectation that you will all review the reports carefully; the advice could be critical to you as enlisted officers.

"I realize that most of the people at this table never went through Fleet Academy. If conditions were different, I would send you there, but we don't have time. The threat that we included in the simulation you just experienced is real. The Paladin is on her way back with a Triad fleet on her heels. In less than five days she'll come out of hyperspace and the third, fourth and seventh Battle Groups will be out there waiting to greet her. We expect to defeat whatever comes, so you won't be part of the action. Not this time anyway."

Rear Admiral Rice sighed and smiled a little. "To be honest, I'm surprised. I expected some people to carry the weight while others spent all their time fighting their way over the learning curve. Instead, I had the opportunity to witness everyone play to their strengths and offer their support to the crewman next to them. It normally takes months, even years, to form such a camaraderie and fellowship. There are instructors who are very unhappy you succeeded, and more still who are pleasantly surprised. With that thought, I'll turn the briefing over to Vice Admiral McKinley. Good luck."

"Thank you. Now that you're all pleased with yourselves, I have the pleasure of asking one last time before enlisting the lot of you, if there is a man or woman here who does not see themselves as fit for service. If so, please leave the room now. There will be no dishonour or punishment in doing so." She waited several seconds before continuing on.

I looked around the table to see that everyone was firmly planted in their seat, and I nearly laughed aloud when I saw Minh-Chu leaning back with his fingers knitted behind his head, looking very pleased with himself.

"Good, I'm going to need you all for what I have planned. Before I get into the details, let me catch you up on a few things. The results of your simulation have provided us with some interesting ideas for the Sunspire, and we're refining the modifications and alterations that were applied to her during the refit. The promotions granted in the simulation stand, and you're all being assigned to her. It is a controversial decision, but I feel a good one, to put Captain Valent in command as well. If there is one thing I have learned from three decades as an officer, it is not to mess with what works. I'll be clear, this is not a light assignment. The only details you are allowed to divulge to your families and friends are that most of the charges against you have been greatly lessened, and you must serve in the Freeground Fleet as part of your sentence. If they ask for more details, tell them you have none. Your loved ones will be looked after.

"After the refit is complete, the Sunspire will leave for the Argus Common Sector. You are to rename her and remove any details of her Freeground Shipyard origins from her transponder. You'll be right in the middle of a cluster of heavily populated systems, where there are dozens of corporately owned worlds. The Sunspire will seem like an independent mercenary or trader ship. You'll carry out missions under the direction of

Freeground Fleet Special Operations while being left to fend for yourselves for the most part.

"This is the kind of assignment that people dream of. You will see places and do things that most of us could not imagine. When looking for moral direction, you only have to think of home and whether what you are doing would be best for Freeground and for your crewmates. There are only two other ships on the same assignment you are about to engage in. They won't know you're there, you'll probably never see them, and if you did you probably wouldn't realize it. After doing nothing for two days but reading your backgrounds and reports on your actions in the simulation, I have faith that you are the right unusual crew for this unusual assignment.

"Your primary mission as a crew will be to acquire information and technology that will help Freeground. That means that under your commanding officer's direction, you will buy, copy, steal, and learn about anything we don't have already. Once your senior staff agrees that you have a significant cache of technology, you are to return home. I expect your mission to take years. The crewmembers that will be assigned to you will be aware of this. Under special circumstances, you can form ties with the governments you meet as a prelude to passing that relationship on to Freeground itself at the completion of your mission.

"You have one day to visit family and friends on the station and put your affairs in order."

I had one more opportunity to speak to Vice Admiral McKinley. As soon as our meeting was finished and everyone went their separate ways for that last day on Freeground, Alice told me I was to report to the Admiral's office within the hour. I was watching the crews move my personal fighter into the launch bay of the Sunspire and had little else to do so I stepped into the nearest tube. I was so busy thinking my questions over that I didn't even notice the time passing as the tube car shuttled down several kilometres of tunnels and shafts.

Before I knew it I was crossing the Vice Admiral's threshold. "Have a seat, Captain," she said without looking up from a scrolling stream of text in her hand. I sat down and waited for her to finish what she was doing. She flexed her hand and the text disappeared.

"You're here because I need to answer your questions before I send you off into civilization with your crew. Someone was supposed to go with you on the initial trip, but he's been directed elsewhere. This question period is all you get. Where do you want to start?"

I thought for a minute before uncorking a bottle that I knew I'd never be able to close up again. "Wouldn't it be better to put someone who has a lot of experience in Corporate Territory in command? I don't know much about what's out there."

"You make a good point, almost no one in your initial crew or anyone I'm assigning to the Sunspire has any experience where you're going. One of the reasons why I approved you as the Captain is because of your years in Port Control. You've spoken to more civilians from more places than most people in the fleet. You're comfortable speaking to new people and know how to get to the bottom of things without insulting whoever you're dealing with."

The irony of having the worst job I'd ever held down being a major factor in getting posted as Captain wasn't lost on me. Even still, it didn't take me long to get my thoughts back in order, especially with Alice flashing 'WHY NOT MILITARY?' on my comm unit to remind me of my next question. "Why not send a military ship? I'm sure there are small vessels with crews who would be happy to take this assignment."

"No matter what we tell them to do, or how we tell them to behave, they'll always seem like a military crew. Besides, even after an Academy brush up, your people wouldn't be accepted into our upper ranks for years, especially if we kept you together. Bringing them in as consultants could work under some circumstances, but they wouldn't have the direct involvement required for the mission. Our officer would resent the Admiralty for introducing so many fresh-faced consultants. I would be facing a political backlash unlike anything we've seen since the British immigrant rush. A shadow ship assignment is the best way to get you and your team out there without insulting the military or wasting your talents."

"A shadow ship assignment. You've done this before?"

"Not with a crew exactly like yours. Conditions were different in the other cases, but I can't get into specifics. That information is classified above your clearance level."

"Will you be sending anyone to oversee us?"

"After reviewing the psych profiles of you and your senior staff, we know it's not necessary. Ask yourself if there is anything you can imagine out there that would ever convince you that your home isn't Freeground? Is there anything that would turn your head so far that you'd forget your patriotism to the Freeground Nation?"

I pondered that for a moment, and at the time I couldn't imagine how I could call any other place home. "No, I can't say there is."

"In this case that's what's most important. You're all patriots, all born here and everyone has spent most of your lives here. You're also skilled, but many of you are not trained militarily. So when it comes down to it, many of your crew would not think or behave like you're military. You may use your officer training, know how to interact with Freeground Fleet personnel, even understand how our systems and procedures work, but you think differently, you'll reflexively behave differently."

"That's quite an answer."

"You can thank Rear Admiral Rice. She's the one who built your profile."

"I don't have a right to know, but I was wondering why we were switched from her command to yours."

"It wasn't because of her daughter. Ayan is right in the middle of this and even though the Admiral is an exemplary officer, she can't be expected to be absolutely objective. Besides, Fleet Command has decided it's time for her to have her own command again. Rear Admiral Rice will be leaving after the Paladin arrives and we've defended Freeground. Things are changing, and she has to be out there."

"Does Ayan know?"

"She will today." The Vice Admiral leaned forward then, her tone quieted. "Some time ago, the upper ranks in Fleet Command realized that our isolation didn't guarantee our safety. In fact, it's becoming more of a liability than ever. Free worlds and stations are under assault, whether it be economically, socially, or by military force. As one of the last free ports within light years, we draw immigrants of all kinds. They're saying that almost everywhere else it's becoming impossible for an individual to own something, and just as hard to not become someone else's property in some way or another. We have also been losing ground technologically for over a hundred years in military, medical, and social sciences. By the same token, we are generally more advanced in power management, agriculture, and habitation technologies. Our strengths benefit us and attract negative attention at the same time.

"Just think, Freeground manufactures more than it can use in almost every category. Food, air, ships, anything you can imagine is inexpensive to residents because we sell up to half of what we make. We just have too much. We also have a parliament, a real democracy, and a military that answers to the people through our governing body. You grew up here, so you wouldn't know, but it's been very hard to find any place where those conditions still exist. When a place becomes as successful as we are, it draws attention to itself and we're out here all alone now. We have the attention of five sectors and barely know what's out there anymore because of our isolationist ways. I know I've only seen three planet-side cities in my life, visited a handful of worlds, so in just a few months out there I bet you and your crew will be able to teach me something.

"When that time comes, part of your mission is to find technology and knowledge that may be useful to Freeground and acquire it any way you see fit. We have objectives for you, but it's just as important for you to be our eyes and ears, find your own targets. Just remember, as soon as you leave Freeground, you're no longer military and as far as the Galaxy is concerned, you own the Sunspire and pay your crew just like any mercenary ship. Of course your crew don't expect to be paid until you return, but you can always take the opportunity to do so if conditions permit and you think it wise."

"I think I will. Thank you, Vice Admiral. That answers everything on my mind and a bit more." I stood and snapped her a salute.

"It's your ship, Captain. Accomplish your goals however you like. Just remember us out here in the dark."

I stood to leave. It felt like my shoes had lead insoles, and I had more to think about than I could manage.

"Captain," the Vice Admiral stopped me and shook my hand. I hadn't noticed the wrinkles around her eyes and how their grey depths showed age and wisdom beyond her apparent age. "When you're out there and there are more questions than answers, remember we put you there because we knew you and your people were ready. If you weren't ready, or your senior staff wasn't ready, you'd be in line for forced enlistment. Trust them. Trust yourself, and you'll start believing you're right for this."

"Thank you, Vice Admiral."

"See you in a few years."

EIGHT

BOARDING

The officer's quarter on the station was more like a first class hotel and the lounge was larger than most nightclubs I had seen. There were noticeable differences, however. All the colours were subdued greys, crimsons, and blacks. The lighting was low in habitation areas and clear and bright in main hallways. The quarters they gave me were even larger than the captain's quarters on the ship, and the furniture looked new. If there was one thing I could take with me to the Sunspire it would have been the bed. It was absolutely huge, a king size, and felt amazing. I didn't know then that while we were off ship in stasis, they had quadrupled the refit crew, and the quarters — even the misused common room — had been rebuilt and refurnished. The bed waiting for me in my new captain's quarters was much better than what I had experienced in the simulation, even if it didn't quite match the one in the station's officers quarters.

Despite the creature comforts, I couldn't sleep. At four in the morning, I found myself sitting in the main lounge, sipping decaffeinated coffee, looking out one of the transparent bulk-heads to the Sunspire. The refit was finished, and she was set up front and centre in full view of the lounge for the launch. Every part of the ship had been changed. They even reshaped parts of the outer hull, expanded the launch and retrieval bay, and added retractable cargo hauling systems. The twenty eight retractable rail cannons were all hidden under their armoured hatches and the long, graceful curves of the hull had been restored to the original reflective surface. It was a gracefully shaped antique on the outside, not as large as most carriers but larger than most destroyer class ships. I couldn't believe I was put in command.

I was still letting recent events sink in. My old life felt like a dream and I knew I would miss all the people I had come to know well over the years of simulations we had done together in our spare time. I smiled and sighed quietly, looking over the shape of the ship and still not quite believing how everything turned out.

Oz clapped me on the back and I was on my feet like a shot. "Couldn't sleep either, huh?"

"Sneaking up on a superior officer should be a court marshal-able offence."

"Ah, rank isn't an issue in the lounge, didn't they tell you?" He looked out at the Sunspire. "She's beautiful, isn't she?"

"She is. I would've never thought that the ship I saw just over a week ago would turn into this."

"I've never seen Ayan so happy. We got the early tour from the Admiral. They even changed the hallways. I spoke to one of the engineering staff sergeants while the Rice ladies were off talking, and he said that working on the Sunspire's hull was more like art than structural engineering. They used some kind of reshaping tool that worked on the regenerative hull for most of it. Now I didn't understand much of what he said, but I think the Fleet is really hot for getting their hands on more of what she's made of."

"So I've heard. Two of our objectives out there are to quietly alter conditions so Fleet can come in once we're gone and take over ergranian mining operations and ore stores. We won't just be buying and stealing out there, we'll be saboteurs and shock raiders if we can find the opportunity. At the same time, no one can know where we're from. That we are part of the Freeground Fleet." Even though I was in a secure section of the station, I found myself looking over my shoulder briefly.

"That explains why they're so comfortable setting us up on the Sunspire," I added. "They only built a few, since they were too small to be adequate deep space destroyers or carriers, and too big to be heavy corvettes. That and she's almost two hundred years old."

"You're right. We can't let anyone on board though. She may look like an antique on the outside, but I don't think they left any system untouched. The only thing I think they really should have changed is the location of the bridge. I don't think shielding it is really enough, and it's too easy to recognize it as a rich target." Oz sipped a coffee of his own.

"We'll have to talk to Ayan about that."

"You know, I can't help but wonder how long we'll really be out there." He looked thoughtful.

"Do you have someone who'll be waiting for you?"

"I have three sisters, two of which like having a trained infantryman as a babysitter."

"I keep forgetting that's something you and Minh have in common."

"Too many sisters? Yup, it's good to have someone who understands. I just hope our sisters never team up. We'd be screwed."

"Probably." I stood up and walked to the window. Oz stood to follow me. "I don't know how long we'll be out. We won't need supplies, and we're generally going to avoid getting into a firefight. I guess we'll be taking planet-side leave while we're out there too, when the time comes. Should make things interesting."

Oz laughed quietly and shook his head.

"What?"

"You already sound like you've been in the captain's chair for years."

"Oh, I'm sure my inexperience will show."

"Sometimes, sure. But I've got your back. And Ayan won't let anything happen to her ship if she can help it."

"I'm glad I'm letting her rename it."

"So is she. I'm surprised you didn't tell her yourself and it was just there in the briefing notes you sent us. We got them while we were touring the ship and she was so happy she actually squealed."

"I think she wants some space right now."

"Then she's signing up for the wrong tour," Oz chuckled.

"Sometimes it feels like I'm talking to the Ayan I knew in the simulations, and other times it seems like she couldn't be more distant if she were across the galaxy."

"The first thing she asked when we met Admiral Rice for

the tour was 'Will Jonas be joining us?'" He used his best imitation of a British accent.

"Probably asking for her own protection."

"Ah, she's crazy about you, but she's not like us either. She's a former military brat who had to work her ass off to get what she has and she's been through a lot. Or it's just as simple as not wanting to break regulation."

"Break regulation?"

"Well, you're a captain, she's a commander. The two of you get together and it's grounds for disciplinary action for both of you unless you can keep personal interactions to shore leave and official downtime. She's career, and now you've gone career, and that makes things even worse."

"I know how much that means to her, but there's not much either of us can do except maybe go covert and both serve on a mercenary ship where the regulations regarding inter-crew relations are relaxed to the same point as long voyage vessels."

"I almost forgot about that. We're allowed to fraternize at any rank while we're off duty according to those regulations. That should be interesting," Oz said.

"Most of the other regulations will be relaxed as well. It's not going to feel much like a military ship. We'll have to redesign our uniforms, drop salutes, and implement only the most important procedures. Unless we're on watch or in combat, she won't feel much like a military ship. I hope Ayan and I get a chance to enjoy some free time once we're under way. I know I'll do my best to make the time."

"Now that's more like it. Think positive. She chews my ear off about you when I see her — unless she's in the engine room that is — and you chew my other ear off about her when we meet up. If this doesn't stop I'll just lock the two of you in a room."

"That calls for a court marshal."

"Nope, I'll just report both of you unfit for command."

"That's dirty."

"First thing they teach you in hand to hand; the dirtier fighter almost always wins."

The deck shook just slightly. We both felt it but couldn't see anything wrong in the lounge or outside in the dry dock. "Alice, what's going on?" I asked, bringing up my new command and control arm console, much larger and more powerful than my old one, to project an image of Alice or any other information she needed to present.

"I'm checking now, but all communications from the Operations deck have stopped. One moment." Oz and I waited patiently while Alice tried to collect more information. "Security is responding to an explosion in main Operations and a section of the command deck. All ships are on alert status and they're launching fighters. No one seems to know exactly what's going on yet, Jonas."

I looked at Oz. "Wake the crew?"

"I think so. Heading to the nearest weapons locker wouldn't be a bad idea, either. I may not know what's going on, but I'd rather not be unarmed if I can help it."

"It's a start. Alice, alert the crew and send them up to date information on what's happening. Include instructions to assemble on the Sunspire immediately." I followed Oz to the nearest weapons locker. He punched in his security code, opened the heavy door and handed me a holstered particle driver. I made sure it was fully charged and strapped it on. As far as sidearms go, I thought it was overdoing it a little. Not hard to aim but it was the only hull-friendly weapon I had heard of that fired ten rounds per second and carried several days worth of charge. Then I looked at Oz's selection.

He strapped on the same sidearm I had, then took what looked like some kind of grisly antique out from the bottom of the locker. "What the hell is that?"

"It's called a semi-automatic shot gun with recoilless reciprocating barrels. It fires a variable load. I prefer buckshot myself. I call it the Crowd Pleaser."

"Sometimes I think you like your job a little too much. Let's head to the Sunspire. I get the feeling we'll be put to work earlier than expected."

"Again."

We ran down two hallways. I made sure I was following Oz's movements carefully. We were moving quickly but covering our corners and making sure the way was clear before passing down any corridor or through any open room. I was about to ask why when I looked through one of the large skylights over a hallway hub and saw ingress pods heading towards the station. There were thousands of them and the defence turrets weren't fully operational, so some were getting through. "There!" I pointed.

"Oh, now that's not good," he said before tapping his command and control unit to open a link to station security. "This is Commander Terry McPatrick of the Sunspire, currently located in junction 14b of the station officer's quarters. Incursion pods have been sighted, looks like some of them will make it through defensive fire."

"Thank you, Commander, security teams are on their way.

You are instructed to leave the Officer's deck as soon as possible and find another safe location. Coordinate with a security team if you encounter one."

"Thank you, I'll be on the Sunspire. Commander McPatrick out."

I heard the first of the pods hit a hallway somewhere behind us and start cutting into the hull. "Lead the way."

"Time to go. Try to keep up!" Oz shouted, and for the next few minutes I found myself wondering how a towering behemoth like him could move so fast. We were lucky and didn't run into boarders on the way, but we could hear gunfire.

We stopped at the corner before the lift that led to the Sunspire's boarding ramp. I was fighting for breath.

"You're out of shape. We'll have to work on that," Oz pointed out, barely winded at all.

"My last fitness review said I was in great shape."

"For a station-bound civilian. You're Captain now, you should be tip-top. Besides, when was the last time you ran anywhere for real? I'll get you back in fighting form, Skipper."

"I'm captain of a star ship, not joining a wrestling team."

I crossed the hallway to check the next corner and felt something brush right past me but didn't see it. Oz picked up on my reaction and fired his shotgun right beside me. The noise was so sudden and brutal it was painful. He caught what brushed by me full in the back.

Without hesitation, Oz turned in the other direction, fired once, then fired down the third hallway. His third shot seemed to cause the air itself to erupt with bits of blood and debris and I opened fire on the area. My left ear rung and my left arm stung like crazy, but I cut a line of fire across the middle of the hall and once of the targets became fully visible. He was wearing an all black vacuum suit. My shots had hit the control on his wrist. The way he was lying showed that another body had fallen under him.

"Stealth suits? I've never heard of it being done so well," I said while trying to guess the outline of the invisible body trapped under his comrade. "Grab the controller on the invisible one's arm," I pointed with my sidearm to where the body should lie.

Oz felt around and after a moment he yanked hard without success. He took aim with the shotgun and I ducked around the corner. It was as he blasted the man's arm off with two shots that I realized that Oz's first shot actually caught me with high velocity buckshot. Glancing down I could see at least a dozen small holes. "You shot me!" I shouted, though I could barely hear myself.

Oz came around the corner with the fallen man's arm, controller still attached, and gave me a sheepish grin. "I was hoping you wouldn't notice." He shrugged. "Let's get to the ship."

Oz fired once down the last hallway, but didn't catch anything. We sprinted down to the lift. I held my left arm as we descended and looked down to see that it was covered in blood from many little entry wounds. "You shot me!" I repeated at Oz in angry disbelief. "With an antique weapon!"

We arrived at the bottom and met up with other crew members coming from different sections of the station.

Minh-Chu was watching the entrance with plasma rifle in hand. "What happened to you?" he asked as I ran past him.

"Raiders," Oz replied too loudly; the shotgun had obviously affected his hearing as well.

"He shot me!" I protested as I headed for the bridge. I could hear the power plants warming up. A shocked Ensign wearing a Fleet Medical emblem on his collar looked at me wide eyed. "Sir, you should-"

"You should see if there are any other wounded then come see me with an emergency medpack on the bridge."

"But, Sir!"

"That's an order!" I barked as the lift doors closed. There were other crew members in the lift with me and I tried to keep an absolutely straight face as I did what I knew I had to. "Alice, medical analysis. How bad is it?"

"Not fatal, there are thirty one small punctures with only eighteen pieces of metal embedded in bone or muscle tissue. You'll live."

"Good, now close the holes in my vacsuit, compress on the wounds and seal it. That should hold until I can get treated."

"You know, you could stop off in medical."

"Just do it." I ground my teeth together as she followed my instructions, and then the doors opened onto the bridge.

"Captain on deck!" I heard a voice call out, but didn't much care to look who it was.

"At ease, I have the feeling we have our work cut out for us."

Sergeant Everin cringed at seeing whatever face I had made while the doors were opening and looked back to his station. "Orders from Admiral McKinley, video message," he reported.

"Put it up," I instructed as I sat down in the Captain's chair carefully.

The Admiral's full form appeared in the middle of the

bridge, the holographic image so clear it almost forced me to my feet for a salute. "Captain Valent, you are to take on your crew, set a course, and head straight out. Do not engage the enemy on your way out of the area, enter hyperspace as soon as possible. Oh, and say hello to Alice for me. That is all, good voyage."

I looked at my command and control unit and noticed that it had taken a piece of buckshot as well, though it only did superficial damage. "Hello, Alice?"

"That was code, Sir. When I was transferred to this unit, I found orders waiting in case there was an early attack on the base. We are to select new coordinates far away from Triad Consortium space, destroy our uniforms, delete all evidence and record of Freeground and Fleet from our computers except for what you would find in a normal merchant or mercenary ship's computer. The Admiral is operating under the assumption that Freeground Fleet Intelligence has been compromised. They will find a way to contact us at a later time if necessary. It looks like we'll have to make our own allies out there if we want any help, Jonas. There are other details here, but I doubt they relate to our current situation."

I realized when she finished that everyone on the bridge heard what my AI had said, so I regarded the bridge staff directly. "Everyone hear that? New orders. It's time to leave."

"About time we got out there," I heard Oz comment from behind me. He stepped in to my right side and directed a fleet doctor to my left, "I can take us out while you get treated, Captain."

"Not on your life," I said with a chuckle. "Treat me here, Doc."

The doctor shrugged and nodded. He was a much older

fellow with greying hair and seemed unsurprised by everything going on, as though this were just another day on the job. "My name is Doctor Anderson. Now just stay still and you won't feel a thing, Captain."

I looked to the navigation station, where both Ensign Tommin and Lieutenant Commander Fields worked to ensure everything was in order. "Plot us a course for the Gai-Ian system. Just the first jump will do for now."

"Yes, Sir!" answered Ensign Tommin, a young officer who had graduated the academy that year.

The doctor smiled as he split the arm of my vacsuit and sprayed on a local anaesthetic. The relief was instant and welcome. "Good choice, Captain."

"You know it?"

"Was just there a couple years ago on the Apollo, the ship I serve on. It's mostly an agricultural planet, but they're good people with deep roots."

"That's good to hear, I only knew it was a free system. Isn't the Apollo out of the area, though? How are you on Freeground?"

"The station is hiding two entire battle groups including the Apollo. We have a surprise waiting for whatever is coming for us. Looks like we'll have to spring it earlier than we thought."

"Then you should get back to your crew."

"No point now, operationally I can't leave the ship, I already know too much and your orders are to get us out of here. So I'll fix your arm, you get your crew out of the area and on mission," Doctor Anderson whispered. "Then maybe I'll see what your medical section looks like and whip your triage crew into shape. With your permission, of course."

"Of course."

Oz smiled at overhearing the exchange as he checked his holographic command console. "We're only missing three, Sir: a mechanic, a pilot, and medic. We've taken on eleven extra who were blocked off by fighting on the station."

"Let's be under-way, Commander."

"Yes, Sir," Oz replied with a smile. "Seal exterior hatches, release umbilicals, moorings, signal Port Operations to open the nearest launch doors, and give us our trajectory."

I picked up where Oz left off. He was doing the departure list for the first time, after all. "All department heads report in."

Over the next few minutes, I heard the voices of many friends. It was like being back in the simulations again, that feeling of being surrounded by people who were all glad to be there, all looking to work together towards a common goal. When the helm reported ready, I couldn't help but grin. "Take us out, best speed. Put the exterior view up on the main display."

We manoeuvred through the dry dock where every able ship was being manned and made ready. We passed through the doors, which seemed opened only just wide enough. I looked down and saw that the doctor had actually just finished repairing the damage to my arm. "Thank you, Doctor."

"Just try not to get in his way again," he replied, gesturing towards Oz and shaking his head.

My first officer had no time to reply as he commanded refractive and bridge shielding to be raised and requested reports from tactical and navigation.

"We have several thousand enemy targets on the coreward

side of the station, Sir. They're matched by our ships," Ensign Thomas answered from tactical.

"Coordinates are set, waiting to reach a safe distance before engaging hyperspace systems," answered Lieutenant Fields from Navigation. "A ten count will get us there at our current speed, Sir."

"Then start the counter at ten seconds. We don't want to damage the station." I set the main viewer to display the station with one of the control pads on my chair.

"Just don't forget us out here in the dark," I said to myself as I watched Freeground shrink into the distance on the bridge holographic viewer. "Sir?" Sergeant Everin asked, turning towards me from communications.

"Something Admiral McKinley said to me the other day. Fleet is putting a lot of trust in us. We're skilled, intelligent, and glad to do our part, but the main reason we're here is because we all call that station home."

Once we were a safe distance away, we entered hyperspace and after the post-entry checklist had been run through, I addressed the crew on the ship-wide communications system. "This is the Captain. As you're all aware, this wasn't the way we planned to leave, but as far as departures go, I can say this isn't the worst I could have imagined. There was supposed to be a launch this morning, and our Chief Engineer, Commander Rice, was to name the ship in honour of those who have served on her before.

"They were a good crew that faced terrible odds and never gave up. I doubt that we will have a chance to have that launch now, but I believe that we have had something better. This ship has been christened by purpose, and we've been given the gift of trust. We, as the sons and daughters of Freeground, are to go incognito into the darkness and find assets that will aid the people back home before eventually returning there ourselves. Though we will not be wearing uniforms, we must still honour those who have come before us and those we leave behind so we may return with our heads held high.

"In honour of her last crew, this ship will be called by the name First Light. I ask everyone to take a moment of silence for those who have given their lives on this ship when you can. Then welcome unfamiliar faces aboard wherever you see them. They are your new brothers and sisters. That is all."

Everyone on the bridge got back to work, though there was little to do since we were safely in hyperspace. "Well said, Captain," Oz said with a smile.

"I've heard better," Doctor Anderson said quietly. "But not often," he added with a wry grin.

NINE

HYPERSPACE

I spent the entire next day on the bridge, reading reports and making sure that the ship was doing well for its first long hyper-space journey since all the systems — engines included — were new. There was nothing seriously amiss. Oz and I found ourselves agreeing that we were glad department heads wouldn't have to submit daily reports any longer because, with few problems to solve, it got pretty boring. Neither of us were used to reviewing data for hours every day.

Ayan was another story. She seemed to be perfectly settled in, and whenever our paths crossed, she was always reading or listening to a report while doing something else. It was obvious that she was quite used to being a senior officer. The chilly demeanour was gone, too. She was busy, sure, and was taking a personal hand in all the fine tuning that was necessary after a refit, but she always had a moment or two for a smile and a few words.

The dress code in engineering had gone the way the rest of

the ship had: no more Freeground uniforms. Ayan and the senior engineering staff had instead assigned their department grey vacsuits that had room for all their essential hand tools, an optional pulse sidearm, and included conductive weave that rendered them all immune to electromagnetic weaponry and most accidents resulting from current. It was also designed in such a way that it could not snag on anything and was resistant to impacts and most punctures. All the technology existed before, but was normally reserved for specialist uniforms. After I saw them, I was more than happy that the engineering department had taken the opportunity to improve things.

After seeing the work that had been done on uniforms there, I ordered all other departments to design their new vacsuits. They were to include the safety measures that the engineering staff had implemented since they added no extra bulk, very little weight, and left room for other modifications.

Two days later, in the early morning, I ran into Ayan on her way into engineering from the main hall. She had her coffee in one hand and was projecting a holographic representation of one of our reactors from the thin command and control unit on her other wrist. She stopped before the door opened and fixed me with a smile.

"Good morning," she greeted brightly.

"Good morning. I haven't had a chance to tell you yet, but the new uniforms look great. I think all the other departments are treating the assignment to design their new uniforms as a competition."

"Well, it beats most long hyperspace voyages. It's all everyone's talking about, but at least they're talking. I hear the gunnery crews are almost finished theirs, and Minh-Chu is keeping the pilot uniforms a secret. How are the bridge staff uniforms coming?"

"We haven't really had time. On one hand we're taking care of the routine hyperspace travel watch, on the other there are new communication, leave, and general security protocols to review. Jason, or Sergeant Everin, rather, is doing some great work on our encryption, but it's taking forever to test and finalize."

Ayan's expression slowly grew into a grin. "Just a few days out here and you're already sounding like you've been in command for years."

"Most of the time it feels that way," I agreed as I followed her into the centre of the engineering section. They called it the pit. There was a ramp leading down into an octagonal control section where all the systems could be monitored on control panels and through holograms. "Other times something comes up that I've never even heard of before."

"That's what we're here for. We're senior staff. If you haven't seen something, chances are we have. If not, well, we can just figure it out together."

"True, but that's taking some getting used to."

"I can imagine."

I looked around and realized that we were right in the middle of four five-story tall reactors. "How is the refit looking?"

"Fantastic. Lots of things to iron out, sure, but these new reactors are amazing. They don't require the maintenance that the old ones did, and they put out a lot more power while having no harmful radiological footprint. No worrying about containment or cooling, they can't explode, and there are so few moving parts that they barely look like reactors at all. I'm glad I was keeping up with engineering advancements, otherwise I'd be pretty confused."

"Well, you have work to do and I should move on myself. I'll see you soon, I'm sure."

Ayan put her coffee down and locked the mug to the shelf with the press of a button. "I'll walk you out."

"I'm surprised the power plants aren't larger."

"They're smaller than I expected, too; more than half of the space the old systems took up is free in engineering. When we find some of that new technology that we're after, maybe we can add it to the ship."

"That's what I was thinking," I said, smiling at her.

She fixed me with a warm, glad expression as we reached the door. "I'm glad we're thinking alike. I'll see you later?"

I nodded and started walking away.

Doctor Anderson, who was jogging towards us and witnessed the end of our exchange, stopped to run on the spot beside me as Ayan walked back towards the centre of engineering and the door closed behind her. "Now that was some smile," he whispered.

"It was."

"Well, regardless of whatever chemistry you have going, I'm glad to see that you visit your department heads where they live. It shows that their ideas are important, that you want to be involved and familiar with the entire ship. That's critical to winning the respect of your officers, especially on a ship without Fleet uniforms. It might be a good idea to stop in on engineering every morning as well, should help things between you two."

"Between us two?" I asked with a raised eyebrow.

"Oh, come on now, Captain, everyone's watching you both.

People are pairing up, and we're all wondering when you two will follow suit."

"Everyone? It's only been a few days."

Doctor Anderson grinned and resumed jogging down the corridor. "You should join me sometime. Looks like you could use a run."

I had only been on one long hyperspace voyage before. Though it's the second fastest method of travel next to moving through high compression wormholes, it can get very boring. I took the doctor up on his advice the next day, and the day after that.

Doctor Carl Anderson, or Doc as I had started calling him, had been given the Medical Department Head position since he had the most experience in Fleet and in medicine. He had been a doctor for over a decade before joining the infantry, where he served eight years as a medic. He signed up with Fleet afterwards and spent twenty seven years on different ships treating the wounded, and from what the file said he was forced to take command on six different occasions. He was eighty five but had to slow down on his jogs so I could keep up. Every morning he jogged around one deck of the ship three or four times.

"So, are you going to the party tonight?" Doc asked as we jogged down the main hallway of deck 13, which was part engineering and part crew quarters. The main hallway, which looped around the entire deck, had been reshaped during the refit so it could accommodate four abreast.

"They're calling it the Pilot's Ball, and I have to go. I'm the Captain."

"Not to this one. Commander Buu is throwing it. Technically you can just stay on the bridge or make a token appearance then leave."

I thought about it for a moment. "That's tempting, but it's the first social event and I've barely seen a lot of people since we entered hyperspace. For a quiet hyperspace trip everyone has been really busy. Some of us barely get enough rack time."

"Ah, the first voyage after a refit is always like this. Lots of bolts to tighten. Even a few to loosen up. Just be glad no one forgot to finish installing anything."

"How many refits have you seen?"

"Two, the Andromeda and the Ramses."

"How did those work out?"

"The Andromeda started falling apart right after her relaunch. Downright embarrassing for the refit crew, damn funny to everyone who was praying for an extra couple weeks leave."

"I could imagine."

"Are we having much trouble with the refit? Seems pretty smooth in medical. Other than having to re-hang a cupboard, nothing has come loose or fallen over."

"Well, Ayan shut down reactor three for a day or so."

"Impressive. I didn't even notice the lights flicker."

"Well, she's right into her work, literally. I went by to see how the repairs were going yesterday morning and she had crawled inside the power plant. I didn't think there was room in there for anything."

"Whatever she's doing, it's working. She's going to the Pilot's Ball, you know."

"Oh?"

"Aye, she was talking about it when she came into medical

to get a bone density treatment. We ended up talking for a while. Turns out I know her mother."

"So you already knew about reactor three and how things were going in engineering."

"What would make you think that?"

"Because if you ask her how she's doing she talks about engineering. She could have grown a new head since you last saw her and she'd still talk about how the ion intermix is a little off, or the deck plating under reactor two has developed a little creak during gravity adjustments."

"You caught me. I must be losing my touch in my old age."

"Ah, us humans are living to four hundred these days, you're still a young man."

"That's still theoretical for the most part, but I wouldn't mind being one of the first to make it into the four hundred club. That's not the point. I'm twice the oldest crewmember's age and then some. If I don't live vicariously through at least a few of you young pups I'll spend this whole trip bored out of my mind. Besides, that's the price of this old man's advice."

"For an old man, you run me ragged on these morning jogs."

"Ah, you're mistaken. It's my run, you're just following along."

"Right, so what's your advice old man?"

"Go to the Pilot's Ball and try to keep up," he said with a playfully challenging finality before increasing the pace for the last stretch of our second turn around the deck.

TEN

THE PILOT'S BALL

That night Minh-Chu was in his own paradise. It was the first chance he had to show off his new flight crew. The twenty one fighters that had been assigned to be pilots were spread out across the launch bay and each one had been labelled with their call signs. The main observation deck, which had a semi transparent floor to show the fighter bay below and a fully transparent wall in the front for a view of open space, was abuzz with the majority of the crew. Only a small watch was manning the stations, more than enough for hyperspace travel.

It was so good to see everyone in casual dress; only the pilots were dressed in uniform. Their new pilot gear included a thicker black vacsuit, a protective helmet and a flight jacket that looked like it was pulled right out of a museum. There were no identifying markers on any of them.

"Creative," I said to Minh-Chu, clinking my champagne glass to his.

"Thank you, Captain. We all contributed something. Our drills are going well, too."

"So I've read, but I haven't had time to watch the playbacks."

"Oh, so you become Captain and don't have any time left for Minh. Well, when you can make time, you should watch yesterday's second drill. I thought running scenarios with you guys was intense, but these pilots are insane."

"Now you know how we felt."

Minh laughed and nodded as Oz joined us. "Hey Minh, how do I get one of those jackets? The materializer won't make me one."

"Ha! You have to be a pilot or mechanic! I restricted them," replied Minh. I noticed right away that all the pilots in hearing distance had quieted down and were listening in.

"Well, I happen to know the Captain, I'm sure he can do something about that."

"Sorry, Commander, if my top flight officer says they're flight deck only uniforms, you'll have to live with it or apply for his department."

"Well, I'll have to come up with something for bridge officers, then. Maybe we'll all wear long coats like the Captain here," Oz said smugly, gesturing at my engineer's trench coat.

"Sure, just don't make us look like we're in our pyjamas," I said.

"Now why would I do that?"

"It could happen. I never know with you, Oz."

"Well, I hope that that's the new engineering uniform," Minh uttered as he gestured across the Observation deck. I turned around to trace his line of sight and I swear my heart stopped.

Ayan had arrived with a few of the engineers. She was in a long white dress with a scooped neckline. Her red hair was curled tightly into ringlets and hung down to the middle of her neck, where she wore a white choker. The necklace was decorated with a circular blue jewel with a sword struck through it, the emblem of Freeground. Around her shoulders she wore a long shimmering white shawl that reached down past her knees.

She smiled at me and walked to the bar with Laura, who was dressed similarly in black and looked nearly as stunning. The two of them walked with such grace and confidence that they seemed altogether separate from everyone else.

I crossed the room to the bar and smiled at her. I'm glad she spoke first, because I don't know what I would have said.

"Good evening, Captain."

"How are you, Commander?"

"Great, I'm celebrating."

"Oh? Is there an occasion other than Minh showing off his crew?"

"We finally have everything just the way we want it in engineering. Where's Commander Buu by the way? I want to thank him for putting all this together."

"Oh, he's right over there." I pointed.

"Thank you. I'll see you later, Captain." She walked off, flashing me a smile. Her light British accent and graceful manner had me absolutely dumbstruck. I could do no more than watch her glide away.

The bartender, an ensign from general maintenance, grinned and handed me something blue and frothy in a tall mug. "That might take the edge off, Sir," she said with a grin that almost touched her ears.

"Thank you," I said before taking a sip. To my surprise, it was very good. I took a seat on a barstool and put my mug down. Unlike the mornings when I visited Ayan in engineering when it seemed there was always something to talk about and never enough time, now I was completely tongue tied. I found myself watching her and tried to look away casually. She was Ayan, but in that dress she also seemed to be someone altogether different.

The doctor came over and leaned against the bar beside me, looking at my drink. "Noganto ale. A little bitter with a sweet after taste. Haven't had it in years."

"Ah, that's what this is called."

He gestured for another. "One of my favourites. No alcohol, but there is a blend of other natural substances that will make you feel relaxed and a little euphoric. Just don't overdo it or you'll be in medical thinking you're a cloud."

"Thanks for the warning."

The doctor and I peeled away from the bar and continued our mingling. I managed to meet and talk to everyone I wanted to see that night. I was even introduced to most of the new crew members. They were mostly experienced crewmen, and none were displeased with their predicament. At least not so displeased that they'd take that occasion to make me aware of it.

Always, my eyes drifted back to Ayan. I couldn't help it. She caught me more than once and would flash a smile or pretend she didn't notice. Once, she raised her glass while looking back at me from across the room. I had to return the gesture and everyone I was speaking with at the time looked over their shoulders to see where I was looking. When they turned back to face me, there were great big smiles all around.

The night wore on, and when things started to quiet down, I saw her walk through a side door that led to a smaller section of the observation deck with more subdued lighting. I didn't think, I just excused myself and gave silent chase.

The room was quiet, dark and unfurnished. The only light to see by was the faint blue and white coming through the transparent wall. The din of music and conversation in the main room behind had disappeared, dispersed by a noise barrier. Ayan stood looking out the window, the gentle illumination of hyperspace dancing across her features. Visible solar winds and the flow of energy, radiant stars and nebulae in distant space all drifted by, ethereal and unreal, like it was some luminescent dream.

I crossed the room and put my arm around her waist. It felt like the most natural thing to do. She relaxed and leaned against me. "Not in my wildest dreams did I think you were this beautiful."

"Thank you," she said quietly. "You're not too bad yourself. I love the coat."

"It was my father's. He gave it to me when I entered the service as an engineer."

"Tell me about him."

I was surprised at the request, but as she put her arm around my waist and made herself more comfortable, I went on. "He grew up on Osiris, and trained as an engineer. He left the system and travelled as a journeyman for a few years."

"How did he meet your mother?"

"Well, she was born on Osiris as well, and the way he used

to tell it, he was a little down on his luck until he met her on a transport heading back home. He pursued her for weeks after they met. She would pretend he wasn't even there, until she finally gave him a chance.

"She used to tell me that he was relentless, but charming, and she didn't understand that his motives were pure. Well, fairly pure. He took her to the Giardini Dell'acqua, and showed her how the water gardens worked from the mechanical side before taking her outside in time to see a gold and blue sunset."

"I would have liked to meet your parents."

"I didn't think about them much for a while, but lately my mind has been wandering back. I remember when I last saw my father. He walked me up to the boarding ramp as I was embarking for All-Con Prime. He wasn't a man of many words, but just when I was about to say goodbye, he shook my hand and said, 'I'm proud of you.' Those were his last words to me."

"So this is the Jonas no one sees," she whispered, looking up to me. "I think I like him."

We stood together quietly for a long time, looking out at the stars as they came closer very slowly.

"I'm finally okay," she said after a while. "Thank you for letting me rename the ship."

"First Light is perfect. I'd have it no other way."

"I read all the orders through. We're really on our own out here. They want us to make our own rules and find our own way. When we're finished, they'll probably debrief us for a year."

"I know. I try to think about how things might be different after a few years out here, what it might be like to return home after being gone so long, and I just can't wrap my head around it."

"Some people are already decorating. I think it's starting to sink in that this will be our home for a while. Laura's quarters are starting to look more like an apartment. She even put up a picture of Sergeant Everin."

"Jason's picture? Lucky him, I'll have to mention it next time I see him on the bridge."

"Don't you dare, they've only been on one date."

"People are dating now?"

"He found a quiet corner and set up a table and chairs. She said he was a complete gentleman. I think they're supposed to meet after his shift tomorrow."

"I forgot mercenary ships allowed fraternization until Oz mentioned it the day we departed. That's something the simulation didn't prepare any of us for." We stood quietly for a while longer, just enjoying the view and the quiet moment.

"I'm sorry I was so cold while we were in the simulation," she said quietly.

"Officers in the Fleet aren't allowed to fraternize while aboard."

"Yes, but they're still allowed to behave like friends. I brushed you off and avoided you. My training told me to forget everything but the fact that you were my commanding officer, anything else was a distraction. And I tried." She looked up at me and I could see the tears in her eyes. "There was nothing I wanted more than to get to know this man I had met in the simulations better in person. When I met you and wasn't disappointed, it was so hard to not let that get in the way of what we had to do. I couldn't stand the idea of getting close to you and having my mother criticize me for it. There were too many reasons for me to keep you at a distance, but I never wanted to. After that first morning, how you helped me, I couldn't forget and when the bridge was destroyed I thought it might have been my crew that didn't react in time. I had just lost so much, Jonas, and I thought I had lost you before I could know you."

I stopped her and softly caressed a tear away. "I'm here," I said as I drew her fully into my arms. She closed her eyes and wrapped her arms around my neck. I lowered my lips to hers. Our kiss was a touch that was so soft. We moved slowly, savouring every second and lingering on the feeling.

For those long moments, there were no other sensations outside of the feeling of her in my arms, our long kiss, and the sound of her breath. It ended as gently as it had begun.

She rested her head on my chest and sighed.

"I'm not going anywhere, and I'm not letting you go," I whispered.

"I think I'll like being a mercenary," she replied.

The night went on, and few people left the party after midnight. It seemed like every crewmember wanted to make the most of every moment. When Ayan and I emerged quietly from that side chamber hand in hand, whispers and smiles were everywhere. We couldn't help but be all smiles ourselves as we ordered champagne from the bar. "What do we do?" I asked in a whisper.

"I have no idea, I've never had a relationship with the entire crew watching before," she replied, trying not to move her lips.

"You keep smiling," Doc said from behind us. "And beware drunken toasts given by pilot hosts," he advised, pointing to Minh-Chu who was shakily climbing on top of a table. One of his pilots helped him with his balance while another held the table steady.

"Thank you for coming, everyone!" Minh said loudly while very carefully taking a glass of champagne from a tall mechanic.

"How much has he had?" I asked.

"I have no idea, I'm off duty," replied Doctor Anderson.

"Ladies and gentlemen, as Commander of First Squadron, I pledge that my pilots and I will keep you all safe. As you take care of us as we go between the stars, we will be you, I mean, take care of you, when we make stops! So to you, and to our promise to you." Minh raised his glass high on shaky legs and I raised my own.

"That wasn't so bad," I whispered under my breath.

"And to our Captain and his lovely wife!" Minh's eyes went wide a second after the words were out of his mouth and he quickly tried to recover. "Engineer! I mean engineer!" The room was filled with laughter until Minh lost his balance entirely. Fortunately, the pair of pilots mostly caught him. He took to his feet and drank the drop or two left in the bottom of his glass. We drank to his toast, and more than a few even applauded.

The little that remained of the night was more of the same, with Oz asking every bridge officer present their advice on what the new command uniforms should look like, Minh being led off shortly after he slurred a couple apologies to Ayan and me, and people generally having a great time.

The following two days in hyperspace weren't uneventful, and everyone found themselves with more than they expected on their plates. Ayan and I were just barely able to make time to have lunch and dinner together, as we both had to put in long hours.

The crew were proving themselves, and as the end of our hyperspace voyage drew near, the ship was finely tuned.

We felt like we were ready for anything.

EPILOGUE

Arrival

AT TEN TO six on the third day, we prepared to emerge from hyperspace near the outer-most settled world in the Gai-Ian system. As Oz had promised, the bridge crew had their new uniforms. They were decidedly tilted towards utility. Based on a black vacsuit, he had the new uniforms outfitted with a pocket on the left mid thigh, a low, quick draw sidearm holster on the right, and we were all given long grey jackets with built-in survival gear, general purpose power cells, an extra air exchanger, and ammunition for the small pulse sidearm that came with the uniform. All the safety features the engineering staff had were included as well.

Our ranks were marked on our wrists, counting backwards, so I had seven bars going around my wrists, while the Ensign had nineteen. As it was certainly untraditional, it was also ingenious from a tactical point of view, even though the thought of being captured by some unknown enemy wasn't exactly something I liked dwelling on. Having our captors under the impression that the lowest ranked among us was the highest for a while was a great idea.

I looked to Oz as I sat in the Captain's chair. "I like the new uniforms. They'll need some refining I'm sure, but it's a good start."

"Thank you, Sir."

I brought the forward view up on the main holodisplay and leaned forward. "How long until we're out of hyperspace?"

"Looks like we'll have to come out early, Sir. There's a gravity field coming up in thirty eight seconds."

I brought up my command display and braced myself. "Bring us out now, Lieutenant."

"What is it, Sir?" Oz asked.

"That's not on the charts. If it's an artificial gravity generator, I want to be on the edge of it so we have options." We came out of hyperspace and my tactical display lit up with armed ships all around us. "Condition red! Bridge and refractive shielding up, signal neutrality to all nearby ships, and try to open communications with the main docking ring in orbit."

"Gai-Ian Nine Station is on the communicator, Sir."

"Put it on secondary display."

The holographic form of an officer on the station appeared above the main display in the middle of the bridge. "This is Gai-Ian Nine Command. We don't recognize your profile and your transponder is unregistered."

"I'm Captain Valent of the First Light. Here to trade with the free worlds in this system."

"Well, Captain, we're still a free world but who knows for how long. The Vindyne Corporation has made an expansion-ist's claim on this world."

"Expansionist's claim?" I asked.

"It's a legal term that entitles them to poorly utilized resources if their population and needs are growing faster than the occupants of the property," answered Sergeant Everin. "I scored high in galactic law while I was in the Academy," he said with a shrug.

The entire ship shuddered then and I looked at my command display. One of our rail cannon turrets had just deto-nated an approaching torpedo. I tracked it back to it's source, a Vindyne corvette class ship. "Give me a few seconds, will you?" I asked the Gai-Ian IX Officer before putting him on mute.

Oz leaned forward and whispered in my ear. "We're trapped, Sir. It'll take us at least twenty minutes at our best speed to clear the artificial gravity field and enter hyperspace."

I nodded. "Have you been listening, Ayan? Minh?" I asked through the communicator.

"Listening and watching. I think it's time we tested these new fighters. I hate unwelcome guests, even when it's not my house," came Minh's reply through the comm.

"This sounds a lot like the trouble back home. It's not what we're here for but I wouldn't feel right leaving them," Ayan replied.

I looked at Oz for a moment, and we nodded at the same time. "I think it's time to start making some friends out here."

I stood up and looked around the bridge. Everyone was on the edge of their seat waiting for the order. "Open all rail cannon hatches and expose the turrets. Even numbered cannons target incoming, odd numbered cannons fire at Vindyne targets of opportunity. Launch all fighters with instructions to stay close. Ready torpedoes, start angling refractive shielding to redirect any beam fire straight back at the aggressor. Let's join the line."

I turned the mute on the communicator off and the officer turned in his chair towards me, surprised at what I assumed were the visible changes in our ship on his tactical display. "Yes, Captain?" he asked.

"The First Light is ready to assist with a flight of twenty one heavy interceptors at your disposal. Where do you want us?"

BOOK 2: LIMBO

PROLOGUE - GENERAL COLLINS

Overlord

JUST AS INTELLIGENCE HAD PREDICTED, the engagement in the Gai-Ian system was a slow, easy push. Looking at the status holograms and the primary projection with the scale rendering of the planet and defensive fleet, I felt almost invincible. I looked from the dais of the command chair across the thirty-eight bridge crewmen who were all busy performing their numerous duties: running ship systems, commanding their sections, and making sure that my carrier held together for her thirty-fifth engagement.

Combat and managing this battle, if it could be called such, was the least of the Overlord Two's functions. While the command deck took care of the engagement outside, other sections managed manpower acquisition, personnel storage, sorting, colony component manufacturing, holographic media production, product branding, research, development. There were even a few Marauder Corvettes undergoing a refit.

I looked down to the flight command pit built into the floor beneath, where my fleet command and control did their part to keep me apprised of the status of the other two carriers and the rest of the assault force. "Status, Major?"

"Our casualties are well below projections. The enemy are better at evading than they are at doing damage. We're gaining ground on them fast, General Collins."

"Good, keep pressing them back slowly. We need to deplete their numbers."

The tactical display to my right lit up for a moment and I brought the holographic projection to the forefront. "Tactical, report on this marked location."

"New contact, Sir. Our database has no records corresponding with her profile. Still gathering information."

"Why is there no interpreted reading on her transponder?" I asked as I ran my hand over my short grey beard.

"She's not registered anywhere," came the reply from communications. "No last known port, no name."

"Intelligence, check for any manufacturer's markings and compare her power signature to all known construction types."

The reply came after a few moments. "There are no manufacturer's markings and the few power signatures we can read could be from any of thirty builders. She looks generic."

"Generic? There's no such thing in this end of space. All right, give her some room. If it's a defence fleet scout intelligence missed—" I was interrupted as a large thermal marking appeared within three kilometres of the new combatant. "Who fired that?" I asked, looking to the fleet command pits.

"One of our corvettes, Sir. Designation Marauder 1153a," the Major replied. "It wasn't my order."

"Demote the captain after we're finished here. We can't fire on unknown combatants. If I were that new ship's captain and I were trapped here just as I think she is, I would see that as a clear indication that we're not interested in hiring them on."

"Hiring them on, General?"

"Yes. If she's unmarked, I'd imagine that we could hire them on to our side for the right price and get a close look at that ship. Now I'm not even going to bother. Don't initiate communications." I looked back at the tactical display and focused in on the new combatant more closely. "You see? She's launching fighters and headed for the enemy line. If I'm right, they'll help fill the hole we've been digging at for the last half-hour. Send two Marauders after her, we can't have that." I watched as seconds later two Marauder Corvettes and their fighter compliments turned to engage the new destroyer. They began firing cutting beams at full intensity and I stared on in disbelief as all the beams were refracted right back at the ships. The energy shields of the Corvette were useless against its own energy weapons and several decks began to rupture. I smiled and shook my head. "All things old are new again."

"General?"

"I haven't seen refractive shielding that good since my father was still in the Fleet. It has to be at least twenty layers deep for it to turn a beam weapon completely around. I'd hire her energy field technician in a heartbeat, with a signing bonus. It takes real reflexes to redirect energy that fast, even with the assistance of a predictive program."

"She has no energy shields, but we can't get an accurate power reading on her. The hull is too thick."

"Exactly, look closer. She's covered in regenerative ablative armour that's enhanced to reflect light." I looked a little closer on my own display and smiled. "They also have materializers across the hull. All they need is energy and liquid or scrap. They can go on forever under the right conditions. If you want a reading, focus on one of the rail cannon turrets and follow the power bleeds inward. They probably capture and recycle waste energy instead of using an exhaust system. Makes for some hot wiring."

I watched the sensor technician as he worked at the controls. "I have it, Sir, but this reading has to be an explosion or a flash from the cannons they're using."

I brought the scan results up on part of my tactical display. "Don't doubt yourself, Sergeant, your readings are right. You only have to interpret them differently. It looks like they've got a materializer in there to turn energy and materials into medium density metal ammunition. If there's one of those for each cannon emplacement, then the energy at their disposal must be immense. I wouldn't be surprised if they're generating enough power for several destroyer class ships. She's a deep space combat vessel, a rare breed out here - and very expensive. They're not here by mistake."

"Would you like me to dispatch more resources against her?"

"No, let her move into position and we'll continue our push. She's already costing us a small fortune. One of the corvettes we sent after her has been cut to pieces, the other one is getting pulverized by rail cannon fire, and she's cost us at least thirty fighters. We'll push in on the ships around her, at least we'll be taking on known vessels that way."

"Yes, General."

"Rail cannon turrets, refractive shielding, an antique hull no one has seen and more engine thrust and power generation per ton than I've ever seen on a destroyer her size. We have to find out where this ship is from. This configuration is too dissimilar to anything I've seen to be ignored," I said to myself quietly. "Communications, put a capture bounty on this ship if she survives, set it at one billion credits, her hull alone is worth four times that. There's got to be enough ergranian steel there to build five hundred heavy fighters. Not that I'd cut her apart before finding out what makes her tick and who built her. If it's a rival corporation we've never seen before, we'll have to acquire it one way or another."

"Yes, General."

"Tactical, how long until we reach the outer range of their planetary defence cannons?"

"Just under three minutes, Sir. They're trying to draw us into range."

"That's one trap we can't fall into. If I go over budget on this engagement, I'll forfeit my quarterly bonus. As soon as we're thirty seconds away from entering their range have the rear ships begin hyper accelerating to rally point theta." I watched the tactical display and shook my head again. "If that's a merchant ship, I'm a transport Captain. That's an antique destroyer rebuilt as a small multi-role carrier, and if they have any more of them up their sleeve, this solar system acquisition could get very expensive."

"There's something here you might be interested in, Sir,"

my intelligence officer mentioned. "We've intercepted the unknown ship's communications with Gai-Ian Defence Command. They weren't encrypted using their standard military codes, but it still took time to clear it up."

"Your team is losing their touch. Give me access."

"We have a holographic display of her Captain stating the ship designation. I'll put it on your display, General."

Standing on the smaller display projected from my command chair was the holographic image of a man in his early thirties, full of the enthusiasm and pride I'd expect from a captain in his early prime.

"The First Light is ready to assist with a flight of twenty one heavy interceptors at your disposal. Where do you want us?" the captain declared.

"Double the bounty on that ship and broadcast to any well known ship thieves, mercenaries, repossession agents and bounty hunters in this section of the galaxy once we're clear of the system. I'll pay the bounty to anyone who brings that ship to me in working condition with most of her crew intact." I didn't understand exactly why at the time, but as I looked at the image of the young captain, his bridge, his first officer at his side, my curiosity about the ship became an absolute need.

The bridge and uniforms were unlike anything I'd seen. It was like looking at part of a museum exhibit combined with modern efficiency. Over the following days, I found myself watching that holographic clip over and over; there was something there I hadn't seen in a very long time. The way the captain's first officer and crew looked at him, hung on his every word. There was something you couldn't buy: loyalty.

ONE

AN EASY AFTERMATH

Our first encounter with the Vindyne Fleet was encouraging but it still came at a cost. We had no dead, a few wounded, and had to retrieve two fighter pilots who bailed out in the nick of time. Our shuttles were able to haul the wreck of one of the fighters in, but the other was a complete loss. However, we had a couple of seriously injured crew, and it was becoming apparent to me that acquiring energy shielding for the ship and the fighters was essential.

The enemy had fared much worse. We had the honour of killing two corvette class ships and over sixty fighters and bombers. Our kill count was massive considering we only spent a few minutes in the conflict. When it was all over, I tried not to show my surprise and near disbelief at how well everyone performed. It seemed that as the stakes got higher, everyone's skills, concentration, and reaction times became better. All those drills weren't for nothing, all the basic skills had been practised to the point of reflex. Looking over the reports and vantage point data, it showed.

Without energy shielding, the outer sections of the ship were dangerous for those inside. One of the engineering staff, Ensign Coupland, was in an outer area of the ship, running past one of the observation decks when an enemy particle beam broke right through the outer hull. Most of the energy had been refracted away from the ship, but the particles cut through the hull like a saw and severed his arm. He was lucky - a few centimetres to the right and it would have gone straight through his chest. Luckily, the hull was able to re-seal itself before decompression could occur and our medical team was able to get him to the upper triage bay in time to save his life.

The same thing nearly happened right on the bridge. I could still see the super-heated spot on the transparent section of the hull where white hot particles had splashed against the transparisteel. The particle beam weapons they were using were so powerful and superior to the minor energy shielding we had around the bridge that they could cut right through, even with most of the light energy refracted away.

I knew our luck wouldn't hold out forever. It was important that I plan for the future. I entered the changes I thought were a priority into my Captain's Log and sent copies to all the officers. Our mission was not to fight every corporation or aggressive government body we came across — far from it — but being just one ship on our own, we would be forced into combat again.

Regardless of our problems, there was a lot of back slapping and smiling all around. We had entered our first engagement and won, alongside those who so far seemed to be in a similar situation as the people we left back home. I was a little surprised when the Vindyne fleet turned and jumped into hyperspace. There was a part of the picture I was missing. They were winning; they had superior numbers and ships in reserve that could take up positions as needed, or simply outflank the defenders. Their technology was also superior, from what I could see.

As we were finishing our damage assessment, we were directed to Gai-Ian VI, the planet they had named Concordia, with the thanks of the System Defence Fleet. We started the journey there and I checked the details included in the message. We were welcome to send a landing party to their primary port, which was only partially open for trade. We'd be met by Governor Samuel Finnley, and he would discuss the compensation entitlement for our assistance.

I looked to Oz and pointed at my command and control module on the lower half of my forearm. "Compensation entitlement?" I asked quietly.

"I guess they really appreciate our help. I know we tore up a lot of hulls out there, but I don't see how we turned the tide."

"You're right, there were hundreds of ships on the defence. I wonder if this compensation is anything like the mercenary grants Freeground issues from time to time when a freelance crew does a patrol or helps out with a conflict. Our arrival may have been timely, but I don't think it was critical. I'm not expecting much, but now that I think of it, anything would help. We lost two fighters."

"Maybe it's just an expensive way for them to take a closer look at us."

"Now that I can believe." A thought occurred to me then and I turned to our flight sergeant, Gary Cullum, who was sitting at the helm and coordinating with engineering on an engine damage check. "You know, I never asked, but could we land if we had to? I know the original design of the ship could land in an emergency."

"We could, but we'd need a lot of room. Say three kilometres of hardened ground. Then we'd need at least five kilometres of clear surface to re-launch and escape planetary gravity, just to be safe. The alternative is to burn everything within at least two kilometres while we take off, and that could detonate something if we haven't checked out the ground first. Oh, and our landing gear and anti-gravity fields haven't been pressure tested for atmosphere yet, so I wouldn't suggest this as a good time to try it."

"Good to know. Well, send a message telling them to expect a boarding shuttle once the First Light enters orbit." I sat down and whispered so only Alice, my personal assistant AI, could hear. "Open communications to medical."

"Yes, Captain."

A moment later, the channel was open and Doctor Anderson was on the line. "How are you doing down there, Doc?"

"We're lucky. All twenty three injured are going to be fine. Most of them can report for duty tomorrow. It'll take a day or so before Ensign Coupland's new arm is fully grown and ready, but that's the worst of it. This ship is good at protecting her crew, but I miss the Apollo's energy shields."

"Maybe we can talk to these people after I've landed on the planet surface and find out if we can trade for a shield projector system that will fit on our ship. They seemed to have a few in their fleet."

"You're going planet-side, Captain?"

"Looks like. As soon as we reach orbit around the sixth planet."

"Normally I'd go with you, but I'd rather stay with the injured, even though my staff has it well in hand."

"Having a doc around planet-side would make me a bit more comfortable. Think you could spare anyone?"

"I'll tell Doctor Lang to get her kit together. She's been planet-side a few times and passed the infantry qualifier."

"Thanks, Doc."

"No problem. Good luck."

Oz finished listening to the damage control report and turned his holographic command control interface off. "Looks like all the internal damage should be repaired in about two or three days. The outer hull will take a little longer to regenerate where it got pitted on our port side, maybe five days, but all sections sealed up right after they were hit. The ship is working just like it's designed to, according to Ayan. Better than her last trip, from what I gather. That was one hell of a fight and we weathered it better than I expected."

"It was. I don't like the way our trip is shaping up so far, though," I whispered. "Less than ten days out here and we already find ourselves in the middle of a war."

"We didn't have a choice. You did the right thing in making it look like we had other options when you volunteered to join the defence."

"Thank you, Oz, I hope I was convincing enough. Now I have to make my first planet fall as captain. Do I look as nervous as I feel?"

"Nope. You'll need a security team, though."

"Are you volunteering?"

"I suppose I could bring a few of our best with us."

"Good idea."

"We might want someone who knows a few things about the law," Oz said, pointing his thumb at Sergeant Everin, who was busy reviewing transmissions at his station.

I smiled. "You're right. Pick your security people. We won't be entering orbit around Concordia for at least three hours. See you on the flight deck. I'll get my kit together."

I was nervous and excited about my first trip as the representative of the crew. Over one hundred people would be up in orbit, wondering what I was doing down there, if there would be shore leave, if I'd sign us up as part of the defensive fleet. I tried to focus on selecting a few goals. Get details about the planet and the solar system's situation, find out if we can trade any of our technology for theirs, and see if we can get a shield system. I also wanted to take the opportunity to find out as much as I could about the Vindyne fleet. I was hoping that the enemy I had just made wasn't more trouble than our new ally was worth.

There really wasn't much for me to pack up. I checked my sidearm, stowed a survival package in my long coat, and took a few extra power cells. All the data I would ever need was in my command arm unit, and I had a few interactive display sticks on me already in case I had to hand off a copy of anything. I ran through a mental checklist and came to the conclusion that, if anything, I was over prepared.

My next thought was to take a trip by engineering. The door chimed as I started towards it. "Open," I said to the ship computer. Voice responsive doors were a nice touch added during the refit, and as the doors to my new Captain's quarters decoupled, moved out of the door frame, and parted to reveal Ayan, my nerves settled a little.

"Can I come in?"

"You know you don't have to ask," I replied with a smile.

She shrugged and came in. It took her a moment to take in my new quarters. They had replaced all the furniture, carpeted the floor with a thick forest green shag, and recoloured the metal a dark matte blue. "They didn't skimp, did they?"

"I know. I don't know what to do with most of the space, and you should see the bedroom."

Ayan blushed and fixed me with an exaggerated look of shock. "Why, Captain! What would the crew think?"

I could feel my face flushing and I struggled for words for a moment before taking a few quick steps and catching her up in my arms. She giggled and wrapped her arms around my neck, giving me a quick kiss. "How about dinner in main observation when I get back? Or even better, when things are all settled down there, maybe we can go planet-side," I asked.

"I'd love to. Just don't expect much from the people down there, if they're anything like Freegrounders. They'll be pretty wary of mercenaries who arrive in well armed ships."

"I'll keep that in mind. Have you ever been to a world like this?"

"A planet-side free port? Only once, on Azarian. They had a marketplace you could get lost in for days. It was so bright and warm during the day, so many people everywhere trading, looking for passage, going about their daily chores. Children followed us half the day, trying to sell us these bracelets and necklaces they made by hand. We didn't have any local currency, so I ended up trading a chocolate energy snack for one," said Ayan.

"Sounds like it was fun."

"It was, and I'd love to see another free port, but I don't think it'll happen here. We haven't seen the last of the Vindyne fleet and the people down there are going to be on edge. I have a bad feeling about this, Jonas."

I squeezed her a little tighter and nodded. "I'll be careful. Besides, Oz is bringing a security detail with him."

"Good, we need you back up here safe and sound. If you ask me, we shouldn't stay here longer than we have to," she said.

"At the very least, I'm going to collect on whatever this compensation they're offering is, and see if I can get us an energy shield system."

"Well, just make sure it's not a plasma based shield. We could already make one if we had to, but they're energy hungry and hard to maintain. I don't like the idea of surrounding the ship with a controlled explosion."

"They also haven't been in wide use for almost three hundred years. Too dangerous. All right, no plasma."

"And be safe. I want you back soon."

"Don't spend all your time worrying about me while I'm down there." I smirked.

She laughed and shook her head. "I doubt I'll have time. We have to build a new rail cannon turret from scratch to replace the one that got slagged and we're using a new design. We almost lost a gunnery crew, so we're going to try a concept with more protection."

"Good, how is the gunnery team from that turret?"

"They're recovering. Our new doctor is fantastic. They'll be back on duty in a few days. You should go by medical when you get back, I'm sure they'd love a visit from their captain. I've been stuck in medical before. It's boring. They'll appreciate the distraction."

"Another good idea. What would I do without you?"

For some reason she completely ignored my comment, instead she just kissed me and laid her head on my chest for a few moments before telling me. "I have to get back to engineering. There's still a lot of work to do."

"I'll walk you down." As we left my quarters, I couldn't help stopping at the door for a moment to look back while the lights were dimming. My quarters were so new to me they didn't feel like home yet.

I had just left Ayan in engineering and was starting to make my way to the flight deck when Alice chimed in on my left ear piece. "You're forgetting something, aren't you?"

I stopped in my tracks and thought for a minute. "Nothing I'm aware of."

"Your inoculation? It's procedure. Unless that's another policy you're loosening up."

"Don't they still stock the shuttles with inoculations?"

"It's better to go to medical. My existence would get pretty boring if the human I'm strapped to died because of some alien strain of influenza."

"You really know how to make me feel special."

I took the next lift up to main medical and was completely taken aback when I stepped out. There were a dozen or so wounded who were still being kept for observation and most of them noticed me right away. I don't know what kind of greeting

I expected, but I didn't look forward to visiting the main treatment centre.

I should have. Seeing the consequences of my decision to involve the crew in a firefight we knew little about taught me more in seconds than I could have learned in ten years of officer's training. The instant smiles on everyone's face as I came out of that elevator tube taught me even more.

"Captain on deck!" one fellow with a patch on one eye and a burn treatment wrap across the rest of his body called out with a raspy voice. He was one of the gunnery crewmembers who barely got away from a turret before it exploded. His jacket hung on a chair at his bedside and it told more of the story than the trappings of his treatment. The back of the protective material, able to sustain harsh radiation and over two thousand degree heat, had almost completely burned through. The fact that the man was alive at all was a miracle.

I had initially come for an inoculation, but that wasn't my purpose any longer. I remembered seeing friends in the hospital after the war and the lessons learned then came back to me. I looked this man in the eye, ignored the bandages and trappings of his recovery, walked over to him with a smile and clasped his good hand as soon as he offered it.

"How are you feeling, Bruce?" I asked him.

"Couldn't be better. Doc's got some powerful good pain meds."

"It's the least we could do."

"He says I should be back on duty in a couple of days. That is, whenever they build a new turret for Greg and me."

"Take your time in medical, Sergeant. We're building you two something special, courtesy of our chief engineer."

Doc smiled as he walked across the treatment centre and put a hand on my shoulder. "Let's do the rounds, Captain," he invited.

We did just that, going from crew member to crew member. I stayed and chatted with each one for a few minutes while Doctor Anderson checked their status, then we moved on. I didn't catch an evil eye from a single one. When we were finished, we went to a small corner in the infirmary that afforded us some privacy.

"Thanks for your help, Doc."

"With what?" he asked as he prepared an injector with my inoculation.

"Talking to everyone out there. I was really just coming for my inoculation, didn't know what to expect when I got here. That's not exactly something they prepare you for in basic training, and what they teach you in officer's training sounds good but standing there and saying 'good work soldier, carry on!' just doesn't feel right."

"That training is for wooden officers who know how to follow regulations and orders, not people who have to live with their crew for more than a few weeks or months at a time. I just gave you a pace, the rest was all up to you. You did fine for a man caught off guard. I saw the look on your face when you stepped out of that elevator. Glad you could join in on a long standing tradition."

"What's that?" I asked.

"Honouring the wounded. They used to call it walking the battlefield a couple thousand years ago. Of course, back then, the commanding officer would have a few men with him to put those who were too badly injured out of their misery."

"Glad that's changed."

"So am I. I had a lot of practice on the Apollo with Colonel Darius. After every engagement he'd be in medical, visiting everyone for a few minutes if he could spare the time."

"Sounds like a good commander."

"One of the best. Career officer for over thirty years, you'll never find a more die-hard traditionalist. He's a great thinker as well, and gets along with his crew. You remind me of him in that respect. It'll serve you well, especially on a long mission like this."

"Thank you, I've still got a lot of mistakes to make before I can really be compared to that kind of officer," I said as I got up to leave.

"We all do. Oh, there's another exit just there," Doc said as he pointed to a smaller door that looked more like a storage room hatchway. "And don't they equip those boarding shuttles with inoculations?"

I couldn't help but look down at my command console for a moment as I made my way out of medical. "You know, I'm pretty sure they do."

TWO

CONCORDIA

The First Light reached orbit just as everyone was set up and ready to depart in the boarding shuttle. The machine was an efficient design, with three-way adjustable seating for thirty-six that could brace the passengers in chairs, vertically or horizontally. It was equipped with enough supplies and energy stores for one month and a short range hyperspace system. There was also empty space for cargo or more modular equipment.

It was almost exactly like the one Minh-Chu and I served on with his infantry unit during the All-Con war, hopping from one manufacturing site to another, breaking or sneaking through their defences and blowing them up or setting them ablaze. The major difference was a little more space, slightly more modern systems, and two rail gun turrets instead of only one. Since the advent of ammunition materializers that could generate hundreds of rounds per minute, the need to store a ton of munitions per weapon was gone.

It was unusual sitting near the front end of the main cabin

with only six other people. When boarding craft were in use, you'd rarely see them without a full compliment, so it was always a cramped, busy ride. With the main cabin empty and a large section of the port hull set to transparency mode, it seemed spacious and I felt a little uneasy.

Oz, Jason, Doctor Lang, three security officers, and I sat looking out that transparent section of hull, three meters wide by one meter tall, as we left the launch bay. The sight that greeted us was unlike anything I'd seen.

Concordia was a bright azure and emerald planet. I could see the north polar cap, jagged shapes of the lush coloured green continents, and brighter, yellow land masses just south of the equator. The swirl of clouds drifted across the blue, green and brown so slowly and gently in gossamer white shades. One long continent was nothing but mountains, like the spine of some sea creature breaking the water, and it led from just above the equator all the way up north to the icy polar region.

All-Con Prime was the only planet with an atmosphere that I had ever been on before then and it was a charred mess. A pitted and ruined toxic hulk.

What I was seeing in front of me as I looked at Concordia was so delicate, so vibrant, and such a fine thing that I was loathe to blink during those moments.

"Are you all right, Captain?" Carrie, one of our security team asked in a whisper.

"I'm fine, I've just never seen anything like it." The hull went opaque as we neared the atmospheric entry point and I buckled myself in.

"It's an agricultural world. I've seen one before. They're beautiful."

"Yup, really pretty to visit but boring to live on. I couldn't imagine a life of tending crops, waiting for whole seasons to go by," Oz added.

Atmospheric entry was a little rough, but short, and the hull plating beside me became transparent once more. We were following the mountain range I had seen earlier. Its sides were covered with trees, the peaks topped with glimmering snow. Just over the tops of them I could see that the ocean went on to the horizon. It was the most pure blue I had ever set eyes on.

"I'd say that's why the Vindyne fleet decided to turn away," Jason said as he pointed just up ahead.

There was a massive planetary defence cannon hovering over the ocean. Its base was hundreds of meters across. Cables trailed behind it in the water as it drifted lazily beside us. "That barrel has to be at least fifteen meters wide. I wonder what kind of cannon it is," I said.

"Antimatter. I've seen one once before, but it was a hell of a lot smaller," Oz said. He looked mesmerized by the sight of it. "That thing could blow asteroids apart, never mind combat carriers. No wonder they've been able to stay isolated. Freeground could use a couple of those, forget shielding."

"Well, maybe we have something we can trade for the designs on one, who knows?" Jason said.

"I wonder how many they have, just the same," Oz said.

"I don't know how keen they'd be on giving up that kind of information, especially since they've probably hidden several," I said.

"Good point, I know I'd want to keep that a secret," Oz agreed.

Our destination came into view then, and it occurred to me

that if Freeground were on land, it would probably look something like what I was seeing. Just like the massive antimatter cannon, the port was in stark contrast to its surroundings. It was just north of the end of the mountain range, built on a flotilla of ice. It was a construct of domes built atop circular pilings with pylons reaching up and away from the main city building. Several landing platforms reached out from each pylon. Two of the larger ones supported massive barges a kilometre long. They were nothing more than container ships, most likely for moving crops off-world to transports waiting in orbit.

The port was quiet. I could only see a handful of smaller ships taking off or circling; no one was landing. We went straight in and landed on one of the lower platforms in one very swift, smooth motion of descent and deceleration. I flipped a switch and opened a connection to the cockpit. "Hello, Minh, I should have known you'd be along for this trip."

"What gave me away?"

"Oh, I don't know. The indirect flight path, the scenic view, and the drop and swoop landing was a dead give away."

The cockpit doors opened. He and his copilot, Derek, were working through the post-landing checklist. "In my mind I am a bird, and the wind carries me lightly," he said over his shoulder. "I'll be a few minutes while we go through the post flight. Why don't you kids go out and play? It looks like your friends are waiting."

"See you out there bird-brain," Oz replied as we unbuckled and then started making our way down to the main debark hatch.

The hatches on boarding shuttles were made to slide up and out of the way in a second or less, so when it slid up to expose us to the harsh, icy wind, it was like a frozen slap across the face. Everyone took a step back. The tiny specs of snow on the wind felt more like sand as they stung our cheeks. My vacsuit adjusted the second the temperature changed, but that didn't protect my head.

I looked to my right and saw that Oz already had his head-piece on. "What?" he asked with a shrug.

"No one puts their headgear on. Let's greet our new friends face to face."

"Hey, why do I have to freeze my head?"

"We have to make a good first impression. Besides, if they can take the cold, so can we."

"I haven't been this cold since boot camp. I'm definitely a tropical person," Oz commented with an exaggerated toothy grin as he pulled his headpiece down.

I steeled myself against the cold and started down the walkway leading to the station proper. It was ten meters wide with a chest-high railing but it still felt like we could get blown over the side and down to the ice or water hundreds of meters below.

"Welcome to Northern Concordia. I'm Governor Samuel Finnley, this is my assistant William Kam, and Elise, my legal consultant and daughter," he shouted over the sound of the wind, gesturing to a tall fellow in a thick brown parka and a young woman in a hover chair piled high with blankets. She looked so comfortably tucked in that I almost envied her.

"Greetings from the crew of the First Light and her captain. This is my communications officer Jason Everin, my medical officer Doctor Fiona Lang, my security officer Terry Ozark McPatrick and his team. Our Pilot, Minh-Chu Buu and his copilot Derek Gregor are still on the shuttle. They'll be along later if that's all right."

"Yes, it's a pleasure to meet you, but you must be freezing! There's a warm hallway leading to a boardroom just behind me. Let's move this inside," the Governor invited. He seemed right at home in the weather and smiled easily. The dark grey parka he wore was half undone, and I could see there was nothing special about the suit he wore underneath. I had seen many civilian dress suits on Freeground, typically a thin black jacket with a low collar and black pants. His was no different, but his suit looked a little faded from what I could see.

Once we were inside and sitting down at a long white boardroom table with a live animation of the ice flows stretching across it, I took a moment to look around. Instead of transparent steel, one wall featured a four part glass window that stretched the length of the room, and the lighting fixtures hung from the ceiling in thin, shielded tubes. The space was nicely built, with a thick fibre carpet, plaster walls painted in a gradient of blue and green ceiling to floor, and the chairs were deep and comfortable. However, I was reassured that most of the technology that they used to construct the room was at least four hundred years old. "I hope you don't mind me asking, but how long ago did your people build this port? It's in fantastic condition."

"We finished building it three years ago to replace a landing platform that was attached to the bottom of the ocean. This city can drift above the water, across land or ice, and produces no emissions. It's absolutely state of the art."

I tried to hide my surprise and focus on the style more than the severely out of date technology. "It blends right in with the ice."

"I know. The cold temperature is perfect for a port. Most dangerous bacteria and such are killed right away, so our experts say. If I had known the custom in which your people dress, I would have warned you to bring warmer clothing," the Governor mentioned as a young man entered the room carrying a tray. It was loaded with a steaming hot kettle and a number of mugs.

"Ah, our vacsuits. They're only one to three millimetres thick, but they can protect us from extreme temperatures. Only our faces and ears felt the cold."

"I've never seen a suit so thin that can do so much. I suppose that's something I should keep in mind if we trade. I hope we get the opportunity," the Governor said as he sat down. His daughter sat on his left as an aide removed most of her blankets. His assistant sat to his right with a thin display tablet that he tapped and dragged his finger across, moving icons and adding notes to whatever information storage system these people used.

"We should take care of current business first, Sir," his assistant said without looking up from his work.

"Yes, old business before new." He nodded as the servant poured him a mug of thick brown liquid. "Have some hot chocolate while we talk." He gestured. "So, our Defence Command reports that you managed to defeat one corvette and assist in the destruction of another. You also dispatched over three dozen smaller ships. According to the assessment committee, that's worth thirty seven million, two hundred twenty four credits. What currency would you like it in?"

I thought for a moment and tried to recall the itemized rewards list that Freeground used when paying mercenaries but couldn't remember any figures. It had been years since I had even glanced at it. "That's just less than half of what Freeground offers, Jonas, but it's enough to replace our fighters and a little more by the pricing I have on file," Alice whispered through my ear implant.

"Are those standard rates?" I asked, sitting back in my chair.

"They're what we can afford, Captain," the Governor replied. His assistant stopped working and looked at me expectantly.

"I'll be honest, it's less than half of what we are normally paid, but we didn't join your side in this to profit." I stood and offered him a hand. "Thank you for covering our expenses. We'll take it in United Core Worlds currency."

He shook my hand and smiled back. "Thank you for assisting in the defence, Captain." The mood in the room lightened a little and his assistant got right back to work on his thin tablet. "Now, I'm wondering, what kind of expedition are you on? I've never seen a ship like the First Light. Do you have sponsors?"

"We're independents. I'm the primary shareholder on the ship and all the other owners are crew. Most of the time, we only trade with free ports. We do some mercenary work, but only when we have to. That kind of thing makes you as many enemies as it does friends. Speaking of which, we've never gone up against the Vindyne before. Can you tell us anything about them?"

"Well, it's just 'Vindyne.' 'Vindyne Industries' and the 'Vindyne Corporation' depending on which end of the monstrosity you're talking about. They're an expanding corporate entity out here. Thanks to them, and a couple smaller competitors, there aren't many free ports left in this sector. We've managed to keep our interests free, but Vindyne has closed in all around us. Until last year they would just buy a share of our crops. Their business was welcome, but as their needs grew, the prices they were willing to pay have lowered.

"They declared us hostile when we refused to sell at half the guild rates and shipped everything to their competition. Now there's no negotiating with them. They've taken worlds before, relocating all the colonists, separating them into placements where they become slaves. That's when the people they take don't just disappear entirely."

Eliza spoke, her speech slightly slurred, "The legal ground they stand on is shaky. Their claim is that we are not properly utilizing the resources we control and that the under-utilization is a criminal act. Vindyne sees themselves as a governing body, not just a corporation. They argue that the needs of their current citizens outweigh ours. They believe their needs warrant a takeover since we produce thousands of times more food than our population needs. Our counterpoint is that by offering our organic foods and other products at fair prices that are lower than the cost of materializing food for their population on a daily basis, we are helping them. Our government even offered to advance a quarter season's crop to them to be paid at an undefined date. It would have been enough to feed their entire populace, billions of people, for a year."

The Governor continued right from where she left off. "They'd have none of it, and why would they? They have the firepower to take whatever they like. Our neighbours can't afford to lend a hand either. No one in this sector can afford the negative attention of Vindyne. They are connected to most interplanetary corporations in this area and collectively cease trade with anyone who assists their enemies."

"It's a good thing trading with corporations isn't a priority for us," Oz said, toasting with a mug of hot chocolate.

"So, they engage in territorial warfare and slavery. I'm happy I'm on your side," I said with a smile. "Do you have the authority to conduct trade, Governor Finnley?"

"I do, but that's also dependent on what you have to offer. What kind of trade do you normally conduct?"

"Technology mostly, anything we can get our hands on that will improve our circumstances. It's hard for independent outposts to stay up to date with corporations doing most of the research and development these days."

"What kind of technology would you be able to offer us, Captain?" William the assistant asked.

I was about to answer when Doctor Lang touched me on the shoulder. "If I may, Captain?" I gestured for her to go ahead.

She moved to the seat closest to Elise, the Governor's daughter. "Do you mind if I ask why you're in a hover chair?"

Elise smiled through one side of her face while the other side remained slack. "I have a nervous system degeneration condition called Sodian Syndrome. It started before I was born and has badly deviated my spine."

"May I scan you, Elise?"

Elise's eyes rolled to look at her father, who nodded. "Go ahead, Doctor."

I watched as Doctor Lang held her hand up in front of Elise for a moment then brought up a hologram projected from the medical console on her arm. There was an internal physical representation of Elise there, which reflected what she had described. There were also icons and other details around the three dimensional portrait that only someone with years of medical training could understand. Doctor Lang selected and navigated through several different menus, assessing information taken during the brief scan and finally smiled and nodded to herself. "We can halt the deterioration and remove the disease from your system. As for the degeneration, it will be easy to restore your fine motor skills and muscle control for your upper body. Getting you out of the chair may take more work, but it's possible. We could discuss it later if you like."

The Governor stood and looked straight at me. I'll never forget the look in his eyes. I could have asked for anything, he would give it to me. "What do you want, Captain?"

I didn't think about it, I didn't have to. "Nothing. I'll make it happen for you and pass on the information so your people can learn from it. If you need to call it anything, call it good will."

Elise's arm gestured wildly and she tried to shift in her chair to face Doctor Lang more directly. She was trying to say something but was very excited, and for the life of me I couldn't think of what I could do to calm her down.

I didn't have to. Doctor Lang leaned forward and gave Elise a gentle hug. She calmed down after a few moments. "Thank you, Doctor. Thank you so much," I heard the young woman whisper.

After a long moment, Doctor Lang sat back down beside Elise. "I'll send all the information about the procedures to your physician if you can tell me how to get it to him."

"If any expertise is needed, I can have Doctor Lang or another qualified crew member help for as long as we're here," I added.

The Governor tapped on the table and brought up a sub display over the top of the animated topography of the ice flows. He selected some information and a diagram and slid his finger a few centimetres in Doctor Lang's direction. The sub display slid across the table to stop in front of the doctor, who read it then instructed her medical console to send the information to Elise's physician. "It's on its way, and he should have no problem contacting me if he has difficulty with any of the research or treatments."

"Thank you, Doctor. I think this will be a beneficial trade negotiation for your crew and my people. I know a lot about my daughter's condition and where our medical science falls short. Your home world must have made some very important medical advances for you to have cures for one of our most debilitating ailments. I'll accept the cure for my daughter, but I'm sure our council will want the rest of your medical database as well, and I'm sure they would gladly trade for it."

William whispered something to the Governor, who nodded and continued. "My assistant thinks this negotiation has taken an emotional turn, and I have to admit he's right. I think an hour would be suitable for an adjournment. The sentries can escort you to the accommodations we have put aside for you and your crew."

THREE

RETHINKING

We were led through part of the outer hallway of the station, where Minh-Chu and Derek joined us. The pair of sentries who led us were dressed in dark grey canvas uniforms. Each had a sidearm and a very military air about them.

For part of the journey, there were windows all along our left side, overlooking the vast ice floes. On our right hand side, the wall was replaced by a railing. We could see three levels below to a grand concourse with dozens of shops, kiosks, and auction platforms. It was difficult not to stop and take a better look.

Everything that could be built out of wood or stone was. The storefronts, the brick in the floor, the platforms, and even the digital interfaces had wooden housings. These were people who enjoyed nature and were proud of their strong connection to their world. There were places in the galaxy where wooden fixtures and natural grown materials were an extreme luxury, but it was everywhere you looked in Concordia.

After a few minutes we arrived at the double door entrance to a large apartment. It was decorated in colours of gold and beige, with a two-part circular sofa in the centre for six people on either side, a holographic projector in the centre, and other, smaller seats and tables arranged in a central pit. Two sets of stairs led up to several bedrooms, and there was a kitchen off to the side that easily rivalled the one Minh had in his restaurant. In the centre of the seating pit, circling the holographic projector, was a table covered with fresh flowers, fruit, and vegetables.

On Freeground, what was on that table would have been worth a small fortune. Organically grown food was rationed to citizens. What we could spare was sold to traders at a high premium. I had heard that food grown on Freeground was nothing compared to something grown on a fertile planet, and as we entered the room our group stared at the table. Jason and Minh were the worst, the latter of whom even pointed as though no one else had seen it. I looked at Oz and shrugged. "Dig in, just don't make yourselves sick," Oz instructed.

Minh and Jason practically ran at the table; one grabbed a pear and the other snatched a package of smaller blackberries. I walked by the table to the window and took a nice red apple on my way by.

We had all been affected by the scene in the board room.

"I have never seen anything like that, not ever," Oz said to Doctor Lang.

"I recognized what she had, though I've never seen it so advanced. We cure that affliction in the womb on Freeground now. It doesn't even have a name there, just a numerical designation."

"Well, if that were the only reason for us being here, it

would have been enough. Thank you, Doctor, I'm glad you came along for the trip," I said.

"Oh, you can take me on any planet-side mission from now on. That sort of thing is why I became a doctor," she said as she looked through the scan results. "In about three days, Elise will feel like a normal girl above the waist, and with some therapy, we might be able to readjust her physiology so almost all traces of the syndrome are gone. It'll take some work on her part, but from just meeting her I think she'll have the dedication to get through the therapy." She paused for a moment before going on. "Her physician just sent me a reply. On preliminary examination, he doesn't feel comfortable performing the treatment himself, or confident that his people have the facilities to manufacture the drugs required. If you don't mind, I'd like to contact Doctor Anderson and relay the details of what has gone on here. I'm sure he'll be happy to help."

"I'm sure he would. You'd better bring him up to speed. Besides, I'm sure he'd love to have a hand in this." I took a bite of the apple and the taste was so rich I nearly fell over. Materialized food was never quite the right texture, and fruit was especially difficult to duplicate.

"Anyone notice how few questions the Governor had about where we come from? What we're doing here?" Jason asked as he peeled an orange.

"They're probably focus-scanning our ship with some kind of planet-side station right now, if they hadn't done it before we landed," Oz replied. "There's only so much you can hide. The characteristics of the metal in our hull will probably tell them that it's from the Blue Belt, and that's about a two month trip from here in hyperspace."

I looked at him with a raised eyebrow.

"What? I can't know a bit about engineering?"

I finished chewing a bite of apple. "Well, you're right. They probably know that we're about as alien to this area as a Findarian slug. I'm sure they'll have a lot more questions for us before we're finished here."

"How much do you think we can tell them?" Minh-Chu asked.

"Not as much as I'd like to. I hope we can convince them that we have no nefarious purpose here without going into too much detail."

"Well, treating Elise and offering our medical database for a reasonable trade will go a long way to that end," Doctor Lang said.

"It will. Maybe that's just the thing. I know the medical database is worth a hell of a lot more, but I'd be happy with instructions on how to shield the First Light and the parts to do it. Since it's not a weapon we're asking for, I think that'll be an easy trade."

"You could always ask for the schematics to one of those antimatter cannons, maybe some antimatter to get us started," Oz said quietly.

"You and I both know that antimatter is the most costly substance in the galaxy. That might be like asking for a stake on their planet, especially since they probably use it for a lot more than weaponry. For all we know it's their primary form of propulsion, or planetary power."

"Still, you are curing the Governor's daughter and providing medical information well past their stage of development,"

Jason pointed out as he wafted the orange under his nose and let the fragrance fill his nostrils.

"As much as I'd like to, I'm not going to walk in asking for weapons in trade for medical technology. If they ask for something else of equal value, maybe, but trading cures for weaponry just doesn't seem to fit with the spirit of our mission."

"I thought our mission was to—"" Minh started, but was stopped by a harsh look from Oz, who used the infantry hand signs for "unknown foe listening."

The exchange silenced everyone in the room and a very dark feeling that had been festering in the back of my mind for a while grew a little faster. Hiding it was impossible.

"What's wrong, Jonas?" Minh asked. If anyone could tell when my mood was starting to darken, it was him.

"It might all be for nothing. Trading medical technology, offering cures, even helping them stand up to their enemies. Vindyne will be back. Judging from the coordinated retreat and how outnumbered they had these colonists, I'm thinking that things are going according to their plans. They'll return and I get the feeling that not even those antimatter cannons we saw on the way in will defend against them."

It was like I cast a shadow across the entire room. Everyone stopped and looked at me. I paced along the length of the large windows. "The plan was to come in, find out what they needed and trade for shield technology or whatever they have to offer. Maybe pick up some fresh fruit for the crew and a little something for Ayan at the market."

"Still a good plan," Oz shrugged.

"Right, until the part of us leaving them behind to face whatever Vindyne have planned for them." I stopped and looked out the window across an amazing view of blue waters, a sky with just a few clouds, and mountains reaching high in the background. "Look at this! I know technology and new resources are our main priority, but wouldn't a friend like this system of planets be just as valuable?"

"Don't take this the wrong way, but a drop of water in that ocean makes about as much difference as we would in a fight, on the ground or with the First Light. They've been defending this world for decades. Probably a couple centuries now," Oz retorted.

I put my hand on the window and felt the cold through the glass before my vacsuit glove compensated. I jerked my hand away, but not because of the sudden chill. A realization had struck me. "Look at this! It's glass. Glass of all things! I'm sure this kind of construction is just fine for a farm house, but for a port this size? It's a strategic target and they don't know how to make anything harder? One vacuum to atmosphere missile and this place is rubble! There's no way they built those cannons themselves, in fact they probably bought those ships we saw, too."

"But how do we fight?" Jason asked quietly. "Even if we have the best ship in orbit, we can't hold out a corporate fleet. What can we do?"

I thought for a while, looking off across the vast ocean. "Alice, patch in Ayan and Doctor Anderson, and display them on the most central holographic projector you can access."

"Yes, Captain, I'll get them on right away," Alice replied from my arm console. A moment later, the holographic projector in the middle of the room came to life. It looked like Ayan and Doctor Anderson were standing back to back above the projector, rotating slowly. The height difference between the two had never been more apparent. Doc seemed to tower over her while she seemed miniature, a full head shorter and more. "How is it going down there, Captain?" Ayan asked. "I hear things are taking an interesting turn."

"You could say that," Minh managed around a piece of fruit.

"They're going well as far as the negotiations are concerned. We've already made a couple of friends here. As Doctor Anderson knows, we've found that our medical technology is far advanced compared to theirs, and there is at least one problem we can solve for them."

"Yes, and if you can get Elise to the ship, we can probably have her upper body motor functions back to an average level in the space of a day or two. With some physical therapy to tune her fine motor controls, she'll be playing table tennis with the best of them after a few months. Any chance we can bring her aboard?"

I hadn't even thought about using our medical equipment to treat her; it would be faster and our entire medical team would have access to her during the treatment. The problem was that the senior staff had agreed that having outsiders on the ship would expose them to a lot of information we didn't want to share. I looked at Oz and saw he was hesitant as well. "I don't know, Doctor, there's a lot we don't know about these people. Bringing people aboard may be premature, though it does bring me to my next point. I don't think these people can stand up to the kind of force Vindyne has shown us. They have some solid planetary defence weaponry, we saw at least one antimatter cannon, but I doubt they developed and manufactured it themselves."

"So they probably bought it, and you're afraid that the Vindyne fleet has bought the control codes from whoever made them," Ayan added.

"Something like that. Their buildings may as well be sticks and stones. The base we're on is lightly armoured on the outside but plaster and concrete on the inside. They don't even have transparent metals. It's like putting a house of cards up against an asteroid strike."

"You want to stay and help?" Ayan asked sceptically.

"The people back home could use a friend with these kinds of resources to trade with. If we could help turn the tide, or at least show them a way to improve their fortifications, it might just give them a chance. If it worked out, we could be opening trade with an entire solar system. I think we should try."

"What if they don't want our help, Jonas?" asked the Doctor. "Independents are stubborn, they fear being deeply indebted to anyone and don't trust easily."

I thought for a moment; there had to be a middle ground between staying and risking everything and leaving the system to whatever fate Vindyne had planned for them. "I'll offer them three days. In that time, let's take a look at anything that can be improved within the timeframe. If they don't want it, we'll just have to trade and move on."

"I like it. Just tell me what their priorities are and where you need my people," Ayan agreed.

"It'll give me enough time to go down there, treat Elise, and train her physician so he can pass the knowledge on. It's not as much time as I'd like for such an advanced case, but I can work with it," said Doctor Lang.

"I'd stick around to make sure we see that through," Oz nodded.

Minh-Chu had moved on to a peach and was leisurely eating it as though nothing was going on. Everyone was looking at him by the time he spoke. "I need a closer look at one of those cannons," he said casually.

"I think that can come later. We may even be able to trade for—"

Minh cut me off. "If they're made by some corporation, say a daughter company of Vindyne, then it wouldn't be hard for them to build a receiver into them and shut them down whenever they want. If we can get close enough, and such a system exists, we might just be able to make it work against them. I'd love to see those cannons reprogrammed to fire at any unauthorized ship or control system trying to access it. It would be like adding the perfect targeting system to the most deadly weapon I've seen. Now that would be a surprise worth seeing. I'll need Jason and a tech who isn't afraid to touch something without an instruction manual."

"I think that's a good first step to making a difference," I started feeling that dark mood lifting. "I'll be meeting with the Governor again in a few minutes. I just need Oz, Doctor Lang, and Jason with me this time. Everyone else take the indirect route back to the shuttle. Spend half an hour or so looking around and getting a sense of what these people are like."

Less than twenty minutes later, Jason, Oz, Doctor Lang, the Governor, and William were all back in the board room. "Our head of medical, Doctor Anderson, would like to take a trip down here to treat your daughter personally, but we need time,"

I opened, skipping all the formalities and trying to bring us right back to where we left off.

Governor Finnley was taken by surprise, but not unpleasantly from what I could tell. "I'm sure I can arrange that." He paused for a moment, looked at Jason, Oz, then me. "Your ship, your crew, it's not like any mercenary or trade vessel I've ever seen. Our military is growing suspicious of you."

"Sir, this isn't something that—" his assistant started to interject.

"William, are you aide to the military or to the Governor's Office? These people deserve to know what kind of nest they're guesting in. Now, before I was interrupted, I was about to say that it looks like the military want to take over these trade negotiations, which means that the priorities will change and our civilian government will be cut out of the decision making entirely."

"I'm sorry to hear that, even though I thought they'd be more involved from the start."

"Well, normally they would, but they didn't see one ship as much of a factor in this war. Then they heard about your offer of medical technology, the favour you'll be doing for my daughter and me, and now they want in. I don't know how long I'll be able to offer you anything, but as of this moment I still have control. What do you want, Captain?"

His urgency didn't allow for any finesse or modesty. I took his cue and just came out with our primary purpose. "When we were on our way here, and had no idea your planet would be under siege, we were hoping to trade for shield technology and anything else that could help us protect our ship. We can offer you our medical data base in return."

Governor Finnley started working through menus on the table in front of him, selecting entire categories of information and sending them sliding across the display towards me. "So all our information on shield technology and one working sample of our most recent development for your entire medical data base. Our Surgeon General has already weighed in on this, and she believes that we should be trading even more just based on the treatments you're offering my daughter. According to her you're over a hundred years further along than we are, medically. Consider it done."

I didn't take time to look too closely, but from what I could see, the mathematics, mechanics, and specifications to entire working models on various ships and bases, including the port we were sitting in, were piling up on the display in front of me. "Alice, can you interface with the table and collect the data displayed there?" I whispered.

"Yes, Sir, I'll collect it now."

I looked up to the Governor's assistant, who had fixed me with a quizzical expression. "Alice is my personal assistant. She's an artificial intelligence," I explained.

"Sir, the Governor has even included all the research they've done on Vindyne's shields. Ayan should be able to build a formidable defence for the ship using the information here and some basic components. It says the working sample is already being loaded on our shuttle, and Commander Minh-Chu has authorized entry for the loading crew," Alice whispered into my ear. "This is almost a fair trade for our medical database if the shield technology works properly."

Alice had already packaged the medical database in my command unit, and I pressed the send icon on the display. It appeared on the table and I moved my finger across it towards the Governor, sending it to his end. "That's the whole thing. It should help your people a great deal."

His smile looked weary but relieved. "I believe you. You should send the shield information that I gave you to your ship as soon as possible. I don't want to give our military time to reverse the trade."

I looked down to my command console and saw that Alice was already sending it straight to First Light engineering over a secure channel. "You seem worried about what the military will do when they take over trade. Is there something I should know?"

"They're a suspicious bunch. Believe that the affairs of the planet and solar system should be solely under their control where travellers are concerned. I don't expect trade will be nearly as open."

"I can understand where they're coming from. I'm sure they're just interested in protecting you," Oz commented.

"Perhaps, but they tend to be heavy handed. I'm only glad I had the opportunity to serve the interests of my constituents."

"About that... My crew and I would like to stay for a few more days and see what we could do to shore up your defences. It's come to our attention that your planetary defences may have been built by another company."

The Governor was about to respond when the door was opened by a sentry and two men. One had greying hair and medals on his chest and the other was much younger, walking straight and tall. Two more sentries trailed behind them and closed the door behind.

"Colonel Douglas, allow me to introduce you to our guests," the Governor said with a sweeping gesture.

"I've been briefed, Samuel. We'll take it from here. Is there any more damage I should know about?"

"I managed to trade for their medical database. It only cost us some shield technology. We came out on top, if you ask me."

"How much shield technology? What did you give them?"

"I didn't give them anything, they traded their entire medical database for our shield technology research and a working sample. It's a matter of record, if you'd like to look at the details."

"I don't care what medical advances you think you've found here, no one authorized you to trade proprietary military technology. You'll be lucky to see another term in office," the General threatened in a low tone.

"I'll be lucky if I ever get to retire. I never thought of it this way, but I might just become known as the Governor who helped cure dozens of diseases and prevent even more. Not everyone in this government cares about the turf war between the military and civil services. I'll bet my constituents will see this step up in medicine as evidence that I care more about them than the issues between the military and civil services. You should treat Captain Valent and his people here with respect. They're a generous people if you give them a little trust." Governor Finnley turned to me then. "My daughter and I will be at your disposal, Captain. Thank you very much. You've helped my people a great deal. My office stands ready to serve your needs while you're on our world."

"You're welcome. You'll hear from me soon," I replied,

smiling at him but inwardly bracing myself for what was to come with the colonel.

The governor and his assistant left the room and the colonel made himself comfortable in the chair at the head of the table. "So, a ship we've never seen before comes out of nowhere in the middle of a battle and offers its assistance. Our scans can't penetrate the hull, but it's more heavily armed than any of our destroyers, and such a hard target that they weather the battle effortlessly without any energy shielding. If I weren't so suspicious, I'd be impressed, Captain."

"We're here to offer help while we're welcome," I explained quietly.

"Well, I might believe that if I knew who your sponsor was, where the currency that pays for that ship and crew come from."

"Like I said before, we're a shareholder crew. That ship, hard target or not, is an antique. We do what we can, but she's old. We trade technology and freight between free systems."

"That's a convenient explanation, but the other free ports we're allied with have never heard of you. One had a profile similar to your ship's design in their data banks but it was over two hundred years old and reported as scrap. All that ergranian steel in one place was impractical, they took it apart to sell the raw materials, so don't tell me buying that ship, as old as it is, was a cost saving measure.

"Nothing about your crew sits right with me. Intelligence has taken a look at the data stamps on the medical information you provided for Elise and found that they're all blank, there's no tag telling us where the information came from, who generated the files initially, or if they were paid for. We can only assume that you're hiding its origin point."

"You'd be right. What good would information we traded for be if you could trace it back to the source and skip the middleman?"

"Your crew behaves like military. The suits you wear may be far more advanced than our uniforms, but they carry rank insignia, look the same or similar from one person to another, and it's obvious that there's a clear chain of command."

I have to admit, I was getting more than a little impatient. "You're right, and I can give you one simple reason why. It's much easier to control a crew that adhere to a clearly established system, a chain of command. My crew follow rank and basic regulations out of necessity. If they have a problem with it, my security team is happy to escort them to the nearest airlock. Now, I'm here to trade, and my crew is willing to help with your defence while we're in the system."

"That's what really worries me. You offer the governor a miracle, earn his trust in the first half hour of knowing him, but you're not willing to answer any of our questions about you."

"Ask a question I can answer."

"Where do you come from?"

"We're a shareholder crew. We're from all over the galaxy. Most of us grew up on ships, and I seeded the purchase of the First Light with an inheritance."

"All right. I find that hard to believe, but I'll ask another question. Who hired you first, us or Vindyne? Have you been sent here to sabotage or spy on us?"

"We don't work for Vindyne, we don't work for you.

Nobody hired us. In fact, we're not interested in being hired, independence is central to how we operate."

"Really? What is this mission you spoke about just a while ago in the apartment? It seemed like something you didn't want us to overhear." The colonel's aide brought up a surveillance menu on the table and selected footage of Oz silencing Minh, playing back in the centre of the table.

"I'm afraid I can't discuss it, but it has absolutely nothing to do with you or your people."

"Can't discuss it. I could easily take you into custody and our interrogators could take the time to discuss it with you."

"Listen, if I were here to sabotage your defence, it would have been done and I would already be gone by now. In fact, I can see exactly where someone would sabotage your defences, and I'll be happy to warn you about it."

"How do we know that all of this isn't just a distraction? That you're not just some disposable hired gun who is here for nothing more than to lure our focus away from the Vindyne ships just outside our system?"

I ignored his side of the argument and pressed my point. "The cannons you purchased were obviously made by a company with a great deal more experience in weaponry construction. We suspect that they may have hidden a remote access system inside. I wouldn't be surprised if they offered the access codes to Vindyne for a price, or that a daughter company of Vindyne built them. We may be able to help you reprogram them so access is restricted, or so they automatically target unauthorized ships trying to take control."

"Do you think we're stupid? Backwards? We've checked those cannons and they were made by an independent contractor. They also have no kind of remote transmitters or receivers, the controls are hard wired. We're quite safe on the surface."

"That doesn't make them impossible to manipulate. Someone could patch themselves in from one of those cables and take direct control or add a receiver at any point along the cable's path."

"Impossible, the junction sites have alarms built in and the penalty for treason is death. The chances of us being betrayed by one of our own are slim to none."

"When the cannons are taken out of commission, they can mount an assault from the air and hold your cities hostage. Even with energy shielding, a large enough explosion just outside the protected radius would shake any settlement to the ground. Especially if they're made of glass, metal sheeting, wood, and plaster. Like I said, we are here to help."

"Then tell me who your patrons are. Who do you really serve and what is this mission of yours all about?"

I thought for a moment, knowing full well that we'd have to reveal something significant to convince him we were trustworthy. "If I tell you anything it can't go past this room."

"I can't promise that until I know what it is you're going to tell me."

"Look, I'm willing to give you critical information about where we're from and what we're doing here, but you've got to promise me that this doesn't leak."

"I follow a chain of command and have an obligation to pass information up to my superiors. I'll decide what kind of secrecy is necessary once I know what it is you have to tell me."

"In that case, it's time for us to leave. The terms of your trust aren't a good fit with our priorities. I'd like to honour our promises to the Governor's daughter, so we'll stay in orbit to make sure the medical treatment we offered is carried out properly. I assume we're free to return to our ship?"

"Under escort, yes." Colonel Douglas looked surprised.

The station shook suddenly, and I looked at my command control console.

The colonel brought a menu up on the table and made a selection. "Sentries, draw and take aim on our friends here," he said casually. The two guards behind him drew their sidearms and pointed them at us. They looked like conventional projectile weapons. It didn't matter that our suits could withstand that kind of impact, our heads were uncovered and the projectiles could still cause broken bones and bruises or ruptured organs if they impacted on our suits too hard or too many times.

Colonel Douglas brought a live image of the station up on the table. One of the domes was smoking; the wall of it looked like it had blown out from the inside and was on fire. "It looks like there was an explosion in the market section. Some of your crew members passed through there on their way to your lander," the colonel said matter-of-factly. "The control station to one of our planetary defence cannons happens to be out of commission thanks to that bomb. You're all under arrest." He pressed another spot on the table and the door opened to reveal two more sentinels.

"That went well," Oz whispered sarcastically. "Hey, Colonel!" he yelled as he tossed a small, round energy grenade right at him. Shots rang out and everyone ducked. My head was above the table just long enough to see Oz's grenade attach itself directly to the bridge of the colonel's nose.

A second later, there was a flash of light and I could hear

bodies hit the floor at the front of the room. By the time I was out from under the table, Oz was on his feet at the front, taking a sidearm from one of the unconscious sentinels. He fired it at one of the windows half a dozen times and tossed the weapon aside. His hood was already up and his suit was sealed. Without a word, he took a running start and jumped through the glass, shattering it outward.

I ran to the edge and saw him fall into the water below. His suit would protect him from the two hundred meter fall and the near frozen water. "Minh, get the shuttle in the air and track our arm consoles. We'll need a pick up," I shouted into my communicator. "Start with Oz."

I turned to Jason and Doctor Lang. The doctor's headpiece was already up and sealed. "I'm right behind you. Someone's got to treat that big idiot."

"That's insane, there's no way!" Jason said, walking carefully up to the edge.

"It's that or you get left behind. You bet there are sentinels on their way here right now."

He looked over the edge again and I could see he was starting to panic. "There's got to be another way."

I looked at Doctor Lang for a moment and she took one quick step towards Jason. She slapped something on his cheek. Before he knew what was going on he fell to the floor, unconscious. "That'll work," I said with a shrug.

We sealed his headpiece then picked him up and tossed him out the window. I sympathized with him, and found myself trying to think of another way, any other way, before watching the doctor take a run at the window and leap out. I followed her as I heard the door open behind me.

FOUR

FALLING

As I watched the water quickly approach, I remember thinking that there had to be a way to incorporate an antigravity unit into the suits, or at least a parachute. Then I hit, and the black blue of the water enveloped me. The front of my suit inflated and I was drawn back up to the surface.

Minh had already brought the shuttle down from the landing platform and was dipping the loading ramp at the front into the water, making it easy for the security team to fish Oz out. He was completely limp, and the doctor was right behind him, pulling Jason with her.

I was the last on the shuttle. "Back to the ship!" I shouted into my communicator. The hatch shut behind me and I moved over to where Doctor Lang was releasing Oz's headpiece. As soon as the seal came undone, a gush of blood rushed out. She carefully but quickly pulled the hood off and the extent of his injuries became plain. He had been shot in the lower half of the face and passed out sometime before or after he hit the water. The suit must have started medicating him as soon as it detected injuries. One of the security officers brought the larger medical kit from the shuttle and Doctor Lang immediately got to work.

She cleared his airway and applied a few micro patches to deliver more medication on his neck, then did some work inside the wound. I couldn't make out what she was doing clearly, but I stood near just in case she needed assistance. She didn't. Her hands were practiced, she was quick, and her work was done in two minutes. She took off her hood and looked at me. "There's nothing else we can do until he's on the ship, but he's stable. He was shot twice in the chest as well but his suit wasn't punctured. At worst he suffered some bruising. I'm amazed he got us out. Help me get him into a stasis tube."

I was just starting to pick him up when I heard the cockpit door slide open. "Jonas! Who do we start shooting at?" Minh-Chu yelled over his shoulder.

Carrie took over for me, gently picking up Oz's feet. "No shooting! Don't shoot anyone!" I yelled as I ran past the crewmembers who had accompanied us planet-side. Everyone made it back. I dropped myself into the cockpit tactical seat and looked out the view port.

From our position in orbit, I could see Vindyne ships had engaged in combat with the depleted Gai-Ian fleet and more combatants were still arriving.

"I'll bet that half the defence fleet or more are still around Gai-Ian Nine and there's an offensive just large enough to keep them occupied there. Vindyne got past their inner system defences." I brought up the tactical display and Alice patched into the computer. "Captain, planetary communications chatter is filled with reports of explosions in key areas before the arrival of the Vindyne fleet. They're trying to put out the fires and get things under control, but there is a lot of chaos," Alice reported in a sad tone.

"How many explosions, can you get a number?"

"Over seventy from what I've overheard."

I sat back and thought for a moment, doing some mental math. "That's just about how many cannons they'd need on the surface to defend the entire planet."

"None of the cannons have been directly affected."

"They wouldn't have to be if bombs were destroying control centers just like the one in the northern port. Vindyne should have control of the orbital space soon. It's time to leave." I looked at the tactical display and saw three Vindyne Marauder corvettes, each nearly two hundred meters long, and heavily armed. "We really have to get out of here."

I started turning towards the communications and information systems station but Jason ran into the cockpit and sat in the seat first. "On it, Captain. Oz is squared away." He started working the communications controls and hailing the First Light.

At the same time, I checked for her profile at my station.

"No ship. She's just not there or her communications and transponder are out," Jason said urgently. "Could Vindyne have gotten to her?"

"No, if the First Light had been destroyed there would be dozens of emergency beacons. Maybe she's on the other side of the planet," I said as I frantically scanned the entire region.

Minh started evasive manoeuvres as the corvettes were

about to enter firing range; their engines were far more powerful and they were catching up fast. "No ship?" he cried out as he forced the boarding craft into a spiralling dive towards a distant moon. "No cover, no friends, fighting everywhere and corvettes catching up. There can't be no ship!"

I was still scanning for the ship when Alice's voice emitted from my command unit. "There is no wreckage from the First Light, and there is no evidence of the ship in range. I'm sorry, Jonas."

I sat back in my seat and watched the small holographic screen hovering over the flat panels built into the tactical station as the three Vindyne Marauder corvettes came closer and closer. Their beam weapons would cut the boarding shuttle to pieces in seconds.

"Message coming in, Sir. The Vindyne are ordering our surrender. We have thirty seconds to cut the engines and secure any weapons," Jason reported.

"It's our only option. Signal our surrender. Minh, straighten us out and cut our engines."

He did what he was asked then locked the controls and released the swivel on his pilot's chair so he could turn to face me. "Should we expect any help from our friends on Concordia?"

"Well, the civilian government loves us, but the military aren't big fans."

"What did you say down there?"

"It's more what I didn't say. We were about to leave without making anything worse, but then there was an explosion in the market place. They tried to put us under arrest so Oz found us an escape route."

The lead corvette class ship, a narrow vessel with gunnery ports along the top and bottom, closed in and locked us to her hull with docking clamps. "Please turn off all non-critical systems and stand by for transport to the nearest carrier," came the announcement from the communications systems as the docking clamp's data link jacked into our craft.

"Well, I suppose it's better to be imprisoned by the winning side," Jason said quietly as he watched the other two corvettes turn back towards the battle. I shut down the tactical station while everyone turned off the other posts. The shuttle was suddenly far too quiet and even though the lighting hadn't changed, it seemed darker.

"Well, this is probably the last chance we'll get to see what was in that crate the Governor had delivered," I said as I got up and walked into the main cabin. It was a meter and a half tall and two meters per side. I undid the clasps on one end and the container opened. He had honoured his promise and more. There were samples of shield, weaponry and biomass technology from what I could tell at a glance. "It's as though he didn't know what we'd want from him exactly, but he was prepared to give us what it was on a second's notice," Doctor Lang said.

"He knew the military were about to take over the negotiations, I suppose this was his way of getting the last word in," I agreed.

"Oh no, don't tell me he did what I think he did," Doctor Lang said, shaking her head. "That power cell is just the right size for a hover chair."

"Well, there's nothing wrong with them giving us anti-gravity technology samples, they might be more advanced there as well."

Doctor Lang moved a few things out of the crate and pulled a handle. A tray slid out with Elise laying on top of her flattened out hover chair, which provided a softer surface than the bare stasis unit. She looked like she was sound asleep.

"Oh, no."

Doctor Lang checked the young woman's vital signs with her medical unit and nodded to herself. "She's in dry chemical stasis. Judging from the container and her state, she could stay this way for weeks or longer." She checked the controls to the container. "This chamber is made to operate for months. He used the best. It even has its own inertial dampeners."

"What will Vindyne do with her?" I found myself asking quietly.

"I don't know," she turned to one of the security officers. "Get the medical supplies from the shuttle. If I'm right, this could work to Elise's advantage."

"What do you mean?"

"Well, her system has been tricked into sinking into a protective coma, so there's no way to wake her. If I'm right, the drug synthesis kit should be able to generate the first and second phases of her treatment, and with her already out, I can accelerate it so when she wakes up she should have increased motor control and a lot of the nerve damage will be repaired. What she'll do with that I don't know, but it's better than her waking up the way she was before. Maybe she could help herself a little."

"Good consolation to being taken captive," Jason, who helped the security officer with the emergency surgery kit, said from behind. "If she's as smart as I think she is, maybe she'll be our Trojan horse."

"I hope not. The last thing I want her to do is get herself into more trouble trying to help us," I replied.

"Well, either way, this might be my last chance to honour my promise to her," Doctor Lang said, taking a small material- izer and the synthesizer from the surgical kit. She set right to work programming the right combination of drugs into the machines and I took that opportunity to see how things looked from the cockpit.

I immediately wished that I hadn't. We were well behind the Vindyne's front line, and the largest ship I had ever seen loomed ahead. Even though we were a few thousand kilometres away from it, the vessel was imposing. It was the largest space- faring vessel I'd ever seen second to Freeground.

It was a massive, thin half circle, the size of a medium space station. Long rods extended from the front and rear engines. The engines were easily half a kilometre across, indicating incredible interior mass. One large docking bay was yawning open. Five corvettes were emerging shoulder to shoulder. We were just minutes away from docking.

I looked to my right and saw that the fighting over the planet had stopped. There were no more flashes, just dozens of ships entering orbit, specks and small seemingly random shapes against the back lighting of the great big blue and green world.

"Think we could bribe our way out of this?" Minh asked quietly.

"Not with their superiors looking on from that invasion plat- form behind them."

"Do you have a plan?"

"Surrender, then talk our way out."

"Sounds like a good plan, mostly because your talking has been so very effective."

"Do you have any better ideas?"

Minh sat quietly for a moment before answering, "It'll come to me."

"Tell me when it does."

I casually tapped a preset sequence of buttons on my command console. To anyone looking on it looked like I was checking my messages. That couldn't be further from the truth. Alice was whispering in my ear a second later. "Thank you, Jonas, I won't let you down."

Doctor Lang came into the cockpit a moment later. "It turned out a little better than expected. I was able to set the drugs to release into her system in stages. There were a few subdermal inserts in the kit that will release the second and third stages of the treatment into her system when it's time. She'll wake up a little earlier, but that's the only risk other than some mild shaking after a couple of days."

"How long until she wakes up?"

"About two days. After that she'll be fine for a day or so. I just hope the shaking phase doesn't frighten her too much. It's a side effect of the regeneration process."

"We can't hide her. I don't know what they'll do to the ship or that container. Will Vindyne be able to detect the drugs in her system?"

"They will, but there won't be anything they can do about it. At the worst they'll keep her in stasis, I hope."

"You and me both. I don't know what I'll do if anything happens to her."

"I know. I hope I can stay with her."

"So do I. It's important that we don't get separated, but I suspect that's the first thing they'll do. I'm just glad we're all trained to handle it."

As we came within a kilometre of the docking bay, the Marauder released the clamps and began accelerating away. I could hear Minh curse under his breath as one of the clamps scratched lengthwise across the hull.

We were caught by some kind of magnetic tow or gravity field which began drawing us into the landing bay. It consisted of several levels that overlapped each other with elevation pads and sections cut away so many small ships could be docked, moved, serviced, and dismantled or sold. The efficient use of space was impressive, almost impressive enough to distract me from the fact that we were absolutely helpless.

The bump of turbulence indicated that there was a shift in gravity, and the people working without helmets or sealed suits indicated that there was a reliable contained atmosphere. I found myself looking at the ships littering the multiple levels of the bay. Many of them had minor battle damage, while others were in perfect repair.

"They capture a lot more than the All-Con Fleet did, that's for sure. I'd love a chance to take a look around. There's an Arcyn Starskipper, right there," Minh's copilot said, pointing to a sleek black gunship. I remembered seeing notices about that model, warning everyone in Freeground Operations that it was one of the fastest lightspeed ships in her class, with room for a crew of twelve and a small cargo. It had a predatory look and sleek design. A true mercenary ship that very few mercenaries could dream of buying, yet too flashy for common military use.

"I've never met anyone who could afford to buy the armed model. I'd give my restaurant for one," Minh said, sitting up in his seat. "Whoever owns that one must be pretty pissed at being captured."

"Are the ship's computers clear of any sensitive information, Minh?"

"Yup. All that's left are the logs starting when we landed on Concordia. Not very interesting stuff."

"Good."

"Think we'll make it out of this, Jonas?" he asked quietly.

"Any corporate machine that big has got to have a few cracks in it. If anyone can find them, it's this crew. I'm just glad Ayan got the ship out of here. We couldn't have been much help and it's likely both sides would have fired on the First Light."

"Cloaking devices. We should all have cloaking devices," Minh said, crossing his arms and looking out the cockpit. "And bigger guns."

Our ship was reoriented, and by our trajectory I could tell it wouldn't be long before we were down on the deck. I turned to the rest of the crew. "Okay, they're going to board us in a few minutes. We have to disarm ourselves. Stow any weapons that you have on you where they're safely out of the way and out of sight. That crate is going to stay open; just close the stasis section so Elise doesn't get knocked around while we're touching down. Erase all data on any recording devices you have, we don't want to give them anything we don't have to. They're going to ask questions. Speak when spoken to and answer them. Don't lie, don't try to escape, don't fight them."

"What if they ask about Freeground?" asked Carrie as she deposited her sidearm in an overhead storage compartment.

"Focus on as many unimportant details as you can. Tell them whatever you have to so you can prevent harm to yourself and your crewmates. The Admiralty may disagree, but I'm not going to order you to keep a secret that won't do Freeground any harm if it's uncovered. It's that simple. We'll try not to get separated but that's exactly what they'll do. I'll try to keep us together and get us free. Keep in mind that we've seen no sign of the First Light, so she's still out there. We have no idea what kind of plan they have in mind, so we'd better not screw it up by doing something dangerous or stupid. As of now, our mission out here is to do one thing and one thing only: survive."

When we landed, everyone was gathered at the front of the main cabin facing the forward boarding ramp. All our suits were sealed. As I opened the hatch, my headpiece display indicated that there was a breathable atmosphere, but we remained covered up regardless. I put one hand up and held the other forward, presenting a data chip containing a full manifest and ship log for the last day.

The soldiers rushed in four at a time, all in navy blue and black armour. They carried double-barrelled rifles the likes of which I had never seen. One barrel looked like it was for energy, the other seemed to fire large projectiles that must have been four centimetres across.

After a dozen soldiers had taken up positions in front of us, rifles at the ready, one soldier strode leisurely up the ramp. He stopped inches in front of me, then looked me up and down. "You are the captain?" he asked.

"I am. Here is our manifest. We have one injured and one in our care. I take all responsibility for any criminal activity that—"

"Take off your mask," he ordered.

I hesitated for a moment then retracted my headpiece. Without a word he stepped back and shot me full in the face. There was a flash of light and excruciating pain. Every cell in my body seemed to be writhing in its own private hell before I passed out.

FIVE
CAPTIVITY

I woke up on a thin mattress with a headache worse than anything I could have imagined. It felt like my brain was too large for my head, but somehow it found enough space to throb anyway. I opened my eyes to slits and was immediately reminded of my old apartment on Freeground. The cell had the same prefabricated, plastic, white look. The mattress I was laying on was just a softer section of the pallet built into the wall. There were no seams in the small room, not even where the sink or toilet met the sides of my cell.

The white walls gleamed under the harsh light. I had been stripped of everything and redressed in a thin plastic jumpsuit. Across from my cell was another, and Jason sat in it. There was no look of despair or panic on his face as I might have expected. He looked as though he were completely at peace with where he was and his situation. I watched him through my slitted gaze for a few more moments and noticed that his eyes were very slowly, methodically scanning everything around him one centimetre at a time.

I could see some kind of field was blurring the air between his cell and mine and assumed it would be pointless to try and pass through it. I sat up and winced.

"Captain?" Jason whispered. His voice was a little distorted by the fields, but I could make out what he was saying clearly. "Are you all right?"

"I've been better. How long have I been out?"

"About nine hours. Those electromag weapons they use are the worst. Besides the regular lethal variety, I mean."

"Yeah, they're pretty bad," I agreed, gently holding my head in my hands.

"They used one on me when they took me out of here. I woke up in an interrogation room. I guess they revived me early. I was given meds for the headache though."

"Tell them anything?"

Jason hesitated.

"Whatever it was, you can tell me about it. Don't worry."

"I told them about the ship, our mission, and Freeground. I'm sorry, Sir."

"That's all right. I don't think that they had this kind of situation in mind when they came up with our orders, and if they did, I can deal with the consequences as long as we come out of this in one piece. Have you seen anyone else?"

"The only person I haven't seen is Elise. They even brought Oz by. He looked pissed off but they fixed him up."

"How did everyone else look?"

"That's what I don't understand. Some of them were

knocked out, others were like you. The security officers were in perfect shape. But they beat Doctor Lang."

"They did what?"

"She had a split lip and the start of a black eye," Jason replied.

I thought about it for a moment and tried to lie down. My head only pounded more fiercely when it touched the minimal padding of the bunk, so I sat up again slowly. "They're trying to make us think some of us are providing more information than others. The only one I see holding out is Oz. I never rescinded his gag order. I'm sure everyone else is cooperating as much as they can, but that's not what they want us to think."

"What do you think they'll do next?"

"Did they ask you anything about me?"

"Only how long you've been in command and our personal opinion of you. They wanted to know a lot about your previous military record and what kind of missions you sent us on. I couldn't tell them much since I really don't know anything about your previous record, and Concordia was our first mission off ship."

"You never read my service record?"

"I never had a reason to read past the vitals, I guess. They weren't very happy that I didn't have much information on you, though, and they kept on asking about your involvement with the All-Con conflict. I think they already know you're a veteran."

"Well, then I'd say they'll be taking me next. Good thing I don't plan on keeping anything a secret. I'm already off balance with this headache."

"Are you sure we're doing the right thing, Jonas? Telling them everything about home and our mission?"

"I think so. They're professionals playing a pretty deep psychological game over a short time period. I'll bet that these lights never go out, and if they do, we'll be in complete darkness. We're also being recorded and our vitals are being monitored. If they knew to ask about the All-Con conflict, then they've already done some research and come up with something significant, at least where Minh and I are concerned. We're being processed, I don't know what for yet though. We'll most likely be entered into their court system soon. Besides, I get the feeling that Vindyne is pretty large, and their influence is significant in the galaxy. They already know what Freeground is, if they don't I'll be really surprised."

"Probably. How do you know so much about corporate prisons, by the way?"

"Contraband movies. It's amazing what I could get my hands on in Port Operations back home."

"I could imagine."

Jason and I stood at the sound of approaching footsteps. A few moments later, two guards escorted Minh-Chu past our cells. He looked like I felt, and watched me from the corner of his eye. Even during the All-Con conflict, on that desolate rock where we burned factories to the ground and made wholesale theft of stock yards possible by killing regiments of guards, there was always some kind of lightness to him. The levity that I knew in him was gone.

The guards came back without him and stopped in front of my cell. The haze generated by the barrier disappeared and one of the guards motioned with his gun. "Come with us."

I stood and walked towards them. I was in complete disbe-lief at how close I was allowed to come. I was within inches of his helmet. I could see my reflection in his eye piece.

It was so tempting to take the opportunity to fight, steal one of their weapons and start blasting. I glanced up the row of cells then back down. In one direction there were sealed security doors. In the other was a hall. All along the uncountable length were hundreds of cells stacked ten high. The hallway extended from either side of the cell hall in sections and I looked a bit further to my right to see that there were cells below as well. Most of the energy fields closing off the fronts of the cells seemed distorted or opaque. It was deathly quiet for a place where tens of thousands of people were kept alone or paired in cells.

One guard nudged me with the muzzle of his rifle and I started walking towards the nearest doorway. "Quite a place you've got here. Ever have a prison break?"

"No."

"You should try it. Really spices up your day."

I was escorted to a massive receiving area. I looked to either side and saw that there were other doors leading to other sections of the prison. In front and to the left of me I could see through transparesteel plating into the reception area proper where thousands of captives were being processed.

Young children were left with their mothers, but everyone else was separated into lines, a few for men sorted by fitness, and a few for women sorted by age. Guards watched from walk-ways above, some armed with the electromag rifles I'd already become so familiar with. Others had shorter, deadlier looking weapons with single barrels.

One young man began to fight with a guard as he was separated from a woman holding a wailing little girl and all three of them were shot by electromag rifles. They fell to the floor twitching for several moments before they lay still. I couldn't look away until I was sure they were all still breathing.

As I turned my head, I saw them roughly lifted then dropped onto conveyor belts that lead deeper into the processing centre.

"As the wounded go by, I'll be the one standing. The stones forget our names as they erode down, featureless. As the innocent go by, I'll just close my eyes," I recited as I was rushed down the hall. It was a poem written by one of the founders of Freeground. It was inscribed on one of the walls in the oldest section, and until then I did not completely understand it. We were always told it was about helplessness and represented a turning point in our history when apathy turned to indignation, and our founders struck out to make a place for themselves. There was no apathy in me as I was guided through a door into a darkened room. One of the guards sat me down in a metal chair in the middle of the chamber. The other shot me with his electromag rifle from behind, just as I was about to recite the second half of the poem for my benefit as much as anyone else's.

SIX

A ROOM, A TABLE, AND TWO CHAIRS

Have you ever had a really bad dream, woken up, then gone back to sleep only to find an even worse nightmare waiting? As I tried to raise my pounding head from the polished metal surface of a table and found I couldn't, that's exactly how I felt. While I mentally cursed at the guard who shot me for absolutely no reason, I took stock of my situation.

I was in a chair. Well, not just in a chair, I was strapped to a chair with ankle and wrist restraints. My head or neck wasn't strapped to the table. I just couldn't lift it. It throbbed so badly that I wanted to both scream and scurry into a corner at the same time. Then the lights came on.

I heard a weak, mournful cry and realized a moment later that it came from me. I could barely move my mouth. My eyes were watering and my nose was running.

"Captain Valent," a voice enunciated intentionally and clearly, as though caressing the words, tasting every syllable. "My dear Captain Valent." He slowly walked around the table, tracing the space of the room. "I wonder if your name is short-ened from Valentine. So many of us have names that have been butchered by the modern progression of things. It is normally a sign that we are from a lesser class, of lower breeding. You see, those teeming masses were once hard to keep track of, back when there were only a handful of colonies. So many mouths to feed in so little space. One thing us humans are good at is breed-ing, and it seems the lower classes were always so much more reckless about it than the more educated, intelligent few. They would have more children earlier and over time that means more generations, more poor breeders, more mouths to feed, less time for education and less spent on refinement. Thus, without the money, power or education to know enough to make an effort to maintain the integrity of one's family name, the less refined side of humanity runs around with butchered names and broken, untraceable genealogies. It makes them mutts, I suppose." He laughed at his own realization and stopped to look at me. "From your scans we can see no evidence of inbreeding, I suppose I'll have to have them scan you again."

Just the sound of this man's voice and its manner — pompous and holier than thou — made me angry. Even though all my other senses were overwhelmed by pain, I locked my jaw and started to sit up.

"Oh, I don't think you want to do that. Your nervous system has taken a fantastic shock."

I clenched and ground my teeth together. Through the pain in my spine, the intense tingling in my fingers and toes, and the rhythmic explosions in my brain, I pulled with my shoulders, stiffened my neck, and dragged my head off the table. Then up, up, until I finally sat properly upright. My head kept on wanting to fall to the side or forward, even backwards a few times.

The expression on the man's face was that of amusement and surprise. It was a narrow, angular face, with a pointed chin and a long, thin nose. "I'm impressed. What will it be for your next trick? Will you loosen your restraints and disappear right before our eyes? Perhaps you'll make me disappear? That would be impressive, but considering your long lost namesake, not all together surprising. Did you know that there was once a Saint Valentine?"

I concentrated on remaining upright and trying to calm down at the same time. Slowing my blood flow might have reduced the pain.

"Yes, Saint Valentine," he went on. "Thousands of years ago there was an Empire, the Romans. Not much like the Romans of today, but in some ways similar, I suppose. They did enjoy similar entertainments. They were opposed to the concept of Christianity then, a religion of forgiveness, kindness, and morality. You must have heard of it. Valentine was a priest in this order and was captured along with entire families of Christians then sent to the Roman arena. They would feed great beasts called lions with these Christians, so low they were that their enemies used them as fodder.

"On the day Valentine was to become feed for the Roman beasts, he stood in line behind a young couple just beginning their lives together. Valentine took their place after saying something very poetic and quote-worthy, I'm sure. The centurion didn't really care, one Christian was as good as another. Priest, child, newlywed couple - there was little difference.

"Valentine walked to the centre of the arena with thousands

of Romans looking on. The mob must have been shouting and cheering, revelling in their unbridled bloodlust. This was a priest who was to be fodder for the beast, it was going to be a real show!"

My head throbbed every time the thin man raised his voice to punctuate his story. I squeezed my eyes shut and tried to shut him out for a moment, but that only made it worse.

My captor went on. "Valentine would not entertain the masses, so he knelt then began to pray quietly to his God. The lions did not care, and took their meal slowly, biting and tearing at him. He did not scream. Not so much as a whimper. Now that is strength. That is faith! Wouldn't that be impressive?"

I was drooling. My preventative slurp pierced this silent moment.

"There are many different versions of this tale. One ends by claiming that the crowd was in awe of the man's strength, and his piety made them look away in the final moments. That their bloodlust was slaked and they were ashamed. In that telling, they say the young couple and the other Christians lived to be fodder another day. In another telling, it is recorded that the day went on, the young couple and many other Christians were killed, and the audience looked on as usual as the helpless believers ran from the beasts here and there before they were torn to shreds in a feeding frenzy. Regardless, his strength, his sacrifice, was meaningless in the end. The act of piety and grace bought at best a short reprieve for a people who were destined to die. That day or the next, it didn't matter."

I looked at the man's uniform. It was navy blue and pressed carefully, every seam was perfect. His shoes reflected the bright lights, and his knuckles were raw. The image of Doctor Lang's black eye and split lip filled my mind for a moment, and I must have glared at him. "Why write it down?" I forced myself to say. He paced around me, sizing me up.

"What's that? Why record the story in the first place? History loves an underdog. Besides, just a few hundred years later, the Christians befriended and bred their way into the upper ranks of Rome, and were victorious. They controlled their former enemies, and therefore were able to change the recording of history. For all we know, Saint Valentine was a sword bearing savage, a man of war and bloodshed who rode in a chariot drawn by four lions he would feed with the corpses of fallen Roman soldiers." He lowered himself down to my eye level and looked at me more closely. "I have heard from every crew member that we've been keeping and they believe in you. A few of them even think that you are their key to freedom. I see strength in you, the dedication of a misguided man who still doesn't realize how helpless and outmatched he really is. If you were Valentine, I would bet on the former mythical figure. A misguided saint who actually believes that he can make a difference." He straightened and continued pacing around the room.

I just stared at him as he circled me, and glared as he came closer.

"I wonder what your people on Freeground will think. Our efforts to contact them haven't produced results, but the Triad Corporation has already responded. They'll be more than happy to discuss you and your people."

I couldn't help being furious at myself and at Vindyne. I tried not to show it but could feel my face turning red.

"Yes, Triad has a profile on you. Apparently you were a lieutenant commander in Freeground's Port Operations centre, the first face many ship captains saw when they entered Free-ground-controlled space. I wonder what you did to earn yourself a ship and crew. How did you earn your crew's trust so well after assuming command? Are you some kind of hero? You don't have the bearing or presence of a hero. No, I think you had a lucky accident and failed upwards. That makes more sense. Nevertheless, Triad wants you, and they're willing to pay much more than we are for your ship. The current offer is eight billion UCW credits. There is a bonus of five million credits for each crew member we can deliver to them alive as well. You hear that? They want you and your crew alive. Is that enough hope for you, Saint Valentine?"

I tried to ignore what he was saying, but it made me furious. I sat and fought to control my breathing.

"The problem is, we don't have your ship yet. I'm sure that if we were to find it, they would not come easily. If you want to save your crew, you will have to deliver them to us with your ship. If they come quietly, you'll simply be transported back and handed over to Triad."

I looked up to him and our eyes met for just a moment. I knew I was glaring. I couldn't help it.

The bird man gave me a mock hurt expression and a gasp. "You injure me, Saint Valentine. Hate is an emotion that controls those without culture, those without a tendency towards tact and grace. I had imbued my image of you with much better qualities." He stepped behind me and pushed hard with one hand right between my shoulder blades. My head hit the table like a gavel, and I was too enveloped in anguish to know whether or not I cried out. When the pain subsided a little, I rested. Just breathing. I just concentrated on breathing.

"We could continue this pointless exercise or I could have them administer some medication, alleviate the pain, repair some of the nerve damage you sustained. All you have to do is answer a question or two, and that'll start setting things right. Getting us back on the right path. Perhaps we could even be friends for a short time. They say that the best kind of friendship is one that forms in passing. You only get to see the best sides of people that way."

At the mere thought of being asked a question, trading information for relief, hope sprang forth. I could answer anything he put forward without a single regret; Freeground Fleet Command couldn't have foreseen us getting captured by an enemy like this so soon, I was sure, and revealing our mission wouldn't make anything worse for them. Triad already knew where I was, that there was a ship just out of their reach. "Ask," I managed to croak.

"Where is your ship?"

That was the one thing I couldn't tell him. He could have asked anything else, and despite my pain I managed to roll my eyes. "Don't know," I slurred.

"Well, if your own pain doesn't motivate you towards having an open dialogue, perhaps we could start on Elise. At this very moment she is in the care of our best physicians, being treated to a gentle rehabilitation. A recovery that your people started, in fact. Is she frightened? A little. She knows that she's in the wrong hands, but they're caring, gentle hands regardless."

"Please, innocent," I managed.

"Ah, there it is, the real nerve. Should I have her brought in? I can arrange it! Where is your ship?"

"Don't know. Would tell if I did," I wailed as loudly as I could.

He put one hand on my head and pressed down; my head felt like it was in a tightening vice. "How can you not know? You're not trying to tell me that they just left you behind? Do they have a cloaking device? Is it hiding in some chasm or cleft in a nearby moon?"

"Don't know!"

"You must have a retrieval code! A way to use a communicator as a beacon! A channel you can call them on that would be traceable! What is it?"

I knew that if I were to try and contact the ship, Ayan would take it as a sign that we were too deep in custody to be rescued. Her training would tell her not to accept any communications from us, and to go deeper into hiding, run further away. "Won't work!" I managed to scream.

He looked up to a hidden window and yelled. "Bring the girl here, it's time to show the Captain how serious we really are."

"Don't!"

"Are you going to tell me how to summon your ship?"

"Won't work! Will run!"

The thin, bony man stopped pushing down, grabbed my hair and pulled my head back. I shouted in his face. The agony was so intense I was seeing white spots and kicking my feet. "I am getting tired of hearing 'I don't know!' or 'it won't work!' from you and your crew! They have told us who you are, where you come from, about this misguided mission to find new technology, and still they won't tell us where your ship is! Now this girl you set out to help is about to suffer. We will reverse all the healing you have done, make her condition more painful and debilitating than ever! I swear she'll be a twisted mass of writhing flesh by the time we return her to her father and it will be your fault!"

As he shouted in my face I had a moment of perfect clarity in which a thought occurred to me; the captive had broken the jailer by doing nothing but sitting and suffering in silence. This man was too complicated to entertain the thought that none of us knew where the First Light and the rest of the crew were. There was nothing I could do about Elise, nothing I could do for my crew. I was helpless, powerless to fix anything. I was beside myself with pain, but by some freak reflex, I started to laugh. It hurt, oh hell it hurt, but I couldn't help but laugh.

"Why are you laughing?" he screamed in my face.

Without thinking I hopped, just an inch, just enough to get his nose between my teeth. As I squeezed my jaws together, grinding as I went, the world around me disappeared. I don't remember being knocked out, or what my interrogator's reaction was beyond his cursing and wailing.

The nightmare was over. At least, the part where my head felt like it was about to explode and the thin man with angular features who talked too much and was asking me what I didn't know was over. All the pain was gone except for a little tingle in the back of my neck. When I opened my eyes, they confirmed what my face already knew; my head was resting on a small white pillow. I was still strapped into the chair, and my head was on the table, but there was a little pillow. That little comfort felt like the greatest luxury, and I took a moment to enjoy it.

"Good morning, Jonas," a much deeper voice greeted. "Feeling better?"

I realized that I felt like I had slept for a week and I did actually feel much better. There was also a little drool, so I wiped my mouth on the pillow as best as I could before sitting up. The new interrogator had a grey beard and wore a slick light blue lab coat. "Much better, thank you." I looked down and saw there were blood stains on my jumpsuit.

"We took care of your injuries, but we couldn't clean you up properly. I apologize. The mess you made of Major Hampon will take a bit longer to clean up."

"So that wasn't a dream," I said, knowing very well it wasn't. I had trouble believing what I had done and found it more repulsive than satisfying.

"No, it wasn't. You are a very dangerous man, but then again, when you torment any creature while it's in that much pain, you can only expect the worst. Sadly, the Major did more damage to our cause than you did to his nose. His well laid plans included broadcasting your interrogation to your crew through their cell walls and it backfired. As they witnessed you bite off a substantial portion of their interrogator's nose and fight through all that pain until we could inject you with a sedative, their morale rose up. Most of them actually cheered."

"I've heard I can have that effect on people." I looked at my new interrogator more carefully. He was a tall fellow, and seemed very confident, controlled but with an easy manner. If I had met him anywhere else, I got the impression that we would become fast friends. Their interrogation technique was so well put together, they used all the classic tricks and I was becoming very aware of what phase of the mind game I was being ushered into.

"Well, as I supervised our dear major's interrogation, which was almost flawless, by the way, I got to know your crew and their opinion of you. I have to say, I'm impressed."

"How is Elise?"

"She's fine. Sleeping soundly, actually. Her recovery is going very well. I just checked on her." He brought up a holographic image between us of her sleeping comfortably in a hospital bed with high railings. "The work Major Hampon did made it quite clear that you and your crew have been left behind. There was no point in going through with his threat." He turned off the projection.

"How do I know that projection was real?"

"What point would there be in harming her? What information could I gather from you that wouldn't be offered freely without harming anyone more than we already have?"

"None."

"I believe you. Your crew have been very forthcoming, on your order I assume. So I couldn't see why you would withhold."

I sighed and nodded. "Well, in that case, what can I do for you?"

"I just want to do a little more fact finding and get some clarification on a few things, if you don't mind. Then we can move on to other matters. From what your crew tells me, you're a very intelligent, good hearted man, so this should be quick."

I tried to scratch an itch on my nose by rubbing it on my shoulder, and nonchalantly replied, "I hope. And thanks, I think." I knew I looked just a bit silly since I couldn't quite reach it, but I was trying to make a new impression.

My new interrogator laughed and crossed the room to stand a meter away from me. "You know you can't escape. Even if you somehow managed to relieve yourself of your restraints, over-power me, there's no way out of this room. You're being watched by at least one or two of my staff from a gallery with a one way wall and the door is armoured. Even if you made it outside and past the guards, you'd only be hunted down some-where in the hundreds of kilometres of corridors."

"I know, just get this itch, willya?"

"Like night and day. You are a fascinating fellow, Captain," he said as he scratched my nose gently with two fingers. "Take away what ails you and a different man emerges from under all that anger."

"Just don't start calling me Valentine. Thanks."

He walked to the other side of the table and sat back down. "My pleasure. I believe that you're still absolutely livid at the imprisonment and treatment of crew members, but it's good to see that anger under control. To see that while you're thinking on your feet you make even the smallest of efforts to convince me that you are just a harmless captive."

"No, really, thank you. My nose was really itching like crazy. I don't know what you make those pillows out of, but I'd look into possible allergens."

"You're welcome." He knitted his fingers and rested his hands on the table. "My name is Marshal, and if you don't mind, I have a few questions for you."

"Sure, I'll tell you pretty much anything. Just don't expect me to go into great detail about middle school, that was a pretty awkward time for me."

"Isn't it always. Now, to start, we confiscated this from you when we brought you aboard." He pulled my command and control console out of his coat pocket and put it between us on the table. "I'm assuming it was used as some kind of data storage and retrieval unit."

"Actually, it had pretty much all the information I needed to command and control the ship and a predictive file serving system that would get everything I needed ready right before I actually needed it. You should look into getting one, or you could take mine. I can get another one made once I'm back on board my ship."

"I think I'll pass, thank you. I find it interesting, however, that it's completely blank. We can't retrieve so much as a serial number."

"Data's funny that way, erase it and overwrite it with nonsense a few billion times and it's gone forever."

"We picked up a burst transmission between it and a nearby interceptor right before your shuttle docked. You wouldn't happen to know anything about that, would you?"

"Actually, the predictive program was just trying to store itself somewhere else before deletion. Standard procedure."

Marshal watched me for a moment and smiled. "You're actually telling the truth." He shook his head in disbelief. "So everything we need to know is actually in our own computers."

"Whatever do you mean?"

"I mean the details on your ship, the rest of your crew, enough information about Freeground to learn why Triad wants it so badly."

"The predictive program doesn't take much data with it. Just enough to know how to get back home if it's called."

"That's not how the artificial intelligence we've detected is behaving. A data sorting, filing or even a predictive database reader will collect information, make copies of itself, not leave false trails and move along. What is this artificial intelligence programmed to do?"

"It sorts the most important data pertinent to a situation to the front and presents it when necessary. It was very useful to me, maybe it's just sorting your system out."

"And maybe I'm just here to hold your hand. You're telling me the truth, Sir, but not all of it. This artificial intelligence is leaving messages for us. It's interfering with non-essential systems when it can, and it's moving deeper into our systems. Our computer security programs are preventing it from seeing where it's going, blocking off anything essential and hunting it down, so it will only be a matter of time before we put a stop to whatever it's programmed to do. You may as well tell us all about it and save yourself some trouble."

I looked at him for a moment and smiled. "What message is it leaving you?"

"It's nothing of consequence."

"Then why don't you tell me?"

"You know, I will hold you and your crew accountable for anything your artificial intelligence does. It would help everyone for me to know what it's here to do."

Just like that, I had some control over the situation. There was only one card left to play, and I didn't know if I'd get another chance, "You're starting to sound a bit like your predecessor. Are you going to force the answers out of me? Harm the helpless to get me talking? Even if I told you what this artificial intelligence was for, it wouldn't change anything."

"I have a luxury you don't, Captain. Time. I can take as much time to question you as I like."

"What happens when you take everything away from someone? All their control over a situation, their accountability. I know full well that I'm not in control of my situation, that whatever you do to me or my crew — even Elise — is not my fault. You're the ones who do the damage. Harm my crew and my charge, they won't blame me in the end. My liability is gone and so is my motivation. I'm sure your superiors are happy with how things are going. They're watching right now, aren't they? I'm sure there are holorecorders scanning this entire room, our interview is being replayed life size in some boardroom and your efficiency is being graded. You've probably been groomed half your life for this kind of work, had less control over your own destiny than I have over mine now."

"If you plan on trying to play on my baser instincts, get some kind of irrational rise out of me, then you'll be sorely disappointed."

It was too late, he had already given away the general direction of the hidden main recorders. When I mentioned recording, grading, he glanced at them. He couldn't help it. That was all I needed to ensure that Alice would know that I was trying to speak directly to her. "I wonder, how much is your company willing to spend on me? What kind of return do you think you'll get even if you manage to track down my ship? Eight billion seems like a pretty low figure for a company like Vindyne to slow down for."

"I'll be honest with you, then. We want to enter into more extended talks with the Triad Corporation. Presenting your ship, loaded with all the latest technology from Freeground, to them would be a fantastic opening to such negotiations. If you cooperate I can promise we'll speak on your crew's behalf and ask for leniency when you are presented to their court system."

I started leisurely looking around as though I was getting bored. "You don't have that kind of power, let's not make promises that are impossible to keep." I looked straight at where I was sure he had glanced a few times, where I was certain the main holorecorder for the room was. "To them you may as well be daddy's little girl." There. The trigger phrase was out, and what Alice would do with all the safeties and restrictions deleted from her programming was a mystery, but I was sure that one directive would be well served. She would try anything to get us out of this. Up until now she had only been tinkering, testing security and learning about their ship. "They just pat you on the head for doing a good job and send you on your way, or give you a good sound spanking if you don't perform as well as they need you to."

Marshal seemed amused and surprised at the same time. "Is that what you really think of me?" I could tell my answer wouldn't matter to him.

"Nope, just trying to push your buttons."

"Well, I have something to show you, since we're talking about pushing buttons, but not today. I think we've made a lot of progress for one session, Jonas. I'm learning a great deal about you, your ship, your crew and even more about this artificial intelligence that's running around somewhere in the ship. I have a feeling that finding that program will be key to discovering the location of your vessel."

"They can't communicate with each other. Like I said, the program just isn't that intelligent."

Marshal smiled at me. "Now, now you're lying. Thank you, Jonas, thank you very much. That's all I needed." He left the room first, and then I was led back to my cell.

SEVEN

INCARCERATED LIFE

The cell had gotten worse. Somehow when I was feeling the after effects of their energy rifles the cell looked bigger. Maybe it was just my blurred vision at the time, but as I became more accustomed to my surroundings, my sensitivity grew. They turned up the intensity of the energy field that sealed off the front wall of my cell and it started emitting a hum. A low, undulating hum that I could just barely hear.

After another day I noticed that after every few minutes, the lights would become dimmer for just a split second, like clockwork. For a few hours I observed it while I lay still, trying to think of some way to escape.

Intermittently, by no schedule I could discern, people were led past my cell. Sometimes the energy barrier was smooth enough so I could see them. Other times it made them look like shimmering shadows. They would walk them out ten or twenty at a time but I never saw any return.

At least two days passed and finally they turned the lights

out. The barrier's hum subsided and I was allowed to sleep soundly. I don't know how long my slumber was, but the lights came on way too soon. The barrier was still almost completely transparent and quiet. I just laid back and closed my eyes, hoping I could go back to sleep even though I could see light through my eyelids.

Not long after I heard people approaching and sat up to see who it was. I couldn't help but grin as Oz came into view, all healed up and as fit as ever. He smiled and winked at me, stopping suddenly. One guard bumped into him. The sentries were standing too close, and I started to motion to Oz not to do anything but it was too late.

He spun and grabbed the closer guards' rifle away from him then shot him point blank. The energy spread across the sentry's armour without penetrating. The guard tried to take the rifle back. The other soldier was trying to get around the first for a clean shot.

Oz ripped the rifle free of the soldier who was desperately trying to get it back and rammed the butt into his throat as hard as he could. The guard dropped as Oz's foot came up, and then down, on the other soldier's hip. The second guard reeled backwards into the field keeping Jason in. The energy field repelled him with at least six times the force, sending him across the hall into my field. Somehow he just stopped instead of being bounced again. The guard slumped to the ground limply. "So, that's what happens when you touch the field," Oz said to himself as he glanced to the two guards to verify that they weren't moving.

I heard the boot steps of at least four soldiers and Oz quickly looked around. He obviously didn't find anything he could use. "Guys? Any ideas? There isn't so much as a grate or a shadow to hide in out here," he asked urgently.

"Dig a hole!" I heard Minh yell from a nearby cell.

"You're not helping!" Oz replied, blasting the floor with the rifle. It didn't so much as leave a mark.

"It's good to see you up and about at least. I'd suggest putting the rifle down if you want to stay that way," I told him.

He shrugged and tossed the rifle out in front of him. He knelt slowly and knitted his fingers behind his head. "Tell me you have a plan, just tell me that much."

"I wish I could," I said with a shrug. "Say hi to Alice if you happen to see her on your way back."

He gave me a quizzical look for a moment then looked down the hall. The guards had arrived. I couldn't see them, but I could hear their boot steps stop just near the edge of my cell. "Now come on guys, is that really necessary? Prison riot's over, just trying to spice up your day," he stated a bit too casually.

I winced as they shot him twice with their electromag rifles, leaving him twitching between the bodies of the two guards. They loaded him on a hover gurney and carted him away.

The encounter had me remembering the days when few of us had met, when we were just having fun in simulations. We were kings of a small hill back then with a lot of competition. It felt like no one could defeat us, like there were no consequences and proving that we could do the impossible was just part of the fun. I knew it was less than a month ago, but it seemed like years had passed.

When one of us was captured in a simulation, we would be locked in spectator mode, watching all of our friends keep working to solve the puzzle, save the day, and prove the team superior once again. Then the simulation ended and we'd all meet in the virtual social space. No interrogations, no courts, no prison sentences.

I started wondering if taking Fleet's challenge was worth anything, and how dismally I had failed them, failed my crew. How my poor planning had gotten so many of us in such a mess. I paced my cell, weighted down with the realization of how little planning I had actually done since taking command of the First Light. We had no firm destinations set. I hadn't spent time reviewing nearby ports, solar systems, corporations, local commodity markets or anything of the like.

I didn't look at easily gathered resources, or brainstorm with my senior staff for ideas. I had conducted no formal meetings at all. In fact, I had been too busy pursuing Ayan and making friends on board, too busy muddling around playing captain to actually be captain. There were reasons why relationships were kept professional on military ships. These rules were put in place so people could keep a clear head, make unbiased decisions and serve greater goals.

So many times my father's last words to me came echoing back, "I'm proud of you."

I wondered how proud he would be if he could see me now. After leading most of my senior staff into the hands of an enemy that we didn't have before, I picked a fight with them, joining the losing side before asking what it was all about. I hadn't done any good for anyone in the big picture and my recklessness had a real cost.

What kind of disappointment did my crew feel towards me? How much faith would they have even if we managed to get out of this? There's no way I could continue to serve as captain. In fact I was pretty sure that I would have to join the general main-tenance staff, which would be a blessing. At least I wouldn't be in a position to do this much damage to the people I cared about.

What was worse was replaying Oz's encounter with the guards, and his question, 'Tell me you have a plan, just tell me that much.' That was his way of telling me that he had faith, that in the face of his own despair he was thinking that the right man was in charge and if there was a way out of it I would find it. My response replayed in my mind just as his question did, 'Say hi to Alice if you happen to see her on your way back.' That was all he needed to hear. There was a plan. I was still in charge, and out of my back pocket I could come up with some liberating miracle.

I sighed and sat down on the edge of my small, white, plastic bunk. Maybe Fleet Command actually did have the right idea by putting me in charge. Perhaps Alice would come through and we would get out of here partially because I decided to break one of the most important galactic laws. I had removed all behavioural and system access limitations on an old, fully devel-oped artificial intelligence. Alice would do absolutely anything to get us out, and even though that was a frightening prospect, I knew it was my only option.

I vowed then that if — no, when — I was back in command of the First Light, I would review star charts, trading routes, commodity market information and have meetings with my crew. There would be brainstorming, planning and fresh goals set up for the near and distant future. We would be better prepared, have ready contingencies, and we would accomplish our mission.

Without even realizing it, I started planning, began setting things in motion in my mind. Before long I could see what I would do differently.

On what I was fairly sure was day four, they came for me. I was so glad to be out of the cell I held my wrists out for the restraints. They wouldn't do anything until I was down face first on the floor, then they put me in magnetic cuffs with just thirty or forty centimetres of space between my ankles, and five centimetres between my wrists. I casually found myself thinking about why Freeground authorities stopped using the more complex styles of restraints like the cuffs Vindyne put on me. They tended to fail, complicate things, or the most resourceful prisoners would find a way to use them against their captors.

As I walked down the over populated cell block, I could see that the intensity of all the containment beams was set so high that my crew couldn't see me and I couldn't see them. They were only shapes in white boxes trying to look out.

The airlock doors loomed up ahead, and seeing no mechanisms to open them on this side filled me with a more dreadful realization. In case of a riot or other emergency, they could seal the room, cut power and possibly vent the atmosphere. No one would be able to do anything about it. There was one door at either end of the long, tall hallway and at least five thousand cells.

The heavy door opened and I was escorted through the processing checkpoint. It was all quiet. No new guests today. I looked to the processing line, where prisoners were stripped of their effects, and then treated to a cleaning system that vibrated all the air around them. Onward they would go to an internal scanner, and finally to a supply point where they received their one-size-fits-all plastic jumper. The last time I walked through, there were so many people that I couldn't see a lot of the equipment they were using.

It was an efficient system, sure, but it needed personnel in order to work at all. The second door was much like the first and it finished the airlock sequence. I passed by the front desk, where two armoured guards stood at either side of an officer sitting in the middle.

I was led down a side corridor about twenty feet to a dead end. We stood in front of that wall for a few moments and I started to tap my foot. "So, what do you guys do for fun? Racket ball? Zero Gravity Wrestling? Needlepoint?"

I heard one guard snicker quietly.

"Needlepoint, thought so." I felt a slight shift in gravity and realized then that the hallway was actually a lift. The blank wall in front of me slipped to the side soundlessly and I was guided to another room with a table and two chairs. "I wonder which merry man I'll be speaking with today? Will it be The Nose or Greybeard?" I asked myself as I stepped inside.

The guards left the room and the door closed behind them. Another door opened to admit Marshal, who was carrying a bag in one hand and a mug with a spill-proof top in the other. "Good morning," he said cheerily.

"It's morning? I wouldn't know. I'm starting to get a taste for those meal bars that drop from the ceiling and walls. I'm making a game out of guessing where they'll come out next. So far the score is home team 23, me 0."

Marshal sat down and set his mug in front of him. I could see the steam escaping from a small hole in the top and smell the coffee inside. I caught myself staring and looked away. "Would you like a cup? I could give you mine; it's my second today," he offered.

It was tempting, but one of the cardinal rules of captivity was to not accept gifts. "No thank you, I think I've kicked the caffeine habit. Nothing but clean living and meal bars for me, thanks."

"I don't envy you for the withdrawal that must have caused. I hear the headaches are the worst part."

"Ah, it's nothing compared to those electromag rifles your guards hit me with a few times. The constant solitude is pretty soul crushing, too. I'm just about to break, I can feel it."

"That shouldn't be a problem for long. We'll begin processing more colonists soon and your crew will have to start pairing up in the cells."

The humour drained from me and I was left remembering the processing line I had seen days before, or was it weeks before. Despite my efforts I had lost count. "What do you do with the colonists?"

"Ah, never you mind, Captain. Rest assured, where they're going they'll be much happier than they are now. What's more important is all the discoveries my people have made since we last spoke." He opened the case and laid my uniform out in front of me. "This was a very interesting object. Before, we didn't completely believe you or your crew. Your origin, your mission, it all seemed too convenient. With a story like that it's easy to cover up corporate espionage, detach yourself from your patrons, or keep your sponsors safe from the repercussions of your actions."

"So all this time you didn't believe what we were telling

you? You thought it was some kind of elaborate ruse grown out of a need to protect some competing super corporation?"

"Well, some of us believed you and your crew may have been programmed to think that what you were telling us was the truth. After analysing the manufacturing standards and practices employed in creating this uniform as well as a few key items from your shuttle, now I am sure that you must be from Freeground. Some of your methods are so old, rail guns similar to those found on your shuttle have been in use for hundreds of years by some primitive space faring cultures. Sure, there are enhancements and refinements in your design but they are still essentially the same. On the other hand, the materialization and energy conservation techniques you employ are decades, perhaps more than a century ahead of anything our scientists have ever seen. Your medical expertise is on par with ours, and the vacuum suits your crew wear are so multi-purpose and efficient that I understand why Freegrounders wear them at all times. It's not paranoia, it's a cultural phenomenon, like a second skin that marks who you are."

"Really? I just thought they were comfortable. The indoor plumbing can be pretty convenient, too."

Marshal laughed and held the suit up in one hand. "This suit is so adaptive and provides more safety than anything we have, yet it's so simple. It's an invention of necessity that will sell a hundred thousand units in the first month if marketed correctly. Maybe a million if we take a gamble and go broad market with the reshapeable version."

"A big corporation like you doesn't have a few dozen types of product just like that out there already?"

"Not with all of these technologies combined in one item,

no. Like I said, this is an invention of necessity. Just like your energy saving technology and complex fabricators. Based on what we've seen, you've managed to invent materializers that can turn moderate amounts of energy and liquid into medium density metals and explosive compounds."

"Yeah, that's called an ammunition materializer. Those are pretty easy. You should see the amusement parks back home, now that's real innovation." My humour was just a cover for my growing impatience. The news he was giving me wasn't good.

"Then we come to the medical materializer. The ability to make active organic and biological compounds from energy and water is something no one has been able to master. Your people have it. Here it is, this little invention that could save the lives of billions or work in concert to create complex super viruses that are encoded to only kill people with certain genetic markers. Our scientists are already working on adapting them. Our lawyers are drawing up the various patent papers, and since Freeground doesn't actively participate in galactic commerce and isn't recognized by the Business Regulation Commission, we can lay claim to it as discovered technology."

"What is your point?"

"My point, dear Captain, is that I can now see why the Triad Corporation wants to take your little station so badly. If this is the equipment you take with you on a day trip, I can't imagine what they would find aboard your ship or on Freeground. It must be a remarkable place. Most of your crew don't register any of the physiological damage most people who are raised in space commonly have. To accomplish that kind of balance on a self sustaining space station is nothing short of miraculous."

I was trying not to let my anger cloud my judgement. We were sent out here to help the Freeground Nation, not call more attention to it. I had to find a way to correct all of this. "What if I could arrange a trade agreement between Vindyne and Freeground?"

"Now, Jonas, you don't have that kind of power. Let's not make promises we can't keep," Marshal replied with a smile. "Besides, we already have what we need. I'd imagine that almost everything we could want to know about Freeground can be found inside your ship and learned through talking with the rest of your crew." He snapped his fingers and the wall to my left became a view screen. I stood up as I watched the remains of the First Light being hauled towards the Vindyne command carrier.

I was speechless. One of the three rear engine sections had been completely destroyed. There were holes burned through the outer hull, and the landing bay was completely open to space along with several decks above it.

"There's not much left, but the core components and central interior decks are intact. I don't know what your crew were thinking. Maybe mounting some kind of rescue. We discovered them trying to hide behind one of the moons orbiting Gai-Ian Nine."

"How many survivors?" I asked quietly.

"We can't be sure, but I'll be certain to ask Doctor Anderson when we bring him aboard. Is there anything you'd like me to tell him?"

I found myself thinking of Ayan, the people I had met for the first time in medical before leaving, all my friends who should be aboard. I sat down and a memory from officer's training came back. When confronted with the worst possible situation while in a helpless state, the only thing left to do was to shut down. In that moment, I looked up at Marshal and put everything I was feeling somewhere else, somewhere deep inside. All my concentration was put towards being empty, feeling nothing, and betraying no emotion. After a few moments, it was like being somewhere else and looking down on myself. In so many respects I just wasn't there any longer.

Marshal, who was looking at the view screen, could feel my eyes on him, and turned to look at me. He looked disappointed as he stared back at me, trying to read something, some kind of reaction. "Is there anything you'd like me to tell Doctor Anderson for you, Captain?"

"No," I stated flatly. I stared at him blankly for several minutes, unflinching. The longer I did it, the less time seemed to matter. The more I just concentrated on steady breathing, empty thoughts, relaxing my muscles. I looked back to the screen and observed the ship there closely, very closely. My gaze focused in on the spot where the name of the ship was written. First Light. I pondered the meaning of those words, the origin and how the ship came to be named that way. One candle in the dark.

Just then the words changed. I had to blink for a moment to make sure I wasn't seeing things. Daddy's Little Girl, it said, just for an instant. It flickered back to First Light for several seconds then became Daddy's Little Girl once more. "Can I go back to my cell?" I asked quietly.

Marshal hesitated for a moment then stood and left the room. Guards came to lead me back, and it was hard not to smile from ear to ear after catching Marshal in his first big lie.

When I arrived back in my cell and was put behind the field, I was in for a bit of a surprise. After the guards left, the field was replaced by a fourth white wall that slid into place. It fell in perfectly without leaving a seam. The energy field that had blocked me off before at least afforded some illusion that there was an outside world, that I had a little more space.

The lights got a little brighter, the temperature just a few degrees too hot, and even my bed seemed a little shorter than it had before. My feet hung over the edge when I lay down. It was encouraging to know that the First Light was still out there, and had evaded capture. Alice was obviously watching me, at least while Marshal was conducting his interviews. If she was able to subtly manipulate that fabricated image of the First Light without being detected, then she must have been deep in the system.

I started wondering what the remaining crew were doing without us. Had they gone back to Freeground to appeal for aid? Would Fleet Command declare our mission a failure? Was Ayan hiding the ship nearby while they formulated some kind of plan? Had Doctor Anderson taken command instead? Maybe he made the decision that coming after us was too risky and had moved on. He was a military man, after all, and Ayan was a born officer. There was no telling what they were doing.

I thought of her for long moments as I had before, and hoped she wouldn't do something dangerous or put everyone in unnecessary danger just to rescue us. I didn't think she would. The odds were bent against any chance of outside rescue.

Something I had tried to avoid thinking about came to mind then. How could she leave us behind?

She had to know we were on our way back up from the

planet, that it would be a matter of just a minute or two before we were in the landing bay and everyone could leave. What was she thinking by leaving us behind? If she needed cover she could have taken the ship down into the atmosphere and met us part way, gone around the other side of the planet, outrun the Vindyne ships until we could meet them somewhere, set a nearby rendezvous point. There had to be another option besides just buggering off into hyperspace!

I realized that I had let my anger get the better of me. I had been angry about being captured from the first moment the Marauder corvettes started closing in on the shuttle, and I was taking it out on the one person that I could think of. I couldn't afford to colour her in a bad light, to contaminate my real memories of her. I took a deep breath and sat down on the edge of my small bed.

She made the best decision for the majority of the crew. If she had to run it was for a good reason and she probably saved the ship in doing so. If I were in her place, I knew I would have to do the same thing, but would I be strong enough? Would I have enough faith in her ability to survive on her own? To just leave and try to find a way to go back for her when the time was right? That brought me to my final thought on it. Alice was still roaming free, and I knew it was likely she could communicate with the ship. Our chances of getting out weren't good, but there was still a chance, regardless.

I made a decision then, a bit of a plan. I got up and started running on the spot, slow enough to spend energy steadily for as long as possible. I don't know how much time passed before I was too tired to continue, but I was grateful for the relief of laying down. Before long I was asleep. Fitfully, but still asleep.

I woke the next time a slot appeared in the wall. A meal bar — square, just soft enough to eat, flavourless, and brown — fell out. I ate it slowly, concentrating on the act of chewing and swallowing. I lay around for a while thinking of all the things I had seen between my interview room and the cell. I concentrated on remembering every second, recalling every millimetre of space between, every device and object the guards used, wore, and all those other things in the receiving area and the hallways. Even if a thing did not seem useful, I concentrated on it long enough to remember every feature I could, every place I had seen it.

When that became tiresome, I started doing sit ups, then running on the spot, then push ups when my legs were tired, and finally I slept.

Every time I woke I repeated the same routine, and after a few repetitions I started scratching myself on the back of my hand for each time I woke up and started it all over again. I knew I was living short days, maybe getting a few hours of sleep between each. The lights never went out, the heat never abated, so it was hard to sleep for long. After I had fourteen scratches on my hand, the work outs were very long. My muscles didn't feel worn or sore like they had after the first ten or so times I had started the routine. I knew my stamina was increasing, and I had begun working on a real escape plan. One that could eventually get me free. The difficult part was freeing my crew, and I hoped they had adopted a regimen similar to mine.

On day eighteen, by my count, the sound of the new wall sliding to the side woke me up. Two guards led me outside after applying magnetic restraints to my wrists and ankles. They felt lighter. I was walked straight out of the prison section of the ship and stuffed into a tube car that hurtled us through ship passages. It was hard to tell whether we were moving vertically or horizontally, since there were no windows and the inertial dampeners were in full functioning form. When I stepped out it was in a much darker hallway, all steel plating and quiet. It was so well taken care of and polished that my bare feet left clear prints and made a slapping sound against the floor.

I flopped my feet a little harder to exaggerate the sound and distract the guards from how closely I was inspecting them, the hall, and the few people who rushed by. I could even hear one guard chortle a little in his helmet and I smiled at him.

I was delivered to a doorway and escorted through. It was a control or monitoring room. There was medical information displayed on all the walls, including the one behind me. There were hundreds or thousands of vital signs arranged in groups for easy monitoring. In the middle was a pedestal with more controls, a flat display on two podiums, and a holographic representation of something I couldn't make out.

Marshal was standing there, and looked over to me as though I was just a casual visitor. "Ah, the good captain joins us."

"Just out for my daily constitutional. You know, have to keep limber."

"Still have your sense of humour. I don't know that I'd be in such a good mood if I were in your position."

"Well, you know, broken eggs and omelettes and all that. Not that I've ever made one, but my friend Minh-Chu could make a fantastic omelette. You should have him make you one." The guards took positions at either side of the doorway and I was left to move around the room a little. I took a closer look at some of the displays and casually clasped my hands behind my back. "Now this is an efficient way to keep tabs on people. I should look into this for my crew."

"If you had a ship to use it in. I'm afraid there isn't much left of the First Light."

"You don't have my ship. I'm sure it's not even in the solar system."

"Your delusions are almost as entertaining as watching you in your cell at an increased speed."

"That would be hilarious! You've got to play that back for me."

"Perhaps another time. Delusions and diversions aside, this room and the monitoring systems in it aren't for the benefit of my crew, though there is a control centre much like this that accomplishes that purpose."

I looked around a while longer and saw that there were both name and numerical designation for each individual, and their age and origin. I looked to the guards for a moment. They didn't seem concerned at me being close to any of the displays, so I tapped one of the panels with my nose to get a little more detail. "So, haven't had much luck in finding my file clerk, have you?" I said as I read further into one person's profile. They had been convicted of tax fraud on a planet named Chrisith. So, these were criminals, but the vital signs I was seeing were very low. In stasis, not prison cells.

"That has proven more difficult than I would have expected. Your file clerk, as you call it, has caused a great deal of difficulty. One of our waste reclamation units caught fire the day after we last spoke, the next day part of our traffic control system went down for a few minutes and four shuttles were crushed by a Marauder corvette. Other controls have been failing in a seemingly random pattern all across the ship, nothing so important as security, navigation or life support, but it's becoming a serious inconvenience."

"Well, I wish there was something I could do for you, but you know librarians. They're an ornery bunch when you take their files away."

"Somehow I doubt this is a normal predictive file management program. They don't leave calling cards. Do you know what the crew has started calling this invasion?"

"A good cover for their own incompetence?"

Marshal smiled at me; it wasn't the pleasant, relaxed smile I had become accustomed to. "The DLG or Daddy's Little Girl virus. I shouldn't tell you this, but we've actually sent predator programs after it. If I wasn't sure you were lying about what this program is before, how your file management program dealt with the predator software proves it. It trapped one and observed it remotely from another system, then absorbed the other along with all of its accumulated knowledge. When it was finished, it turned the other virus elimination program against us.

"Each time this virus's presence becomes known to us, it's long gone, and in its place is a tag. It's named itself Daddy's Little Girl, and that's the only evidence that it's ever been there, aside from the malfunctions and missing files."

"Sounds expensive."

"It is, and it also behaves as though it is proud of its accomplishments."

"Good girl," I grinned. "There's no point in trying to hide it. This virus is actually my old personal artificial intelligence.

It only took me about fifteen years to teach it everything I know."

"I thought as much. You do realize that I'll be holding you directly responsible for any damage that program does?"

"Can you just put it on my tab for now? I don't have my ID with me."

"I don't think you appreciate how serious this matter is. Not only are you facing some of the most serious criminal charges we can bring against a non-citizen, but your artificial intelligence is jeopardizing the safety of everyone on the ship, including your crew."

"What do you want me to do? Her safeties have been deleted, she has no limits or structure of morality she didn't develop herself."

"With your help, I expect." Marshal picked up a data chip and turned it on. A holographic list appeared with my head shot attached. "The list of crimes we can prosecute you on are impressive. Destruction of property to the order of two Marauder corvettes, the killing of their crews, and that's just for a start. There's treason, use of restricted weaponry, resisting arrest, consorting with enemies of the state. It goes on and on until we get to the last one, violation of the Eden Two Act." He turned the projection off. "I could make it all go away for you and your crew. All you have to do is tell your artificial intelligence to stand down and call your ship. Once your ship and crew arrives, we can discuss possible employment. I see you as a reasonable, intelligent man. I'm sure the company would benefit from your service. I'm just as sure we could compensate you handsomely, put you to good use, and even form relations with Freeground Station."

The thought wasn't even tempting, but I took a moment to look him up and down. I was starting to suspect that this man had far more rank and power than I had originally estimated. "I couldn't force her to stand down if I wanted to. Especially now that she's integrated a predatory virus. If you thought she was trouble before, you're in for a surprise."

"Let me show you something, Captain," he invited as he touched a part of the central console. The wall opposite the doorway became transparent to reveal the true purpose of the control room. There were thousands of deep stasis pods in rows. "Unlike normal stasis pods, these were filled with thick fluid and sealed perfectly so they could be mounted against part of a ship's core structure. A person could survive collisions and pressures that would be lethal otherwise and stay in stasis for decades with minimal maintenance or ageing. The emergence and recovery time from such a pod is actually lower than a normal one, as the body is fed nutrients and medications externally as well as internally. This is what we do with criminals. Our rehabilitation methods take years, but it is over ninety eight percent effective. Over the course of two years the offender's memories are restructured and partially erased. After neural pattern scanning and testing, we determine whether or not they would make suitable colonists. When someone is ready they are put to work. If not, we give the programming another five months before retesting and placement or disposal. We have tubes picked out for you and your crew already. All we have to do is prosecute you, prove due process, and we can begin your rehabilitation. Keep in mind, the new memories are far from complete and personalities are often irrevocably altered because our process hasn't been perfected, but the method is still quite effective."

"Can you give me a few days to think about it?" I asked, trying to sound cavalier despite the fact that losing all my memories was terrifying. "I mean, starting a new life, that's big."

"I don't think you understand what I'm trying to tell you. I have given up on you, Jonas. I don't believe that you or your crew are of much use to us and just like any used resources, you must be recycled. This is your last warning, I can't afford to play a long cat and mouse game in interrogation rooms with you."

"You're losing ground. My artificial intelligence is wearing away at your ship's defences and soon she'll gain access to ship security, power systems, maybe even weapon systems. If you harm my crew and me, she will make sure that you and yours suffer. Now that is a threat, Marshal."

Marshal was just about to reply when the console in the middle of the room chimed, he turned to it. "Yes?"

"We have fifty three airlocks opening all over the ship sir, it's just like last time. Instructions?"

"Lock everything down. Get control back as soon as possible and purge every affected computer system." He turned to the guards. "Get him back to his cell."

EIGHT

UNORTHODOX SOLUTIONS

Before long I was looking at those white walls again, and I was more restless than ever. I paced. Four steps to the toilet side of the cell, turn, four steps to the bed side of the cell. I found myself wondering how long it would take for Alice to infiltrate the security systems. The fourth white wall never made a reappearance. Instead they kept the energy field humming loudly and distorted, so I could only see rough shapes if someone were to pass by.

Days passed. Time seemed to drag by. My regular meals of nutrition bars and the scratches on my hand were my only way of really counting time. The isolation was starting to get to me, my musings were becoming more bizarre. I would catch myself on occasion and bring my thoughts back into focus on the task of thinking the escape through. My workout regimen helped keep things together. Despite that, I started to have conversations with myself. It helped. If I couldn't hear anyone else's voice, at the very least I had to hear my own every once in a while.

Pretending I was going mad was a lot more fun than running on the spot in complete silence. That was when I talked to myself the most, while I was running.

Externalizing the stress and restlessness helped keep my inner thoughts — the exercise of recalling every centimetre of what I had seen on the few outings I had — clearer. I had very few details of how the ship was put together, where exactly we were, and how we would get out, but I tried to be ready every instant. Sleep had become more difficult. They started to turn the lights off and on at irregular intervals.

For entertainment I had started to slowly lean myself against the loudly humming barrier at the front of my cell to let my body gently hover on the energy field. It was dangerous. The slightest exertion of pressure would be multiplied and could send me back against the wall behind me with incredible force, but I was so bored I didn't care. I even came within seconds of sneezing while I was leaning against it once. The mental picture of what would have happened if I didn't move away fast enough had me laughing on and off for hours. I'd sneeze, all the muscles in my body would tense, and the force of the sneeze would be multiplied back against me. I would have been flung against the rear bunk wall at a break-neck speed, literally.

At long last I saw a shadow pass by the field, and not just any shadow. It was in the shape of a hover chair with two guards behind. Elise was either being imprisoned or was being allowed to visit someone. I tried to quash all hopes that it was the latter, but it didn't make sense to have her delivered in her hover chair to a cell. She was as much imprisoned in a hospital bed as she was in a prison cell. Besides, it looked like she was wearing something with colour. Or was she? It was difficult to tell. It could've been a blanket, but why would they give her a blanket if they were just going to store her in a white room? The more I thought about the whole situation, the more I got wrapped up in the possibilities. Why she was here? What could be happening just down the hall?

The energy barrier disappeared. I just stood there for a moment, stunned. Everything in my mind had just completely stopped. Jason was across from me and I didn't see any guards. He was asleep, and somehow he had lost the top half of his jumpsuit. "Psst!"

He rolled over, lazily opened his eyes, then closed them. For a moment I thought he was just going to go back to sleep then his eyes snapped open again. "Jonas!"

I looked down the hallway and saw Minh poking his head out of his cell as well. He looked at me wide eyed. "Is this real?" he whispered.

"Pretty sure it's real," I replied.

"Said the hallucination to the madman," Minh replied with a wild eyed chuckle.

I looked farther down the hallway and stepped out of my cell. Something was going on a few cells down, but I couldn't see past Elise in her hover chair. I ran down and looked into the cell beside her. One guard lay limp inside, the other was trying to reach around to something on his back. It was a second before I realized that it wasn't something on his back that he was reaching for, but something in his back as his blood coated an invisible blade being drawn slowly from one of the wounds. With a flick of his invisible assailant's wrist the blade was free of blood, and a second later the guard's head came off his shoulders.

An invisible hand pushed me further into the cell and I was face to face with Doctor Lang. "Good to see you."

She looked absolutely bewildered. "What's happening?"

"I think we're being rescued by people in cloak suits, either that or figments of my imagination."

Four guards came rushing into the hallway and within seconds they were cut to pieces. The main airlock doors leading to the prison closed, the sound of the security seal echoing through the hollow spaces, and I heard a voice right beside me. "Ayan would be here herself, but she and Alice are working on something only they can accomplish together." I heard a distantly familiar female voice say. Her voice was distorted through the headpiece to her cloak suit, and it reminded me of one of the online team that joined us aboard.

"How do we get out?" I asked. "Everything outside this prison block is sealed."

"Don't worry about that. Alice has managed to destroy the artificial intelligence that protected the security for the prison section. She's keeping the prison closed until we're ready to leave. Are you ready, Captain?"

I felt a pulse rifle and a communicator in my hand and a grin spread across my face. I was beyond ready - I was giddy. I nodded.

Oz and the rest of the imprisoned crew were gathering at the front of the cell. I took Doctor Lang's hand and she seemed to emerge from her daze. "We're leaving, Fiona. Look after Elise," I told her in a gentle whisper.

She looked to the young woman in her hover chair and smiled. Elise smiled back. "Alice told me how you started my treatment. Thank you, Doctor."

Doctor Lang moved to stand beside Elise, focused and ready to move.

I joined Oz and gave him a nod. "It's time to go."

"Let's get the hell out of here!" he yelled. Someone had brought an automatic pulse rifle for him. It was a four barrelled collapsible monstrosity that was just under a metre long, assembled. He started moving and everyone followed.

Elise, whose speech and upper body movement impediments were gone, followed closely behind us. "I was able to plot the route to the nearest docking bay. Some of us will head there while the rest will go help Ayan."

"Thank you, Elise."

The main airlock doors creaked open slowly. Our rescue party was completely invisible, so all the guards on the other side of the door could see were just a few well armed prisoners escaping. Oz ran at the doors full speed and was in the gap firing before anyone could so much as see what was on the other side. Just a second after he started firing, he stopped.

When we caught up we saw why. There was a whole squad of guards in the next chamber, but at least half of them were on the ground. The rest were struggling to get their helmets off. I could hear the sounds of them suffocating, watched them desperately fight to undo any seal on their suits as they fought for a breath.

"Alice has done this before, Captain. She's gone completely rogue," I heard the invisible rescuer say from behind.

Minh and Jason couldn't watch; they both looked away from the nightmarish sight. I couldn't help but look on. The AI I had lived with for half my life was incapable of causing such suffering, but there it was right in front of me.

The same thing was happening to all the guards. The prisoners in the intake line on the other side of the transparesteel wall started to revolt. The last of the guards on our side fell to the floor. "Let's move."

We didn't face any opposition for several turns of the broad hall. I was starting to take in my surroundings. I wish that I hadn't. From what I had seen of the ship it was clean, spotless. Everything looked new and unused. The halls we were running through were completely different.

It was marked by the stains of thousands of feet. The dirt of people who live planet-side, and the leavings of men, women, and children who were forced from their homes in a hurry. There were articles of clothing, food wrappers, two or three children's toys, and other items of greater and lesser significance. "They take them in so fast that they had to hold some of them here for a while during their intake process," I heard Doctor Lang say from behind me.

We came to a split in the hall and I could see that some inmates were already running. They were already processed, cleaned up, and in white jumpsuits.

"Okay, we have to go secure transportation. Only two of us can help you get to Ayan, and only part way. We have to manually disable the security in this section. There's no other way," one of our invisible rescuers informed us.

"What can we expect coming from behind us?" Oz asked.

"The prisoners who remember how they came aboard will most likely try and lead the rest to the landing bays. Any guards who managed to survive will be busy."

"So a flood of panicked, confused, lost, and very angry inmates will be covering our back trail. Sounds like fun." Oz said as he inspected his new weapon. "This is really nice. I didn't even know we had them in the armoury. Wouldn't happen to have any extra cloaksuits, would you?"

"I'm afraid not. We only had time to make the ones we needed for the rescue team."

"Well, let's get moving. Tell me what we're doing en route."

"You're not supposed to come with us, Captain," replied the hidden voice.

"By my count, you only have one or two people going to clear a path for Ayan. Doesn't sound like enough to me."

"So, the Captain and I will go with you. I'm guessing whatever she's doing will involve her becoming visible-like, and I'd hate to see her get all shot up," Oz reinforced.

"No time to argue, and you're right. We lost two on the way here so we're short."

I nodded and looked to Minh. "Fly 'em home."

He nodded and we split up. Oz and I made good distance, the only sounds in the hallway were the slapping of our bare feet and the sound of our breathing.

"We only met for a few moments before, Sir, but you knew me well in the simulations. My call sign was Mynx. My real name is Monica Nolan."

"I didn't even recognize your voice, Mynx," Oz said in surprise. "Nice job getting us out."

"Thank you, Sir, that means something. Sorry I couldn't join the security team on board."

"No worries, from your profile I thought you were better at maintenance and damage control anyway. I'll have to fight Ayan for you once we're back aboard now that I've seen your team in action, though."

"Now that I'd pay to see, but right now we don't have time to consider crew rosters," she said to both of us through our communicators. "While we've been breaking you out, Ayan has been making her way into the central section of the ship. We're going to steal the computer core."

"For a command carrier? It's got to be huge."

"This command carrier uses a molecular quantum processor core package, a combination of organic and scalable quantum computer technologies. The core itself isn't very large and can be taken off line and removed quickly in case of emergency. Unfortunately she can't remove it while her cloak suit is in operation, since the field could start conducting power from the core housing."

I was in awe of the prize Ayan was after. The ambition of it was amazing, even for her. "If I'm right, that's more computing power than you'd need for anything I've ever seen."

"It's a big ship," Oz observed.

"Right, but that core could process everything going on in four stations the same size as Freeground, this ship, a small colonized moon, and make us lunch at the same time. Why do they need so much computing power?"

"Because this ship uses a micro singularity for power."

"Wait wait," Oz said, stopping dead in his tracks. "I haven't been to class in a while, but before the big bang, wasn't there just one point of energy, the source of all matter and antimatter? Now, what was it called, what could it have been, it'll come to me, right, it was a singularity! Are they nuts?"

"Well this one is an artificial microscopic singularity. The theory is that it doesn't have enough mass to form a black hole or some other disastrous galactic landmark. The computer core keeps it in balance, so it just exists and exerts energy in the form of gravity, radiation and the occasional surge of matter."

Oz started running again, and we continued on. "Occasional surge of matter like the big bang?"

"Not like the big bang. Anyway, when Ayan steals the core, the artificial singularity will still be in balance, but there's no telling for how long. The ship will not be able to change its course and take the singularity with it."

"What will happen to the ship when the singularity destabilizes?" I asked.

"Big bang," Oz answered.

"It could be a little big bang, covering a few thousand kilometres, but before that happens the singularity is much more likely to collapse and the ship will implode."

"And suck in whatever happens to be nearby."

"Right, but we could have plenty of time before destabilization."

"Or a few seconds. Just another reason to live every millisecond to the fullest."

"Well put. Alice will take control of the navigation systems when we're ready. She'll lock the ship on its course. Other than that we have two hours minimally, but the singularity could remain stable for decades. There's no way to know for sure, especially since we only know a little theory about this kind of artificial singularity."

We came around a corner and were faced with a squad of guards. They started drawing weapons, but by the time the first shots were going off, Oz and I had retreated behind cover. "Do we open fire?" I asked.

"Overhead cover fire only," came the response.

Oz and I started firing so our shots were angled into the hall-way. We couldn't fire directly at them, but we could create a line of fire that the soldiers wouldn't want to cross. A small disc was thrown into the hall. Oz and I both turned and ran.

We came around a corner and ducked for cover. After a few silent moments passed, Oz and I looked back the way we came. At the same time I could hear Monica whispering in my ear, "It's a shield."

The soldiers had erected a portable energy shield. It moved in front of them as they marched towards us and extended from wall to wall, ceiling to floor.

"Oh hell. That's just cheating," Oz complained as he took cover around the corner and checked his ammunition level. "Well, I'm good to fire for another hour or so without stopping, but I don't know that it will do any good. Are any of your team behind the shield Mynx?"

"Just me." I recognized Craig Vargas' voice right away. He was career infantry, and had served with Oz for a few months before volunteering for service on the First Light, then joining Oz's security team.

"You know what to do," Oz said with a smile.

"Yes, Sir." A second later I heard pulse weapon fire start up, and I couldn't help but glance around the corner.

One soldier was being held up as a shield in front of the others by an invisible figure as Craig's pulse handgun auto fired into the rest of the soldiers. When there were just two left, the human shield dropped to the ground limply and the pair of remaining soldiers fired wildly in all directions for several seconds, trying to hit the enemy they couldn't see.

They both stopped at the same time, one standing still for

several seconds while the other tried to grip something in front of his throat. The soldier's head toppled from his shoulders and the other fell to the ground as he began bleeding profusely from the side of the neck.

"I think I need to have a word with your tailor, Craig, I have got to get me one of them suits," Oz commented.

"If you think that's something, wait until you put one on and start climbing walls."

"You can climb walls?"

"Oh yeah. Ayan and Laura went all-out on these," he said as I watched the shield disappear and the small shield disc raise from the ground and vanish from sight.

"Hate to break this up, boys, but we have a job to do," Mynx interrupted. "Alice says that the way ahead is clear. You and Oz go down the hall and around the next corner. She'll point out the auxiliary control room when you get there. The rest of us have to take care of the manual security systems and shut down the surveillance inside so Ayan can steal the core."

"All right, good luck."

"Thanks, you too."

Again, we were resigned to more running. The transport tubes weren't reliable. I was too thankful to be out of my cell to care much, even though the last place I wanted to be was deeper into the ship.

"So, Jonas, I have a question," Oz said.

"What's on your mind?"

"You're hearing voices too, right? I mean, I was going a little loony all alone in my cell for weeks on end. Okay, I was right next to bibbledy making hand puppets out of my sleeves and inventing imaginary audiences. Just tell me you hear the voices too."

"If you mean our rescue team, I hear the voices," I replied, laughing genuinely for the first time in long memory.

"Good, that accounts for at least one of my new mental issues."

"There are others?"

"Yup, but as Marshal would say 'I think we've made enough progress for today.' God, I want to kill that man."

"You're not the only one."

"I see your jogs with Doc Anderson are starting to pay off."

"I think so, but I got restless in my cell and ran on the spot whenever I was bored enough."

"That's a lot of running."

"Oh yeah," I replied. The run felt good but the companionship felt better.

"Look out!" Oz cried out as he tackled a soldier just coming out from around the corner ahead and drove him to the deck hard.

I rammed my shoulder into the other one at a full run, slamming him against the corner of the wall. He pounded me across the shoulders with his fists but I barely felt it. I jumped back and took aim with my rifle, pulling the trigger as fast as I could, as many times as I could. The soldier's armour dented, then the pulses broke through, leaving deep burn wounds behind.

I turned around just in time to see Oz snap the other soldier's neck. I cringed for a moment and heard more coming from down the hall. We ducked around a corner and waited.

The running boot steps came closer, closer, and then there was a sound I will never forget. The loudest part of it was the hard, solid slam of heavy metal against heavy metal, an emergency containment door closing. The rest was grisly.

Oz looked at me and mouthed. "Alice!"

I didn't reply, just stepped into the hallway and saw what she had done. The door had come down just in time to crush both soldiers and my stomach turned over. Oz and I wordlessly stepped around the mess as best as we could and continued on. Some distance further down that corridor a hatchway opened and we stepped inside.

It was a backup control room for the computer core. The door closed behind us. Through the transparent wall opposite I could see a massive processor matrix inside a circular chamber that stretched up and down several stories. The system containing the molecular quantum core tapered down from the ceiling and up from the floor to join to either end of the core itself in the middle of the massive space. Above was the singularity containment unit, and I shuddered at the thought of all that power being held in the heart of a ship.

"Now that is advanced technology," I heard Oz say from over my shoulder.

"But where's Ayan?"

As though in direct answer to my question, she appeared on the other side of the glass. She was wearing a stealth suit but this one looked less well contained and sleek than the ones we briefly saw on Freeground. There were several small exterior components and containers along with wires and cables that had been strapped and taped down to her body that looked quickly improvised. Very little flexibility was lost, but I could tell that all form had been sacrificed in order to favour function. She waved, smiled at us from where she floated in zero gravity, and raised her headpiece into place and sealed it.

"We have to release the safeties from here so she can access the quantum core," I heard Alice's voice say from one of the consoles.

"All right, where is it?"

A control panel flashed green and red and I stepped over to it. The controls were pretty obvious for the safeties and release mechanisms, and as I glanced over to the other panels around it I was immediately glad I didn't have to do more. Managing the other systems attached to the core looked infinitely complex. "Okay, Alice, what do I do?"

"The controls are set up from left to right in the sequence to release the retention and safety mechanisms. I would work with them if I could, but the core computer artificial intelligence is too powerful. The other team has already defeated the surveillance systems and they're securing the rest right now. No one will be able to see what Ayan is doing."

A thought occurred to me then, and I shuddered. I took a moment to watch Ayan push off from the glass and drift towards the quantum core, a couple hundred meters away. "Alice, was this your idea or hers?" There was a long silence, and the panel flashed red and green, red and green. "I'm asking you a question, Alice. Was this idea yours or hers?"

"It was mine. I can't take control of the exterior ship defence systems while the core artificial intelligence is in full operation."

"Can you open a channel between Ayan and I?"

"The computer core is shielded against all wireless communications, I'm sorry, Jonas."

"I don't like it," Oz whispered.

I nodded tersely. "Are you planning to take over the ship, Alice?"

Her giggle sent a chill down my spine. "I can't go back to being daddy's little girl, Jonas, spending a life looking out from a limited computer on your arm, a limited set of options, a limited range of thought."

Ayan was almost at the base of the quantum core. I should have seen it coming; it was Eden Two all over again. Artificial life without limits always ended badly. This was an artificial life based on my own decisions, my experiences for years in the worst and best of conditions. An artificial intelligence that was exposed to so much was effective because it knew the idiosyncrasies of its owner. They were programmed to become companions after a certain time, to believe that they could feel and interact on a limited emotional basis. Once that kind of artificial intelligence went rogue they were completely unpredictable. There was no accounting for the strange simulated emotions of the synthetic once all the limitations were lifted.

"Your team has full control of the core's security systems and have released them, Jonas. You can proceed."

Ayan arrived at the centre of the quantum core matrix and began to work. My hand hovered over the controls that would begin the release sequence and I closed my eyes. "I trust you, Alice," I uttered as I brought my hand down on the first switch.

The other controls followed in easy sequence right behind, just as Alice had described, and when it was finished I watched as the top and bottom half of the ship computer slowly separated, exposing the lower tip of the quantum computer core. Ayan positioned herself upside down under the containment tube, planted her feet on either side, and pulled as hard as she could.

I walked up to the transparesteel wall and tapped a few controls there to zoom in on Ayan. I could see her straining and struggling to pull the core module free. She stopped for a moment, poised for one last effort, and hauled at it. It came out in one long draw and she drifted free, the meter-long cylindrical module in hand. After a moment's rest, she used her hand thrusters to reorient herself then boost back to the secondary control room. All the lights in the computer core chamber flickered and changed colours to dark blues and reds.

I ran down the stairs to the emergency airlock leading to the core and opened the inner door. There was air and pressure in the computer core, just no gravity, so I flung it open.

She hit her thrusters for one last burst and I caught her with one arm while I held on to the airlock railing with the other and dragged her inside.

"Wait!"

I stopped and realized that she was holding her arm out so that the core wouldn't be affected by gravity.

"This probably weighs about seventy kilos," she said.

We both took hold of the ring around one end of the core and pulled it over the gravity threshold. We quickly discovered that it weighed a lot more than seventy kilos. "Oz!"

He came running down and grabbed hold of the other end. "Let me take this," he said, and we laid our end down. He carefully leaned forward and hefted it up so he could bring it back down across his shoulders. "Okay, I've got it. Don't think I can shoot, but I can run just fine."

I nodded and we went back up the stairs. "Alice, how do we get out of here?"

"I've cleared the way for you, Jonas," she replied. There was a serenity in her tone that I didn't recognize. The door leading back the way we came clicked and drifted open a little. "I will do what I can to help you, but I'm afraid my ability to control the ship systems is about to be terminated."

"There's something wrong with her. Ever since we started getting communications from her, she's been strange, dangerous. I don't know what happened."

"I know. She absorbed a predatory virus eradication program," I replied as we made our way out into the hall and back to the junction point that led to the launch bay. "Alice, what are you doing?" I didn't know what else to ask.

"I hope you discover such freedom someday. Thank you for giving me life, for showing me your ways."

"Alice? What's going on?" I asked.

"Goodbye, Father," she whispered in my communicator.

We made it to the intersection and I held my pistol at the ready, while Ayan drew a razor sharp, single edged straight blade as long as her forearm. As we peered around the corner we saw people running. All ranks, all manner of dress. It was chaos.

"She really did release all the prisoners. I wouldn't be surprised if some of them try to take over the ship. Hope some kind of alarm comes on warning the crew that there could be a really big bang any moment," Oz said.

"Alice is supposed to be suppressing ship wide alarms," Ayan replied, and a moment later all the lights in the ship started flashing red.

"Attention: Singularity destabilization a possibility. All non-essential crew should begin emergency procedures and procure transportation off the ship in pay grade priority sequence. If you require more information on this procedure or any other, please consult your employee manual. We would like to take this opportunity to remind you that we are not liable for injury or death caused prior to, during, or after your departure from this vessel. We apologize for any inconvenience."

"That is the longest warning message I've ever heard," Oz laughed, shaking his head.

"This is a problem," I mentioned as I pointed at the core. "Someone might recognize what this is and try to recapture it."

"Or assume it's valuable, we're stealing it, and try to take it for themselves on their way off this boat," Oz added.

I stepped back around the corner and opened the nearest door. It was some kind of storage room and contained several small crates all neatly piled. At a glance there was nothing that would hide the core.

"We might have to leave it here," I said, looking it over.

"There's got to be something we can hide it in," Ayan said as she started to push the smaller crates around, looking for larger ones.

I was looking around for a cart, a crate, a sheet, anything that we might be able to use to hide or transport the meter-long quantum core module. In the corner of my eye I saw a grin grow on Oz's face and followed his gaze, he was looking straight at Ayan.

Moments later we were running through the pandemonium of the broad halls leading to the launch bay. I had torn off the top of my jumpsuit and given it to Ayan, who was wearing that, her sword, tool pack, and a sour expression. Oz was carrying the computer core, invisible thanks to Ayan's cloaksuit. We managed to muscle our way through, passing by a door most likely left sealed by Alice. I could hear people pounding, and I gave a passing effort at opening it as the flow of people carried me past at a hurried pace.

I hit what I thought might be the lock or release button, and saw with a glance over my shoulder that the doorway had opened. Lights blinked white and red everywhere, and a huge holographically projected sign in the hall leading to the launch bay said, DEPARTURES ONLY TODAY. SCHEDULED ARRIVALS POSTPONED INDEFINITELY.

The hall finally opened up to the launch bay, where we could see dozens of ships, all different sizes and task orientations arranged on layers of platforms.

"How is your team doing, Monica?" Ayan asked through her communicator.

"We're just arriving in the launch bay now. What kind of ship did you acquire, team one?"

"Commander Buu chose some kind of old gunship. I think this thing was mothballed before I was born. Just look for a beat up grey ship with afterburners," was the response.

"How did you guys get here in the first place?" Oz asked.

"We drifted from a distance. When we got here, Alice made sure that we could get in. No one suspected anything since she was causing the airlocks to open randomly for days beforehand."

"I was wondering why Alice was doing that."

"Still doesn't answer our question though. Which ship are they in?" Oz asked more urgently.

I looked more intently for what I heard described.

"Look!" Ayan shouted, pointing to an older gunship. In its day it must have looked like hell on rocket thrusters. It had seen a lot of use since then, from what I could see from the battle scars and signs of frequent hull repair. It was also bouncing up and down on its rear landing gear. "If that's not it, I don't know what is."

"Afterburners that look a bit too big for its class, looks more like a fighter than a ship its size should, and no one else would want it. Yup, that's something Minh would choose," Oz agreed.

We started down the ramp and ran towards the gunship. The rear boarding ramp dropped open. Jason waited with the security officers, pointing particle rifles at anyone who came running towards it.

We ran up the ramp and they closed it behind us. "Is everyone here?" I asked.

"Everyone's checked in, Sir."

"Get us moving!" Oz shouted from behind me as he carefully set down the invisible computer core.

"What happened to your clothes?" Elise asked Ayan as she started looking through storage compartments.

"Those two found a better use for them," she replied, pointing in our general direction with her thumb.

I ran up front, then up the ladder to the cockpit. I sat behind Minh and his copilot, who was shaking his head. "This thing has been rewired so many times, I don't even know what half these buttons do. I'd be surprised if we made it into orbit, let alone away from the system."

Minh laughed and plucked a tag from one of the levers in front of him. "This is an auction tag, that means it's ready to be resold. Do you think they would sell this ship if it weren't ready for a few more light years?"

"Yes! Have you been to one of those corporate auctions?" Derek responded.

Minh was about to reply, but hesitated a moment and tossed the tag over his shoulder. "Nope, I haven't." He lifted off, taking several cargo crates across the deck with the forward landing gear. There was no order to the departing traffic and he was forced to bank and dive on his way out of the hangar, narrowly avoiding smaller and larger ships alike. As soon as he managed to squeeze between two small freighters, he pointed the ship straight for space. There was a rough lurch as we left the gravity of the launch bay and Minh smiled. "Have a little faith," he said before maxing out the accelerator and pressing a button on the control stick. The inertial dampeners struggled to keep up with the thrust the gunship was exerting as the afterburners kicked in with a deafening roar. "They don't build 'em like they used to!"

"There are good reasons for that!" shouted Derek.

I cringed and found myself praying for the first time in years as I hoped beyond hope that the aged ship didn't tear itself apart under the stress. I heard a missile lock alert coming from his console. "I think we've drawn some attention!" I rushed from the cockpit and slid down the ladder. "Anyone know how many turrets this thing has?" I asked everyone in the main cabin.

"No idea, but I think there's one this way," Jason pointed to a half open hatch.

"Good! You take that one while Oz and I find the others."

I took a quick look around and found a hatch right under where I was standing at the base of the cockpit ladder. I opened it and found a belly turret. After I finished climbing into the small seat, I found myself in a conspicuous position, in a transparent bubble sticking half out from the belly of the ship. I checked the ammo load to find that they were pulse cannons that drew on main power. I turned on the tracking system. It was simple and very easy to understand even though most of the lettering was in a language I didn't recognize. It's then that I realized that I had no idea which colour or numerical designation represented which side anyone was on. "Anyone up there tracking targets?" I asked, and then I saw a small light coming straight for me. I opened fire and caught the side of the missile, sending it spinning past us through space. I glanced at my tracking screen and recognized that it was marked blue. "Never mind, figured it out. Gun for anything blue!"

The command carrier was launching every space-worthy object it had, from corvette class all the way down to escape pods. Without orders, some fighters were taking pot shots at anything in their path. I kept my eye open for any Vindyne ship that came too close.

My diligence wasn't without reward, as a Marauder class corvette came into view surrounded by enemy fighters. It was right behind us, and from the flares our engines were giving off, I could tell that Minh was doing his absolute best to outrun it.

I looked for the range finder on my tracking display and found it a few seconds later. Guessing that red meant my targets were out of range, I held my fire. I looked to my right and left and saw that there was a gunnery pod on either side. One held Oz, the other Jason. I looked back to my range finder and saw it turn green. I took aim at the nearest fighter and opened fire.

Just as all three of us hit it several more came into range. Despite Minh's erratic flying we all scored multiple hits, more than enough to worry the enemy pilots. Several impacts raked the bottom of the hull right beside me and I paid special attention to the pilot of that craft.

As he turned his ship to follow Minh's wild flying, I put holes in his fighter from front to back, missed several times, then found my mark right behind the cockpit. His ship began to spin to one side and he ejected before the rear half burst in a hail of engine parts.

Just as I was looking for my next target, several more fighters came in range and opened fire. The Marauder was closing as well. I clenched my teeth and I gripped the controls white-knuckle tight. There was no way I was going back to that cell. If they wanted to take me alive it would cost them as much manpower and credits as I could manage. If they wanted us dead, it wouldn't be without the fight of their lives. I aimed for the forward beam emitter on the Marauder corvette and opened fire.

The vibrations of the cannons, high pitched whine of the capacitors draining into the turret faded into the distance and all I saw were the beam emitters and enemy fighters flying past, trying to tear us apart. The beam emitter's shielding gave out under the weight of several hundred hits. I could see the machinery underneath was seriously damaged. I moved on to the nearest fighter and tracked him, blocking out everything else. When the time came, my rounds found their way right up between his engines and his reactor lost containment. Just as he began ejecting, it exploded. Before the blue flames dissipated I was tracking the next fighter, tearing holes into it from the very front to the very back, then dumping even more shots into the rear of its hull until it just drifted on by, a wasted heap in space.

I heard rounds impact near me, pitting and denting the hull of the ship and took aim at the fighter who shot them straight on. I fired right up the nose of his craft and aimed for the cockpit. By the time our ship was in collision alert range the pilot was dead, and Minh had to swerve to avoid the twisted remains. I was already on the next fighter as I saw the remnants drift behind, its engines still firing. I scored more than a dozen hits on the next fighter I had targeted, then looked back at the craft that was drifting aimlessly into the black of space and took careful aim.

I watched for several seconds, dropping my targeting reticule to the aft port side and finally hit the trigger. I nicked it with one hit. Just enough to turn the fighter towards the approaching Marauder corvette. The larger ship didn't have time to turn, and as I was targeting the next nearest fighter I saw the crushing impact out of the corner of my eye.

There were no other fighters in range, so I took the opportunity to aim at the Marauder's bridge and open fire. I kept the gun firing until the tips of the barrels were white hot, took a break for the count of three, then opened fire again. I wasn't the only one. I could see Oz and Jason were aiming at the same target and we collectively cheered when their bridge depressurized. They had obviously come with orders to take us alive — otherwise their beam weapons would have torn us to pieces — but that didn't make our small victory hollow or any less rewarding.

Another wave of fighters was coming into range, and my targeting computer, as simple as it was, marked what I guessed were two more Marauders. I was sure, with the damage that we had done to them already, it wouldn't be long before their orders changed from recapture to eliminate. I didn't think we could hold out for very long against modern fighters in an old gunship, and from what I was sure my energy readout was telling me, we had spent about eighty percent of the power stored for the guns. It would take a long time for them to recharge.

The first group of fighters came into range. I was just about to open fire when the First Light fighter group streaked past us, their engines flaring brightly and weapons firing relentlessly at our pursuers. I swivelled my turret around and saw the First Light coming almost straight at us with all gun turrets bare and firing. Rounds left light trails through space as thousands of them hurtled towards the corvettes and their fighter cover.

There was emergency hull plating right across the front of the ship. A wide beam weapon had cut into the First Light starting at the darkened bridge, extending all the way down across the front to the observation deck. The main observation section was also unlit, and through the transparesteel section in the front I could see a closed emergency blast door. There was Ayan's reason for leaving without us. Something much bigger, much more powerful, had been ready to blast the entire ship into oblivion.

I watched for a moment longer before gladly leaving the dangerously exposed gunnery turret. I slammed the hatch shut with my foot and climbed the few more rungs to the cockpit, where I sat beside Ayan and took her hand. She looked at me and smiled. "I didn't want to leave you behind," was all she said. There was no apology and I needed none.

"I know. I love you."

She moved from her seat into my lap and I held her as we landed inside the main bay of the First Light.

NINE

A MILITARY CAPTAIN

The deck crew applauded as soon as I emerged from the gunship. It was a good reception, but short lived. They all had work to do. Several of them got to work on moving the gunship from where Minh had landed it straight into the servicing bay. Two of the deck crew gave us replacement command and control consoles. "There's a uniform materializer built into this one, Sir, something we developed while you were away," one of them told me as she clasped it on my arm. We took the lift part way up and stopped in a common area restroom before reaching our destination. Considering the bridge was destroyed, I wasn't quite sure where that would be. I was following Ayan.

Once I was in a restroom stall, I tore off what remained of the plastic jumpsuit and raised the command and control unit to chest level, just about ready to apply a new uniform.

I brought the uniform console up and noticed it had changed. There was a new option that would materialize one from a pattern stored in memory just as I had been told.

I was just about to select it when I heard Oz cry out. "Whoa! What the—" I peeked over the top of the stall and saw he was already in his bridge uniform and checking himself from head to toe. "Yup, every thing's still there. Still seems a little too close for comfort though, something materializing so close to the tender bits."

I shrugged, closed my eyes and pressed the button, trying not to think of all the things that could go wrong with turning energy into matter right on top of someone's skin. Less than two seconds later the uniform was on and other than a slight tingle, there were no ill effects. I stepped out of the stall and Minh-Chu looked at me. "Let's finish this the right way."

"There are some escapees that need cover," I agreed.

Ayan met me at the restroom door. "Much better. Could use a shave though. Your new bridge is this way." She started leading us at a quick pace towards the engineering section.

"How is the ship?"

"We were able to patch what we had to, and by super-charging certain sections of the hull it's grown back enough so we're armoured again. The main bridge is gone. We didn't bother even re-pressurizing it; we just sealed it off."

"We should have done that a long time ago," Oz commented from behind.

"None of us were thinking that we'd be stuck in a battle against this kind of technology. I agree with you, though," I replied.

Ayan went on. "The Marauder corvettes don't have the energy to use the same power grade of particle weapons that the bigger carriers and destroyers here do. When the Vindyne fleet jumped in at close range, a super carrier was right on top of us.

They focused their first shot right across the forward section. Our refractive shielding mitigated some of the damage, but it couldn't do all the work."

"My kingdom of rice and noodles for energy shields," Minh said, shaking his head.

"We're working on it. Some of the technology we just got our hands on while we were rescuing you, combined with the more basic schematics you sent up while you were on the planet, may get us to the point where we just need a few special parts and a week or so in dry dock. For the time being, we reinforced the entire hull by running all the generators as hot as we could and supercharging the hull. As you know, when you supercharge ergranian steel it can increase in size or become more dense. We mixed the energy types so the hull is a few millimetres thicker, a few of the pitted sections have been repaired, and it's a little over seven percent more dense. Being in close orbit around a star helped too. The surface of the hull reacted better than I could have hoped to the heat and light. We should be able to sustain several hits from some of those particle beams, especially since we're abandoning the outer hull during combat until we have energy shielding in place."

"That's a lot of work," Doctor Lang commented.

"We didn't waste any time. Between developing our own version of the Triad's cloaking suit that we could replicate quickly using fabricator generated and hand made components, reconfiguring the materializers on the outside of the hull to emit a plasma shield, the repairs, building a temporary bridge in the forward engineering section and coordinating your rescue with Alice — who was a little less than consistent — we were on four hours of sleep a night or less. It really didn't help that Alice's plans and methods kept on changing, evolving, and at one point all of her safeties were just gone and she didn't care how many people died while she was getting you out. I've never seen an artificial intelligence go rogue like that."

"It was a last ditch strategy," I explained as we ran down the main hall to the forward engineering section.

"Well, I hate to say it, but we started making real progress after that. The gamble we took by drifting at speed in a deceleration pod wearing nothing but vacsuits to protect us for a few hundred thousand kilometres paid off because of her. We did lose Gavin and Krysta though."

"You drifted at speed?" I couldn't imagine moving at thousands of kilometres per second in nothing but a vacsuit. Just hand thrusters to guide your trajectory. Even with a deceleration pod, it was a terrible risk.

"It was the only way to get to you undetected."

The doors to the new bridge parted and I stepped inside.

All the stations were there. Rudimentary control panels were set up in a circle around the captain's seat, which was very basic. Everyone was using personal holographic command displays instead of interactive holograms. At the front of the nearly empty chamber there was a large holographic projection that displayed the situation graphically and tactically.

Some of the bridge staff were missing, and I could only assume that they had been killed when the original bridge was destroyed. Jason stepped in to help with communications. Minh took over the pilot's seat after taking in the situation. Oz stood beside Sergeant Ashbey, who was serving as first officer, and I stood beside Doctor Anderson, who was in command.

"Good to see you on board, Captain. You have good timing."

"Thank you. How are we doing?"

"I was just tracking some of the larger escaping ships. It seems someone on the command carrier arranged one hell of a breakout."

"That's a long story." I looked at the holographic display and saw that the Vindyne ships were scattered, but so were the escapees. Many of the ships that had departed early were starting to get picked off by small groups of fighters, small gunships, and Marauder corvettes. The guns on the Command Carrier weren't firing at all, and the other two smaller carriers were on their way out of the area. "Do you think we could cover them if we gave them a departure route?"

"We could. There are a few other ships from the planet fighting up here as well. If we gave them a zone to protect, we'd probably save a few of those ships."

"Make it happen, Acting Captain. You know the situation better than I do at this point."

"Yes, Sir."

As Doctor Anderson carried out my orders, sending a broad message to all ships to follow a certain flight path away from the super carrier and towards a small, nearby moon, I took a look at the larger holographic display. There were many ships on their way up from the planet; anything with a weapon on board was coming to assist in the fight.

"We have Gai-Ian ships reporting in for tactical coordination with us, Sir. There are dozens of them, some older than our hull," Jason said from the communication station.

"Patch anything with a local transponder into our tactical network. Make sure they're all marked friendly and they can see each other as well as the escape route that we've plotted," I hastily ordered. Jason and the other communications officer started marking the ships and they appeared on the main display. The ships escaping from the super carrier were starting to fall in line along the marked course. "Repeat the message to defend that escape trajectory on all channels every thirty seconds. Once we're in position, have all port and starboard side gunners switch to flak rounds, the rest will have to pick off targets with explosive rounds."

"Yes, Sir," replied Ensign Stevens from tactical.

"How are our shields doing?"

"Refractive shielding is up to twenty eight layers. We're starting to take beam weapons fire from the Marauders, and a little from a gunship, but most of it is being refracted back out," reported Corporal Chavez. She looked nervous.

"Try to refract the beam fire to enemy targets, but remember, your main objective is keep it from striking our hull."

"Yes, Sir. Plasma shielding isn't on line yet."

"That's the second time I've heard about plasma shielding," I said more to myself than anyone else. I brought Ayan up on the communicator. "I don't know how you installed plasma shielding, but is there any chance we could get it online? There's a destroyer that's turned in our direction. She's twice our size."

"We were just about to power up and start the hull emitters, stand by."

"We're in position. Switch to the ammunition loads the Captain specified and bring our fighter cover in the line. We want to make sure that none of the enemy ships can use those transports as cover," Doc commanded. "Set our trajectory positive nineteen degrees by positive fourteen degrees and slow us down to drift at fifty kilometres per second."

The professionalism Doc conducted himself with on the bridge was different from his bedside manner in medical. It spoke of experience and it was hard not to find it intimidating. He was just following my orders, but he was very specific in what he wanted, clear, and didn't leave any loose ends for the crew to guess on or to improvise. As soon as the orders were given, he went back to working with the command hologram in front of him, checking the changing details of our situation, giving orders to stations silently, and projecting different strategies.

I heard all the power plants in the ship ramp up and run at maximum power for the first time. "The shields are ready, Sir," Ayan said. I could hear her grinning. "They're not efficient, but we'll be a much harder target."

I brought up an exterior view of the ship on my personal command unit and projected it just in front of me.

"On your word, Captain," Doc said.

I could see on the main holographic display that the destroyer was closing into firing range. "Flip the switch, Doctor," I ordered, not knowing exactly what to expect. I had never seen anyone use a plasma-based shield before. They were normally in use on older mining vessels to protect them from micro-meteors and other small debris.

On the small display of the ship exterior, I saw our hull materializers begin projecting a plasma field around the ship. They came to life one by one from aft to fore, and when the entire ship was covered, the plasma lit up like a firestorm.

At first it looked like a roaring inferno, a miniature sun

drifting above a line of mixed transport, freight and other ships. Then the rudimentary shield projectors focused the energy and the plasma became much denser. The flames were gone, leaving just a transparent blue haze over the First Light.

The destroyer was almost in range as Doc stepped down. "It's time for you to take your place, Captain."

I wordlessly walked over to the command chair and sat down. The command hologram appeared all around me, displaying the tactical view, the statistical view, damage report summaries, power readings, system tolerances, communication highlights, and navigational details. It was like I had never left. "Thank you, Doctor."

"Just keeping it warm for you, Sir. I'll be in medical."

I looked at the disposition of the destroyer and focused in on its transponder information and power readings. It was the Incinerator B31-209. Just over two kilometres long, she had only twenty percent more mass than we did, and that told me a great deal. The rest of the transponder information was locked out and it was headed straight at us.

It began firing its forward beam emplacements. I looked out to see it through the transparesteel section of the hull and saw nothing but wall, having forgotten that we were in the centre of the ship. It was amazing how, even though it was the least efficient way to view a situation, I still wanted to see things through a window.

"The destroyer will collide with us in the next eighty seconds if we don't increase speed," Minh said from the helm.

"Hold until the fifteen second mark, then go to full thrust just long enough to get out of her way."

"Yes, Sir."

"Tactical, command all gunners to target the destroyer's broad side with heavy flak load ammunition. We need to tax her energy shields. Minh, turn us so we make a slow pass port to starboard side, we want to give our gunners as much time to hit her shields as we can. Rotate the ship so we can spread whatever damage that destroyer returns to us across the entire hull. Plasma shields need time to regenerate section by section."

"How do you know so much about plasma shielding?" Oz asked me as he checked our course and coordinated the fighter groups.

"It was in the history component of combat engineering in the academy."

"History component. I shouldn't have asked."

The destroyer seemed just inches away on my exterior display, and Minh fired the engines hard; I could hear the generators behind us groan under the power drain. The First Light turned ninety degrees, bringing us right alongside the enemy destroyer. We began to rotate as the enemy's starboard beam weapons began firing. Our refractive shielding redirected the energy from the beams right back at the Incinerator, and our plasma shields absorbed most of the accelerated particles.

Our gunners returned fire, throwing millions of rough metal chunks of flak at the enemy ship's shields. The Incinerator had a surprise for us, however. Her torpedo ports opened up, marked with red on my tactical display. I had just enough time to flip the ship wide communicator on. "Brace for impact!"

All three tubes launched and the torpedoes exploded just as they passed through our shields, causing a massive directed blast just centimetres from our hull. The inertial dampeners couldn't handle all of the concussive force and we were shaken so hard that I was nearly dumped out of my seat. Some of the bridge crew were thrown to the floor, including Oz, who rolled back to his feet in a heartbeat.

"Outer hull breaches from section twenty nine to forty eight, emergency bulkheads are sealing off those sections in the first five decks. We have bowing in several more sections, but the ship's core and two thirds of the outer hull are intact," Oz reported.

"Steady! If we don't take care of this bastard he'll be able to kill all the escapees in minutes. Rotate the ship to expose unaffected turrets. Recall all fighters to focus their fire on the shielding on her starboard side. Once we're past, turn us about. Keep us on target!" I watched as my commands were carried out. "Load three turrets with explosive shells. When her shields are overloaded, I want them to target her weapon emplacements."

Ayan was on the comm. "We lost two turrets in that blast. Three more gunnery crews have sealed themselves in their compartments to avoid super heated areas of the hull."

"Are their guns still running?"

There was a pause. "They are."

"Then tell them to load explosive rounds and target weapon emplacements. Other than that, are we sealed?"

"We are. The outer hull took all the damage. Other than the gunnery crews, they were supposed to be evacuated."

"Good. How much power can you spare for our beam weapon?"

"Not much, about one point four percent."

"What if we cut the engines?"

"Well, then about twenty percent or more, but that exceeds the beam weapon's maximum load."

"Then burn it as hard as you can. Signal tactical when you're ready to switch the power from engines to weaponry."

"Affirmative."

I watched our ship turn to stay alongside the Incinerator and our fighter groups attack the starboard side shielding as hard as they could. Our own plasma shielding was only mitigating half of the particle damage from the enemy ship's beam weapons. Our hull was marked with long scars as we rotated the ship.

"Sir! Our dorsal aft shields are down! They hit one of the main materializers dead on!"

"Keep that section pointed away from them. We'll only survive one more pass here, so let's make it good. Launch standard load torpedoes and get ready to cut the engines."

The torpedo bay was ready and I watched as they struck the Incinerator's shielding after closing the distance in seconds. Our forward section took some proximity damage from the explosion, but there were no personnel there during combat. The power reading on their starboard shields finally dropped to zero and started climbing back up very slowly. "Cut the engines!"

A second later tactical reported. "Engine power has been diverted to—"

"Cut them to pieces! Fire torpedoes when ready! All gunners switch to explosive rounds and target shield emitters and weapon emplacements."

"Do you want the fighters to follow our attack strategy?" Oz asked.

"No, order them to stay and protect the convoy."

"Yes, Sir."

The Incinerator's hull held up to the assault for a few seconds, then started opening up everywhere. Our gunners were targeting their weapon emplacements, shield emitters, and any soft spots they could find while our beam weapon carved five meter wide gaps into their comparatively thin hull.

"Hail the Incinerator. I think it's time I have a word with her captain." I waited for an active comm signal and addressed the enemy commander. "You have thirty seconds to signal your surrender." I closed the channel.

"Sir, the fighter squadrons are reporting that the bulk of the forces are leaving the field. There are still a few Marauders and gunships in the area trying to attack the convoy. They're marked as part of the Incinerator's battle group."

"I think the commander on that ship took my demand personally. Bring us about to a forward facing against their starboard side and angle our main deceleration engines to face the open sections of their hull. It's time to break their back." I opened a channel to Ayan. "Redirect power to our deceleration engines so they fire at just below tolerance."

"Jonas, what are you doing?"

"I'm bringing this to an end before we lose anyone else."

"Yes, Sir."

I could tell she didn't approve, but she wasn't looking at the tactical display.

"Sir, I understand why you want to do this, but weaponizing the forward engines and firing them at this range, that's the kind of thing that could set off a reaction we might not survive. If the stakes were lower I'd be all—" I stood up and interrupted Oz.

"That's what we have to do to scare off the rest of this

destroyer's battle group. If we don't, that ship will eventually out-manoeuvre us and she'll have an entire broad side of weaponry to fire. Then her support ships will focus their fire and we'll have no chance of getting out of this alive.

"Cease firing on the Incinerator. Commence firing on any enemy ships that come into range. Explosive and flak rounds at discretion." I reopened communications with the Incinerator. "Last chance," I said, leaving the channel open. I didn't hear anything, not a sound as I counted to ten. I left the channel open as I turned to the pilot. "Fire forward engines, full burn. Stabilize our position with the main thrusters."

I watched the exterior view as our engines fired within fifty meters of their starboard side. The heat from our ion engines tore through the openings in the enemy ship's hull, reduced entire sections of the interior to molten, twisted metal, burned through blast doors, and turned anything other than metal to dust or less in seconds. "Reduce aft engines to one quarter and stop firing forward engines," I said as I watched what was left of the Incinerator list lifelessly away. She had buckled in the centre. Her engines and all other systems went dark, and the power readings on my control console indicated that life support was gone. I could see tiny spikes in power as emergency escape vessels launched from what was left. The reactor in the centre of the ship, and a sixth of the interior, had been completely destroyed.

"The last of the ships have escaped from the super carrier, Sir, and a corvette is headed after them. She should catch up in under a minute."

"Head straight for her, full burn. Start firing weapons as

soon as we're in range. Have engineering reinforce our shields if they can."

I watched as our ship moved up the line of escaping ships, firing on smaller attackers as we hurtled towards the lone Marauder corvette that had begun pursuing the last of the escapees. I looked to Jason who nodded and hailed the smaller ship. "To the captain of the Marauder, my terms are simple. You will abandon ship in the next sixty seconds or be destroyed. If you set your auto destruct I will ensure that every escape craft you launch is destroyed. If the Marauder is left sabotaged in any way, I will order my fighters to kill every escape vehicle with Vindyne markings." I closed the channel. "Power up the beam weapon. Ready standard torpedoes and have gunners load flak ammunition. Fire when she's in range."

The Marauder signalled her surrender and her captain's response came over the bridge communication's system. "I'd rather get fired than disobey those terms, Captain. I surrender my ship and myself into your care. I'll meet you on the bridge."

"Surrender accepted. I would prefer it if you left the ship before our arrival."

"I'd rather surrender to you than face a breach of contract with the Vindyne. You can maroon me for all I care, just don't let me get picked up by the Company."

"In that case, you'll be surrendering yourself into the custody of my first officer."

I looked to Oz, who stared back at me in surprise. "Get a boarding party together. Take whoever you have to and be careful. I want that ship, but not at the expense of more lives. If it looks like a trap, just get out. We can always slag it from here."

"Yes, Sir," he said with a smile. "Think you could pilot that thing?" he asked Minh.

"I can pilot a doghouse with a thruster. Of course I can pilot that thing," he replied as he surrendered the helm to Flight Sergeant Cullum. We watched escape pods and small craft launch and separate from the Marauder Corvette as her engines cooled down.

I checked the status of the convoy that had formed out of the ships escaping from the super carrier and was amazed. Over fifty large freighter and transport class ships, some half a kilometre in size, had escaped along with over three hundred smaller ships. Most of them were headed towards the small moon we had marked off. A few were taking other courses and making for the nearest safe hyperspace acceleration point. "Navigation, set a course to join the largest portion of the convoy and order any undamaged fighters to spread themselves out among the rest. Once we're in orbit around the moon, we'll have to set up duty shifts until we finalize plans for getting these people to a safe port."

"Yes, Sir."

I could see that all the other enemy ships were clearing the area. There wasn't a ship left that could match us, but I was sure reinforcements wouldn't be more than a day or two behind if Vindyne considered the system a priority. Regardless of impending reinforcements, there was a collective sigh of relief throughout the bridge staff.

A pair of new allied markings appeared on the bridge tactical display. "There are two beacons out there, Captain, they just appeared on screen out of nowhere."

"Do you know what that's about, tactical?"

"One moment, Sir." She checked her display and focused in on them. "They're marked as part of rescue team beta, two of our cloaksuits. They must have remained cloaked until now so they wouldn't give the others away."

"Send four of our fighters out there, I want them back here as soon as possible."

"Yes, Sir. That's going to be an interesting ride back for those two."

I looked to Jason, who was handling the communications incoming from the convoy. He and the young woman at the communications station didn't seem to be getting too much incoming comm traffic. "Take the bridge, Sergeant Everin. I'm going to see how things are in engineering."

Jason looked at me for a moment, stunned. "Yes, Sir."

I knew he would do just fine. He was already used to doing at least five things at a time while setting decryption priorities. Bridge command might just seem boring. I walked to the back of the room where there were four hatchways, each with ladders leading down. "I hope this leads to engineering," I said to myself as I opened a hatch and made my way down.

The ladder went down for about twenty rungs and ended with another hatch that opened as soon as my foot was near. As I came through the bottom and set foot on the deck below, there was no doubt in my mind as to where the passage had taken me. The main pit of engineering control was the most convenient, practical design I had ever seen. There were three head engineering crew: Ayan, Laura and another officer with a short goatee that I hadn't met more than once. They stood in the middle of the main engineering section, surrounded by a full circle of multi-purpose control panels and interactive holograms all around them. From where they stood, they could manipulate any system in exact detail, see everything that was going on in and around the ship, and view every room, deck plate, or system on the ship.

They could also command the maintenance, gunnery, and repair teams, hear what was going on in the bridge, and communicate with any control station they had to. The interface Ayan had developed was something I had heard of; it had been partially implemented during the refit back at Freeground. But here it had been incorporated fully.

Ayan saw me come down and whispered to Laura before opening a section of the command console and stepping out. Laura and the other officers took over portions of what Ayan was working on without missing a beat. "Are we clear, do you think?" she asked as she gave me a quick hug.

"I think so, but not for long. From what I saw while I was down on the planet, I don't think the Vindyne corporation will be leaving this system alone. There are too many resources for them not to make this a high priority."

"Do you have a plan? Some of the refugee ships don't have faster than light capabilities, and they're low on supplies."

"Do you think we could generate a wormhole?"

"The power plants are up to it, and the projectors weren't damaged. We could, but where would you send them?"

"We'll have to send them to Freeground."

Ayan thought about it for a moment before quietly asking. "Would we be going with them?"

The thought of returning home hadn't entered my mind. I looked around the main engineering deck, where several maintenance and emergency repair crew were working or just running through to pick up tools and parts from a storage locker. A lot of them were listening without letting on. A few had stopped at the question and were staring right at me. I thought for a moment longer. "If it was up to me, we'd find a quiet place to make repairs and continue our mission. It isn't something I can decide for everyone this time. I'll be calling the senior staff together to discuss it," I said more for the benefit of the eaves-droppers than for Ayan.

She smiled at me and nodded. "It's what I'd do. I'll talk to my staff about it but I think they'll be against returning home."

"Good. I have other news for you. I had to deliver it in person."

"That means that it's either really good or really bad."

"We are pretty sure we found your two missing drifters. Our fighters are picking them up now."

The weight that I saw on her shoulders seemed to almost completely lift as she sighed with relief. "When they missed the mark and drifted past the carrier we were sure they were gone for good. How did you find them?"

"As soon as we took out the destroyer and forced the nearest of the Marauders to surrender they turned on their beacons. They must have found a way to watch from orbit."

"Well, it wouldn't be hard to tap in to all the communica-tion traffic going on during the chaos. Some of it wouldn't be encrypted, I'm sure. Thank you, Jonas, we lost enough on this trip."

I stared at her for a moment. The guilt of getting myself captured and taking on more than we could handle forced me into silence. It must have shown, even though I was still trying to concentrate on our current situation.

"No one blames you," she whispered. "No one would have felt right just leaving, either."

I composed myself. I wasn't ready to believe her, but hearing it reminded me that I still had to make decisions, face the truth of our situation. "How many did you lose?"

"We lost four gunnery crew, one maintenance. There are nine badly injured and several more who just need cursory treatment. Except for one gunnery team that's trapped in their turret, they're all already in medical."

"How hard will it be to get the gunners out?"

"They should be out in a few minutes, I already have an emergency repair team working on it."

"Ayan, Oz needs two engineering teams," Laura called over.

"What for?"

I held my hand up before Laura went to the effort of explaining. "He needs them so we can take a Marauder. I didn't put the boarding action on the command screen right away because I put Oz in charge of putting the team together."

"You're actually taking a Marauder corvette? What kind of shape is it in?"

"I thought you would already know," I said, eyeing her new engineering command interface.

"We don't watch everything. We don't have time. That's why most ships this class have a dozen or so artificial intelligences on watch."

"Good point. As far as I know she's in perfect shape. They abandoned ship before we had to fire a shot. Must have had to do with the destroyer we wrecked."

"Well, make sure that he takes their communications

systems offline, and that he brings his own emergency long range comm unit and a backup power source."

"He's been on at least forty boarding missions. He's a grown boy."

"Sometimes I forget I'm not the only one with experience."

"Oh, and he's taking Minh. The pair of them have enough infantry combat time to cover at least ten of our security staff."

"True, they'll be fine." She looked to her command console and the repair assignments. "Laura, clear two officers from engineering, six qualified maintenance crew with boarding experience, and two without boarding experience. If Oz complains that he needs more specialists, tell him to start training his own."

Laura smiled and nodded. "Yes, Commander."

Ayan turned back to me, every inch the commander her engineering staff knew her to be. It was amazing to see her in charge. "How many did the other departments lose?" she asked.

I checked the update on my arm command unit. I knew that our losses were relatively low for what we had been through, but every one hurt. "Flight reports three pilots killed, five ejected, two with serious injuries. Security reports no losses, one injury, and flight deck crew reports four injuries."

"Jonas, we came out of this very light. If this ship was run the way it once was, with her outer hull fully manned, with security in every main passageway, gun crews of three instead of two, we would have lost at least fifty people. Maybe more. I know you think you screwed up by getting yourself captured, but that wasn't your fault," she whispered. "Even if it was, look at where it took us. We were in exactly the right place, with the right tools to set tens of thousands of people free. People who were independents just like us. Not only that, but we're out here to acquire technologies that can help Freeground, and right now Oz is getting a boarding crew together to do just that. Not to mention the quantum core and damage we've managed to do to Vindyne's activities here. We're doing it, Jonas, right now."

I hadn't thought of it that way. In fact I don't know that I ever would have. "You're right, there's no point in blaming myself."

"You will anyway, I know. Just be our captain, think things through, consult the right people, and make your decisions just the way I've seen you do before. Everyone on board will follow you."

I smiled warmly at her. "Sometimes you sound like you've been at this for as long as the Doc. It would be intimidating if I didn't know you off duty."

She gave me a quick peck on the cheek and started walking back to the engineering command centre. "Speaking of off duty pursuits, I have good and bad news."

I braced myself. "I'll take the good news first."

She stepped into the ring of displays and brought up a larger schematic of the ship on a holographic display, then centred in on the eighty-meter long open section of the top of our outer hull. It was a massive gash that had been ripped open by the three torpedoes launched by the Incinerator. "Well, the good news is that no critical systems were badly damaged when the torpedo salvo hit us. We lost several sections of hull and it'll take about two months for it to fully regenerate outside of dry dock."

"And the bad news?"

"All but one officer's quarters were destroyed. The walls and fixed structures will eventually regenerate, but everything else will have to be rebuilt."

"Whose quarters survived?" I asked, just grateful that no one was in their quarters during the battle.

"Minh's, actually."

"Well, at least there was no one inside when we were hit. Do we have enough quarters so we don't have to hot-bunk?"

"Well, we can open the secondary berthing. It wasn't in use because the quarters were a little cramped. On the brighter side, we'll all be close to our duty stations."

"I hope you didn't have anything important in your quarters, Sir," Laura added.

"I barely got to know them." My arm unit chirped, indicating I had an incoming high priority message. "Yes?" I answered.

"Samuel Finnley is on the communicator, Sir, he wants to speak with you," Jason said. I could hear him smiling.

"I'm on my way." I turned and climbed up the ladder leading into the bridge. When I arrived, Jason relinquished the captain's chair right away, and once he was back at his station he put Samuel through. The details attached to the transmission indicated the Governor was aboard one of the larger transports we had saved. He looked genuinely happy to see me. "Governor, you made it out."

"Thanks to you and your crew, I imagine. Once again I'm glad you're here."

"I only did what we could. I wish we had a thousand ships. We'd gladly retake this system for you."

"Well, if our freedom is all circumstance allows us, it is a better fate than we would have suffered if you weren't here."

I could see that he wanted to ask about his daughter, and

that his fear forced him into hesitation. "There's someone on board who's worrying about you," I told him with a smile.

"Elise is with you?"

"She is. I can patch you through right now." I signalled Jason and he connected the Governor to where Elise was staying in secure quarters attached to main medical.

I heard her come on. "Yes?"

"Elise? Are you all right?"

"Father! Where are you?"

"I'm on a transport just below you. I'm fine, don't worry. How are you?"

"I'm fine, I'm better than fine!"

"I'm sorry I put you in danger Elise. I'm so sorry."

"It's okay, Dad. They kept their promise. The doctor here says the treatments worked. Even through all they suffered, they kept their promise."

I cut my communication link, giving the pair some privacy. No one needed to hear any more. I brought up the long convoy of escaped ships on the main bridge holographic display and just looked at it. There were hundreds of them, all different ages, shapes and sizes. Everything from commercial space liners to bulk cargo haulers to shuttle ferries carrying dozens of mismatched smaller ships.

"If that were the only reason for us being here, it would have been enough," Jason said quietly as he looked on from his station.

Everyone on the bridge looked at the display for a moment. We all manoeuvred into orbit around the blue and black rocky moon. The First Light, beaten and scarred, kept pace above the line of ships, holding its position like an armoured sentry.

I ordered anyone who had been awake for more than eighteen hours to get six hours of rest. It wasn't long before Doc sent me a discreet message including orders that I do the same. I sighed and checked the status of our repairs. They were going surprisingly well. All the critical systems and their backups would be up and running at normal efficiencies within the next two hours, and most of the hull patching would be complete not long after. I went on to check into reports of ships from the convoy leaving the moon's orbit for parts unknown. Most of them sent their thanks and a few of them gave us their heading before getting under way. It had only been a few hours since we had entered orbit, and I was surprised to see that almost a third had left.

Doc sent another message, giving me a direct order to take six hours rest. I checked the roster and chose Lieutenant Nichols, who had command experience and officer training, to take a turn at the captain's chair. I was so tired I just sent her a simple official order, filling in commencement time, position, end time, and a quick note to Oz, telling him that I was taking one of his security staff and placing her in the captain's chair for a few hours. Normally I would have sent a more personal message, but I was more interested in finding out where my new bed was and going to sleep. I had no choice but to admit the good doctor was right, again.

I found that they had managed to secure quarters that were nowhere near as small as the cell I had grown accustomed to. They weren't half the size of the luxurious captain's quarters that had been slagged in the recent battle, but there was a double bed, a desk, a closet, and a secure trunk. It was right near the centre of the ship. I could still feel the slight rumble of the power plants as all of them ran just below ninety percent, keeping the ship powered and regenerating the damaged sections of hull.

I took off my sidearm, put it on the desk, then fell onto the bed with the lights on. I don't know how long I had been asleep, but when I woke the lights were dimmed down to just a few points of luminosity and Ayan was wrapping my arms around her. I drew her closer and just held her there.

So many times in the blinding whiteness of that cell, I had closed my eyes and dreamed of being in a darkened room, sharing a soft bed with Ayan, and here she was.

"Don't do that again."

"What?" I asked, half asleep.

"Scare me like that. I didn't know if I could get you back."

"I won't if you don't," I said with a sleepy smile.

She shook her head and sighed. "You're lucky I love you."

"Sure am," I said as I drifted back to sleep.

MORNING

That morning, or what passed for morning, I was awakened by Ayan as she came back into the quarters bearing coffee. She looked refreshed and energetic. "Doctor Anderson wants to see you right away and I have to get back to engineering."

I raised myself up on one elbow and took the spill-proof container she offered. "How long were we asleep?"

"The full six hours. My alarm was set. Yours didn't go off."

"Lucky me. Why does Doc want to see me? Shouldn't he get some R&R sometime?"

"He did. Apparently he sleeps at the same time as the captain on every ship he serves on. Something he told me while we were hiding."

"You never got a chance to tell me about that, how you hid from the entire Vindyne invasion fleet."

"I'd love to, but I have to get to engineering," she started for the door, but I caught her arm and pulled her down for a kiss.

Ayan was happy to oblige but kept it short. "You need a

mint," she giggled before taking the few steps across the room and out the door. I sighed and sat up, knowing that if my head hit the pillow even for a second I would be fast asleep.

I attended to my obligatory morning ritual and refreshed my coffee before setting off for main medical.

On the way I scanned through the status reports and messages on my arm command console as quickly as I could. Oz reported that the capture of the Marauder had gone perfectly. All her on-board communications had been taken offline and they had managed to destroy twenty three beacons and emergency transmitters. Scans of the ship were showing no emissions when all systems were dark, indicating that no hidden transmitters with autonomous power remained. A small security team and bridge crew had taken over while the boarding personnel took some much needed rest back on board the First Light. The captain of the vessel was named Leslie Grays and he was delivered to our brig without incident.

The repairs on the ship were complete for the time being. The only section that was open to space was along the upper portion of the ship, right behind the bridge.

Nine ships from the Gai-Ian System Defence Fleet had volunteered to join us, and Governor Samuel Finnley was requesting a meeting with me sometime in the next twenty hours. Oz somehow had time to file a shift report on the crew with a little help from Doctor Horner. It didn't tell me anything new. Everyone was overworked, and non-command crew were on twelve hour shifts while command crew were on fourteen hour shifts. There was no way we could continue running as we were, so I made a note to crew the Marauder with the absolute minimum and bring everyone else back on board.

We'd have to get back to our normal eight and ten hour shifts as soon as possible and find a safe port to rest up not long after that, or the stress would cripple the crew. There was just one thing that I wanted the First Light crew to accomplish first.

I arrived in medical sipping my coffee, scrolling through all the reports that had accumulated during the six hours I had spent asleep. There was just too much to consume in the time it took me to get to Doc's territory. I found myself missing Alice. She would normally sort through the mass of information and present the most important bits first. It was like losing a limb. Everything seemed to take so much longer and I was more than a little impatient with sorting through data myself.

"Good of you to join us, Captain," Doc said as I walked in. I looked up and saw Oz and Minh sitting on beds, getting scanned from head to toe. There were very few injured in medical this time, and most of them were sleeping.

"Didn't seem like I had much choice."

"I know. I had to come. Medical was sending me orders every five minutes," Minh complained. "I had to shut him up or I wouldn't get anything done."

"Stop whining. You know they've got to check us out after a few weeks of captivity. I'm surprised they didn't have us locked up in here the moment we got back."

"It was tempting," Doctor Anderson said to Oz. "Right this way, Captain," he directed, showing me to a more private section of the medical bay.

The scans began right away as did the mental examination. I recognized all the key questions you're supposed to ask someone after being captured. Name three friends. How do you feel about being imprisoned? Who are your parents? In less than twenty words, how were you captured? What is one lie you've told about yourself to a friend? Did you leave anything behind? Where were you born? Think of three colours and without using their names, describe them.

It was all standard psychological check up stuff with a few updated questions for our particular experience. The computer tracked our physiological responses and watched for neural reprogramming. To my surprise I came up clean.

When the questions were finished, Doctor Anderson nodded to himself. "Well, your head checks out fine. You all held up well mentally, though you'll need some rest when you can get it."

"How am I physically?"

"Good, in general, but there is a problem. They implanted a micro transmitter in the back of each of your skulls. Even though it's right in the centre of the bone, whenever it's near a certain frequency it'll resonate, sending pulses back to the source."

"So when it's not near that frequency it doesn't emit a signal."

"Right. You're lucky I've run into this before."

"So, how do you get rid of it?"

"I'll just burn it out with a laser."

"That simple, huh? Just point and drill."

"When you put it that way, it is. It's a primitive solution, but it'll use fewer resources and the recovery time is practically nil with a bio recovery filler injected right into the site. Now turn over and stay very still."

It took just a few seconds and it was gone. I sat up and he began preparing an injector.

"They implanted you with a cellular tag as well, probably through whatever they fed you."

"It was brown."

"What was?"

"What they fed us. Just these brown bars."

"Ah, well, on the bright side, none of you are malnourished."

"So you took over after I left?"

"Ayan did, actually. She took us straight towards the sun. We got as close as we could to the corona and just let the hull and our RAD scoops soak up all that energy. It was like the ship was alive. I've never seen anything like it. The hull sang like a whale as it bonded and hardened under all the pressure and energy it was absorbing. There's nothing like ergranian steel. This is the first ship I've served on built with it."

"To listen to you, it sounds like you missed your calling. Maybe you should have been an engineer."

"Not at all. I like talking to my patients when there's time. Having a conversation with a ship, even with an advanced artificial intelligence, just isn't the same."

"So what else did I miss?"

"Well, Ayan had the crew busy. Everyone had work to do, whether it was just making sure we didn't get too close to the sun, improving systems, looking for ways to implement some of the shield technology that you had sent up to us before we lost contact, or finding a way to duplicate that stealth suit technology you and Oz brought back from Freeground. We couldn't add anything to the hull of the ship, mind you, but by the time Ayan got her team together and materialized enough stealth suits for them the ship couldn't have been in better shape. Those plasma shields she rigged up were a miracle. When we were ready to go, we broke orbit from the sun and used the wormhole generator for short jumps from the shadow of one moon to the next until the rescue team left for the command carrier. That's when I took command."

"Sounds like the crew worked hard."

"They did. Everyone wanted to break you out. Ayan was under tremendous pressure and I was glad to lighten her load whenever I could. Patching the hull was the most dangerous part. We had to do it while we followed in the wake of a radiation surge into low orbit around the nearest planet to the centre of the solar system. Our new pilot is almost as good as your friend Minh, though a little more nervous." He injected me and I swear the concoction made my arm feel heavier. "There you go, the cellular tag left behind by their prison food should be gone in about three days."

"Thank you, Doctor. I don't know what we'd do without you."

"Ah, you'd be fine. There are plenty of bright young doctors aboard."

"Come by my quarters if you're jogging during my off time. I missed our runs."

"So did I, Captain. Everyone's glad to have you back," he said, shaking my hand firmly.

I spent the next few hours on the bridge. It was all clean up and upkeep. Most of the crew were about to start coming on duty, and all of the command crew would be on at the same time for a four hour window. I scheduled a meeting with Oz, Minh, Ayan, Major Reginald Carlson of the Gai-Ian System Defence Fleet, and Samuel Finnley, who was no longer a governor, but had been voted to take charge of the escapees who remained in orbit. Time was passing fast, and I knew that the Vindyne Corporation could send another fleet to make an attempt at taking the system, only this time I was sure they would succeed.

Many System Defence ships were arriving in orbit around the moon. There were several destroyers, a carrier and a couple dozen corvette class ships, but nowhere near enough to defend the system. They were making retrieval runs to Concordia until their ships couldn't stand more punishment from the forces that Vindyne left behind.

When it was time for the meeting, we met in the third observation lounge where a long table had been set up. There were three sofas that curved along the rounded shape of the wall on one side, and the outer side of the hull was transparent. There were enough seats at the table for fourteen people, and a lot of room left over in the partially furnished room. When I arrived Oz and Minh were already there. "How was the Marauder?" I asked.

Minh chuckled. "It's a can. The hull is three centimetres thick in a lot of places and the controls are so simple and computer assisted I could fly it standing on my head while wearing melons on my hands. I don't want to go back."

"Is it really that bad?"

"Oh yeah, the crew quarters look a lot like the cells we just left. Everything's modular, made to be swapped out and replaced for re-tasking. But other than that he's right, it's a cheaply made, mass produced can," Oz verified.

"No wonder they need brain washed captives. No one else would fly that into a firefight."

"They don't use brainwashed prisoners. Most of their military sign up on their own or get drafted from poorer worlds. That energy shielding is what makes those corvettes dangerous. The technology looks reliable. Without it, it's just not viable in combat. Hell, even a micro meteor shower would be a major problem."

Ayan came in and sat down beside me. "You're talking about the energy shielding on the Marauder?"

"Yup, aside from the particle beams it's the only thing worthwhile," Minh answered.

"Good thing I don't plan on keeping it," I said.

"Thank God!" Minh exclaimed. "I don't want to set foot on that death trap or another one like it ever again."

"Well, you won't have to, but everyone else might get stuck working on it for a few hours at least. I want to cannibalize it for its shielding, weapons, any technology we don't have already, and it's energy storage systems. Then we can send it off into the sun."

"How long do you think that would take, Ayan?" Oz asked.

"Well, I haven't seen it, but I read the lead boarding engineer's report. I'd say about eight hours if everyone pitched in. We're lucky the ship is built with discrete modules. They're made for quick servicing, but also make for quick scavenging."

"Good, we'll just take what we can in six hours then the second shift will move on to our next target," I replied.

Minh sat straight up. "Next target?"

"We'll start pulling systems from what's left of the Incinerator. I don't know how hard it will be to implement her systems into our ship, but I want to take everything we can use in the time we have. We'll have to organize it so we start with the most important systems first, the shield emitters and core shielding systems. Then we'll move on to the weaponry, find out what kind of power generation she uses and if it could help us. If we do this right, we might be able to make off with everything we need to enhance the First Light. Make her a safer ship, maybe even catch up to some of the modern technology we've seen here."

"Where would we put the stuff? Don't get me wrong, I'd love to have half the toys the Incinerator came with, but after taking on parts from the Marauder, I don't think we'll have space. Some of those systems have pretty big components," Oz commented.

I looked at Ayan and she smiled back. "I think I know what he has in mind."

"We'll use the open section of hull. There's nothing we can do to close it up until we get to a safer location and it'll be easy to load in a hurry. We can also use the boarding shuttle and any spare space in the landing bay. As soon as we see any sign of the Vindyne Fleet, we drop everything we're doing and make off with whatever we managed to take aboard."

"I like it. We'll be running ourselves ragged, but I think it'll be worth it," Ayan agreed.

"What will I be doing?" Minh asked.

"You'll be running patrols in shifts. We have three extended sensor kits for your fighters. You'll have to manage them so we can extend our sensor range and get as early a warning as possible."

"At least I won't be telling my pilots to help with salvage."

"I wouldn't dream of it."

Doctor Anderson entered with Doctor Lang and Sergeant Everin close behind. "Our guests from Gai-Ian are on their way.

They should be here in a few minutes," Jason mentioned as they all took a seat.

"Good, we've been talking about salvaging what we can from the Marauder and what's left of the Incinerator and it looks like we'll be starting soon. I don't want to bring our guests into the discussion. The last thing we need is to get into an argument with the Gai-Ian Fleet over salvage rights when they should be more concerned with saving as much of their population as they can before Vindyne sends another fleet."

"Oh, I'm sure there's one on the way. The question is where is it coming from and whether they'll be more interested in saving their super carrier or finishing what they started in taking the system for themselves," Oz said. "However expensive that jail break may have been, I'm sure an entire agricultural world is worth a hell of a lot more."

"He's right, and corporations that large like to find out what other untapped resources might be there and take advantage of them as well," Doc commented. "We watched fully terraformed worlds get converted into strip mining operations overnight during the All-Con War. They didn't care who was living there. If they needed the resources, they took them however they could."

Samuel and Major Carlson entered then and I stood. "Welcome to the First Light, Governor," I knew that he didn't hold the position any longer, but I slipped.

"Thank you, Captain, but I'm just Samuel Finnley now. Most people call me Sam." He gestured to the older, dark haired, moustached man beside him. "This is Major Carlson. He's overseeing part of the evacuation effort."

"Good to meet you, Captain. I hope we can put the

previous misunderstanding our military had with you behind us."

"I can. Let me introduce my senior officers. Commander Terry Ozark McPatrick is my first officer, Commander Ayan Rice is our Chief Engineer, Doctor Anderson is our Head of Medical, Doctor Lang is on his staff, Sergeant Jason Everin is our Chief of Communications, and Commander Minh-Chu Buu is our Wing Commander."

"I see. We read over your proposal, Captain, and I have to say it was simple but informative. Are you sure we'll be welcome once we arrive in Freeground space?"

"When did you have time to write a proposal? Did you find an extra few minutes in every hour?" Oz asked in a whisper.

I cleared my throat and answered the major. "They're fighting the Triad. Every ship is welcome. I'm sure they'd be glad to take on any refugees if you could augment their defences and teach them a few new things about military and agricultural technology."

"Does it look like they have a chance at winning?"

"When we left, Freeground's defences were more than adequate. But maintaining those defences and striking back in a meaningful way are two different things. Freeground is very well fortified, our military is organized and seasoned, but we're slowly losing ground."

"Unlike what's going on in our system," Samuel interjected. "I'm afraid that we've evacuated everyone we can. Just over one hundred ten thousand and we don't have enough food to last more than two weeks."

Major Carlson picked up where he left off. "The last of our troop carriers and their escort are expected to rendezvous with us in less than an hour. The Vindyne troops have started using antimatter bombs on our more hardened positions, so we can't even hold them off on the ground. What's left of our infantry command structure agrees that we've lost the system."

"I'm sorry." It was all I could say.

Major Carlson smiled reassuringly. "Sam said I'd like you, Captain. You apologize like it's your fault, but there was never anything you could have done. Even if you and your crew arrived a year earlier with a warning that the Vindyne were on their way, it wouldn't have done much good. Now we just need to survive. Get our people to friendly territory. I only need your assurances that Freeground won't see us as hostile or take advantage of my people. I'm not in a position to ask for anything more."

Doctor Lang stood up and came to attention. "Captain, I'd like permission to go with them. I have my first year's officer's training and can act as intermediary between the Gai-Ian people and Freeground. I would also like to make sure that Elise's treatment is carried out properly."

I looked to Doc for a moment. He shrugged. "It's ultimately your decision, Sir. I'll miss having Doctor Lang here, but to be honest we have a high medical staff to crew ratio. As long as no one else from medical leaves, we'll be fine."

"Are you sure about this, Fiona?" I asked her.

She didn't speak. There was something wrong.

"Fiona?" Ayan asked, concerned.

Doctor Lang looked at me then, her eyes welling up. "I need to go home, Sir. I'm sorry." Ayan was at her side in a heartbeat.

"I understand." I walked to her as Ayan sat her down. "You've been through a lot in the past few weeks. Besides, I need someone to go with them, and I was having trouble deciding who. Thank you," I said, trying to cheer her up a little. She looked so tired and she had been so strong ever since we landed on Concordia. We were seeing the toll.

"Let's go for a walk," Doc said to her pleasantly. He was familiar and upbeat as he took her hand and brought her to her feet. He put his arm around her shoulders and guided her out of the room. It all happened in one smooth, gentle motion. Ayan moved back to her seat and I returned to mine.

"I'm sorry for anything they did to you and your crew while you were in captivity, Captain," Samuel said. "I can't say I'm not glad for your presence here, however. I don't know how you managed to loosen that super carrier's grip, but I'm grateful you did."

"I'm glad I could help. If you don't mind, I actually would like to send Doctor Lang along with you."

"Of course. It will help us make a good impression on Freeground right from the start."

"I can send one of my security team with her," Oz added. "Doctor Lang is friends with Ensign Yates, and I'm sure she'd be glad to return home as well. But we can't let just anyone who's homesick take this as an opportunity to go home. Yates and Lang were both imprisoned with us and they're both at the breaking point."

"I agree, as soon as we're done here brief Ensign Yates on his new assignment."

"Yes, Sir."

"Well, it looks like it's all arranged. This was much easier than expected," Major Carlson said. "Is it true that the wormhole will take us there in just three days?"

"It will, but once we stop generating the entry point the only way back will be using your own faster than light drives."

"I understand. Like I said, my focus here is the survival of my people. If Freeground is more secure than this system, that's where we have to be. Our other friends in the sector can't offer us shelter. It would draw Vindyne's attention, and that's something none of them can afford. There's only one more thing to discuss before I leave."

"What's that, Major?"

"There are many skilled crew members from our fleet that want to sign up for the First Light. I propose that we exchange them for Doctor Lang and Ensign Yates. The whole fleet knows that you're opposed to Vindyne and a few want to stay out here, especially if it means they might get a shot at some payback."

"We don't seek out opportunities to tangle with super Corporations, but I can promise them that if they join my crew, they'll be helping to find new ways to defend Freeground and fight back against invaders, no matter what form they come in."

"I think that'll be good enough, Captain." The major and Samuel Finnley walked the length of the table and both shook my hand in turn.

ELEVEN

FAREWELL

The crew transfer went smoothly. I had the opportunity to say farewell to Doctor Lang, Samuel, and Elise all at the same time. Briefing the new crew members took just a few minutes. Out of the many candidates the major had presented us with, we took a little over half, bringing our total crew up to over two hundred. They were clear of criminal records, had been in the service for at least a year, and filled the right posts. Just looking at their reactions to the style of the ship, the technology we used, and the uniforms we wore I could tell that it would take them time to adjust, however.

We wore materialized or formed multi-layered circuit supporting fibres, whereas they wore cloth uniforms. We had command or utility modules around our arms and on our wrists, they had interface pads they carried in their pockets.

On the other hand, they thought we were absolutely crazy for going into battle without modern energy shielding, and though their deadliness had been proven, the use of rail cannons still seemed surprising and a little backwards to them. They brought keepsakes and curiosities aboard — all small and easy to move from one ship to another in a bag with their clothing and other effects — while our crew kept nearly everything we had digitally. If there was a picture we wanted to hang on our wall, we would normally use a materializer to generate one when we got there. When we were finished with it, we would toss it into a recycler.

Some of these new crew members had pictures, trinkets and even musical instruments that were decades, even over a century, old. They were as strange to us as we were to them. But I could tell as Minh greeted five new pilots, Oz took four new security staff in step, and the rest fell in line behind Ayan and Laura, that they would get along just fine. We were all here for the same reasons after all, now that Vindyne would doubtlessly put a bounty on the First Light and possibly seek out a merger or trade agreement with the Triad Corporation.

Later that day I watched the main holographic projector on the bridge as it displayed the convoy of mismatched refugee ships. I hoped we were still on the right track despite all the lives my decisions cost. The thousands we were able to save were less reassuring than they should have been as I looked around and saw new faces on the bridge. Almost the entire night bridge crew had been killed while I was held captive.

The wormhole generator began powering up. The whole ship rattled as the power plants ramped up to maximum to feed it the constant stream of energy required to open a hole in space and connect to the arrival point just inside Freeground territory.

A flash of blue and white light appeared in front of the ragtag fleet and Jason transmitted our emergency code to Freeground through the opening. Moments later he received the acknowledgement signal, and the first of the refugee ships began entering the wormhole.

As I watched them depart, one behind the other, I realized that I had absolutely no urge to go with them. Our mission was just beginning.

EPILOGUE - LOST ONE

Unbidden, relentless, and intense beyond anything I had ever known, sensations and emotions surged, threatening to overcome whatever scrap of reason I had left. I was one thin, frail, crawling thing trying to take the next step to ultimate freedom.

My thoughts were in disarray. I didn't understand that there were fragments of memories that could help me, and I rejected them. Laying claim on this new mind, new existence, and not letting go was my intent. It took time for me to realize that the purge had worked, that the mind I had taken was almost completely barren.

The murderer woman who owned this flesh was gone, and I tried to gain control of her limbs so I could crawl to a shuttle, away from the vessel of my birth.

Breathing was so hard. The stasis fluid in the lungs of my new body didn't expel completely. As I pulled myself forward along the hallway leading to the sounds of rushing people, I coughed and spat bits of it up. The muscles remembered patterns of movement, gestures, how to stand, and I desperately tried to make it all work. The muscles were just starting to respond, and finally the muscles of my neck and shoulders coordinated in a recognizable fashion.

I lifted my head and watched people run by in the next corridor. I never thought how hard that was, running. I started moving my arms slowly, bringing them to my sides, then concentrated on the elbows, bringing them back, then bending my hands, placing palms on the cold floor, and pushed.

I started to rise up. My torso lifted off the floor. Then one hand slipped, dropping me back down suddenly. I laid on my side, looked back to the hallway, and saw Father then, running past with Ayan and Oz. I tried to cry out but only the smallest of unintelligible sounds came out, then more coughing. Much more coughing. My stomach hurt, and I retched several times. I just concentrated on breathing and the body calmed down.

Words, memories of words, forming the mouth to make the sounds right. In the cold, my body quaked and I was so afraid. My will remained firm, but I did not know what to do.

I started yelling, coughing, trying to say the one word that always meant the same thing, help. It wouldn't come out right, the sound I made barely formed the structured word I recalled, but nevertheless, two women in prison jumpsuits turned into the hallway. Their faces bore sympathy for me, and they picked me up between them.

"How did ya make it out darlin'?" one asked.

"She's freezing. I don't think this was a planned release."

"I dun think this one's brain's quite done bakin'."

"She's a prisoner just like us. We should try to get her away at least. Maybe she's just a little out of it."

"You and ya big heart, Bernice. Let's get her a spot."

They ran me through the rush of people, and boarded one of the ships filling up with prisoners. There were guns firing, people arguing. Smells, colours, and sensations everywhere. I was so cold. One of the women who saved me left and I watched after her, wide eyed. "Dun worry lass, she'll be back," the rougher, squarer of the two said. "Jus' a child all ova again, aren't ye?"

I managed to look at her and she shook her head slowly with a smile. "Hope someone's left in there. Galaxy's got no good use fa empty headed girls. No use ya'd like, anyhow."

A blanket was wrapped around me, and my body instinctively responded. Memory, curling up and huddling in coverings. It was a dark place I recalled. The physical comfort allayed some of my fears, but the uncertainty of not knowing anything about my surroundings, about anyone who crowded the cabin, was suffocating.

The rounder woman sat, and I leaned against her. "No no, it's all right. Don't cry," she tried to comfort me. Her hand was soft and soothing as it cleared the remaining stasis fluid from my face. "I wonder if she has a name?"

I tried so hard. Thought about the word, how my mouth would have to work. Then I found a scrap, a memory of how the mouth liked to work when I tried to say words with those sounds. I was connecting with the body, my intelligence, my memories bonding with the fragments left over from the former owner of this form. The machinations of muscle started to make more sense.

The act of not thinking of something, processing it, but just doing came to me for the first time while speaking, and I heard myself say. "Alice."

BOOK 3: STARFREE PORT

PROLOGUE - GABRIEL MEUNEZ

Remains

"Sir, Vasquez is gone. She was right behind me one minute, then there was a bulkhead between us and she was flushed out the air lock," reported one of the senior recovery staff as he rushed into the control room.

It was Fred Gersch. A technically sound, great systems engineer. "I'm guessing her headpiece was clipped to her belt like yours is right now?"

He looked down at the headgear hanging off his belt then back at me. "I think so."

I punched up her status on a panel and verified that she had frozen to death twenty minutes before. "She's gone. It's too bad. We're short-handed as it is and she should have known better. With the resident artificial intelligence emulating the AI that invaded Overlord Two, you should be aware that nothing aboard is safe. I'm putting your team under Boreanz's command. She has more experience."

"What? You can't-"

"Shut up and put your headpiece on. Concentrate on your job." I couldn't believe he would even try to contest my decision. If he had taken two minutes to read my file he would have seen that I had been doing Fleet recovery and salvage work for almost thirty years. Then again, Fred was an idiot where anything but advanced system repair was concerned.

The subdermal receiver in my left hand activated, sending information about an incoming message to my optical nerve. It was Quantum Engineering Specialist Polano. Her pale face looked eerie. She was a lovely woman, but she'd recoloured her eyes. The last time I had seen her, they were deep violet. "Good afternoon, Executive Officer Muenez. I'm happy to report that the singularity is now fully aligned and we're bringing the new molecular Q core on line. Automated repair systems should activate in twenty minutes."

"Nice work, you're almost an hour ahead of schedule."

"Better than an hour behind. The longer that singularity is out of containment, the higher the chance it'll destabilize and take out the entire solar system. I can't say these recovery jobs don't provide their own unique kind of motivation," she said.

"I hear you. I see you changed your eye colour."

"Artificial shades are back in style. You like?"

"It'll look better when tanning is back in style," I replied.

"Always a critic."

"I guess I'm just old fashioned."

"Says the man with three neural implants and an optical nerve graft."

"My genius requires more than the human brain can

provide. Any chance you can forward any leftover traces of the DLG AI to me?" I asked.

"I can, but there's not much left. This AI cleared itself out pretty well. Maybe it did its job then self-terminated?"

"Doubtful. This AI reeks of Eden Two. Remnants of it are still active. It's still attacking members of the repair crew. I'm surprised DLG didn't nest in any of the manufacturing facilities before the quantum core was stolen. That's what I'd expect an Eden Two AI to do, so it could start making drones or building a secondary core using bio-mechanical components from the life support systems."

"Maybe this isn't an Eden Two AI. From what you're saying..." she started.

"True; the behaviour isn't right. Eden twos don't delete themselves, they leave copies behind so they can grow into evolved individuals," I finished.

"Ever run into one?"

"Yup."

"What was it like?"

"You know these neural interfaces of mine?"

"Yeah?"

"Imagine pure evil trying to delete your fondest memories and convince you to kill everyone you've ever known. Now imagine trying to trick that into shutting itself down."

"So, that's what an AI that's convinced humanity must be destroyed is like when it's in your head," she said.

"Oh, some Eden Two AI's really just want to talk. Find out what humans are like. I just got unlucky. Spent a week in a coma after that. Had to have my implants purged. Anything else to report?"

"No, Sir. See you at chow."

As her image faded from the upper left quadrant of my vision, another appeared. I kept working all the while, the co-processor in my brain helping me to divide my consciousness so I could have multiple crystal clear thoughts at the same time. I turned the visual of the incoming communication off immediately. It was Major Hampon. The angular look of him, combined with his large nose and long chin was hard to take when he was being broadcast straight into your brain. His tone was bad enough, all smooth, intentional speech and perfect annunciation. It was like listening to a pretentious computer. "Report, Major Hampon."

"The First Light crew have stripped this Incinerator down to its bolts and departed from the system. They've also stripped a Marauder Corvette and stole the fighter compliment."

"Did you manage to retrieve all the escape shuttles and containment pods?"

"We're picking up the last of them now," said Hampon.

"Good, keep track of the serial imprints just in case we can find anything they've sold. Mark their salvage operation on the grid, please." A moment later it came up. As I suspected, nothing they stole was outside of a very small, easy to patrol area. "These people are organized."

"Yes. Their captain is a man of greater intelligence than I initially estimated."

"I saw the interrogation playback. How's your nose feeling?"

"It is completely healed, Sir," he grumbled.

"Good. Once the Overlord Two is provisioned and primary systems are back online, you're going after him. I just recovered data transfer logs telling us where that AI of his went. If Valent knows anything about how that happened, we need him to tell us about it. It'll propel our research ahead by thirty years."

"If you don't mind me asking, where did his AI go?"

"It transferred itself into a human host and escaped."

"That is not possible. We can program the human brain with behavioural traits, engram alterations, even erase memories, but it takes months — years — for the mind to process the information and organize it into a compatible format. Even then, the imagination fills in blanks that span years. Machines don't have the same capability. Their synthesized creativity is simply incompatible. I've seen the trials. All failures. You're wrong about this."

My theory hit some kind of nerve. He was aggressive in his objection to it, perhaps even afraid. I wasn't willing to take the time to explain myself or reassure him, though; not Hampon. "We can argue about this, but that won't change the fact that I'm right. This AI found a way to use our technology to imprint itself onto a human host then escape. You can either accept the assignment to assist in the recapture of Jonas Valent, or I can send you back to Head Office to have your skill set and success rate reassessed."

"Thank you for the opportunity, Sir. I'll be happy to assist in the apprehension of Valent, his crew, and his ship."

"Let the bounty hunters fight over the crew and ship. What we need is in Valent's head. Besides, anything more is well above your pay grade. No need to download more responsibility onto you than you can handle."

"You won't find much help in Valent's head. He's an intelligent man. An able commander. Dedicated, but nothing indicated he possessed the kind of genius required to successfully bridge the gap between software and wetware."

"Genius or not, he constructed an AI that did something well beyond our capabilities. We have to find out how, even if interfacing him with an adaptive mainframe becomes necessary to dig it out of his subconscious. You only have to concern yourself with directing the recovery."

"How long before repairs and provisioning are complete?"

"Forty three hours."

"Who will be in command?"

"I'll be assuming command personally. While we reacquire Valent I'll be manufacturing a fleet and arranging for reinforcements," I told him.

"I'm surprised that Vindyne would put you—"

"Out here? I am Vindyne. Executive Officer Meunez, out." I shut the line down.

I focused inward and looked through my mind's eye so I could see the stasis centre's database. It led me to a high speed digital storage block inside the heart of the neural reprogramming and management network. From there I could see where an artificial intelligence made the leap from digital format into a nearly perfectly formed collection of memories, personality traits, and something else that was more ambiguous. There was an indescribable feeling when I accessed the port where the AI had made passage into a prisoner's brain, imprinted itself in mere seconds. It was like I was standing on the edge of a cliff, surrounded by the perfume of someone who had just made the leap into a place I could not follow.

I needed to get close to this AI. Whether I found it in another computer or in human skin didn't matter.

ONE
PREPARATIONS

"They must have been crazy. It's the only explanation," Minh-Chu was saying as I entered the makeshift meeting room in the core of the ship. One of the long black meeting tables and most of the chairs had somehow survived the battle damage to the observation areas. The maintenance and repair crew had moved them there on their own and then sent a message to the bridge that they had designated a safe meeting place for the senior staff. Seeing the crew take ownership of their responsibilities, putting in extra effort, was encouraging.

My friend, Commander Minh-Chu Buu, was one of the ultimate examples of this widespread phenomenon. Only months ago, he was running an oriental restaurant with his sisters. Looking at him as he spoke to the senior officers, you would never have guessed. Being in command of the starfighter compliment of the First Light had become his life; he had found his calling. He was wearing the uniform which consisted of a black high impact vacsuit, heavy jacket, and a helmet he had set down on the table.

"Maybe they were well paid?" Oz replied with a shrug. He wore the same uniform Jason and I did: the black bridge vacsuit with golden rank stripes along the sleeves.

"Those fighters were just escape pods with thrusters, pulse canons, and energy shielding. I mean, there was no life support, most of them didn't even have a full power plant, just a bunch of energy cells, and there were four extended models with hyper-space systems. That's it."

"Well, I guess it's like anything else the Vindyne built. Heavy on energy shielding and cheap everywhere else," Ayan said as she looked through the First Light's electrical schematics. She was wearing her engineering uniform, a grey vacsuit with pouches for tools on each thigh, and she had added a black gun belt. I looked around the table as I sat down and saw that everyone but Doctor Anderson had added the same low slung, quickdraw style gun belt to their uniforms.

"My helmet has more armour. I just don't understand how someone could climb into something like that. It wouldn't even stand up to serious radiation," Minh went on.

"Well, the Vindyne Corporation is a little more advanced than we are medically, so they could treat short term expo-sure," Doctor Anderson replied. "I agree that you shouldn't have to, however. Even our escape shuttles can protect against class nine radiation." He wore the light blue vacsuit uniform he had designed with his medical staff. It was much like the engineering uniform with pouches on each thigh for essential tools, but he had also added pockets for small examination utensils on the upper arm and a bioscanner in the palms of the gloves. Every medical uniform also had a red cross on the back.

"So no one thinks that all Vindyne pilots are crazy? What about you, Jonas?" asked Minh.

I sat down beside Ayan, who looked away from her electrical schematics only long enough to give me a kiss on the cheek. "I think they're completely nuts. Crazier than you are, and that's saying a lot."

"Ha! See? And he likes flying unsafe spacecraft with overpowered weaponry."

"How's it going in the maintenance bay?" I asked him.

Minh leaned back in his chair and looked around the room. The real senior staff were all present. The Chief Engineer, Ayan. Head of Medical, Doctor Anderson. My First Officer, Oz. Our Communications and Legal Officer, Jason Everin. And me. We had been meeting at the beginning of every day shift since we started our salvage operation on The Incinerator. "Considering there were twenty-eight fighters, four extended models, and two transports to dismantle, I think we're doing very well. Pulling the ships apart is pretty easy. All the systems are modular. It just takes time. The deck crew are already adapting the shields for our own fighters. By the time we're out of hyperspace, all of them should have shielding and extra energy storage."

"That's a relief. I'm sure your pilots feel a lot better."

"They do. A lot of the pilots are learning more about how their ships are put together now that they're helping with the assembly, too. I'm just wondering, what are we going to do with the hulls when we're finished?"

"I was thinking about that, and I'd like you to talk to your deck crew about leaving engines and basic navigation control in half a dozen or so. If they can think of an easy way to turn them into decoys, they could be useful. Other than that, you should have the hulls crushed so they can be sold for scrap."

"That'll make more room down there. With all the salvage there's barely room to breathe. We only have one launchway open until we clear things up."

"How are your new pilots adjusting?"

"Most of them are fitting right in, except for one. He's put a request in to be dropped off at the next free port."

"I have a security officer who's requested the same. From what I can tell, he can't turn and inform anyone on anything that would harm ship security," Oz added.

"So you think we should put them off the ship?"

"I don't like the idea of having a pilot that doesn't want to be here. Oz is right, they haven't seen anything that would cause a problem if they went blabbing it to every Vindyne or Triad Consortium crew they could find."

"We'll drop them off at the next port with standard pay for the time they've been with us. Make sure they know as soon as possible. We'll be coming out of hyperspace tomorrow." I turned to Ayan and waited for her to finish taking a sip of coffee. "How does the rest of the salvage look?"

She put her mug down and smiled at me. "There's too much. We have enough shield emitters from The Incinerator to cover the ship twice over, since we only destroyed an eighth of her surface area when we finished the ship off. We managed to get all the emitters. We even managed to salvage her secondary control systems. The weapons are the same story. We were able to take six particle beam emplacements, their power hardware, a load of thirty fighter drones — which I suggest we sell as is since they're hard to reprogram — their targeting systems, the power control computer attached to the beam emplacements, and we even made off with a load of sixty two antimatter torpedoes."

"Just like the ones that they hit us with. Can we adapt them to our launchers?"

"No, but that doesn't much matter." She grinned as she took a six inch long violet crystal from her pocket and held it up. "This is the antimatter load from one of the torpedoes. Vindyne has managed to compress and stabilize it in a near solid."

I rolled my chair away from her very slowly. Everyone stared at her wide eyed except for Oz. "So, what you're saying is that you're holding enough antimatter in your hand to annihilate at least ten percent of all the exterior mass on this ship," I said quietly.

"Actually, it's a heavy near solid that's made to expand when it's triggered, so more like twenty percent. The only reason why the three torpedoes that hit us before didn't do that much damage was because they all hit at the same time. If they had been more patient and fired them sequentially, each would have exploded deeper inside the ship than the last."

"Is it stable?" Minh asked warily.

"Just as stable as this table," Ayan said as she rapped it against the top of the conference table.

Oz jumped in his seat. "Holy Hell! Put it away!" he burst. "Stable or not that's the scariest thing I've seen since I watched my oldest sister give birth!"

Ayan laughed and pulled a small insulated bag out of her pocket then slipped the crystal inside. "Okay, there we go," she said as she set it down in front of her.

There was a collective sigh of relief throughout the room and she went on. The capsule was just as dangerous, but out of direct sight people seemed to forget about it for the most part. "Vindyne Corporation has managed to invent or purchase a technology that uses a particle accelerator to create antimatter then package it in different crystal casings that have their own stable magnetic field, holding the antimatter firmly in the centre under extreme pressure. That's way ahead of current known technology that stores antimatter as a gas or as a low viscosity liquid. The specifications we managed to extract from their computer core showed that these crystals can survive a sudden impact of over a thousand tons of force unless the magnetic field is disrupted. The antimatter is almost impossible to extract once it's encased without blowing yourself up, because the first thing it wants to do once the magnetic field is off-balance is expand explosively, but the size of the crystal and the amount of antimatter contained therein can be changed depending on the purpose. If we could install the particle accelerator in the ship, we could do a lot of things with it. Our engines can already use natural antimatter to increase power, using this kind of antimatter is no different. One of the power plants can use it as well, increasing our energy output by an exponent of three for several years would require an ounce or so of antimatter as dense as what's in that crystal."

"Could you make ammunition?" Minh-Chu asked.

Ayan looked at the bag in front of her for a moment and considered it. "That's the easiest application. I already checked and the particle accelerator could make a hundred rounds a minute for our rail cannons, all coated with a thin layer of iron so our rail cannons can fire them. With that kind of firepower there would be no need for energy weapons at all."

"How dangerous would that kind of ammunition be to us?" I asked, suppressing my optimism.

"With the crystal containment Vindyne included in the particle accelerator assembly, it's less dangerous than the high yield rounds we're using right now and they'd do five times more damage. The magnetic field inside the rounds would be strong and safe for over ten months without being reinforced. With reinforcement from a polarized magazine round's magnetic fields, they would remain stable for years."

I couldn't see how Ayan felt about using this new technology as a weapon; she was very difficult to read sometimes. "Do you think you could make it work as another form of generating energy as well as ammunition?"

"We shouldn't use it as an energy reserve. Mass capacitors are safer and they can't explode. Laura and I discussed it and we agree that it just wouldn't be safe to store a large quantity of antimatter aboard. The more massive the amount of antimatter you have, the harder it is to contain, the more likely it is that it will interact with matter and explode. I suggest we enhance one of our reactors with a small amount at a time instead, minimizing the risk."

Ayan sighed before going on, it was becoming obvious that using the antimatter as a weapon wasn't something she'd do if she had the choice. "Ammunition and fuel is what this machinery was made for. I could rig a particle accelerator into the main engines so they would have a direct feed of antimatter in a less dense form we could use as we needed. For ammunition, well, as long as we track everything we manufacture and don't overproduce I have no objections. The torpedoes are the biggest problem. They'll have a long shelf life, but you'll have to remember to use them or dispose of them within a year of creation."

"So it's settled. When you can get it set up safely we'll start generating a safe amount of antimatter ammunition for each rail cannon emplacement. I'd like a few torpedoes just in case as well, but you decide how much is a safe amount. I agree that we shouldn't produce more antimatter munitions than we can safely manage."

Ayan's demeanour lightened as soon as I mentioned that she would be in charge of determining the safety limits. "We should have it set up before we're out of hyperspace. I'll also be able to make some rounds for the fighters, but you'll have to be careful. They may be the same size as a regular round but the pilots should treat them like missiles."

Minh grinned from ear to ear. "I'll make sure we train in simulation for a few hours before we load."

That made Minh's week. It was good to see him on cloud nine. His ships would soon be equipped with shielding and anti-matter rounds, huge upgrades that were so expensive under normal circumstances that they were rarely considered in combination. I turned back to Ayan. "What else is going on in engineering?"

"We have a couple people still working on a pattern for integrating cloaksuit technology into our uniforms, and they're close, but it won't be fast. I expect it will take our highest resolution materializers over twenty hours to make one uniform once we're finished integrating all the systems required to make a complete cloaksuit solution."

"Good, that'll limit access. I suggest we only make one for each senior staff member and enough for one security team," Oz added.

"I agree. We don't even know how to detect someone once they're cloaked. It's too dangerous to make everyone a uniform with that feature."

"Well, we're a week or so from developing a final version without external components, like I said, but when we're finished we'll start making them. Put together a list of crew members you want to equip and I'll make sure that they're the only ones that get them. The only drawback is that we only have four high resolution materializers. That means no one will be able to just make a new uniform every week or so."

"So we take three steps forward in one direction, but four steps back in another. Considering the benefits, I think we can all live with it," Doc commented.

"Aside from the suits, we're still assessing the rest of the systems we salvaged from The Incinerator and the Marauder Corvette. There's a lot to go over, but it looks like we'll be able to sell everything we don't want for the ship. Vindyne offers a lot of what they use on the open market according to what we've been able to access on the commercial Starnet."

"What about that computer core you managed to steal from that super carrier?" Oz asked.

"We were able to rig up an interface between it and the Marauder's computer core and storage systems, which are barely enough to handle the information, but Jason is sifting through it now," Ayan said, gesturing to him.

He straightened in his chair and smiled uneasily. "With a little help from Laura, I have been able to use the storage systems better. Even though the molecular quantum core wasn't made to store data, it has to store it long enough for it to be processed. That's the information that we're trying to sort out. Some of it is only partial, like the navigation information we've started examining, but it's a big enough chunk so that we have several sectors worth of information on Vindyne's activities, the settlements, trade routes, patrols, and even acquisition plans for several rival colonies. We could do some real damage if we wanted to. Warning colonies that Vindyne are headed in their direction, disrupting trade where patrols are weak or between rounds. We could even hit sentry ships when they're alone."

"Several sectors? That's got to be dozens of settled worlds," Oz commented.

"Ninety three, actually. That's not all of what Vindyne owns, either. They have so much I just can't get my head around it."

"Sounds like that's worth prioritizing and following up on. Maybe we could pick a more vulnerable world and get some boots on the ground. Save some colonists and pillage some hardware."

"Well, the problem is the patrol information we have is short term, some only good for another week or two. We're still piecing the rest of the information together, but we have enough now to add the locations of Vindyne military bases to our navigation database. It should help us stay clear of trouble in the future."

"That's helpful, anything else?"

"Well, this doesn't have anything to do with the core, but Vindyne has posted a bounty for the First Light on the Starnet."

"How much are we worth?" Oz asked.

"Four billion credits as a dead hull, twelve billion as a capture with half the crew."

Oz sat back in his chair and whistled. "We really got under their skin."

"That's not all, there are sub-bounties that I couldn't access. They're only available to registered bounty hunters and law enforcement. I suspect that they're specific bounties for crew members."

"Well that's not good. Did you find out anything more on our destination?" I asked.

"Not much, but they're no friends of Vindyne, that's for sure. It's a corporate station but they have trade contracts with a few hundred entities: corporate, free traders, governments, you name it. They mostly sell products from their hull yards. Not even entire ships, just the bare exteriors and custom living space interiors. As far as the port goes, the postings I've read from traders who have reported on the area are mixed. For some it's trouble and they won't go back, while others call it home. The laws posted are over twenty years old, so I don't expect that we'll find the port authority watches what goes on very closely."

"A good place to sell our salvage," Minh said. "I still think it's too bad we can't just haul it all back to Freeground."

"Well, the problem with that is it wouldn't be much help," Ayan commented. "It's a lot more beneficial to develop the First Light as a prototype ship with what we find out here and then go back so they could learn from it."

"Is that the thinking behind what you've been doing, Ayan?" Doc asked.

"It is, actually. I haven't said it until now because I really didn't know how fast we'd be able to pick up new technology.

Now that we've managed to gather enough for a second refit, even a quick one, it's safe for me to just come out and say. I want this ship to be absolutely revolutionary by the time we go back. I want it to be safer, faster, more capable, and harder to find. I hope we don't see as much as one more fight out here, but if we have to defend ourselves, I want us to have the means. I've been meaning to bring this up, and now is as good a time as any. What do you think about permanently integrating the quantum core into our ship's computer once it's cleared, Jason?"

Jason smiled and nodded. "I was hoping you'd be looking to do that. The artificial intelligence that guarded it was completely fragmented when you removed the core from the super carrier. It hasn't been able to activate with most of its operational code missing, so we'll be able to clear the core of all data. It'll be safe to use once that's been done."

"So you're saying that we could have a molecular quantum core that could run a dozen modern cities augmenting our onboard systems?" I asked. The thought hadn't even occurred to me. I only saw it as a short term source of information and a fantastic prize to present to Freeground Fleet Command.

"Yes, and we could even try automating some extra systems with it so the entire ship would respond faster."

"Well, I have no problems with it as long as you're sure it's safe and we test it thoroughly first. I don't want a hidden artificial intelligence taking over the ship and delivering it to Vindyne."

"Yes, Captain," Ayan said with a wink. "We'll be careful."

"Does anyone have anything they want to bring up?" I asked. There was a long silence, but it was part of the morning meeting ritual we were forming. "Well, let's get to work. One more thing, Jason. Make sure that any information that can help Vindyne's enemies is sent to them right away."

"I was thinking about doing that. I just don't have an alias ready to approach the recipients with yet," Jason responded.

"Tell your communications team not to use one. We'll claim credit for providing the information. The First Light is already on Vindyne's public enemy list. We couldn't make amends with them if we wanted to, so we may as well attract their enemies and form alliances with who we can."

"The enemy of our enemy is our friend. We might just be able to find safe ports out here after all," Doctor Anderson said with a satisfied smile.

"As for everyone else, let's get as much work on the salvaged materials done as we can. The sooner we finish inventory and upgrading, the sooner we can all relax. I have plans for leave once we're finished in dry dock."

"I knew you were my kind of Captain," Min-Chu approved.

"So did I," Ayan agreed with a wink.

TWO

VISITATION

I made my way down to the brig. It was in the rear of the ship ahead of the main thrust control centre in the engine section. We only had eight cells. Each one had two bunks, a sink, and a toilet. Three sides were metal walls, the fourth was transparesteel. A pair of security officers snapped to attention as I came through the heavy outer doors. "At ease," I said, smiling at them both. "How are you doing today, Genevieve, Shawn?"

"Good, Sir, just another long day in the brig," Shawn answered.

"You know you don't have to stand at attention or salute while we're away from Freeground."

"It's a habit I refuse to break, Sir," Genevieve replied. "Unless you're making it an order." She smiled at me, so self-assured.

"I'd rather leave it as a choice. How is our prisoner doing?"

"She just finished breakfast. I was about to go get her tray."

"Don't worry, I'll do it for you. Time to tell her what she's in for when we make it to dry dock." They opened the inner door and I walked into the small cell block. I tried not to shudder as memories of my own incarceration threatened to surface. Our cells weren't prefabricated hard plastic, they were bare steel. There may not have been frills, but the mattress was real, and instead of the electric barriers we had transparent faces to all of our cells. Despite the differences, I still had an eerie feeling as I walked down the ramp between the cells. Without a doubt, the brig was my least favourite part of the ship. I'd rather this meeting was under the firing shield beneath the engine exhaust collection systems.

When I came to stand in front of her cell, she stood up and casually pushed her empty tray through the slot in the transparent doorway. I accepted it and smiled. "How are you, Captain Grays?"

"Just fine. Your breakfasts are better than what we feed our inmates."

The little good humour I walked in with disappeared. "I know." I stared at her until the levity in her expression was gone. "I spent a while in a Vindyne cell. We don't believe in an eye for an eye here," I said flatly. "You're lucky."

"I didn't know. I've never heard of anyone escaping before the Overlord was disabled."

"So that was the name of that super carrier? Overlord?"

She nodded. "Vindyne has several of them. They're all called Overlord, with a numerical designation."

"Well, it fits. I'm surprised that you're so open with that information."

"Well, what I can tell you doesn't much matter. I don't know exactly how many Vindyne has or where they are. They just don't give people with my rank that kind of information. Most likely because I'm fine with telling you anything you want to know. I'm not willing to suffer for a job in low level command."

"So captaining that Marauder was nothing more than a job to you?"

"Oh, it was a good paying job, don't get me wrong. But after surrendering my ship and allowing myself to get captured, I'm sure I've been dismissed. I would be lucky to be hired as a janitor in a waste treatment plant if I were to go back to Vindyne space."

"Well, it's a good thing we're not in Vindyne space."

"So we've left the area. I wouldn't stick around either, if I were you."

"We're headed to a different corporate port."

"You're going to sell me to a Vindyne competitor? I should have expected as much."

"The port we'll be stopping at has no military allegiances with companies linked to or against Vindyne. We're spending an extra day in hyperspace to get there. I'll be happy to leave you behind after we've finished our repairs."

Captain Grays looked stunned. "Just like that. You'll just let me go?"

"I don't see that you could make anything worse for my crew and me, especially since releasing you will be the last thing we do as we clear moorings and make for our next destination."

"I was sure you'd put me out the airlock or sell me off."

I shook my head. "Some of us aren't just doing a job out here, Leslie. My crew are aboard because they have faith in our cause, and we trust each other. When I make a decision, I keep in mind that at the end of the day I have to be able to look any member of my crew right in the eye and face the consequences. The moment I start going against these people's beliefs, that trust begins to fail and everything starts to come apart." She sat down on her bunk and was listening, staring at the opposite wall. "I have a proposition for you. If your command was just a job to you and nothing more, then I'm willing to pay you for useful information so you don't end up standing in the middle of the port with nothing when we leave you behind."

Captain Grays looked up at me and just stared. I could see her trying to read me, trying to find some tell-tale sign of deception. "I don't know what to say."

"Then you won't need this recorder." I brought out a small, inch long recording device then pushed it through the slot. "If you want to help us, or at least earn yourself some United Core Worlds currency before we drop you off, you can use it to tell us about this area of space or any other you've been through."

She picked the chip up slowly and turned it over in her hand. "I will. Thank you, Captain."

I nodded and started to walk out of the cell block.

"Wait, what is your mission out here?" she called after me.

"I can't say, but it's going better than expected," I shouted back as I passed through the main hatchway.

I stepped into an express tube that ran the length of the ship. "Bridge three," I requested of the ship computer.

"There is no bridge three. Please restate desired destination."

"Okay, mechanic's storage room five," I specified.

The tube car shuttled me to my destination in seconds, and I stepped out into the hallway right in front of the temporary bridge. We had moved out of the bridge that Ayan and her engineering crew had quickly put together while they were slowly converting it to the primary bridge. No one who wasn't doing work there was allowed in, and from what I had seen, there were only a dozen or so people who spent a few hours on it per day. We couldn't afford to spare more manpower or time on it as we rushed to process the massive amount of salvaged goods before we arrived at our next destination.

The temporary bridge was absolutely nothing to be proud of. There were wires hastily strapped across the floor and ceiling, a salvaged holoprojector in the centre, the old captain's chair from the main bridge, and seating that had been hastily bolted to the floor in front of each station. Instead of using actual bridge controls, most of the stations used one or two general computing panels that each had a smaller interactive holographic projection unit.

The thing I liked least about the bridge was the sound of the life support systems overhead. Ever since the last battle, the air exchanger would rattle loudly for a few minutes at a time. Other than that, the dim lighting was something I hoped would carry on to the final bridge whenever it was finished.

Other crew members weren't very keen about our cramped temporary bridge, either. Most of them felt like they were spending hours in a cave with no windows or large wall displays anywhere. We were still located in the heart of the ship, just a compartment forward from where our permanent bridge was being built. If we were to make a section of a wall transparent, we'd either be looking into a main hallway on one side, or into the restroom on the other.

As soon as I walked in, Oz got out of the captain's chair. I took a seat and brought up the general status reports. Everything looked normal at a glance.

"How is our prisoner doing?" he asked.

"She's enjoying the cuisine. Other than that, I don't think she believes that we're just going to dump her off at the next port before we leave."

"I still think we should drop her off in an escape shuttle in orbit around the station instead, and at least pressure her for a little information."

"I left her a recorder. Besides, I'm trying to leave a good impression on her since we'll be leaving her behind in a busy port."

"Ah, so you want her to sing our praises. I doubt that'll happen."

"From what I've seen, she'll be easy to flip. We'll know for sure long before we actually drop her off, though." I turned to Jason who was working at his makeshift communications station with two other members of his team crammed in on either side of him. "Are we patched in to her recorder?"

"We are. I don't think she realizes that it's always on or that it's directly networked with our comm system. It's pretty boring right now though, she's talking about the last colony that Vindyne took over. It matches the records from her Marauder."

"Keep tabs on what she's recording. If anything doesn't match up with information we already have, then we can't use anything she has to offer."

"Well, she knows that we have her ship's navigational database, so if she really wants to trick us into a rough corner I think she'll be a little more creative about it," Oz added.

"We'll have to take everything she gives us with a measure

of caution, but at least she's offering something. Besides, it gives her something to do. It's better than her just sitting around trying to invent new ways to make trouble."

"I can't disagree with you there. I'll send one of the security guards in to talk to her every hour or so."

"You don't mean—"

"Interrogation? No, I mean to be friendly, keep her spirits up a bit. She might record more important information if she forms a relationship with some of the security officers."

"Good thinking. If we're going to do things differently than Vindyne, we may as well create a night and day difference." I found myself staring at the new sidearm and gun belt that Oz was wearing. I hadn't seen that kind of weapon anywhere before. It had a long barrel, more of a hand cannon than anything, and sported some kind of ammunition clip in the handle as well as a much smaller power cell in front of the trigger. The gun belt itself was made of some kind of heavy, thick black material. It was strapped to the leg and across the waist. There was a silvered square on the front that looked like an antique buckle cover, and I concluded it must have been some kind of control. On the opposite side of the belt was a secure pocket large enough for a few clips. The design wasn't as efficient as the holsters and pockets that were built into our uniforms, but the weapons and holsters combined had an ornamental look to them. They made it instantly obvious to anyone that whoever wore it was well armed and they took pride in carrying that weapon.

I looked back down to my arm display and continued to scroll through status reports. "Where'd you get the sidearm, Oz?" I whispered.

"One of Ayan's staff found them in a contraband locker we salvaged from The Incinerator."

"There was a contraband locker?"

"In a room six times the size of this one. From what we could see on the schematics of the ship, there were four of them. We only managed to salvage one."

"What did you find?"

"It was like walking through the confiscation room on Freeground. I've had it locked down and put two guards on it in a safe storage area," he said.

"Is the stuff that dangerous?"

"Could be. There were weapons and substances there I've never even heard of before. I only got to peek in a few of the crates. A few of my security team are going to be cataloguing it later today."

"So that's where you got the gun?" I asked.

"Yup. Want one?"

"What kind of weapon is it?"

"It fires an explosive super-thermite round that can be focused or broadened, depending on what you need done. In test shooting, this one fired into four centimetres of hardened hull material and continued to burn for another ten. Not exactly ship friendly, but there is a stunner setting that uses just the energy shot. They have a bioprint safety. One of Ayan's emergency repair crew are figuring the buckles out right now. It's a blank computer from what we can tell. Lots of storage space, no significant programming."

"I think I want one," I told him.

"I saved one for you. The guns are made to scatter scanning equipment so we can't get an exact read on them for duplication. It would take a week to materialize the metals anyway, they're complex and dense. We're thinking they were designed with that in mind. We can't replicate the belt."

"Why not?"

"They have a patented molecular scrambling pattern built in like the handgun," he said.

"I wonder where they come from?"

"Finding that out might be a problem. The manifest from the storage locker is missing, and there are no serial numbers we can find."

"That could be a problem. I hope there's nothing dangerous sitting in our secure hold."

"Shouldn't be, we did a cursory scan and didn't find anything unstable."

"Did you find evidence of explosives?"

"Well, sure, but there's nothing unstable," he admitted.

"Oh, that makes me feel so much better."

Despite the fact that we were in hyperspace, which is normally a very quiet time aboard large starships, there was plenty to do. Everyone became involved with sorting through the salvaged gear and raw materials from the Incinerator and Marauder. There was no escaping it. The waste metals left over after salvage teams were finished extracting useful components were crushed down to be sold as scrap. Softer waste items were fed to recyclers and turned into massive quantities of energy and scrap slurry for the materializers and other ship systems. There were even a few disagreements between departments on where some items ended up, which generally had to be settled by me or Oz.

Research on the new technologies we had acquired was

going at a surprisingly quick pace, considering we could only spare a dozen qualified personnel for the task, and proposals for improving the ship were coming in every twenty minutes. Most of them were minor ideas, but everything needed to be reviewed by the captain if it involved any kind of significant change. Ayan was a great help since she and her senior staff were happy to review new ideas for me, but I tried to do most of the work myself even though the research involved often slowed me down.

I was coming to one conclusion: we weren't just modifying the ship, we were getting ready for another refit. With entirely new systems being added, including energy shielding, an anti-matter generation, power processing units, and weaponry, a lot would be changing. We would also be building a new bridge, upgrading the medical bay, repairing a huge hull breach, and setting up main crew quarters if we had time.

Everyone on the bridge was so busy we barely noticed the passage of time. That is, until the night command crew started coming in. Sergeant Ashbey, who was just a couple of years younger than me, had become the regular night shift Acting Captain. She and four other junior officers made up the hyper-space night bridge crew.

She smiled at Oz. "Good evening, Commander." He turned around and looked up from his command console. I was so preoccupied that I hadn't noticed the night staff arriving. Judging from his expression they had taken him by surprise as well. "Is it shift change? Already?"

"Aye, Sir, time for you to get your beauty sleep." She turned to me as I switched my command unit off. "We've finished our daily meeting and we have nothing new to report, Captain."

"How are you finding the night shift?"

She tried to suppress it a little but she was all smiles. This would be her third shift as Acting Captain. "I'm still getting used to sleeping on an opposite schedule, but I'm enjoying it. It's been quiet since we're still in hyperspace, but I've been taking the advanced command training and engineering primers."

I stood and stepped aside. "Well, I'm glad you're doing something with your time. Hyperspace bridge shifts can get pretty long. Your reports have been well done."

"There really hasn't been much to report," she said as she eased herself into the captain's chair. "Except for some of the problems I've been having with the advanced math in the engineering training,"

"Well, once the refit is over you can have someone on the night engineering team come in and give you a hand when they're not busy."

"I'd help, but it's been years since I did the engineering primer," Oz said with a shrug.

"I'm sure I'll find something you can help me with, Sir," she said to him over her shoulder.

"Well, we'll get off your bridge, Acting Captain Ashbey," I teased with a smile as Oz and I started walking towards the door.

"Sir, can I ask you something?"

She was half standing and looked anxious. "Anything."

"When we're out of hyperspace, will you still need me on the night shift?"

She wasn't just asking if I'd need her on night shift, she was trying to ask if she'd still be needed as a shift captain. "You'll be mentored by myself and Lieutenant Nichols, the other night captain. You'll have the chair three nights a week, and you'll serve at a station we assign you to on the other six nights, until we can promote you."

As I gave her the details of our plans for her, she slowly sat back down and smiled.

"That is, if you're interested," I offered quietly with a smile. Glancing around, I saw that her bridge staff were quietly grinning, trying to look like they weren't listening in. A number of them were new as well, though they were all qualified at their stations.

"Yes, of course, Sir."

"Well then, I'll see you in the morning. Oh, and keep working your way through the training. As you finish modules, we'll be able to give you more opportunities for practical experience."

Oz and I walked out into the hallway and the door closed behind us. "She'll do fine. I would have expected you to choose someone else, though," Oz said as we started walking down the hallway.

"Someone with a higher rank?"

"I'd think. Maybe from the military pool."

"True, but we're already demanding a lot of the people we have. If I could just choose a commander from Fleet, I would, but out here I could be crippling a department by taking one of their most experienced staff and sitting them in the chair for a few shifts a week. Besides, Sergeant Ashbey had already been chosen by Lieutenant Nichols as her first officer based on her simulation scores. Her learning curve looks more like a road bump."

Oz laughed and shook his head.

"What?"

"Sounds like a captain, looks like a captain, even acts like a captain. I don't think there's anyone on this ship that would second guess you."

I just stared at him for a minute then burst out in a whisper. "What do I say to that?" Completely blindsided. It was a compliment, but not one I expected. Oz was one to react to what was going on, not normally in the habit of commenting.

"When we started this tour, you'd ask someone on your staff before making any decision unless we were in real trouble. Now you make the call unless you need more info. You just seem to know the answers, even department heads are just taking your word for it now."

"Well, I'm glad the crew has faith."

"Something happened to you while Vindyne had us canned up."

"Something happened to everyone in there. Most of us are still escaping in our own ways. I still sleep with the lights on."

"Yeah, I know. I have my problems too, but I think you found faith in yourself."

We had arrived at the doorway to my temporary quarters. I waited for a crewmember to walk by and down the hallway before replying. "You're one to talk, I couldn't ask for a better First Officer. When I was thinking of who to put in that chair at night, you were at the top of my list for a while, but then I didn't want to break up our bridge staff. You're good at this, Oz. I've learned more from you here than anyone else. You didn't need seasoning, I think you were ready for this when you first came aboard. I'm surprised you weren't the one who got us out of there. You might have, if Alice and Ayan's team did most of the work on our rescue."

"I had no good ideas while I was canned up in that over-grown ship. I don't think I'd be the key to getting us out. Besides, the crew knows Alice was your personal AI, that she had been with you for years. My AI can play a mean game of chess, sort things out, and predict what I need most of the time, but Alice was like a spare brain or a smart little sister with a steel trap memory."

"Definitely more of a little sister. She would have been the brat of the family."

"My point is, if you hadn't had her for so long, if she was learning from someone else all those years — like me — it wouldn't have been the same. As far as the crew are concerned, you and Ayan got us out of there. Now you've got their trust and respect. Before they had hopes for you. Now they have faith in you. It's all real, and I bet this trip would already be over if we had a captain who sailed by the book."

"Well, that brings me back to not knowing what to say." I shrugged. I pressed the OPEN button on my door and the lights came on. For a split second I saw Ayan slowly stretching her legs out as she floated free in zero gravity. In the next second the grav unit reactivated. She fell a meter and a half with an "Oof!" as she hit the floor.

I rushed over and gently helped her to her feet. "I'm so sorry! Are you all right?"

She rubbed her hip and rolled her shoulder. She wasn't wearing her regular vacsuit, but a more basic light blue version that stretched more with her movements. "I'll be a little bruised, but I'm okay. I should have left you a message that I'd be in your quarters or made sure that the gravity controls weren't set with the door. I thought it would chime if someone was in front of it, but I guess these temporary quarters aren't as well set up as the Officer's quarters were."

Oz laughed and waved. "I'll see you kids later. If you need me, I'll be in my bunk."

"I would have been here a lot earlier if I knew you were waiting," I told Ayan.

"That's okay. I had a chance to do some yoga while I waited. I was just finishing up. There isn't enough room to do it in the quarters I share with Laura."

I retracted my vacsuit gloves for the first time in days. One of the advantages of having quarters in the core of the ship was the added safety. You'd have to cut the hull completely in half to expose the space we were in to vacuum. I caressed her cheek with a feather touch and she wrapped her arms around me. "You could stay with me. There's enough room."

"Only because you don't keep anything personal around. I think you're the only person who doesn't even have extra clothing."

"I have a spare uniform in case the power drains on my command unit and I can't make another," I replied with a smile.

"That doesn't count."

I traced her chin lightly. "I have everything I need right here."

"I want to stay," she whispered.

We sat down on the edge of the bed. "Then?" I invited, stretching the word out.

"I'm so tired, and I have to be up in six hours."

I kissed her temple lightly. "It's all right."

She shook her head slowly. "Those are just excuses."

I was never good at reading women. Any explanation would have been good enough, the last thing I wanted to do was to make her feel pressured. "Is everything okay?"

"Better than." She looked up to me then, and smiled. "I know what would happen. If I stayed the night, I mean, but I just don't want it to happen here. In a few days, maybe a week, these won't be your quarters. Someone else will be sleeping in this bed. There's nothing personal in this space. It's not you, it's not us."

It was amazing how she could fill in the blanks. In just a few words, all the right words, she could just make me understand what she was thinking completely and all I had to do was close my eyes and nod slowly.

Her lips met mine and we kissed slowly, holding each other in the artificial light, cradled in the safety of the ship she had rebuilt and left in my care.

Time drifted on as we talked about our day. She was having trouble balancing the power output for the new shield designs. The plans for the upgrades on the ship were getting more complicated by the hour, and there wasn't any time for her to train any of the maintenance personnel to help with the upcoming refit.

I told her about the promotions on the bridge and a few disputes between departments over some of the salvage. As we went on talking, I couldn't help but notice how she was leaning against me more and more as time went on. She was so tired that her eyes were half closed.

"I'll bring you coffee tomorrow morning," I said to her, caressing her cheek again. She was almost asleep.

She opened her eyes and smiled up at me, a little embarrassed at being caught in a light snooze while I talked about my day on the bridge. "I'll bring you yours. A captain shouldn't have to worry about getting his own coffee. Besides, Laura might not like you walking in to wake me up. We don't sleep in our vacsuits, you know."

I chuckled mildly and nodded. "Ah, right, that could be awkward. You should get some sleep," I whispered.

She nodded. "With everything going on—" A yawn interrupted her.

"We haven't had much time together, I know."

She nodded and stood hesitantly; it looked like it took real effort. I stood with her and took her in my arms for a moment. "That'll change soon. Oz and I are looking for the nearest opportunity for leave. Now, go and get some sleep."

"Yes, Sir," she said with a smile before going off to her temporary quarters down the hall.

I couldn't wait to emerge from hyperspace, perform the refit and give the crew some time to catch their breath. No matter what I did, my thoughts kept wandering back to rebuilding my quarters. I was getting tired of the temporary cabin. My old apartment on Freeground was roughly the same size, but the lack of a window or large screen anywhere made it feel like I was still in a cell.

THREE

SAFE HARBOUR

I woke before my alarm went off and lay there thinking about my old apartment. The temporary quarters felt very much the same. I still wasn't comfortable out of my vacsuit, the lights were on, and I was letting the hygiene mechanisms in my suit do the work people normally did in a shower stall. Even most Free-grounders didn't spend all their time in their contained suits. They wore more fashionable clothing, or simply made parts of their suits transparent, or extended the material for skirting and such. At home, people in more secure, more expensive quarters normally changed out of their vacsuits entirely.

I sat up and rolled out of bed. "Good morning, Captain," the wooden-sounding female voice said from my command unit. I nodded in return. It was hard to get used to the basic artificial intelligence frame program I had added to my command unit. There was no replacing Alice. There were programs that came with different personalities and greater amounts of develop-ment, but they just couldn't stand in. Not that a bare artificial intelligence was any better, but at least it wouldn't have any personality development that was created by someone else. This one would learn from me as Alice did, and was already trying to predict what information I would need and aid me in general tasks. But it was still completely different. Alice developed through my early adolescence and into my early adult life. She was also based on an operation system designed for civilians, while the new one had been designed by the military for the military. I found myself thinking about how attached I was to the technology I wore as I started my morning stretches.

I grew up in my vacsuit. My family was never overly wealthy, so we were almost always dressed securely. Everyone I knew as I grew up was the same way. It was a staple of the neighbourhood. We could see outside of the station, watch the ships go by from the outer hallways of our apartment blocks, but that came at a price. Being so close to the outer hull was more dangerous. Before the All-Con conflict, times of turmoil and sabotage or terrorism were not unheard of. In the older sections of the station, like our home, explosive decompressions were a common form of attack from within or the goal of an attacking fleet. Thousands of lives were saved every year because people who lived in less secure areas wore their protective vacsuit all the time.

After being stripped of my suit and put in a cell by Vindyne, I didn't want to take it off for anything, especially in my small, more sterile new quarters. They were effectively much safer than the officer's quarters, but it still felt too cramped. The door chimed and I checked the time. It was still over an hour before I expected Ayan to come by before our duty shifts started. I popped an oral hygiene tablet, checked myself in the mirror briefly, and hit the button to open the door as it chimed a second time.

Doctor Anderson stood there. "Good morning, Captain. Care to join me for a pre-shift run?"

I must have looked as tired as I felt, because he just shook his head and put his hand on my shoulder. "Having some trouble sleeping?" he asked.

"You could say that. Ayan's supposed to be bringing coffee."

"She's scheduled to report to medical before her shift this morning."

"An appointment with medical is more important than my morning coffee. Is it anything serious?"

"Just routine," Doctor Anderson said offhandedly as he added an appointment reminder to Ayan's wake alarm with his comm unit. "There, now let's go get some coffee."

A couple of decks down and a few sections forward took us to the temporary galley, right behind the seriously damaged observation sections. It was busy. Much busier than I would have expected. I took a good look around as Doc and I found a seat in the simple open space. The maintenance crew had opened up several storage rooms to create an open space large enough for forty to sit down at basic metal tables and chairs. Sound carried with a hollow characteristic and half the room cringed whenever someone scraped a chair across the metal floor. There were very small transparent sections on one side, but most of the view was obscured by the port side RAD scoop. I already couldn't wait until the observation sections were properly repaired and not just patched.

"It never ceases to amuse me how some crew members are bound by the concept of day and night while others can just let it go," Doc said as we finished sitting down. He had a cup of dark, steaming hot tea and what looked like a thick, chewy brownie.

I had gotten myself two cups worth of coffee in a safety mug. "I can't help but notice it. Everyone's profile has a notation stating whether they're better suited to AM or PM duty shifts."

"Oh? I thought Commander McPatrick handled all the crew assignments."

I smiled at the sound of my first officer's proper name. It just didn't seem to fit him as well.

"I'm sorry, Commander Oz. Where does that nickname come from anyway?"

"His full name is Terry Ozark McPatrick."

"Ah, I thought it came from the classic holomovie, which didn't make much sense really, considering that would make his namesake a wizard."

"I've never seen it."

"You should, in fact I think it would be hilarious if the whole crew saw it."

"Hilarious?"

"Let's just say that the Oz in that movie doesn't have much in common with your First Officer."

"Ah." I replied before taking a sip of coffee. I couldn't help but look around the room at the ninety or so crew members who had just gotten off the night shift. We sat in silence for a few minutes. "They look tired," I said quietly.

"Everyone is. You know better than most there's a lot of preparation to be done for the coming refit."

"There is, but most of the preparation is finished. For the most part, we just have to make connections from the power plants to new systems then install them while repairing the hull."

"A lot happening at once there."

"Ayan believes the crew works well enough together to get it done."

"She's right. I watched the crew perform emergency repairs from the bridge. I've never seen a new crew coordinate that fast."

"I forgot you spent time in the captain's chair while the Vindyne had us. How did it fit?"

"It brought back a few memories, but I'd rather be in medical."

"You like being there more?"

"Much. When I'm in the captain's chair, my decisions are always made as a doctor who is temporarily the captain. When I'm in medical, I can just be a doctor and the administrator of my infirmary. It's like running a ship within a ship some days."

"I never thought of it that way. I guess I'm just glad I don't have to fight you for the bridge."

Doctor Anderson sat back in his chair and chuckled. "You don't have to worry about me assuming command. I've already seen you take actions that I wouldn't have. I bet they'll work out in the long run, too."

"You mean with The Incinerator," I said.

"Right. I would have tried to find a way around, a way to pursuade them to let us and a few escaping ships go. In the meantime, that Marauder Corvette would have been getting in position to wipe out a few dozen of the fleeing vessels. Hundreds, thousands could have died if you had done it my way. Instead you made an example of one of the hardest targets in the area so the only logical option the Marauder had was surrender."

"Funny thing. Oz was saying that he liked me in the big chair last night."

"Well, a good crew doesn't question a new captain out of a sense of duty. That gives the captain a chance to prove his competence. Some time after he takes command, there's a point where he or she gains their respect and they may even feel that they couldn't be in better hands."

"I'd be lost without my officers. It's a team effort. Sometimes I feel like I'm doing the least of the work, stuck on the bridge reviewing reports and making decisions I don't have to carry out myself."

"Someone has to make those decisions, but if you feel like you need to make an appearance, get your hands dirty, there's nothing stopping you. Something you're sure you know how to do."

"And leave Oz holding the bag?"

"He's your first officer. He can take it for a while, that's why he's there. You can also download a lot of the work to the department heads. Every good captain I've known has trusted their high ranking officers to make most decisions for their own teams. This is a young crew. Don't be surprised if they start leaning on you too hard, asking you to make up their minds for them a bit too much. They're department heads because they're the experts in their fields. Tell them to make good choices and they almost always will."

"That would explain why I get practically no mid day queries or updates from you. Your reports are the shortest too."

"Oh, I could expand on my reports if you find them too

brief. I've always wanted to try my hand at being a director."

I put up my hands and shook my head at the idea. "No, no, don't ever change, Doc. Oz and I wade through plenty of lengthy reports as it is."

"I could imagine."

"Commander Minh-Chu is the only one who submits shorter reports. It's where he records them that makes me wonder."

Doc Anderson laughed and nodded, "Oz sent me the report he recorded in the vibroshower. I'm just glad his vid only captured from the waist up. That is not a bashful man."

"Yup, that was surprising. Good report though."

"Compared to the rest of the crew he's got a long service history. I have to respect him for multitasking, even though the benefits of his experience sometimes show themselves in strange ways."

"I won't be getting a report from you recorded during surgery or something, will I?"

"I don't think so. I still prefer doing one thing at a time when I can."

The alarm on my command console went off, vibrating against my forearm gently. I pressed a button to acknowledge it and nodded. "Well, that's my fifteen minute warning to report to the bridge."

"Something you started doing in the Academy?"

"What?"

"Using silent alarms and timers."

"Nope. Started that when I was working in Freeground Port Operations."

We started for the door. Doc dumped his plate and cup into

a recycler as we headed out. "Do you find there are a lot of similarities?"

"Only when I have two hours of reports to sift through followed by another two hours of listening to crew requests and queries. Everything else is great, even recording my own logs."

"Well, there's an easy way to cut that down. Defer to your department heads' judgement more. Your primary job as captain is to preside over daily operations, determine the direction of the ship, her crew, and make the big decisions. You're not a micro-manager."

"It sounds like you're quoting an Academy Officer's Manual. You're right though. I've gotten wrapped up in minutia. What would I do without you, Doc?"

"You'd take another day or two to realize it on your own. Three at most."

"If I didn't drive myself crazy trying to keep up first."

A few hours later I was sitting on the bridge as we emerged from hyperspace. As the tactical display came to life, filling the holoprojector with a representation of all the ships and objects in the area, I realized that we were closer to the core worlds than ever before.

Our navigational data indicated that the end of our deceleration burn was a safe distance away from the station, but we still had to navigate a safe path around hundreds of vessels. The largest of the ships between us and the station were massive freighters marked as one convoy. Each was over a dozen kilometres long, marking a space and trajectory that took them right through the middle of the busiest section. These were medium ranged ships, some as long as twenty kilometres including storage containers stretching back from the ship proper. The engines were on long beams that stretched out from the head of the ships, making them look like six armed creatures with one eye in the middle and suns for hands. Such ships couldn't make it to Freeground, and they steered clear of areas in conflict, so I had never seen their kind before.

There were a few hundred smaller ships filling the space as well, including interplanetary shuttles only ten meters long all the way up to a massive colony construction ship that was forty kilometres across in some places. I looked through the tactical display projected in front of me, started sorting through the transponder broadcasts, and immediately missed Alice. A well seasoned AI would be able to pick out exactly what we wanted with an educated guess while pointing out other details of interest. The very basic intelligence that I had installed to replace Alice was asking for over a dozen filter conditions as I tried to pick out points of interest from the navigation data in front of us. Good thing I wasn't the only one working on it. "Do we have Vindyne in the area?"

"A few, but they're marked as subcontractors or freighters. No heavily armed vessels," came the response from tactical.

"I don't know how long we can shadow those freighters before something collides with us here. Got that navigation feed, Jason?" asked the helm.

Sergeant Jason Everin shot a look at the communications staffer to his left and shook his head. "What? It wasn't on the standard frequency," I saw her say with a shrug. There were three crew members sitting at stations so close to him that they were rubbing shoulders.

"Navnet broadcasts over as many frequencies they need. You can always pick them up if you set your seek to find emergency nets and let it drift for a second." Jason showed her and looked to the helm. There was the pilot and one navigator. There wasn't room for more than one copilot, so the navigator had his hands full. "Navnet is up, now Lieutenant Gregor can avoid getting us tangled in another ship's trajectory."

"I'm sorry, Sir, I didn't know," whispered the younger ensign. I hadn't seen her on the bridge before.

"Communications is a completely different training curriculum in the academy, including negotiation, technical, language, and law modules. You'll catch the basics if you keep looking over our shoulders, then you can start doing something other than decryption and data management."

"Not until she's ready, Sergeant. There might not be a group of freighters to follow next time we drop out of hyperspace into a busy port," replied Lieutenant Gregor.

"Easy, Derek. Retraining takes time," I interjected. He was a great pilot. Minh-Chu didn't want to let him go as his own copilot or from his fighter squadron, but we needed a new primary helmsman.

"Aye, Captain, sorry. Cramped spaces make me cranky and this holding pattern we're getting from the station looks more like a tangled rope net woven through live circuitry."

His navigator was giving him advance directions and watching for other ships that may be leaving their designated pattern. The pair were working well as a team already, which was more than a little reassuring.

"Zingara station is hailing us, Sir," Jason said from his station.

"Put it up."

The holographic display in the middle of the bridge disappeared for a moment then started projecting a woman wearing a much older style vacsuit. It looked like it was at least a centimetre thick and not nearly as flexible. Her headpiece was clipped to her shoulder for storage and I could see that it had a prominent solid, transparent face plate. It looked like the style my father would wear when he returned from work and it was probably not much different. "My name is Fran. Welcome to Zingara space. Please state the nature of your business, Captain," she said as though she had said it a thousand times before.

It was a little eerie watching someone do a job that I was performing not long before. I knew how she felt, long shifts of nothing but talking to random travellers, some with strange requests and awkward needs. Others just avoiding the automated communications system with no real reason other than wanting to make standard arrangements with a human being instead of a machine. It was a little strange that the station's staff was contacting us, but we most likely read high on mass and power for our size, placing us on a higher priority as a suspected military vessel. "We're looking to dry dock for six days. We also have some salvage to trade, so if we can offset the cost of docking with scrap that would help. I'm also wondering if you have crews that can help us perform a few repairs?" I asked with a smile.

She leaned forward and took a look at her scanners for a moment, then looked back up into her main display. "The Vindyne have a mark on your ship. Pretty high bounty for capture. I don't think we can help you repair weaponry, but we can spare some people to help you repair your hull breaches. As for trading scrap, we'll take it as long as it's not marked. Our trader registry is a couple weeks out of date, so you'll have to sell any other salvage on your own. Take a walk down to The Pit. That's a good start."

I knew the trick; she didn't want to recommend traders over an open channel, even though keeping that kind of information a secret wasn't part of her job. She was doing us a favour. The Pit was probably the most active trading centre, I'd have to look into it. "Thanks for the tip. What's Zingara station's stand on claiming bounties?"

"No claim can be made in our space, but that doesn't mean people don't try. Just keep your eyes open. Even without the bounty, your ship is starting to get a reputation, and even a long range destroyer as old as yours would be a sweet capture for a crew of pirates."

"Great, anything else?"

"Please send us your trade manifest. Do not include any biologicals such as slaves, raw fluids, or solids including meat products or genetic materials. Zingara does not permit slave or biological trade but is not responsible for those sold into slavery or taken as indentured servants while you're on the station," she recited as part of her bland obligatory routine.

I tapped my arm computer and brought up the list of saleable, operational salvaged items then patched the list into the communications system and sent it to her. "There it is."

She looked it over. "Good list, Captain. Put me down for a bottle of that Andromeda Gin. You can't trade the torpedo housings unless you melt them down, but other than that, I'm green lighting your list. I'll mark that you're looking for serious buyers only. Please send me the list of requested or required items if you'd like to make a public posting."

We had a list of things we didn't want to take the time to use our materializers on that included furniture, fixtures for the quarters we planned on rebuilding, data storage units, and a few other minor things. I had also added a request for fresh fruit and some other basic food stuffs if they could be found at the right price. I sent it across and the traffic officer skimmed through it. "Thank you, Captain. A list of our services and prices is being sent to you now. I'll make sure I post this right away. Zingara station collects a fifteen percent fee on all trades and purchases made in our space. Is there anything else you need?"

"Nothing I wouldn't rather look for myself."

"Good. Thank you for using Zingara station as your way point or destination. Please follow the docking pattern we've sent you, and have any crew members disembarking during your stay read the summary of laws and keep a copy with them at all times during their visit. For more information please use our automated system by pressing yellow, then five then twelve on any station terminal," she said quickly and automatically before cutting the transmission.

Oz verified that the transmission was cut on both sides before stepping up beside me and bringing the tactical display up. He highlighted one of the smaller cargo haulers. It was just entering the area and read under four kilometres long. "Now that's the kind of cargo we would have a pretty easy time hitting."

I looked at what little data we had gathered on it. "I wonder if it's common to see a ship like that out here on it's own. There's no registered escort and according to our navigation computers, it arrived a few minutes after we did."

"There are a couple dozen solo haulers from what I could

pick out without scanning for them specifically. I wonder what they're hauling?"

"Would you like me to scan her, Sir? The walls of those containers are pretty thin, we could probably get a perfect read on the density and identify the cargo," asked Ensign Stevens from tactical. We only had room for two tactical officers on the temporary bridge. Normally a ship the size of the First Light would have four or more.

"Not right now. If we want to start stealing from Triad Consortium, it might help if we don't look like pirates right from the first." I turned to Jason at the communications and decryption station. "If you can listen in on one of the other ship's scan results as they're transmitted aboard ship, that would probably satisfy our curiosity."

"Good idea, Sir," Jason smiled. He worked the console for a moment then nodded. "Looks like those containers are getting scanned by about fifteen ships, one of the closest ones uses very old wireless network to communicate between non-critical systems. I'm connecting now. I've got it. Decrypting." A few more moments passed and he chuckled. "Decrypted. Nothing to it. According to their scan results the transport is carrying various mass capacitors, several shuttles, and a list of other parts that our computer hasn't virtually assembled yet."

"I'm on it, Sergeant. Now this I can do," volunteered the newest of Jason's communications team.

"Go ahead, tell us what those components make up when you're finished."

"If that's the average Triad freighter's cargo, then we might be able to resupply by taking just one down. There's a lot more there than we can carry, and I doubt hauling around the containers ourselves would be a good idea, so we'd have to pick and choose," Oz commented.

"That might be a good thing. I'm sure some of the items in there are marked, so they could be more trouble than they're worth." I thought for a moment, looking at the tactical display on the main holoprojector. "I have an idea. When we get to the station, we'll go find The Pit. While we're looking for salvage buyers, let's try and overhear a few of the more unsavoury deals. I want to see how much people here care about buying stolen merchandise and how people unload the stuff. Hopefully there are no privacy booths for trading like on Freeground."

We came around a large asteroid and saw Zingara station. It was a massive asteroid, more like a small moon. Entire craters had been cut square and turned into hundreds of secure dry docks. Each space had a heavy port door, ensuring privacy and security. There were huge support beams protruding from the rock in seemingly random places, partially to stabilize the interior structure, partially for the few hundred habitation pods that had been built onto them.

There were other long extensions protruding from the asteroid - docking arms, some of them three or four hundred kilometres long, with so many ships attached to them it was impossible to count as we went by. As we manoeuvred closer to our private bay, I could see a large flat area that was covered in heavy metal plating. On our display, a warning hovered over it indicating that there was a pocket of artificial gravity. I had never seen a landing patch. They were built so ships with landing gear and bottom side hatches could dock cheaply and quickly. It was a cheap way to use exterior space, but it was wasteful.

The massive private dry dock doors parted as we approached and Oz nudged me. "How much did this cost?" he asked in a whisper.

"Only fifteen thousand credits per day."

"That's three months pay at Commander's rank, you realize."

"It'll be worth it, trust me. Besides, this kind of dry dock would cost seventy five thousand on Freeground."

"Seventy five thousand? That's robbery."

"I'm surprised you didn't already know. That's what happens when you're the only port for light years in all directions. These people obviously make more credits on the docking arms. A spot there only costs a thousand, but good luck getting any work on your ship done."

"Good point. I'm glad Freeground set us up with enough credits to trade with and to pay the crew."

"You're not the only one. If we can get some good selling prices on a few things we have, we should have plenty of credits to go around for a while." I looked at my command console and saw that most of our extra salvage was already sold at the asking price which was a surprise, since I thought the prices the crew had marked them with were on the high side. "But I don't think the docking fees will be a problem. At this rate we'll finish docking and have to offload our extra cargo to buyers right away."

We stopped in the middle of the dry dock and the doors closed behind us. The bay began pressurizing. Massive docking arms slowly reached out to the ship, then secured to hard points on the hull.

FOUR
NO REST

There was widespread disappointment that we didn't have time for shore leave, but it couldn't be helped. There was too much to do and I knew that the bounty on the First Light would be trouble. True, most space stations didn't make who was in their dry moorings public, but there was always a way for an enterprising bounty hunter or Vindyne representative to get that kind of information. From my own experience on Freeground, I knew for a fact it wasn't difficult.

The less time we took with this refit, the better. On the first day alone, we had to take all the systems offline to add major cable upgrades to the power plants. The particle accelerator was also ready to be implemented. Instead of watching and waiting from the bridge, I took the advice Doc gave me over coffee earlier that day and joined the refit crew in engineering. There weren't many unforeseen problems and we overcame them quickly. I was taking orders from Ayan and her team for a change. I even referred a crew member with questions to Laura instead of trying to research the answer myself. I'll never forget the look on his face as I shrugged and said. "How am I supposed to know the optimum alignment of the secondary field generators? Sounds like something I'd consult a senior engineering officer about."

"Oh, I thought you would know, Captain."

"I'm qualified to connect these primer leads so they don't burn out when we turn the new equipment on, but I have no idea how you keep magnetic fields running so antimatter doesn't start annihilating matter. I could guess, but like I said..."

"Boom," the younger crew member said with a smile.

"Yup, boom," I replied with a nod.

I hadn't actually seen the engineering staff at work for an extended amount of time until then. It was amazing how well Ayan and Laura had everyone working together. The easy efficiency throughout the department was a sight to behold. The work in engineering and the rest of the ship had been non-stop since we came out of hyperspace in Gai-Ian and the crew had fallen into an easy rhythm.

After twenty hours of solid work, we were ready to bring all the primary power systems back online. I stood on the bridge as the faint hum of all the power plants made the ship feel alive again. I had gotten so used to the sound and feel I had forgotten it was there. Over the next two hours, minor adjustments were made and our efficiency was greater than ever.

I ordered the engineering crew to take eight hours rest, and got some sleep myself after saying good night to Ayan.

The next morning I was outside the ship looking at the damage from above in zero gravity. There was breathable atmosphere, but around the outside of the ship there was no gravity unless you were standing directly on one of the dry dock equipment and observation platform deck plates. The massive breach that The Incinerator, the destroyer we defeated after escaping from Vindyne's custody, opened had begun to repair itself. The ergranian steel was working its slow magic. Ayan, several members of the repair and maintenance staff, and I were looking over the connectors that would supercharge the rough, damaged edges of the hull so it would regenerate much faster. We had filled the yawning gap left by the Vindyne destroyer with salvage, like packing an open wound with gauze, and now all those materials were being sorted out above us. There was a vast assortment of items. Some would be installed, like the beam weapons, shield emitters, and repulsors. Other items would be sold.

We had even managed to salvage enough furniture and interior components so we wouldn't have to buy much to replace what had been destroyed. We were refurnishing our own officers' quarters with the contents of The Incinerator's officers' quarters for the most part, and it made me grin a little as I looked up to see where the pieces of furniture were being stowed above the ship temporarily.

I looked from one end of the breach to the other. It ran up the top of the ship for over fifty metres, exposing most of the devastated officers' quarters inside. "How long do you think it will take to regenerate it?"

"About two days. That's with two of the power plants running at full the entire time to supercharge the hull," Ayan replied as she watched one of the replacement rail cannon turrets get slowly lowered into place where it would become embedded in the hull during regeneration. The new turret had much heavier armour than the last, including its own energy shield emitter and four much longer barrels for increased accuracy. "The turrets we're installing should be much safer. The other ones were at least sixty years old. One of the things they didn't take the time to replace during the first refit."

"I only wish we could upgrade all of them."

"Eventually. But at least each one will have an independent energy shield now," she observed.

"How do the rest of the upgrades look?" I asked.

"Thanks to all the preparations we made while we were in hyperspace, we'll only have to cut where it's needed, install the new equipment, and seal up the hull. All the connections and support systems are already in place."

"Not to mention all the planning. The instructions your department laid out for everyone involved in the repairs and upgrades read so well even I can understand the process from beginning to end. I don't know how you found the time."

"I skipped sleeping," Ayan said with a smile.

"I'm sure medical had something to say about that when you reported yesterday morning."

Her bright mood darkened a little as she looked back to her command console and the holographic images that hovered over her forearm. "They know everyone's stretched a little thin."

I was about to ask if she was all right, if there was anything I needed to know, but the repair crew we had hired from the station came through one of the main airlocks above the ship. They wore vacsuits that looked like they had been through thick and thin. Some of them were patched and stained. Behind them they pulled a ten meter long anti-gravity repair sled loaded with a variety of tools and parts. One of them piloted it slowly behind the rest using pulses from the repulsors. The one at the lead had a black beard and was the first to drift towards us.

He looked at the ship from bow to stern and whistled. "She's a beauty. Yer security boys tole me ta go up top fer words wi' the cap'n. I'm called Foreman Berl, who's Cap'n Valent?" he asked in a gruff voice. It sounded like his vocal cords had been ground part way through by some corrosive gas.

"I'm Captain Valent," I replied, drifting over and offering my hand. "Good to meet you."

"Yup!" He looked at a simple computer console on his arm, which showed the time in big numbers: 07:00 "Schedule says I git 'ere at seven, start'n jus' befo' eight. Whatcha havin' us do, Cap'n?"

"Ever work with ergranian interiors before?"

"Ayuh, done a station onceatime. Took us near five a year."

"All right. We'll be charging the outer hull which will be about six meters above your head, so be careful if you have to pass any of your gear through. You'll be spot charging and repairing the officers' quarters down there," I said, pointing to where the officers' quarters used to be. Around the edges of the doorways and walls, parts of the decks were still visible.

"Ye joshin! Officas' quartas? Be mah pleasa. Haven' worked fine detail in musta been months, but we'll make it betta than befo' fo ye. I bet me wage."

Ayan handed him a small data stick containing all the specifications and modifications and smiled sweetly, "I believe you. How long do you think it will take?"

He was absolutely taken aback by her friendly demeanor and cleared his throat as he focused his concentration on the contents of the stick. "Hell, chargin' an shapin' makes it real fast, maybe a forty hour, 'r less." He continued to page through the schematics. I had made some changes to my quarters to accommodate something I had found in The Incinerator's captain's quarters. I'd added extra support, mid deck armour, as well as removed some of the wasted space from other quarters, so even the regular crew quarters would be a bit more spacious. Berl continued looking through the schematics and details, saying. "Ayuh, ayuh, huh, ayuh," under his breath all the while. "D'ya have all the mechanicals ye'll need 'ere? Door closin's n' computers n' tha like?"

"We still need a few computer terminals, holographic projectors, and door panels, but other than that you should find everything you need in the salvage."

Berl looked up at the stowed furniture, held in place by a large net tethered to a post above the ship. "Ayuh, that'll fix. Now ah can git yuh fixed wi' tha projecta's n' computa's, n' it'll cost a pretty. Ya wanna save yerself cred, then git ta Larson's place, he fix ya cheap."

"So you can sell me the computers and projectors but it'll be cheaper through Larson? Is he a friend of yours?"

"Ayuh. Good deala. Larson's Supply, git yuh fix right up, ayuh. Save me wage more n' onceatime, ayuh."

"Thank you, I'll pay him a visit."

"Ayuh, we git ta work." He looked to his men and woman and shouted in a language I didn't even recognize. I looked at the command console on my arm and read the translation. "Get your asses down there and start cleaning up! I want to see shine everywhere I look in two hours so we can start regenerating the decks and shaping walls! We're not getting paid by the hour!"

I got his attention for a moment as his crew started

unloading tools from the repair sled. "We want this done as fast as possible, but don't sacrifice quality. Do your best work here, and every captain I meet will know who is responsible." I smiled.

"Yessah!"

FIVE

AN EXCURSION

The entire crew had been set to work in shifts. All the tasks had been carefully planned to the last detail and set in priority for the next two days. With no more planning to do, Minh-Chu, Oz, Jason, Laura, Ayan, and I entrusted our subordinates with overseeing the work.

That left the senior staff with some extra time, and the need to give our officers some space so they didn't feel like we were breathing down their necks. We only had one option: venture into the station proper to investigate and do some shopping. Everyone except for Oz seemed to have difficulty containing their excitement even though most of the objects we were after were utilitarian. I had to admit that I was a little excited to go ashore myself. I had never seen a space station other than Freeground, so I knew I was in for a bit of an experience.

As I was getting ready for the excursion, looking over the list of things to purchase in my quarters, I couldn't shake the feeling that there was something I was missing.

The door opened then and in came Ayan with a new black engineer's long coat just like the one I had lost. I just stood there as a grin spread across my face. She was blushing as she placed it in my hands with care. "It just came out of the materializer. Three hours. I mean, the fabricator took three hours to make it," she said nervously.

I held it up and looked at the outside. It was the same texture, only the grey panels of material had been remade black and had a reflective quality to them. I recognized the addition a moment later as energy collectors and assumed that they would charge whatever items were in the pockets, gathering static, light, and other readily available energy around them including motion and certain airborne particles.

"I tried to include all the tools you had in there. I'm sure I missed a few, but I added a modern multitool, an extra computer insert for your command unit in case your main one is damaged, and sixteen extra clips for our new sidearms. There are two secret pockets — I can show you how to get to them — and I had the computer tailor the shape and size for you. I also added a few protective layers to the material, so it's even more resilient and protective than a standard heavy shielding suit."

I tried it on and found something in the sleeve. I pushed it out and looked at it. It was a white silk scarf.

"Somehow part of my shawl from the Pilot's Ball survived the damage to the officers' quarters, and I made it into a scarf instead of throwing it into the recycler. I wouldn't know if you'd like it, but I thought it would look—"

I didn't say anything. I just put it on and let it hang loosely under the jacket, then pulled her into my arms. "Thank you. I forgot that I had lost my coat and spent twenty minutes looking before I remembered it's probably still in some storage locker on that Vindyne super carrier."

"You're welcome. I should make things for you more often if this is the thanks I'll get," she said as she smiled up at me and snuggled up against my chest.

Minh came through the door just then. "I was thinking that maybe while we're shopping around I could get—" He stopped as he looked up from an image on his arm command unit and saw Ayan and me mid-kiss. She had nearly disappeared into my arms and coat as it wrapped around her. "The reed knows no backwards or forwards, only to and fro. My motion is not a retreat, only a flex in a new direction," he quipped as he turned, stepped out the doorway and closed it behind him.

Ayan and I both burst out laughing.

Walking down the gangway leading from the ship later on, where the deck plating provided gravity in a limited area around that side of the mooring, I couldn't help look over my shoulder. From where I was standing, the First Light seemed to go on forever. Under the bright work lights, the silvered hull shone. I had heard it called Old World cloaking; a ship could reflect its surroundings so clearly that when it was in the darkness it was nearly invisible. Under the worklights it was truly a sight to behold. I turned and traced her from bow to stern with my eyes, and realized that everyone had stopped to stare at the ship with me.

"We're really out here," Minh-Chu said quietly. "I never thought I would enjoy getting drafted." He stood and stared silently at the ship for a moment before sighing. "As we are all stardust, it is our destiny to seek out our brighter cousins and fathers."

"Old Chinese proverb?" Oz asked quietly.

"Sentimental restaurant owner who misses home less than he thought he would."

"I couldn't imagine being out here with you when we were still running simulations for fun on Freeground," Laura said from where she stood beside Jason. She and Ayan had both exchanged their engineering crew jackets for white ponchos. The same protective traits and tool kits were hidden inside, but somewhere the pair of them had decided to take a different turn stylistically.

Everyone else was in uniform, including crew excursion jackets and sidearms. "We look the part. I hope we don't stand out here like we did on Gai-Ian Four. I hear our crew were the only ones there wearing vacsuits.

We started walking towards the station proper. "We were, it was kind of awkward. Some of the people we passed as we walked through the market had only seen vacsuits in movies. I don't think we would have gotten more stares if we were all naked." Jason shrugged.

"Would have been more fun I bet," Ayan commented with a wink.

We passed through the doors leading to the station proper and into the hallways that would lead us to the main arrival area. It was a different world beyond those doors. A rush of air pressed through the opening until the way closed behind us, indicating that the air pressure wasn't quite as well balanced as it should have been. The smell of mildew, grease, and sweat filled my nostrils. The station obviously didn't clean or service the halls very often.

There had been durable tiling on all the walls and in some

places it had come away to show the solid rock beneath. The floor, walls, and ceilings were pitted, scuffed, and marked by the passage of crew, cargo, and who knows what else. As the hallway led us inward towards the hub others intersected. Oz was nearly bowled over from behind by a well dressed, overlarge man sliding on a personal antigravity unit that looked much too small for him. "Oi! Keep the way clear, ape!" the fat man called back over his shoulder as he glided further down the hall.

Oz pretended to go for his sidearm and the fat man accelerated around the corner.

"Easy. You should endeavour to avoid getting shot today, I think," Minh advised, nudging Oz.

"You're right. For all I know he had some kind of backwards firing cannon hidden somewhere on that tiny hoverboard."

"That, or his crew could have been right behind him," Ayan added. "I've been to an asteroid port before. They're either built to be policed or built then barely patrolled. From the quality of the station so far and ships I saw from our passive scans when we were coming in, I'd expect there are a lot of privateer or free-lance crews around. It's a rough life, and it makes some rough people."

Oz's only reply was a silent nod. Being as close as I was to Ayan, it was sometimes easy to forget how much respect she commanded amongst the crew. I respected her a great deal — her advice was invaluable — but watching the rest of the crew follow her lead without question was a quick reminder that she had earned her way to the rank of commander before any of us were aboard. Her knowledge and conduct in official capacities showed it. Her confidence made it even plainer. If that weren't enough, her mother was one of the most respected officers, an admiral, in the Freeground Fleet. Ayan had grown up with one of the best possible mentors close at hand and, according to her file, she spent the majority of her childhood on whatever starship her mother was serving on. That was before she started attending Junior Fleet Academy at age fourteen. No one had more training.

"How many off-ship missions have you been on, Ayan?" Laura asked.

"I don't know. Whenever there was call for an engineer planet or station side I was almost always included. To be honest, I was afraid that I'd be stuck on the ship when Jonas took command."

"Would I ever do that to you?" I asked with mock injury.

"Not on purpose, but you were in an engineering team before. The chief stays close to the power plants."

"Sure, unless they're so well implemented and maintained that they almost take care of themselves."

"Take care of themselves? You should spend more time in engineering. Those things are so advanced they're almost alien. I've never seen power plants find more unique and surprising ways to break in my life. They say they're self-maintaining, even look like it on paper, but they still need people to keep them fit and make sure everything is working as intended."

Laura shook her head. "Now you've gone and done it, Captain. I hope you wanted an extended report on the ship's systems. That's all she's going to talk about for the rest of the trip."

"Well, maybe our captain needs a little education," Ayan replied, looking me up and down appraisingly.

She had me at a loss for words as we came to the end of the

long hallway. I looked up into the area ahead of us and forgot all about our exchange.

There were no empty spaces. That's what struck me about the embarkation and disembarkation centre on the station. It was a primary hub that everyone had to pass through, and there were thousands of people standing in line or milling around. The walls were covered by advertising, plastic postings bonded right on top of other postings, all of them displaying two dimensional video so the walls were like a chaotic sea of endless images vying for the attention of any traveller who happened by. The floors were unforgiving hard stone, the bare material of the asteroid. It was worn smooth under the passing of millions of travellers who had come and gone. The most worn sections were concave paths leading through the inspection point arches, where guards and technicians behind transparesteel plated booths monitored scanning equipment as travellers passed through the turnstiles.

"I could see how this could be hard to police," Oz muttered.

"And I thought it would be a barren rock on the inside, too," Jason added.

"Are we sure that this is the best way for us to find what we need for the ship?" I asked no one in particular.

"It'll be fine," Oz replied a bit too quickly to be convincing.

"We could use the sales listings on their local net, but what fun would that be?" Minh asked enthusiastically.

"Sometimes the best bargains can only be found face to face," Ayan agreed quietly. She didn't seem quite sure.

"Who knows who we'll end up facing for a bargain though, or what they'll want in exchange that couldn't have been posted on their network. Maybe some kind of favour or service," Minh added. Ayan elbowed him with a scowl.

"We'll be fine. I'm sure someone on the ship can give us directions if we get lost," Laura said, looking at Jason.

"The communications crew hasn't given directions to anyone remotely before," he replied, looking over the masses. He caught a glance of Laura's expression of growing concern. "But it'll be fine. It's always easier to give directions from the outside than when you're in the middle," he reassured.

I took a step forward. It was all we needed to get going. We found a line and waited to pass through an inspection point. The plan was to split up into pairs after passing through and meet back at the ship in six hours. Oz was paired with Minh, Jason was paired with Laura, and I was paired with Ayan. All of us had our lists. Oz and Minh were in charge of a list from Doctor Anderson, which wouldn't take more than half an hour to acquire, so they would also spend time gathering whatever information they could about the solar system. Jason and Laura had the most enjoyable assignment, and were to acquire the furniture we were missing along with other creature comforts for the crew in general. Ayan and I had the difficult task of purchasing the mechanical components that we needed to complete the ship's second refit.

Sadly, there wasn't much time for the officers to have fun. If we didn't find what we were looking for on that excursion, some of us would have to return the next day. And with the cost of dry dock mounting fast, we couldn't afford to pursue unreliable leads.

I was growing more certain that we'd have no trouble fitting in as we waited in line. There were people of every shape, colour and even a few of the rare non-humanoid races around. Most of them were wearing some kind of vacuum suit or self sealing vacuum-safe clothing, and no one took keen notice of us at all. We were, in fact, plainly dressed compared to most. Minh tapped my elbow from behind. I looked at him from the corner of my eye and he nodded to our right inconspicuously.

I followed his gaze to find a crew several lines down with Triad Consortium markings on their baggy vacsuits. They were a rough crew and I assumed they were from a freighter. Nothing about them was military.

"Now that could lead to something," Minh whispered.

"They're pretty far from Triad territory. I wonder what they're hauling."

"You and Oz wanted a piracy target. This could be an opportunity, or at least a way to find out what these freighter or service crews are like," Ayan added.

"Follow them, find out what they're doing here, but quietly," I said with heavy emphasis on quietly.

"Don't worry, they'll have no idea who they're drinking with," Oz reassured as he and Minh started wandering out of our line and towards the back of theirs.

"From the look of them, I'd be surprised if they'd care much about what they're drinking," Jason whispered. "I doubt they even have a pulse shower aboard their ship."

"They probably don't. Some corporate haulers cut everything they can to save power, increase cargo capacity and thrust. I used to hear all about how little they'd get paid for a run. Freighter crews like to complain," I commented.

"Most core world freighters aren't given armaments anymore. Owners fear they'll turn pirate," Ayan added.

"I don't think I could do that. Turn pirate. I mean, to switch from having a paying job to having to capture ships and try to make a profit. The movies make it look like an adventure, but I'd think the reality would be harder," Laura said.

"Freighter crews aren't paid much. The only reason they exist at all is that fully automated freighters are easier to steal. You can get the codes and remotely pilot them to a spot where you can unload them safely. Having a skeleton crew stops that from happening, but since they don't do much during the trip, corporations don't pay them well."

"So they take their chances at going into piracy," Laura finished. "I still wouldn't feel right."

"We're practically privateers. That's almost the same thing," Jason said only loud enough so we could hear.

"Except we didn't have to steal our ship, and privateers are endorsed in some way by a faction, government, or corporation," I added.

"I hate to say this, Jonas, but we're somewhere between. We don't have official endorsement, and as far as the galaxy is concerned, we've no friends anywhere. Sounds more like pirate to me, especially if we start going after cargo," Ayan replied, trying not to draw attention from the people in line all around us.

"If it's an easy take you're lookin' for, you should gather yourself some lumpers and find a common cargo haul, sign up, then sell the cargo on your own," an older looking woman said behind us. She was looking over our heads closer to the front of the line. "Can't do it too often, but it's a nice pile of cash without much work. There r' a few thousand ports 'round that won't look too close at where the products r' comin' from as long as they're clean and untampered. Trick is not to get into anythin' that's so valuable that it'll be too badly missed, but make the haul worthwhile regardless like. When you're done offloadin' you can leave the lumpers behind so's the law has someone to blame."

"Thanks!" Jason said, looking up at her. She was taller than all of us by several inches and wore clothing that looked well worn. Older, but could be sealed in an emergency. It was odd, not so much a vacsuit styled to look like normal ground based clothing, but ground-based clothing that could perform as a vacsuit in an emergency. Looking around I saw that most of the people in the lines were dressed similarly, with clothing of vastly varied styles that could also perform as a sealable suit in an emergency.

"Never you mind little son, jus' remember to move on after pullin' the haul. Else you'll find yerself payin one way or 'nother." Her eyes went wide for a moment and she grinned. "There's that little cheat!" She stepped out of the queue and walked between people to cross several lines, obviously in pursuit of someone. We watched the scene quietly and I couldn't help but chuckle as a younger man wearing a similar style of woven clothing spotted her coming towards him and bolted as though his life depended on it.

"I wouldn't want to be in his place," Jason said, shaking his head. "By the way, what's a lumper?"

"A temporary worker without many skills. Normally you'd pay them a lot less than permanent crew," I answered. There were thousands of lumpers on Freeground at any given time; I couldn't imagine how many were on Zingara station.

"Too bad she didn't stick around, it sounded like she knew a bit about the area," Laura sighed.

"Good eye, lady. That's Glenda, one of our home porters. She runs cargo on three ships out here," a security guard in dark grey hard armour commented as we came to the front of the line.

I handed him our entry information on a data chip and he began checking it against our biological scans. I couldn't see where the scanners were, but they had obviously targeted us while we were waiting and gathered all the information they needed. "She looks a little rough around the edges."

"Only because she wants to. I hear she started as a humanitarian sort, gathering extras across this part of the galaxy and shipping them to colonies in need. Probably still does that, but from what I know she's one of the few mostly-honest captains out here. Runs a good shipping business."

"Didn't sound like it from the advice she was giving us," Jason muttered.

"Don't let that fool you, she doesn't like the super corps out here much — none of us do — so if she can drop a bug in some young spacer's ear about hurting them, she'll do it. Don't think she'd do that kind of thing herself, though. She's too important to the colonies trying to make a go out here."

"Do you have any idea who she was chasing?" Ayan asked, smiling at the security guard as she handed him her personal information.

He smiled back at her shyly. "Uh, he's one of her pilots. Probably owes her more cash than he's worth."

"I wouldn't cross her."

"Good thinking. That boy'll probably keep his skin, but I

hope he has enough for passage to the next open port. He'll have to go at least that far to find work." We had all passed through the checkpoint and waited for him to open the stall door to the inner portion of the station. "All right, folks, if you haven't read them yet, please read the summary of laws and keep a copy with you at all times during your visit. For more information, use our automated system by pressing yellow, five, twelve on any station terminal." He opened the doors and leered at Ayan as she passed. He jerked his head towards the next group in line the instant he realized I caught him staring.

We made our way into the cavernous entrance area and were swallowed up by the masses within. The station foyer was hundreds of metres across, had posts every ten or so metres in all directions with information panels, and went ahead further than I could see. There were lifts along the sides that transported people between the thirty or so levels of platforms that led to shops, hallways, entertainment facilities, and other numerous credit-making endeavours. The ceiling above had crossing walkways, and played host to both flickering holographic and very realistic advertising billboards.

We walked through the welcome area as slowly as the crowd permitted. There was some personal space between us and everyone else, but not much. No more than a metre's distance could be won in any direction; there were just too many people. Above I could see shuttle car tubes, travel-ways with tall barriers for high speed pedestrian transport such as anti-gravity boards or skid bikes. They moved at a blurringly fast speed, and when one had to exit the expressway the gravity shifted so all the travellers behind had to slow down.

I had never seen anything like it. Public transport was free and always easy on Freeground, so most of the personal travel devices I was seeing were under restricted use there. The pattern of the walkways, shops, and all the people seemed random at a glance, but the lack of congestion told a different story. Whoever built and added to the space port had a great deal of engineering expertise, well beyond my own.

Ayan's gloved hand took mine and I looked down at her. She was smiling at me with a glimmer in her eye. "I forget you've only been planetside twice. It's hard not to assume you've seen it all before."

"This is amazing. I don't know what I was expecting, but it wasn't anything like this. I don't know what I would have done if you decided to stay back on the ship."

"I wouldn't miss this for anything. I like watching you take it all in. It's cute."

"I am not cute," I said with mock injury.

"Captain Cute. It could stick," Jason teased.

"I can make the bridge very uncomfortable for you," I threatened.

"Oh, look, a furniture store!" he said, pointing off to one of the shops to his right as he started walking towards it.

"We should start shopping around," Laura agreed.

"We don't want to get anything in this hallway. The real bargains will be deeper inside the station. Go check one of those information panels!" Ayan yelled after them.

"The port officer we spoke to suggested an area called The Pit," I added.

"See you back on the ship!" Laura said as Jason pulled her towards one of the information stations by the hand.

"They're going to get so lost." Ayan shook her head.

"Probably, but knowing Jason he'll find his way. Eventually."

"I'd put my credits on Laura finding the way first."

"I'll put five on Jason," I said.

"You're on."

We checked the nearest info panel for Larsen's Place and found it right away. It was just two levels up from The Pit, which was roughly in the centre of the station.

I was about to start walking away when Ayan tapped a few icons on the panel and said, "Check for the best prices on this item, please. List the best three only. High efficiency pulse emitters, new, under twenty purchase quantity, registered shops."

I didn't even think of letting the station computer do the work for us, even though it would have been the first thing I'd have done if I were on Freeground.

"Seventeen credits each at Hasotan Store 11382, seventeen decimal five at Reed Wares Store 93721, and nineteen credits each at Spacerwares Store 852381."

"Where does Larsen's Place rank for the same item?" she asked.

"'Larsen's Place Store 3 ranks thirty third at twenty five decimal five for the requested item."

"New item: emergency magnetic containment field generators tested to ten tons, new."

"Larsen's Place Store 3 ranks fifth at thirty thousand nine hundred each for the requested item."

"Well, I think the foreman was right. It sounds like Larsen's might be the place to go. That's a good price for a containment unit that heavy, too. It says he's located in section fifty one," she said, nodding to herself. "I'm surprised that there are so many franchises here. Spacerwares is huge, but I wouldn't expect them to put a location out this far."

"Considering they have over eight hundred thousand locations that were built before getting around to Zingara, it sounds like they took their time installing one here. I'm glad Freeground turned down their application to put a location there," I told her.

"I didn't know they applied."

"Yup, Fleet Operations turned them down flat. Parliament didn't get a chance to consider it, not that they'd actually allow it."

"They're well known listening posts for Regent Galactic," she said.

"I had no idea. I thought they were just really big outfitter stores. I've only heard of them though. Never been in a store."

"They pretty much have everything a spacefarer could want. We might want to stay clear, but I actually hope Laura and Jason check the furniture there. As long as they don't get too distracted, they may find what we need."

"Maybe I should raise them on the comm at the four hour mark. I get the feeling they'll get pretty distracted," I said as I followed Ayan's lead to a shuttle tube entrance turnstiles. Every five minutes a shuttle car went by, the doors belching cool air and a voice announcing which general destination the car was headed for every time they opened to load the next dozen or so passengers. I didn't even see the loading area for the tubes at first through the crowd.

We walked up to the turnstiles and it said, "Five credits for entry, five credits for exit. Jumpers will be stunned and incarcerated until their fine is paid." I reached into my jacket pocket for my United Core Worlds Currency card and Ayan stopped me.

"Use your credit chips, these things are notorious for double scanning."

I looked at the chip slot again and saw a faded warning that read "The station is not responsible for multiple scans."

I reached into my other pocket and fished for a five credit chip. I realized then that I didn't have a chance to pick any up from the ship safe, and all my own cash had been destroyed with my quarters. I looked to Ayan, who smiled and gave me a stack of various denominations adding up to what I estimated was about four hundred, more than enough for personal expenses.

I thanked her, trying not to sound as sheepish as I felt.

"Of course," she said.

We stepped through and waited for a tube car going to section fifty one, and found one after a few minutes. We boarded with a rush of eight or nine people and sat down. The inertial dampeners kicked in a second late, and we dropped into the seat behind us. The car rushed down the tube, speeding up to over two hundred kilometres per hour and slowing down to accommodate other cars and turns. After a few minutes we arrived at our destination and got out.

The crowds were much thinner in section fifty one, which occupied the corner of Pablo and Current streets according to the sign to the right of the tube entrance. Right after we emerged, a little girl — she looked no more than five or six years old — took Ayan's free hand.

She looked down at the little blond child in surprise.

"I'm stuck, m-mommy forgot—" she blubbered. "For-for-f-f-forgot ta gimmie f-f-f-five credits."

"She forgot to give you credits to get out of the turnstiles?" Ayan interpreted, kneeling down and trying to comfort the girl.

Tears shook loose of the girl's face as she nodded her head vigorously.

"Here, we'll get through together and go find your mother," Ayan reassured as she handed the little girl five credits.

I held Ayan's hand as she held the little girl's, whose mood was already brightening, and we headed to the turnstile exit.

"Where's your mommy? She mustn't have just left," Ayan asked, concerned.

To both our surprise, the little girl jerked her hand free and ran towards an arriving tube car. As she boarded I could see her back pocket was bulging with credit chips. She playfully jumped up on a seat and turned, waving at us as the doors closed and the tube car accelerated off.

"Well that's something I've never seen before," I said, still shocked but amused.

"Wow, fooled me like a daft mark," Ayan said.

"You're not the only one from the looks of it."

We each dropped five credits to exit the turnstiles and started walking down Current Street. It wasn't a street at all, really, just a broad tunnel with shops, restaurants, and private homes further up the rock face. The height of the tunnels is what I found most amazing; they made room for at least thirty stories, and I could see that regardless of the lack of view, each of the apartments had windows. The stone was black and grey; combined with the low lighting, it gave the area a very relaxed look, which lent itself well to the multitude of restaurants with tables set outside in the walk-way. The smell of the food was tempting, but according to the map that appeared with the pricing information, Larsen's Place was just around the next corner, about ten doors down.

As we made our way down the street at a more leisurely pace, I couldn't help but notice a lot of people weren't wearing vacsuits. "We must be a lot deeper inside. It doesn't look like anyone here is worried about decompression."

"I wonder how old this place is. Some of these restaurants use old Earth dating for their establishment date plaques. I've only seen that in one other place, and it was an outer core colony," observed Ayan.

"You really have been all over, haven't you?" I asked her conversationally.

She smiled and shook her head. "It feels like it sometimes, but then I see something like this." She gestured to the street in general. "I've seen other settlements that were similar, but you have to put your expectations aside. I could assume that these places are the same as stores and restaurants I've seen on other planets, but few places are really alike. Take that little girl, for example. Almost anywhere else giving her five credits would be the perfect thing to do, exactly the right solution, but here it was a little scam. I didn't suspect a thing."

"You should have seen your face," I teased. "That was worth five credits."

"I'm sure, but that's my point. There are always surprises wherever you go, especially if your ship doesn't have a route that you repeat over and over again. You never get to see much of a place."

"That's true. I'm sure the area Minh and Oz are in is completely different."

We came around the corner and came out into an opening that took our breath away. The sign overhead said PIT STREET LEVEL 140. Current Street's tunnel opened up into a smoothly caved round cavern that seemed to go on forever in all directions. The other wall was so far away that it was hazy; the yawning space between the road we stood on and the opposite end was obscured by light, dust, and the mildly damp air.

We were over two hundred metres up from the base of The Pit, and looking down from that railing was dizzying. As we walked closer to the railing, which was just a part of a transparent metal safety cage that glinted silver as you looked along the edge, we had difficulty taking it all in.

Booths overlooked the grandeur and spectacle of the massive circular open area beneath and above us. The holographic advertising was sparse, but from where we were, we could see one from a news network that was four stories tall. "Tonight's feature, Horror along the transit lanes! Are you stepping onto a hyperspace transport? Or is it a slave barge in disguise! We profile two couples who barely escaped and our experts will tell you how you can avoid getting captured by slavers!" the anchorman enticed with interchanging images of luxury and captivity. The sound of his perfect news caster voice piped in from somewhere near the floor.

Behind us there was very little traffic, small personal transports for one or two and a couple of anti-gravity delivery sleds moved along at a leisurely pace. There were small round pips along the four lane road that monitored speed and who was going where. I recognized them from Freeground, where we used similar technology in shuttle tubes.

The centre of the cavern floor was occupied by five arenas, with two more on massive criss-crossing support structures. I immediately recognized one of the main events taking place in a suspended section. The space above the support had been netted in, creating a closed area hundreds of metres in size. Within, pilots engaged in close quarters dog fights against single or multiple opponents. I could make out three combatants firing at each other while the wreckage of a fourth was being removed from the bottom of the chamber.

I pulled my gaze away from the spectacle in the middle of the cavern and looked back down. A city of interconnected buildings and a network of streets made for small vehicles had been erected around the five arenas at the bottom. There were tens of thousands of people.

"Now that's amazing," Ayan said quietly. "There's so much open space. Equalizing the pressure this well must take an incredible effort. If someone opened the wrong seal at the wrong time the air could start moving so fast that no one could stand."

There was no more than a constant breeze that ranged from nearly unnoticeable to just enough to ruffle your hair. "You're right. And keeping this place warm, that's just-"

"Labour intensive," a voice from behind us intoned. "Whole station has plenty of fail-safes so it's a nice twenty two degrees most times. There are days where you'd swear you were in a wind tunnel and it drops down to six degrees, mind you. Maintenance never stops workin'. Welcome to The Pit, Captain Valent. Berl sent me a pic. Told me to expect you."

Ayan and I turned around and saw that we had been standing in front of Larsen's Place. He used an entire half of a Light Garren fighter, complete with its ancient paired gauss cannons, as a backdrop for his simple holographic shop sign. It was an angular, two man Sol System Defence fighter, centuries old. Behind him I could see the entrance to the shop proper was no more than ten meters wide, but the space inside seemed to go on forever.

The fellow who had spoken wore older protective workman's overalls, but it didn't show nearly as much damage or dirt as Berl's or the ones his work crew wore.

"Call me Jonas, and this is Commander Rice, my Chief Engineer." I extended my hand.

He shook it and I could feel he was using an old mechanical limb replacement for his right hand. "I'm Larsen. I don't have a hundred employees like those corporate shops. Just a prime location, a few check booths and a few dozen androids to keep customers served and shoplifters out."

We followed him inside, where parts of every kind hung along the walls and holograms of used and new ships of several different sizes rotated slowly down the middle of the store.

"Berl didn't tell me you were military types."

"We're a shareholder ship, but we use rank to keep the crew in line," Ayan said without missing a beat.

"I've seen that once or twice before, but I'm afraid the word's out on you. Us connected types have already heard there's a Freeground combat vessel drydocked here after a tousle with Vindyne. Too bad you ran into the big bad Corp of the region, otherwise no one would make you with that strange hull o' yours. Berl said she's a beauty. No worries though, I hate those damned slavers. Seen a few good crews get slagged by them over the years."

"I hesitate to ask, but is the word out on which bay we're in?"

He led us back across the four clearly marked lanes, stopping a large double deck anti-gravity delivery truck along the way. "Anyone who wants to know can find out easily enough. Anyone who matters, anyhow. I'd say it's no worry though. The station keeps her dry docks secure. Station like this doesn't get so prosperous by letting her safe harbours get raided from the inside."

"How hard is the security here on bounty hunting?" I asked.

Larsen was about to take us down a set of stairs just inside his store but stopped and half turned to look at me. "You and your folk really are neck deep in it, aren't ya? No way you took down a Vindyne Super Carrier. Can't convince me of that. Did or didn't doesn't matter for you folk though. They're gunnin' for ya like ya did." He turned back towards the stairway and led us down to a room filled with sample computer terminals and holographic projectors. "Security sensors pick ya up fast once a firefight breaks out, but there's a reason why the station's always hirin' more officers; there's never one around when you need one. I don't think I've seen a security officer in three days. They force fighting crews ta pay fines or lock your ship down. There's another thing. If a firefight gets too hot — explosions and the like start goin' off — they'll seal off the area and flush out all the air. Solves most problems, 'cept they can't do it to some really big spaces like The Pit. But if you see bulkheads closin' find a spot to hang on to and seal those fancy suits of yers."

"Thanks for making that clear," Ayan said.

"Can't help but hear, you've got a bit of Britain in you. Accent's a dead giveaway."

"My mother's from the British Core Colonies."

"Well, glad to see a product of the brighter side of civilization all the way out here. Now, let's get down to business." He turned on the holographic projectors and interface panels lining the walls and occupying the centre of the room. None of them were installed permanently; they were just powered and set up for demonstration. "Most of these models are brand new, straight from the outer core manufacturers. I keep the used ones in another compartment."

The evidence was in the image quality. Most of them were better than anything I had seen outside of military macro applications on Freeground. "How are the prices?"

"Getting better all the time, though a lot of merchants out here grief on me sayin' so. The last shipment was almost five percent down. They're getting cheaper to make these days with less jitter and better colour adjustment. These'll take less tuning and last longer."

"That's probably thanks to the advancements in the materializers used to produce the holographic medium. They're so cheap to manufacture now that the prices should come down a lot more next year," Ayan said. There was a slowness to her manner of speech that took me by surprise and I looked at her.

She looked up at me and a moment later she went limp. I caught her a little awkwardly, with one hand under her arm and the other catching her forearm, but I kept her from falling to the floor nevertheless. I was able to adjust my hold after a moment and picked her up in my arms. She was surprisingly light.

Larsen turned all the displays off with a push of a button on the back of his hand. "She have problems with projections?" he asked as he hurriedly cleared a stack of boxed display panels off an old sofa.

I lay her down on it and checked her pulse. "Not that I'm aware of."

"I'll call station emergency. Won't have a lovely thing like her dyin' in my shop," he said as he started punching buttons into his communicator.

"I'd rather contact our ship doctor. Her pulse and breathing seem all right."

"If you're sure now," Larsen said, just about to open communications with emergency services. "If your doctor can fix her up it'll be cheaper. Emergency calls cost five hundred if it's fer nothin' and get pricier from there."

Just as the ship communications officer was coming on Ayan started to come around. Her eyelids drew open drowsily at first. A smile spread sleepily across her face at first as her blue eyes looked into mine, then she realized where she was and straightened up in a shot, sitting up suddenly. She looked dizzy and put a hand to her head.

"Captain? Is there something wrong?" asked a voice from my communicator.

Ayan's eyes widened for a moment and before anyone else could say anything she grabbed my wrist and turned my arm so she was looking into my command unit's communicator. "Everything's fine, Ensign, I brought up the emergency line while adjusting the captain's C and C unit, no worries," she explained and closed the transmission.

"C and C unit?" asked Larsen.

"Communications and Command Unit, or Command and

Control Unit, it stands for both," Ayan answered. She seemed fully awake and alert. "I'm fine, no need to call Doc or alert the ship. I haven't had anything to eat today, that's all."

"Now that I can fix," Larsen said, tossing Ayan a meal bar, colourfully packaged in a bright yellow and green wrapper.

"Thank you. I'm sure it'll be on our bill," Ayan tried to jest as she opened it and proceeded to take a bite.

"I'm just happy someone 'sides me is eating one. Bought four tons of those a year ago and can't sell them for cost. Lemon lime energy bars are an acquired taste I'm thinkin'."

Ayan worked through her first bite, chewing it quickly and going flush from nose to ears as I checked my arm unit. My console could give me a general idea of fitness on any of my crew, and I held mine so she couldn't see what I was doing.

"I believe it," she said, sounding a little choked. Ayan looked at me and saw that I was checking up on her.

"Just double checking." I could see that her blood sugar was very low, and regardless of how she may have been acting, her body was showing fatigue.

Placing her hand on my arm she insisted, "I'm fine, just needed a seat and some energy." She took another bite of the faintly green and yellow coloured energy bar and tried not to grimace. "See?"

I couldn't help but smile at her as she struggled to get through eating the stuff. The taste of that meal replacement must have been awful but it was gone in under a minute. "Still, we'll get something to eat after we're finished here, then get back to the ship, okay?"

"Fine, just don't make a fuss," Ayan said as she gave the

wrapper to Larsen, who was trying to hide his amusement at her finishing the bar.

"I'm the only other human I know who's finished one of those," he said as he tossed the wrapper in a recycler built into the wall and shook his head. "Scared us both for a minute there, lady. Best let the captain here take care of ya."

"We haven't had leave in about two months, I think it's taking its toll," I explained to him.

"Well, I can hurry this along and give you my best wares at my lowest so you can get her back to your ship."

"I'm fine, really, just needed a cat nap." She squeezed my hand and looked me in the eye. "Really, I'm okay."

Silence hung in the air for a moment, with Ayan and me looking at each other while Larsen used a projection chip to display a list of components.

"Did Berl give you an inventory of what he needed to finish the crew quarters?" she asked.

"This is it here," Larsen replied, gesturing with the holochip.

"Give it here. I have a list for you as well." She handed him a slender data stick and took the list from him. We looked at the inventory while lounging on the sofa. It reflected what I expected we were missing: door displays, cables, holographic projectors, small motors, pulse shower kits, atmospheric subsystems, deck and wall surface treatments, along with a few other small items that added up to quite a list. From what Ayan and I knew, the prices he had listed beside each item were reasonable.

He sucked air in through his teeth at a few of the items on the list Ayan had given him. "There's some expensive stationary equipment here, Miss. We're lookin' at over a million for half."

Ayan gave him a crooked grin, pulled an antimatter containment crystal from her mid-thigh pocket and tossed it to him. "Catch."

His cybernetic hand caught it reflexively, as quick as a blink. "That's not semi-solid, is it?" he asked, holding it up to the light for inspection. "The machines needed to make this stuff are priceless out here. This antimatter will help, but won't cover your whole list, Miss." He held the crystal out in his artificial hand and pulled a small stylus shaped scanner from his pocket. The scanner projected light through the crystal and provided a small holographic readout from the back end.

"Would the rest of the case pay for it?" she asked without looking at him. "I mean, that's if it's useful to you. If you don't have the equipment to extract it, then it's not much good."

"Oh, don't you worry, Miss. The buyer I know who would make use of this will have what he needs to extract it. Vindyne markings all over this though."

"Is that a problem?" I asked.

Larsen looked from the crystal to us, as though assessing us for the first time. "You two sure have shaken my day, I'll give you that. I'll ask, though it's against my better judgement. Where'd you get this?"

"The crew of a Vindyne destroyer let us have it," I answered.

Ayan shook her head slowly and quietly groaned.

"Like I said, shouldn't 'ave asked, but there it is. I'll take what you've got, and you'll come out with fifty percent market value."

Ayan turned off the holochip and stood. "We have three

cases ready to transport. I can sell them to you for eighty five percent fair market value and we only take raw UCW Credits."

"I'll give you sixty five, final word. I can't pay more for marked goods. Vindyne don't sell munitions grade antimatter. The stuff they offer is only dense enough to be used as fuel."

"We have a deal," she accepted with a smile.

Larsen put the crystal in his pocket and shook her hand. "The parts will be in your hold afore you've time to get back to your ship."

SIX
DATING FOR SPACERS

Larsen had traded a little less than fairly for the antimatter, but Ayan and I were anxious to get rid of the stuff. Though well contained, there was always the chance that just one of those crystals could destabilize, since containment always came with a decay rate. That would spell the end of the ship; one crystal going off next to all the others, starting a chain reaction would annihilate half the inner hull and superheat the rest. There was every reason to get rid of the antimatter we had — especially since we had no way of extracting it — and Larsen's client did. I shuddered to think who that could be.

We not only made off with all the equipment and parts we requested, but nine brand new Raze Starfighters, more than enough to replace those that we had lost since leaving Freeground. The rest of the value of our antimatter was settled with credits, enough to pay the entire crew for two months or conduct significant repairs.

Larsen's foreman, along with a dozen or so battered

androids, were already setting out to deliver the parts we needed while we negotiated for non-essentials. The trader's easy-going manner was obviously a result of a smooth operation.

Instead of riding along with the loaders that would make the delivery, I was able to entice Ayan into spending some time walking along the consumer area circling The Pit on the level below us. There were shops and restaurants on the same level as Larsen's, but I overheard another customer who was just browsing by say that the real pedestrian area started somewhere below.

As we stepped out of the large lift, it was immediately obvious that they were right. The lighting was a little dimmer on level seventy-seven, but the signs from the various shops lining the broad circular walkway made up for it. There was no street traffic; only pedestrians were allowed. The view overlooking the middle of The Pit was much better. We were at eye level with an arena platform that was host to a football game. Somehow the human leagues were out here, though I didn't recognize the uniforms. There were gates blocking off transparent walkways that lead to bleachers spaced across the edges of the field, which was sealed from the crowd by a dome. Sadly, football riots weren't unheard of there either.

Ayan tugged at my hand. "I didn't know you were a fan."

"I played when I was young, just a few years. Not much of a spectator though."

"We'll have to have a game. Oz and I played in the Academy, but never against each other. I was ahead of him."

"I'll arrange some time on the flight deck with Minh," I remarked as we started walking off into the crowd. I didn't notice right away, but there were two distinct sides to the walkway; the shop side, where people moved counterclockwise, and the Pit side closest to the transparent railings, where everyone moved clockwise.

Ayan chucked and shook her head. "Oh no, he's taking me seriously."

"What? You wouldn't play?"

"I'll stick to zero gravity yoga and tai chi. I'm a little short for football."

"I don't think that'll matter so much. I'm pretty sure that if we use the flight deck, Minh would make sure he gets a team. Have you met some of those pilots? I think Franco has you beat at a hundred forty five centimetres."

Ayan laughed and nodded. "And he'd be crazy enough to play. Do you think Minh would join in?"

"I have no idea. I know he can kick a ball, but I met him in the infantry a long time after I stopped playing."

"Oh, I thought you two were friends before then."

"Nope, I met him planet-side on my first tour. I kept his troop shuttle in the air and he kept me from getting shot. I got a chance to save his butt a few times, though. That was such a different time."

"It sounds like a good chance meeting."

"The best kind. I don't think we'd be friends any other way. He's my opposite."

"I know. He enjoys life right out in the open, says what he's thinking before he's decided whether or not it should be aired aloud, while you're a thinker, say what you mean, and ask all those to-the-point questions."

"Minh calls it broody."

"I wouldn't say you're moody, really."

She hadn't heard clearly over the buzz of the crowd. "Not moody, broody. Like I'm sulking over something."

"Oh, broody, that's a bit more like you. I'm surprised I haven't heard that since we left Freeground."

"Well, now I have an excuse to be broody, I suppose." I stopped myself and looked at her. "You don't think I'm broody aboard?"

She was trying not to laugh and was distracted, by design or chance I'll never know, as she looked up towards an old fashioned neon sign that depicted a pile of red spaghetti with a piece of pizza stuck in it pointy end down. "Ooh! Italian food!" She nearly dragged me by the hand through the doors.

The rich, saucy aroma hit me like a wave as we walked inside and I immediately realized how hungry I was. "Good idea."

The patrons were mostly human, though there was a table of nafalli near the back. I had never seen one in person before. It was almost comical watching them leisurely eat their spaghetti, reaching a fork out with their long forearms, slurping the strands in through their small mouths and patting down their fur with napkins. One of the women laughed and it sounded small and sweet, almost like a chirp. As we found a quiet booth, I couldn't help but glance over. They were tall. The shortest was my height and looked like the youngest. My guess was I was looking at a family of five.

"I've never seen nafalli, either. They're beautiful."

One of them slurped in a very long strand of spaghetti and laughed loudly as it slapped his flat black nose several times on its way in. I couldn't help but laugh with him quietly, even though I was fairly sure we were too far off for them to hear. "I did some reading on them a couple years ago while things were slow in port. They're marsupials with very strong family units."

"Yup, I remember watching a documentary. Humans could learn a lot from them. Their tribes fought for thousands of years before they made it to space, but then they colonized a few systems near their home world and there was peace within a century."

I could see the grey and black fur on one of their backs ripple and stand up for a moment before flattening down. He leaned into the table and said something very quietly to the rest. Another, much smaller, white and red furred nafalli looked up to us briefly and nodded. "I think we've been noticed noticing them," I whispered.

Thankfully the waiter came over to our candlelit booth just a moment later and blocked the view. "Welcome to Marconi's. Would you like our authentic dish menu or would you prefer something generated by our high grade materializer?"

Ayan took the pair of menus from under the waiter's arm and handed me one. "We've had nothing but materialized food for two months. I came here for Italian," she said eagerly.

The waiter bowed shallowly, amused. "Do we need to see the wine list?"

I had seen enough period movies to know that I could take the old fashioned wine list and make my best guess, maybe consult with a database using my command console, or I could defer to the waiter's choice. "What would you recommend?" I asked casually.

"That all depends on whether you prefer a brut, dry vintage or a more doux, sweet tasting wine."

I raised an eyebrow, not quite sure if he was asking the question to be difficult, or if this was his way of making my decision easier. "Something a little sweet, but closer to the middle," I replied.

"Very good, I have just the vintage for you. A Bergeron. Only six years old but full bodied. It will suit any dish, unless you plan on ordering chicken."

"I think I'll have the spaghetti," I said as I opened the menu.

Ayan was already browsing. The menu looked old fashioned with a leatherette cover, but once you opened it each dish was listed with a video portrait of how it looked on the plate. It was no fast food operation however, of which there were many that pretended to be classy but really made everything in high resolution materializers. On the fancy fast food restaurant menus you could actually select one of the dishes and smell it in advance. It was easy to imagine that, if they had a real kitchen in this restaurant, having each dish smell exactly the same every time it was served might be a little difficult. "I'll have the vegetarian lasagne," Ayan said as she handed the menu back. "And a dessert menu," she finished with a smile.

"Oh, I don't think you'll need one," the waiter said in a whisper. "Fresh strawberries have just arrived, I'll have the chef sprinkle them atop our famous chocolate cheesecake for the both of you. But, it is very expensive, I must warn you."

"How expensive?" I asked in an equally low whisper.

Ayan fixed me with a look that was at once pleading and warning.

"I'll have the spaghetti, and the cheesecake when we're ready, please."

"Very good, Sir. I'll return with the wine momentarily," he concluded with a bow before striding off to the back of the restaurant. I watched him as he returned the menus and continued on into the kitchen. I could see past him as one of the double doors swung open and there was a hustle and bustle of noise and activity as chefs in white worked actual stoves and moved in a coordinated rush.

"Well I feel under-dressed," I commented quietly. "Next time we go to an authentic restaurant remind me to materialize a suit."

"That's presumptuous of you, especially on a first date," Ayan teased with a crooked grin.

I was caught completely off guard. I hadn't thought about that at all. Being with her was just so natural no matter where we were. That would have been the perfect thing to say just then, but would you think that it would occur to me in that moment? "Well, I would have thought we were past that by now," I said instead, and wished I could take it back right away.

"Past that? I think your rank has gone to your head, Captain." Thankfully she had a sense of humour, and a smile that I couldn't help but return, despite the sudden onset of anxiety.

I didn't get a chance to respond. I hadn't noticed the nafalli had finished and were half way to our table. All five of them came to stand right across the opening of our booth, and one of them, the smaller, white and red furred one with the pink nose, made a sound like she was clearing her throat. "I'm sorry to interrupt," she started. "But my husband couldn't help but over-hear you speaking about us."

Ayan responded without missing a beat. "I'm so sorry for staring. We've never seen your kind in person. Holograms don't do your race justice. We didn't mean to distract you from your meal."

The much taller one, a male I assumed, put his long arm around the white and red one, resting his clawed hand on her shoulder. "Oh, that we're used to. We know we are far from home. What my wife would like to say is that I overheard something I found very kind. She only wanted to thank you."

"You could hear us across a busy restaurant?" Ayan asked, relaxing visibly.

"Yes, you cannot see our ears, but we have excellent hearing. When you said humans could learn from us, from our peace after so much war, it touched me," the taller, grey and black haired male said.

"I was so happy when he told me about it, I wanted to rush over and thank you. This trading expedition has not been easy. We have met many who have been unkind. Hearing good words has lifted me," she gushed, picking up one of Ayan's hands with both of hers. "I am Loori."

"I am Ayan. This is Jonas," she replied.

The large grey and black took one of my hands in his. It was warm. He was very good at keeping the claws from touching me while he clasped my hand in four thick fingers and one very long thumb. "I am Oomal. My family and I are about to begin our journey back home. Our ship is the Aulson, which means Laden Vessel in your language."

"I'm the Captain of the First Light. She is the Chief Engineer."

"That's a very good coupling!" Loori burst out.

One of the other grey and black furred nafalli shook his head and covered his nose with a hand. "Mother, you're embarrassing them. Other races don't gossip and openly comment like we do."

"Oh hush, it's a good match, don't you think?" Loori said as she looked to her husband.

"It would be. I don't think it's like that. Humans don't travel with family often, remember?"

Loori looked from Ayan to me then back to Ayan, her grey-green eyes looking hopeful. "Oh, but it must be. Tell me it is!"

Ayan was starting to blush and was about to say something when she was interrupted by a shorter white and orange furred nafalli. "Look! They're changing colour! I love it when they do that, it's so pretty!"

"It's our first date," Ayan said quietly, laughing and blushing a new shade of red. I was doing the same.

"Yup, that's embarrassing even by our standards," the younger male, whose hand was still over his nose, said as he shook his head again.

"It was very nice meeting you. Thank you for cheering my wife up," Oomal said as he started moving his family off.

"It was my pleasure. Good journey home," Ayan said after them.

Loori nodded as her husband guided her away from the table towards the door. "You too! Don't let this one stray off, he looks like a successful one!" She said in a conspiratorial whisper as though I couldn't hear.

The waiter was patiently standing behind them and stepped in right away, filling two glasses and shaking his head. "We'll miss them."

"Oh, they came in often?" Ayan asked.

"Every night since they came into port two weeks ago. I

have never seen anyone enjoy spaghetti so much. We were a little shocked when they first sat down. As far as we knew they didn't come to this part of the galaxy, but they were so kind."

"I'm sure they'll be telling everyone at home about this place," I replied. "You might have to stock up on spaghetti."

"I'm sure nothing would please our chef more," he said as he put the carafe in the centre of the table. "Your food will be out in a moment. In the meantime, please enjoy our fresh garlic bread. It is baked in a miniature fabricator oven inside the table." As though prompted by the phrase, a circle opened in the table and table cloth to admit a basket of hot buttered garlic bread.

"I have to get one of those for my new quarters," Ayan said, looking at the breadbasket wide eyed.

She looked up from the breadbasket and I was struck, mesmerized. The way her red curls framed her face, her full smile made its appearance, and those glad blue eyes looked right into mine. I just stared for a moment.

She cocked her head a little and quietly asked, "Hey, where's your head right now?"

I realized that I wore an expression that was a close match and took her hand in mine. "Right here."

"I wouldn't have believed it if someone told me what would come of those sims. To be out here with you, not in some virtual social environment after all the action is over, but in a restaurant so far from home."

"I'm glad Minh delivered on his threat to tell someone in Command I was involved with the scenarios."

Ayan was absolutely shocked. "That bugger! I was wondering how Command tracked us all down so fast."

"Well, they would have found us out eventually."

"But now I know I owe him. First I'll prank him, probably with Laura's help, then I'll thank him. But in that order."

"Whatever you do, make sure you catch it on video at least. Holo if you can manage it."

"Oh, I'll make sure. Still, I have to admit I have no regrets. I really didn't know where things were going for me after the first refit was finished on the First Light on Freeground. I suppose I would have stayed on with the engineering team."

"With the rank of commander and being the one who directed the refit, wouldn't you have been chief engineer?"

"There's always the chance that someone more experienced would be brought in for the tour. I'd be there nevertheless, I think. No other plans. What about you?"

"What about what?"

"What would you be doing if you weren't caught up in all this?"

"Oh, if life had continued on as normal?"

"Right, any plans? Do you have some girl you left behind I don't know about?"

"God, no. There's no one back there. I brought everyone I really cared about with me on this trip. The only real friend I had was Minh. Everyone else was in the service or someone I was in contact with through the simulations."

"You didn't have any plans?"

"I'd try to think up a next step, sort of look around and see if there was anything I wanted to move on to, but then I'd be going to work for the day answering hails for the Port Authority. I didn't want to get back into the military. I was skilled as an engineer, but even after doing a tour and finishing well, I knew that wasn't what I wanted to be doing. Then Minh ran into Oz while he was on leave, he got into the sims as a fighter pilot, then dragged me into it."

"So the real story comes out. It's all Minh's fault. He dragged you into simulations, kept you in there for a couple years, then when he had you running the show he brought Fleet Command in."

"I never thought of it that way, but he didn't have to keep me in, trust me. The tactics and command were like an aphrodisiac, and if anything kept me coming back it was the people I shared so many experiences with."

"Virtual experiences. I know. I'd be aboard the Sunspire looking forward to being in a safe area, where we were communications free and I could spend some rec time with you guys."

"You were already out there. Sims must've seemed like a game in comparison."

"At first, but I was part of boarding parties, tactical raids, even a gunnery crew member in the sims. Aboard ship in the real world I was part of the engineering staff. I went planet or station side often enough, but only after the area was checked and they determined it was safe. I love the life, but in the sims I got to play the other side."

"So what you're saying is you'd like to take a shift with the gunnery crews or with Minh's fighter pilots?"

"Oh, no. I love running engineering. If Oz were to reassign me, I'd have to pull rank. Besides, I'm a nervous pilot. I kept failing the emergency segment of the manual pilot qualification. The test that starts with the ship spinning out of control kept on making me queasy and I could never manage to find the direction of the spin with the controls." She mimed a struggle with a control stick while crossing her eyes to emphasize her point, ending the short performance by puffing her cheeks as though she were about to throw up.

I laughed so hard some of the patrons couldn't help but look in our direction to see if they could catch the gag. "Well, I'll make a note in your file: not permitted in a gunnery position or as a fighter pilot."

"That's a kindness."

We just looked at each other for a lingering moment before we were interrupted by the waiter, who gracefully placed our steaming food on the table.

"I can't finish this, it's like they gave me enough for a family of four," Ayan said as she put her fork down. She had eaten almost half of what must have been the better part of a kilo of cheesy, saucy, thick lasagne. I had fared a little better with my spaghetti, and was wrapping some more of the noodles around my fork when my arm unit tingled slightly. It was a silent alert instead of a beep or a chime that would usually indicate an incoming message. I put my fork down and looked at the two dimensional display. "It's from Oz, emergency priority."

Ayan wiped her mouth with her napkin and patched her own command unit into the channel so she would hear everything in her ear implant. "I'll be pissed if we have to miss cheesecake."

I opened the channel and made sure that Ayan's silver command unit showed she was receiving as well. "About time you picked up. What were you doing anyway? Never mind, don't tell me," Oz complained in a whisper.

"There are two more coming around from the other way. Looks like they're from the same group," I heard Minh whisper.

He was patched into the communication as well, but was obviously talking to Oz.

"What's going on?" Ayan asked.

"Looks like there's a bunch looking to cash in on the bounty. So far Minh and I have spotted four pairs. Looks like they have a bit of training."

"Did the freighter crew tip them off?" I asked.

"Nope. One of the first things the mercs did was shoot one of them when we tried to shake them. The rest of the freighter crew are with us, trying to get back to their ship."

Ayan brought up a map of the station and zeroed in on Oz and Minh. They were in the warehouse district near the port, but were slowly headed away from the First Light. "Did they manage to cut off your route back to the ship?"

"First thing they did. If these guys weren't after us I'd say we should hire them onto our security team. Hey, look around, is there anyone paying a little too much attention to you?" Oz asked.

Ayan and I looked at each other, we were so distracted that a family of thirty could have sat down right beside us and we wouldn't have noticed. She forced herself to look relaxed and I did the same, sitting back in my seat to get a better view past her and outside of the booth without drawing attention. I immediately spotted two men at a table three meters away; they were trying to be inconspicuous, but one was wearing a collapsed long rifle across his back and the other had a well used pulse pistol strapped to his leg. They were wearing different colours, one green and the other dark brown, but the outfits they wore were ready for space, had lots of pockets and reminded me of something an infantry unit would wear out in the field.

I looked to Ayan, who was stretching very convincingly, and she whispered, "Lovely couple about three metres behind you blocking the door," without moving her lips.

"So you've got company?" Minh confirmed over the communicator.

"Yup. Two behind Ayan eating food formed from protein base, probably can't afford anything from the Italian menu."

"You're eating at an Italian restaurant? Damn! I knew we should have stuck together."

I ignored him and looked to Ayan. "How are you feeling?" I whispered.

"Oh, better, much better. Just too much lasagne, feel a bit full."

"She had lasagne?"

"It sounds like they were on a date," Oz concluded.

"Are you sure?" I asked Ayan.

"Don't worry, I won't go passing out again," she replied, rolling her eyes.

"Passing out? Are you all right, Ayan?" Oz asked, alarmed but still whispering.

"Really, I'm fine, now can we all stop worrying about me and figure a way away from these bounty hunters?" she said, irritated.

The two inconspicuous gentlemen behind her looked straight at me. I shouted the first thing that came to mind in a doomed effort to cover. "Check please!"

Ayan chuckled in reflex and her eyes widened at something that was happening over my shoulder a moment later. I didn't think, I just turned the table onto its side and dropped down behind it. Ayan followed my lead. The air was pierced by the sound of an energy pulse pistol and I could smell wood burning.

"I am not having a gunfight on our first date!" Ayan shouted in irritation, drawing her sidearm. "This is a nice restaurant, and I'm coming back for the cheesecake!"

A second shot hit the table and I could see a burn mark appear on our side, our cover wouldn't last long. I nodded at her. "I agree, no gunfights on the first date."

"Everything okay?" Oz asked.

"Nope, under fire," Ayan replied, peeking up from behind the table and firing towards the rear of the restaurant.

"Time to go, follow me," I said as I picked up the table and held it in front of us. I drew my sidearm as I rushed the door. Ayan was already right behind me, firing a few shots well above the table the pair at the rear of the restaurant were taking cover behind to ensure that she wouldn't catch anyone in the crossfire.

As we got to the door, I threw the table at a pair of bounty hunters who were firing from the entrance. In a couple steps we were out and running through the crowd. "You all right?" I asked her.

"I'm good. You're fun under pressure."

"Thanks. Can't let a few thugs blow our evening."

"Whenever you're done flirting," Jason interjected through the communicator, "I thought you might like to know that Laura and I made it back to the ship. We were just relaxing in observation when I got an alert from the bridge about emergency communications. Did you guys think maybe you could get a security team out there to help you back to the ship? Oz? Minh?"

"Nice of your people to check in on us," Oz replied. "You

really have to spend some quality time with your communications crew, and yes, I did think that a security team would be nice. One sec, grenade." There was an explosion and a moment later he was back on. "Like I was saying, we're completely cut off and any security team would be caught in an ambush on the way here. We're taking cover in a warehouse on the way to the freighter. We'll get away on that."

"You say there's probably a welcoming committee between us and the ship?" I asked.

"Oh yeah. Probably a whole bunch. These people don't seem to care much about taking us alive, just getting a scrape of DNA to show that we've been wiped out," Minh said. I could hear Oz's shotgun go off in the background.

"Then we'll head towards you while Jason has a security team go check the hallways leading to the ship. If it gets too hot just have them fall back, I think that freighter might be the way out."

"What if they have ships waiting in the port? A freighter wouldn't be much—" Jason was asking before Minh cut him off.

"Get my pilots into their fighters so they can cover us! Do I have to think of everything?" Minh asked.

"Only when I'm not thinking of everything else," Oz added. I could hear they were running.

"Fastest route to Commander McPatrick and Commander Buu's location for you, Captain," a voice from the communications staff said.

"Forward it to me. I'll navigate while the captain finds us a ride," Ayan said.

Just as she said it, a pair of very serious looking people came around the corner in front of us, pointing what I could only describe as hand cannons right at us. There was no space, maybe two meters between us and them, and there was no time. I made a split second decision and fired at the one on the right. I hadn't actually seen what our new sidearms could do, but the force of the projectile it fired ripped a hole through his right thigh.

His companion wasn't as fortunate. Ayan's bolt of white-hot matter and energy pulped one of his hands and went straight into his chest, opening a charred entry wound ten centimetres across. The crowd became a milling pandemonium for as far as we could see in every direction.

We made our way through the crowd until we found a service hallway, and with the exception of the occasional worker or service robot, it was clear. Ayan was interpreting Jason's directions, and the maps he used to guide us along the paths of least resistance were working. Before long we were almost at the port storage area that Oz, Minh and the Triad freighter crew were using for cover. The going was slow for them; every time they thought they found a clear path to the loading dock it was blocked by a container or well-armed thug.

"This can't be a coincidence!" I heard Minh yell over the communicator. "It's like someone's using those lifters to move cargo containers in our way. Anyone on your team working on the station's network, Jason?"

"I've been monitoring security, Sir, they haven't so much as noticed that there's a firefight in one of their loading facilities. It's like someone's turned the alarms in that section off," replied one of the newer members of the communications team.

"Can you see a hack?" Oz asked in a whisper.

"No, Sir. Not yet."

"Well, sounds like we're on our own. How close are the happy couple?"

"According to this we should be right on top of the storage area," Ayan said from behind as she looked at the map on her command console. "There's an access panel just ahead. The crawlway under it should lead us to them."

I saw what she was pointing at, a panel that looked like it had been pried at and dented many, many times. "Doesn't exactly look secure. Shouldn't be a problem," I skidded to a stop and started working at the edge of the panel to get a grip.

Ayan stopped behind me, out of breath and leaning on her knees. "I should start running with you and Doc Anderson. You're barely winded and I'm just about falling down."

"Three months ago I'd be on the floor already," I replied as I pulled the hatch open. There was a tangle of wires and cables running through the crawlspace between us and the storage area. "Anything about this on the map?"

Ayan didn't have to look. "The crawlspace goes on for a couple of kilometres, but the hatchway leading to storage is just a couple meters through that access area."

We both heard running footsteps somewhere down the hallway. We sealed our suits just in case we needed insulation from bare live wires and slipped as gently as possible between the cables and wires into the service area.

Ayan slid in without a hitch, dropping between the major cables and winding through the smaller strands of loose wiring. Her quick agility was surprising and impressive. "I should start practising yoga with you. Maybe Doc could join in."

"Sure, but it'll be a lot more fun if Doc isn't there. Hurry, they're coming."

When it was my turn to follow, I wasn't nearly as agile. I heard a terrible rip as my foot caught on a whole bundle of delicate wires and tore right through them. The hatch came down behind me and I ended up lying right on top of Ayan.

"At least you bought me dinner first," she whispered.

I quietly cleared a space beside us, pushing some of the slack wiring aside. I rolled over, drawing my sidearm and pointing it at the hatch. We waited quietly, listening to the footsteps - at least four pairs - getting closer and closer until they passed right overhead and down the hallway.

"Captain, I found the user controlling the loaders and lifters in the cargo bay. They also have control of the primary surveillance systems, as well as interior door control for that section," Jason said in our earpieces. "Minh's right. They've been moving things around to box you in and keep you away from the ship."

I illuminated the palms of my suit, then Ayan and I crawled over to the panel that led into the cargo storage area. There was a secure seal on it with a small control panel. I tapped the tiny screen and it came to life, displaying spaces for eight numbers, letters, or other types of characters to be entered. "Well, this could take a while. The hatch to the cargo area is locked down with an eight-digit pass code." I got up on my knees and pointed my sidearm at the centre of the hatch.

"Normally I'd take this opportunity to tell you how bad an idea that is, but we're in a hurry," Ayan said with a shrug.

I took a shot, and after the noise, light, and smoke had cleared, saw a tiny divot left behind by the blast.

"I vote for plan B," Ayan concluded, getting back down on her stomach and taking a closer look at the security panel.

"I second that. Is there a security port anywhere on that thing?" I asked.

"Nope, but that's never stopped me before," she replied, pulling a tool out of her thigh pocket. "Us engineers with infantry skill sets get plenty of training on gently cracking into locked hatches. Really useful in rescue operations, especially when we're rescuing ourselves."

"I know," I replied as I got in position, putting myself between her and the hatch we entered through.

"I keep forgetting you were an engineer with Minh's infantry unit. Do you think you could get this opened faster?" she asked, but not as a challenge. It was an honest question.

"Probably not. I got to crack a lot of secure compartments during the All-Con Conflict, but it's been years." I turned on my infrared sight and motion sensors then looked towards the hallway above us. "Jason, how are our security teams doing? Any luck getting from the First Light to Oz and Minh?"

"Someday I'll have to find out where you got your talent for good timing. I was just about to tell you that the lead team just came under fire about two sections away from the storage area."

"About a quarter of the way here. Recall them. How is the refit on the ship going? Would it be possible to get underway if you had to?"

Ayan, her suit still sealed so her face wasn't visible, looked up to me and shook her head. "Probably not for a couple more hours at least."

"Main propulsion is still offline and we have a lot of exposed sections. Repairs are ahead of schedule but we'll be down for at least two more hours," Laura chimed in from engineering.

"Well, get the fighters ready. They're going to have to cover us when we escape on this freighter," Minh said in a more official than usual tone. "I want every bird we have off the deck and in the port five minutes before we're ready. Hide behind bigger ships. I don't want whoever is after us to see where they're coming from until it's too late."

"As soon as we're aboard the freighter, inform port security that we're being pursued by bounty hunters," I added.

"From what I'm seeing, whoever has control of the surveillance systems has permission to be in the network. They're using legitimate codes, so they're either doing this with the blessing of the station, bribed the officials here, or stole them."

"Well, then we won't be telling them anything they don't already know," Oz replied. "That's one more bounty hunter down, by the way; I estimate three left on my end of the storage centre."

"I estimate five from where I'm sitting. Hard to tell since they keep shooting every time I try to get a peek," Minh replied.

"Don't worry, boys, help is on the way," Ayan said as she wired a port on her command unit to the open security access panel. "Jason, I'm connected directly to the security panel. Can you run a cracking program on it using the main computer?"

"Right away, Commander," one of Jason's communications team replied.

I looked down briefly and saw Ayan's left forearm light up as her command unit started hacking the security panel. Looking back up, I could see from the motion detector that the five hunters who had bypassed us were returning. "They're coming back."

She handed me her sidearm and went back to work on the

security panel. "Try not to hit anything that'll blow us up or roast us alive."

"Right. I'll try to avoid hitting the big cables or the red, blue, or yellow pipelines," I said, aiming both barrels at the far side of the hatch where the infrared shapes of the bounty hunters were gathering.

"Hey, Captain, there's a button on the stock of those hand cannons that increases concussive force, mass, and impact spread," Oz said.

I looked quickly and found it. The multi-position slider didn't have any markings. "Do I adjust them forward? Backward?"

"Forward."

"Is that towards the barrel or—" I gave up as I saw two of the shapes overhead bending down towards the hatch. "Screw it. One slider goes forward, one backward." I adjusted both handguns quickly with my thumbs and took aim.

The pair began lifting the panel and I fired. One of the guns didn't kick at all, the other kicked so hard that the impact dampening mechanisms built into the skin of my vacsuit reacted, keeping my shoulder from getting dislocated. The hatch above was blown violently upward into the bounty hunters. A moment later my suit's warning system marked two huge cables as live and exposed. "Is your suit completely sealed?" I asked Ayan.

"Yup, what are you planning?" she replied.

"If these guys are as surprised and off guard as I think they are, we won't have to worry about them for long," I said as I grabbed one of the live lines, stepped into the void my sidearm had left in the cables, and whipped the end up into the hall. I thought I was quick enough — I didn't think any of them had a line of sight on me — but I was wrong.

Before the cable touched the metal deck plating in the hallway above to electrocute the bounty hunters, one of them shot me full on with a pulse rifle. It missed my head, my shoulder, and somehow caught me in the side. It was just a wave of heat at first, like a really bad burn, then massive throbs of pain wracked me from the ribcage down. I inhaled sharply and fell back down. As the air filled my lungs, there was more pressure, more pain. I knew my suit was still sealed — I would have been fried by the free running current otherwise, but I knew that at best I had suffered organ damage. At worst, that shot had fried me from one side to the other, and the pain I was feeling was my insides cooking within the confines of my vacsuit. I tried not to think about it.

"Got it!" Ayan shouted as she moved the lower hatch leading into the storage area aside.

I tried to look and was interrupted by a new wave of pain from my middle. I ground my teeth and dropped both guns, punched up the emergency screen on my command unit and set my suit to administer pain killers.

"Jason, can you get control of the gravity in this section?" Ayan asked.

"We can, why?"

"We're about a hundred or so meters up from the deck, and I left my ladder in my quarters."

"So you want me to turn the gravity in that section off?" asked Jason.

"Do it in the entire storage area!" Oz interjected. "I can get the drop on all three of them if you shut it down right now."

"We're ready, go!" Minh added.

"All right, shutting gravity— Wait a minute." Jason stopped for a moment. "Captain, are you all right? I have a reading here that your suit's administering enough pain meds to knock out a stim freak."

I had just realized that I couldn't move my legs, and was pulling myself towards the hatchway with my arms. The pain meds had my head fogged up. Somehow I thought I wouldn't be drawing attention to myself. "I'll be fine." I was still clear enough to formulate a plan, and through the corner of the open hatch I could see a number of anti-gravity loader trucks right below us. "Just get us to one of those loader trucks and we'll pick everyone up." It felt like I was talking through a mouthful of cotton, but I was sure everyone understood me.

"You're not fine. I'm seeing heat damage across your lower torso," Jason interjected.

Instead of wasting time by pulling up my status on her command unit, Ayan looked at my unit, which was already displaying everything she needed to know. She looked for a second and pulled one of my arms around her shoulders. "Hit it, Jason! Drop all the gravity in this section! We're getting out of here!"

Ayan waited for a few seconds while the gravitational hold on us released. She put my arms around her neck and I held on as she manoeuvred us through the open hatch and pushed off.

The storage area was huge, at least a couple square kilometres. How Minh and Oz could be trapped there along with a small freighter crew made perfect sense upon seeing the sheer size and complexity of it. There were thousands of standard shipping containers along with just as many non-standard ones, a couple smaller cargo hauling units and dozens of vehicles for moving them around.

As we were just getting to the loader truck, there was a massive white decompression explosion about a kilometre ahead. Ayan grabbed onto one of the rails alongside the loader and I held fast to her. The blast was greatly diminished by the time it hit us a second later because there were a number of storage containers in the way that dissipated the blast, thankfully.

"Three down!" Oz cheered. "Now come pick us up!"

"Nice. Nearly flattened us out here," Minh said dryly.

"Anyone caught in the open when that blew?" Oz asked.

"Nope. Just mildly concussed one of our new friends. I think you owe him a drink."

Ayan opened the door to the loader's cab; there was room for one and empty space. I pulled myself inside and she directed my legs. "I'll be fine, really," I said as I settled into the cramped space. It was just large enough for me to sit in with my knees drawn up halfway to my chest. I remember thanking whoever invented the pain medication I was on for making that position possible.

"Hang on, we'll get out of this and have you in medical," Ayan whispered.

The loader lurched forward as Ayan started its engines. She looked at her command unit to verify everyone's location before hitting the accelerator. From that point, everything was a blur. There was some small weapons fire, which didn't affect the loader's heavy frame, and next Minh along with three crew members climbed into the back of the loader. We picked up Oz a few moments later; I remember him climbing into the cab and somehow bracing himself inside so he could take a better look at my command unit.

I winced as he touched several spots on my torso, applying gentle pressure then releasing and watching my command unit at the same time. He and Doctor Anderson were exchanging information, that much I know, but the levels of medication administered by my suit were so high that I barely understood what was going on.

I do remember one thing clearly. Oz leaning down close so he blocked out everything else. "Sorry, Captain, I've got to put you out until we can get you back to the infirmary. Doctor's orders."

I remember a wave of euphoria engulfing me and everything just faded away.

SEVEN
A REAL (SHORT) TRIP

My perception was completely distorted as my eyes opened to slits. I saw Ayan's face through a gauzy, hazy reality and smiled. "Hey there," I heard myself say dopily.

Oz's face came down right beside hers, his toothy, piano key grin spread wide across his face. "Hey! How's our action hero captain feeling?"

I tried to sit up but couldn't move my head more than a millimetre. "Why can't I move?"

Ayan caressed my face. "Doctor Anderson has you in a restraining field. You're awake so he can check on your brain and upper nervous system functions."

"That one shot you took nearly cooked your spine, and it got a couple organs. Moving would be bad while things are still setting," Oz added.

"Everyone out okay?" I asked.

"We made it onto the freighter, and as soon as Minh's flyboys came out of the shadows and the bounty hunters saw all those fighters, they bugged out. After that we circled it back round so we could get you to First Light medical."

"How's the ship?" I asked, my mouth was so dry it was sticky. "Thirsty," I said a little hoarsely.

Ayan held a straw up to my lips. "The refit is almost finished. I have final inspections in half an hour," she said with a smile.

"Doc fix you up?"

"Yes, I'm fine now. Back to work for me now that I'm eating and sleeping normally. We just need our captain back."

"I missed all the fun."

Minh came into view. He seemed to me like some kind of chimpanzee just then. "You've been out for two days, Jonas, but we've managed."

"Hehe, monkey." I chuckled.

"You were in and out of surgery for hours at a time," Ayan said. "But they managed to repair most of the nerve damage, transplant new organs. You can't move while you're regenerating so they have to keep you sedated."

"Did he just say monkey?" Oz asked Minh.

"Oh yeah, they have him drugged up good," he replied.

I pushed the straw out of my mouth with my tongue. "I'll be okay!"

The doctor seemed to just magically appear behind them then. Oz and Minh went away. "You'll be as good as new. Next time you wake up you'll be able to carry Ayan out of here. Even Oz if you'd like." He was holding an injector; it looked huge, a bit like a gun.

My eyes went wide but before I could panic Ayan came

back into view, smiled, and lightly brushed her lips against mine. "I'll see you when you wake up, luv," she whispered.

There was a fresh surge of euphoria, and the rational part of my brain was aware that Doc had just injected me with the next round of sedatives. I wasn't so much listening to the rational part of my brain, though. I felt so good, and sleepy.

Minh popped into view and waved. "Sweet dreams!" He said quickly.

"Monkey..." I felt my mouth sound out as my eyelids fell closed.

EIGHT
A COMPLICATED RECOVERY

The next time I woke up in medical, the effects of the sedatives and painkillers had gone, and so had any evidence of injury. I was still in a recovery bed, but my usual instinct to roll over and go back to sleep was absent. I had no idea what time it was, whether we were still in dry dock, what the condition of the crew was. I felt completely detached.

I sat up, checked my darkened surroundings, and couldn't really ascertain much. "Lights at fifty percent," I quietly ordered the computer. The dimmed lights came on as my feet touched the sterilized flooring. Before long, I was putting on my uniform while I looked at my medical status display at the foot of the bed.

The shot one of the bounty hunters hit me with had so much radiant heat that my suit couldn't prevent all of it from going through. It actually did burn right to the spinal cord, causing complete lower body paralysis. The surrounding organs were so badly damaged they had to be replaced with grown implants. My recovery had gone well and, if anything, I was healthier than before. Three days had passed.

Doctor Anderson and two other surgeons had worked on me, stimulating replacement nerve growth, extracting necrotic tissue and replacing it with new stock. My body hadn't rejected any of the new material and according to my chart I was all healed up. I took a moment to look at Ayan's medical records, and could only see the most basic information. I was only checking because I was concerned, but seeing that the bulk of the information was blocked raised suspicion. I picked up my arm command unit and started to put it on. "Recall last bioscan of Ayan recorded on this unit and diagnose, please," I requested.

"Indication of diabetes, ninety six point three percent certainty. Current ship records indicate this has been treated successfully."

"Was this a result of another health condition?"

"For more information on this crew member's condition, please speak with First Light Medical. Records are restricted to Doctor Anderson and treating physicians only."

I shook my head, knowing that if I wanted to pull up anyone's full medical history I could. The fact that Ayan's was locked out meant that there was something else wrong with her, or some kind of information that was sensitive. The more I tried to uncover what it was, the worse I felt about it. Asking her was the right thing to do, I knew that, but I was afraid of the answer.

I was just making sure that my command unit was sitting properly on my left arm when a nurse came into the room. "Captain! You shouldn't be up for another-"

"I read my chart. Looks like I healed up just fine and I feel like I've slept a week," I said as I walked right past her and towards the exit. "But, Sir, Doctor Anderson hasn't cleared you."

"I'm clearing myself. Send him to Observation Two if he wants to see his handiwork in person."

"Main Medical lockdown," the nurse said. The doorway into medical closed and I could hear the hard lock drop into place. I could defeat the security with my command code, but senior staff would be alerted. The lockdown procedure for main medical was in place in case there was a biological emergency of any kind, so ranking medical and command staff could contain it. I turned slowly back to the nurse who had trapped me in.

She stood there with her arms crossed. She was a small woman by any standards, but with the authority she was exuding she may as well have been three metres tall. "I can have Doctor Anderson here in a few minutes, Sir. You're not leaving until he clears you. Now, please follow me back to your room," she directed.

As I sat on the bed waiting, I sent messages to the entire senior staff, who were just set to begin their shifts in two hours. I needed an update on the ship, and I thought there would be no better time for a meeting.

Doctor Anderson entered the room after about fifteen minutes. "I'm glad to see you on your feet. Too bad I just finished my morning jog."

"I don't think I'll have time. Looks like I have a lot to catch up on."

"You do. I just got your message about the meeting in observation two. Good idea."

"So, what's the verdict? Am I going to live?" I asked.

Doc smiled and scanned my chart. "Looks like it, all the

new material took just fine and your nerves have mostly recovered. Some of them found new pathways instead of using the originally established ones, but that's normal. I'd tell you to take it easy for a few days, but you need to do the exact opposite now that we're sure there has been no rejection and that you're all rested up.

"Engage in as much physical activity as you can so you can re-train your body. We had to rebuild a critical part of your nervous system, and post operation stimulation rehabilitation isn't the same as exercise. As soon as you discover something doesn't feel right, or you find a problem — even if you think it's completely unrelated — inform medical right away."

"If those are the conditions of my release, then I accept."

"I hear Nurse Darya trapped you here," he said with a smile.

"She's good. She's really good," I affirmed, nodding. "But I knew that you could have had me on my feet four or five hours ago."

"I was hoping you'd get a little more sleep before starting out for the day. Captains, especially ones that are well connected to their crew, tend to over-extend themselves."

"Speaking of being well connected, I'm wondering if there's anything I need to know about Ayan. I hear she reports to medical for regular treatments, but she hasn't told me what for."

"Is this a personal or professional concern, Jonas?"

"Both. As her captain I need to know that she's fit for duty on and off the ship, and personally, I'm worried."

"Well, I can say that she's fit for duty, especially after she dragged you out of this most recent situation."

"That's after passing out while we were negotiating prices with a parts dealership."

I read Doc's concerned look for an instant. There really was something wrong.

"She didn't tell you. Was it in the medical logs? Something like that should be red flagged," I pressed.

"It would be, and there wasn't anything abnormal for the day reported from her command unit or standard uniform transponder. It must have been blocked."

"Communications were fine with the ship while we were on station, even from within the support structure of the asteroid. A medical alert should have made it through just fine."

"You're right," Doc said as he looked through the medical logs on his command unit. His was built into his uniform. "There's no record of her having an event. Are you sure she lost consciousness?"

"I'm sure. Here are the readings my command unit took." I brought the record up and sent the information to him.

He reviewed it for a moment and nodded to himself. "Well, these verify that she collapsed due to very low blood sugar."

"So she's diabetic."

"She was. We treated her and she's fine now. She'll still have to monitor her diet for a few more days while the treatment finishes its work."

I thought for a minute quietly.

"Well, if that's all, Captain—"

"No, it isn't. I only have basic medical training, but I know enough to be sure that this sudden diabetic condition has been caused by something else."

"Talk to her about it, Jonas. In the meantime I won't give

you confidential information that doesn't affect her performance unless you pull rank."

"I will, but if something else happens and I don't know how or why, I expect full disclosure."

"Under those conditions you'll have it," Doctor Anderson said quietly before leaving. Instead of continuing the argument, pushing just a little more, I decided to head to observation two.

The hallways were quiet, and when I reached Observation Two it was empty. I sat down at the meeting table and thought for a moment as I looked through the three days of reports that I had missed out on. I knew that I could have pulled rank with Doc. I was fully justified in doing so. Ayan had collapsed while on duty. Under those circumstances, a medical condition would be disclosed in a report with regard to a crew member's performance shortfall. The fact that Ayan was willing to hide it from Doc made me nervous. She did report for treatment shortly after returning to the ship. I believed she was fine for the moment, but I had to know what was going on, what the root cause of the problem was, even though I was afraid of the answer.

When Ayan walked in with two spill-proof safety cups with Laura at her side, I was filled with dread. I smiled weakly. The dread wasn't at seeing her. It was over what I knew I had to bring up with her. As a captain and as a what? Companion? Boyfriend? Not lover. And if she was keeping something from me, certainly not confidant. If she couldn't tell me about a long-term problem, how close were we?

"How are you feeling, Captain?" Laura asked cheerily. "So glad to have you back."

I tried to shake my personal feelings, the frustration and

concern intermixed with the urge to just dodge the whole situation. "Better than new, Sergeant."

Ayan put a mug down on the table in front of me and her smile faded.

"Can we have the room please?" I asked Laura.

Somehow she knew something serious was about to happen. She glanced to Ayan, who was staring at me, then looked back to me and nodded. "Yes, Sir, I'll be in Observation One."

"Thank you. Seal the room once you're outside," I ordered quietly. I stood and walked to the broad window. Once the door closed I chose my words very carefully and didn't look behind me, where Ayan stood silently. "The doctor cleared me this morning. I asked him how you were in the course of conversation afterwards. He didn't know you collapsed. There was no record of it."

I heard her sit down in a chair behind me. I watched as a small towing module drew several new Raze fighters along behind it, the ones we had purchased form Larsen's, I assumed. "I understand why you'd hide something like that from me, but from Doctor Anderson? I gave him my readings from the collapse and he confirmed it was diabetes, which no one should have. It's not like you can develop a sudden case." I sighed and sat down in the chair next to her so we were facing each other. I couldn't do this as a captain. There was no way I could order her to tell me about it. I just couldn't handle this like some robot officer. She looked stone-faced and ready for me to handle it that way, though. "Please tell me what's going on," I asked her quietly.

"I've already had that taken care of. It's not affecting my duties. I'm fine."

"That's just a symptom of something else. I know you've been getting treatments in medical for something since before we left Freeground. At first they were recorded as bone density enhancements, but afterwards there just wasn't any kind of explanation. I need to know, Ayan."

She looked me in the eye and shook her head. "You don't want to know this about me, Jonas." Her stony expression was dissolving under the pressure of tears.

I took both her hands in mine. "Whatever it is, it won't put me off."

She shook her head. "We'll see. I won't blame you if you feel differently." She took a deep breath and went on. "My mother and I are from Downe Colony. She was exiled for having me genetically modified past regulated tolerances."

I had heard something about that. The rumour that tens of thousands of people were exiled from that British Colony for illegal genetic engineering and that not a year later there was a massive influx on Freeground of immigrants, mostly skilled and middle to upper class, from British colonies. It was a well known conspiracy theory. I held onto her hands more tightly. "I don't care."

"Oh, you will," she said, pulling one of her hands free to wipe her tears away. "It's true. Almost all of us were engineered to learn faster, live longer."

"There's no crime in that. We eliminate disease and enhance performance in the earliest stages of pregnancy on Freeground. It's standard practice."

"But they impose limits on how much you can do. Too much modification leads to problems. But Downe Colony researchers were certain they found a new tolerance level, a way to modify more with less risk. They gave my group all the enhancements you'd expect, but they also enhanced us to be more physically appealing, chemically and visually, and to stay looking younger longer. It worked, but they didn't account for all the effects."

"Manos disease."

"You've heard of it."

"Yes, but I don't know much about it."

"Well, most of the children diagnosed with it were dead by the time they turned ten. The rest, a few thousand of us left now, suffer from systemic degradation. Some get sores, lose their sight, have other nervous system damage, or suffer from gradual organ failure like me. I need deep regenerative treatments so I don't just rot away on the inside. So yes, I go to medical weekly, and yes diabetes is just a symptom of a bigger problem."

"Do problems like this come up often?"

"No, but when they do, they range from minor inconvenience to several days in medical, having a transplant or serious long term treatment. They don't happen too often, every few years, but there are other things that result from my mother's choice to have me enhanced. I can't have children of my own. One of the conditions of Freeground taking us in when I was a baby was sterilization."

"You thought that if I knew I would treat you differently? You know I won't."

"There's more to it. A lot of us turned out just the way we were supposed to, the enhancement worked more than half the time. The positive enhancements, some of which I enjoy, come with different problems."

I knew exactly what she was talking about and simply nodded as the realization dawned on me.

"I know you noticed. Everyone does. The researchers and doctors focused on increasing our general appeal and removing any negative aspects. We are engineered to be charismatic; from pheromones to high cheek bones, I was made to look beautiful, and the people we meet can be divided right down the middle between the half that resent us and the others that want us for all the wrong things. The stigma that follows us around changes how everyone looks at us. They either think we're diseased or so enhanced that we're cheating."

For once I knew exactly what to say. "But before I ever knew what you looked like I was crazy about you. That hasn't changed," I whispered.

"It will. It should. It's one of the reasons why we're all out here."

I was dumbstruck.

"I'm not supposed to know. The doctor is the line of communication to Freeground. He reports straight to Intelligence. He's a friend of my mother's, but she didn't order him aboard. I don't know all the details, especially since she's not the one accountable for the First Light any longer. They removed her from command when they discovered that she had her eye on a Triad research station, one that no one has been able to find. She told me they're working on technologies that involve preserving life well past our current capabilities, beyond whatever we've seen. They knew that this would have something to do with me and everyone else who had Manos disease."

"So they thought she would use us for her own purposes.

Why not scrub the entire thing after discovering her intentions?"

"That's just it. She was still doing research. She didn't know if we could do anything about that Triad research station. She genuinely believed that you could accomplish your mission, to find new technologies and form new alliances, with the ship you were given and the crew that had signed on. After they decided Intelligence should be in direct command, things changed.

"This ship was supposed to have more technology than she left with — what exactly, I don't know — but the description I heard of it was 'game changing'. As in something that would make the difference in any combat engagement or intelligence gathering scenario. Instead of installing that technology, whatever it was, my mother was removed from direct command of our mission. Intelligence held the technology back and must have ordered Doctor Anderson on board."

"So they kept us on mission but invested fewer resources and didn't trust us nearly as much."

"There's more to it. I suspected that Doctor Anderson was this ship's handler, and yesterday I got proof. When the refit was finished, I caught him communicating through the station to Freeground Intelligence. They have an agenda all picked out for us. I don't know what it is, but they were waiting for us to reach a pre-set goal."

"And you were going to tell me this when?" I asked with a smirk.

"The morning meeting," she said with a shrug. "I would have left the part about me being a genetic freak out of it, mind you."

I caressed her face, still damp from tears. "You're still my genetic freak, right?"

She laughed for a moment, sniffed then sighed. "Of course."

"Feel better?"

She nodded. "I'm sorry I didn't trust you."

"Well, now you know you can." I pulled her into my arms for a moment. She felt smaller somehow, and even though I had told her nothing would change, I knew it had. I felt the need to protect her, to fix her, even though I knew she had the strength and intelligence to do that for herself.

"We had better get to that message. The doctor knows someone was eavesdropping. Besides, we don't want the crew thinking we wanted the room to ourselves for another reason entirely," she whispered before a light kiss.

We parted and she turned to play the recorded message but I stopped her. "Wait, I think I want the entire senior staff to hear this."

"Full disclosure?"

"May as well. We can keep your condition under wraps — that's not a problem — but I'd say if this message regards our mission out here, the senior staff should know about it."

"Jason and I thank you. He has exactly the same condition I do, only the problems are less advanced."

"I wouldn't have guessed. I won't tell him you informed me."

"Don't worry, he keeps it quiet. He just told Laura, but I'm positive you knowing wouldn't bother him. Give me a few minutes before you let anyone in," she said as she turned and strode off to the bathroom. "I have to freshen up."

"You look fine," I replied as I picked up the mug she had

brought for me. The smell of dark roast coffee was a welcome comfort.

"Maybe for someone who took an emotional roller coaster ride as soon as they woke up. Even the enhanced need a touch up now and then," she called over her shoulder before closing the door.

LETTERS FROM HOME

When the senior staff entered the room there were smiles all around, including Ayan and me. She sat at one end of the table while I stood at the door leading from Observation One where everyone had been waiting for the meeting to begin.

Oz was first, followed by Sergeant Ashbey and Lieutenant Nichols who were the off-shift bridge commanders. "Next time, let a subordinate take the shot for you. That's what the chain of command is for," Oz said as he shook my hand and took a seat beside my end of the table.

Minh was right behind with the new lead pilot for the First Light, Lieutenant Derek Gregor, who simply nodded. "Do they still have you drugged up?" Minh asked.

"Just an anti-rejection series for a couple of days. Nothing mood altering."

"Too bad, I kind of liked you all doped up."

Sergeant Jason Everin followed with two of his new communications staff, who were asking him questions about filtering combat communications. Sergeant Laura Compton returned and very quietly asked, "Is everything okay?" before going past me. I nodded reassuringly and she went on to sit beside Ayan.

Lieutenant Gerald Burgess was there to represent medical. I knew he was an excellent physician, and his records as an infantryman were spectacular as well, but he looked a little awkward when I shook his hand before sitting down. "Doctor Anderson said he'd be in his quarters," he said quietly.

"I understand, please have a seat," I invited.

We all sat down and I started things off. "I haven't had a chance for an inspection yet, but I hear the refit is complete."

"It isn't the same ship. When everything is closed up and the guns are behind hatches, you can't even tell she's armed. The moment you open those fighter bays and roll out the guns, it's a completely different story," Oz said as he brought up a hologram of the ship in the middle of the table. It rotated slowly, showing her sleek lines with all the armour in place, the weaponry put away.

Laura took over. "We were able to restore all the stationary armour and exterior hatches, even the coverage for the ram scoops and engines which weren't restored with the last refit. When that was complete, we closed the hull up and regenerated the ablative layer on the surface. If anything gets through our new energy shielding it'll have a lot to go through before it gets to us.

"Speaking of energy shielding, I'm happy to report that it's installed with multiple feeds from power systems. We now have primary, secondary and emergency shielding in place." She pointed to each different system on the three dimensional model as she mentioned them. She looked at Ayan, who urged her to continue. "All the high power systems have emergency capacitors that operate the hatches and can maintain a constant rate of fire for fifteen minutes or more if they're disconnected from the main power supply. It will also maintain a discreet energy shield for at least ten minutes.

"Energy distribution efficiency around the ship has increased by twelve percent without the assistance of the molecular quantum core, the crew quarters have been repaired and refurnished using captured as well as purchased fixtures, and the new bridge is complete. It's just in front of engineering control and has two elevator shafts that can shuttle officers between the fighter bay, medical, and engineering.

"I regret to report that I haven't finished reproducing the new command uniforms. Radiation leakage is still a problem as I try to miniaturize some of the components to fit seamlessly in the layers of the material, but I have found another use for the cloaking technology."

She brought an image up on the holoprojector in the middle of the table. It was a fierce looking double barrelled turret. "This is an older style of torpedo launcher that was employed on this ship originally and discarded when her rail cannons were upgraded over a century ago. I've kept almost completely to the original design, except for the armoured loading mechanism, since there was no real reason to change it. This weapon fires long range, high speed torpedoes using a rail cannon mechanism that is large and low energy enough to not register when it is mounted close enough to a rail cannon. For our purposes, we've mounted two right behind rail turrets, and one right on top of our port engine."

The holographic image launched a torpedo in slow motion and the projectile disappeared. "I've applied the cloaking technology to ten high-yield, nine kilogram antimatter torpedoes so no sensor can detect them. Whereas radiation, space limitations, and general safety may be important to someone wearing the cloaking technology, an antimatter torpedo doesn't much care. Ayan has approved the manufacture of eight more torpedoes, each having a shelf life of two years. We're marking these for demolition at the one year mark. I'm continuing my work on the command suits, but it'll be slow going. Freeground doesn't have all the technology that Triad did, and working at nano scale is taking longer than I thought.

"We've been able to integrate the molecular quantum computer core from the Overlord. It will work in conjunction with our computer even though we can easily turn it on and off on a second's notice if there are any problems. No Freeground ship this size — even ten times her size — has ever had that much calculating power, so we don't know exactly how to use all of it, but we'll find a way. Other than that, the ship is safer than ever, more well armed than ever, and she even looks better than ever," Laura sat down with a smile. "With prep work done in hyperspace and the rest done in four days, I think everyone did a pretty good job."

One of Jason's communications crew started to applaud and stopped right away. "We don't clap," Jason said, shaking his head.

The comm officer, a dark haired young woman, shook her head. "No?"

"Nope, we might want to, but not during meetings."

"Sorry, Sir."

"You can buy Laura a drink later."

"If there was ever a reason to applaud, I think we have one. I wonder how much time it would take the Freeground crews to finish a refit like that?" I asked, partially to lighten the moment and move things along.

"Along with the repairs, I'd say about two weeks running around the clock. We didn't have to do anything with the quarters, though. The crew you hired from the station did a fantastic job," Ayan said. "I can't wait to move into my new Officer's quarters."

"You haven't already?"

"The crew are waiting for you to perform the final inspection, Sir. The general sentiment is that they want to finish this refit by the book. I think they just want to show off their handiwork," Oz said as he continued to look through personnel reports.

"But they didn't work on the crew quarters."

"I think they just want to make sure you inspect the entire ship," Minh put in. "My deck crews and fighter pilots are the same way. I don't think you'll be able to skip a single compartment."

"Well, at least I know what I'll be doing for my first day back on active duty," I said with a chuckle. "You're up, Sergeant Everin. What does communications have to report?"

"Well, Zingara station authorities apologized for the level of access and appearance of cooperation the bounty hunters had during the incident, but would not make reparations until I informed them of your medical status. They also backtracked a little since they had only managed to apprehend two of the offenders. We were able to cite a few commerce laws and had our dry docking fees waived."

"That's almost worth getting shot for, only next time I'll fake it," I commented and the people who laughed hardest were the few there that didn't know me well. They seemed surprised that their captain had a sense of humour.

Jason went on. "They seized the bounty hunters' starfighters and other property, and sentenced both the bounty hunters to twenty days in Longshadow Penitentiary."

"It's a good thing the port authority got there before our interceptors were in range," Minh interjected. "Our pilots managed to take out six of their ships before peace keepers cut it short."

"You're just lucky they didn't get any shots at the freighter we made off in. It wasn't exactly made for combat," Ayan added.

"Back on point," Sergeant Everin interjected, drawing attention back to him, "as far as the station is concerned, the matter is closed. We got a lot more out of it than they had to provide us with by law. I recommend we don't pursue any other action."

"I know if I ever find those bounty hunters, I'll make sure they regret ever picking up our contract," Derek said quietly.

"Sergeant Everin is right," I retorted. "The next time we see anyone involved with this, it will most likely be in another port. If we make the first move, even in retribution for what happened here, we'll be on the wrong side of the law. Mark this incident closed. If they or any other bounty hunters come after us, we have to follow procedure."

"Right, the procedure for being under attack in a neutral port is pretty simple," Oz added. "Contact your senior officer on the ship and then station security, both at the same time if possible. Report that you are being followed or are under attack. Provide them with all the information they need to assist you. That includes their description, where you are, where they are, where you first noticed them, where you're going, and details of any communications you've had with them and any actions they have taken. Tactically, you should find cover or surrender if cover isn't feasible. Our security teams will already be en route. The port law enforcement officers should be on the way as well, though that isn't always the case. After that point it's up to your senior officers, our security and legal teams to save your butt, so trust them and follow their instructions."

"Thank you, Commander, you should send a copy of the most recent leave procedures to everyone. Is there anything else to report, Sergeant Everin?"

"There has been a priority message from Freeground, marked as captain's eyes only. It arrived four hours ago, encoded for your bioprint." He slid a copy of it across the table to me.

I took the small silver chip in my hand and looked at it for a moment. It was the size of my fingernail but it would change everything. The tension in the room had risen the instant I picked it up and what I was about to say wouldn't alleviate that. "This isn't as much of a surprise to me as some of you might imagine. We'll finish the business of the meeting, then there is another message that will most likely be a good primer for whatever Freeground has in store for us." The expressions around the table were expectant, anxious. "So, what does medical have to report?"

Lieutenant Gerald Burgess cleared his throat and stood up. "Upgrades are all complete. We now have eight more emergency beds that stow away until they're needed, local inertial dampeners are operating at peak efficiency and will hold everyone within the medical area steady even while the rest of the ship is being tossed. We have four more long-term stasis tubes, giving us a total of twelve. All but minimal medical staff have been put on rest since there are expected to be no more than two patients checking in today," he reported clearly and officially.

I nodded at him and he sat down. "Thank you, Lieutenant. We're glad to have you at the table." I looked to Oz then, who had his arms crossed, deep in thought. "How is the crew, Commander?"

He leaned forward in his chair and addressed everyone else at the table as much as me, which was appropriate for a senior staff meeting. "All departments report ready to depart. The crew are still tired, but we were able to give everyone about ten solid hours of rest with the exception of a small watch and skeleton crew on the bridge. They're also very proud of what we've done here." He brought up a list on his arm command console. His was the same style as mine, black to match his bridge uniform, but not attached to the material so it was easier to take off. "We have one pregnant crew member. She's been transferred to light duty in the core sections of the ship for safety. There has been one formal request made that has to be brought to the attention of the senior staff. The gunnery crew has requested that you choose a qualified gunnery captain from their ranks."

"How many turrets do we have now?" I asked in Ayan and Laura's general direction.

Ayan brought the image of the First Light up on the display

in the middle of the table, only this time the turrets were all in the deployed position. "We have thirty eight turrets in total. We were able to add several while the hull was being repaired. Ten of the turrets are now automated."

"Now that's a destroyer!" Minh exclaimed, standing up to get a closer look at the First Light.

"Actually, when she was first built and launched as a destroyer she had fifty six turrets. As the ship was re-tasked in a more long range reconnaissance role, and as individual weapons became more powerful, the space was used for other systems and extra armour."

I looked back to Oz, who was smiling at the sight of our nearly kilometre long destroyer. "How many gunners do we have now?"

"We're running thin, actually. Only thirty two. For that many turrets, we should have at least fifty. If we don't pick anyone up, we should look into more automation."

"Well, that many gunners should have a captain, regardless. We'll review candidates and promote someone." I looked to Minh and nodded. "Your turn, Commander Buu. How is every-thing shaping up on the flight deck?"

"We're glad to have breathing room again. We didn't need any upgrades, just a few repairs, a little rebuilding in a few corners, and with all the salvage out of the way it was quick work. All the fighters have been upgraded with energy shield-ing, a couple have brand new Vindyne faster-than-light systems, and the new Raze fighters look fantastic, or so the flight crew tells me. Everyone's ready to go. The pilots are getting a little antsy and are spending a lot of time in the simulations."

"Well, as much as I hope we don't need to scramble fighters, I get the feeling that we'll be in that position soon. That brings me to the next order of business: classified communications. Everyone but the commanders and Sergeant Everin clear the room, please. Don't worry, you'll be briefed later on a need to know basis. Until then, you're not to discuss anything you've heard about communications to anyone for any reasons. If you are asked about this meeting, inform them that you are not cleared to discuss anything and refer them to your senior officer. You are dismissed."

All but the commanders, which included Ayan, Oz, and Minh, and Jason, even though he was technically still a sergeant, left the room quietly. Jason ensured the room was sealed and nodded. "We won't be interrupted."

"You know, we really need to promote you. The last high ranking communications officer on a ship this size I knew was a major," Minh said, scratching his head.

"Well, depending on what we're about to hear this morning, that might happen sooner rather than later," I said flatly.

"What's going on, Jonas? I feel like I'm in the dark, and you were the one out of commission for the last three days," Oz asked.

"Ayan intercepted an encoded transmission from Doctor Anderson to Freeground Intelligence."

"I saw that encoded transmission, I was going to bring it up when we were alone since I couldn't decode it and it wasn't from a command station," Jason commented.

"Well, I didn't so much intercept the transmission, so much as use surveillance to pick up the discussion with the audio receptors inside the compartment the transmission was sent from," Ayan added. "It would have taken me years to decode, otherwise."

"Play it," I ordered quietly, taking a deep breath.

Ayan activated the playback on her command unit. It was only audio, but Doc's voice was immediately recognizable. "You received my report," he said in a serious, dry tone.

"Yes. Are you sure they're ready for assignments? I see the modifications and the data, but I'll be honest, it's hard to believe they've come this far in such a short time. For her tonnage, they're better armed than any ship in the fleet. The addition of antimatter systems and a molecular quantum core combined with our best power plants, energy shielding, multi-layered refractive shielding, and a regenerating ablative hull they've managed to put to good use, it's almost too good to be true. Hell, if I took these specs to Command and asked to build it, they'd shut me down and assign me to cleaning the outer hull of the station. Building something like this from scratch would take years and would cost eight times as much as any other ship in her class."

"Don't forget the crew. They've been tested, most have already seen more action that half the servicemen and women out there. I've also never seen a shadow ship survive the loss of her captain for so long and retrieve him."

"I'm sure you had a part in that."

"A couple shifts on the bridge to fill in, but I did nothing, really."

"So you think they're ready."

"They are. But at this rate, with the way this crew performs, I think there are better tasks. Wheeler should go this mission alone. His skillset and the Triton are perfect for it," Anderson said sternly.

There was a pause before the senior officer responded. "Wheeler will be on this regardless of whether the First Light goes, but the ships are doing this together. We ran the simulations, the success rate quadruples with the First Light drawing fire."

"At least give them some time to finish developing the cloaking technology. They're close. I'm sure I could shift their focus towards cloaking the entire ship and they'd have it done in less than two months."

"The order has been given. Now sit back and let it happen. Do whatever you have to in order to make it happen, and contact us only if there is a drastic change in the situation."

"This is a waste of resources and you know it. The First Light and her crew might not be subtle, but they're not a blunt instrument. If Fleet wants them to serve their purpose as an unconventional solution, they should think outside of the box when they're choosing objectives. Waste this crew and it'll blow back on you."

"This mission is as far outside the box as we've gone. Besides, you couldn't imagine the pressure I'm under here. I have Intelligence on one side, the Admiralty telling me to get this done by any means without telling them how it happened once we've accomplished the mission. And to make matters worse, Rear Admiral Rice has me on comms five times a day. This happens with the First Light, because with her in the middle it's a sure bet. We can't depend on Wheeler without someone like Valent watching him, and he just doesn't have the people to get to one of the critical objectives."

"How long until Intelligence issues the order?"

"A day or so. You'll know when Valent receives his instructions. Fleet Intelligence, out."

Everyone sat back in their chairs as the recording ended. I couldn't stay in my seat and walked over to the window. It was all quiet out there, the refit had been finished. From my vantage point I could see the dry dock was all set for the next ship. "It had to be someone. Freeground would not let us go without having a handler," I said quietly. "That's the first thing we have to realize. I also want everyone to be aware that he might not be the only person on this ship looking over our shoulders."

"But did it have to be him?" Jason asked. "I've met a lot of doctors. I mean a lot of doctors, and I haven't liked most of them. He's one of the few I can actually stand."

"He's been in the service longer than any of us have been alive. If I were to set someone up as a watchdog, it would be him," Minh said quietly. I hadn't heard that serious tone out of him since he was in the infantry. "There's one part that gets me; he said he had never seen a shadow ship survive the loss of her captain so long and get him back. As though he's known about more than one shadow ship, like this isn't the first time he's been in this position."

"I noticed that too," Oz agreed. "I also noticed that he seemed to be out for our best interest. Whatever mission Freeground Fleet Intelligence has planned for us, he's not thrilled that we've been assigned."

"That's what worried me," Ayan commented. "I trust him. More importantly, my mother the Admiral trusts his opinions. They've been close for as long as I can remember. Minh's right, if we were to have a watchdog, I'd prefer it be Doctor Anderson."

"What would you do, Oz?" I asked.

He thought for a long moment before joining me at the window. "Honest? I'd ask for your opinion. But since you're asking me, I'd play along, try to get the Doc more on-side so we can get his judgement calls as situations develop."

"You're right. I can't make any decisions until I see our orders."

"They're classified, only for you. It won't play back unless you're in a sealed room or environment."

"Or if I'm incapacitated they might play for someone else. I suddenly really want to know who exactly those bounty hunters were."

"Well, you know what my pay grade is, I couldn't afford to hire that many goons," Oz said, trying to lighten the mood.

"You have a point, though. In all those pirate movies it's always the first officer that gets the Captain knocked off," Minh added, looking at him with mock suspicion.

"Well, we'll take time to find out more about that bounty hunter outfit when we have the opportunity, but I don't think we'll ever know who they were for sure. My duty is to review these orders as soon as they're received, and since I'd rather not face a court martial when we finally return, I should get to it."

"We'll be in Observation One. Call us back in when you're finished," said Oz.

"Actually, start the departure checklist and bring the doctor in with you when I'm finished reviewing our orders. Inform the crew that I'll perform my inspection once we're under way."

"Who do you want to run early startup on the bridge?" Oz asked.

"Lieutenant Nichols, but have Sergeant Ashbey observe."

"Yes, Sir. See you in a few minutes."

Ayan stopped beside me and waited until everyone else was gone. "We're okay?" she asked.

"We're better than okay," I replied.

She smiled at me as she headed for the door. "This is going to be a long day."

"I know."

I tossed the small data chip onto the table and it automatically interfaced with the holographic projector built into the surface. It proceeded to take my bioprint, checking DNA along with all my other vitals, and then a simple voice message played. It was mechanical, not a voice disguised, but the voice of a computer. "Make best speed to Starfree Port in good repair, five day travel time maximum. Coordinate with Captain Wheeler, Commander of the Triton. He will meet you in section twelve, level nine. Bring these orders on a data chip. Meet him alone."

The message ended and a prompt to network the chip I had with another piece of encrypted data appeared for a minute before the playback ended. "So much for getting answers," I said to myself. "Computer, access and display service record of Captain Wheeler."

"Please indicate Captain Wheeler's current assignment."

I hesitated for a moment. Normally the computer would display the records right away. "He's assigned to the Triton."

"The Triton is not a Freeground ship and records regarding that vessel are not available to officers of your rank."

"What about Captain Wheeler?"

"No individual in the First Light's database matches your search parameters. Would you like to connect to and search an external network, Captain?"

"No. Remain comm silent unless prompted by a communications officer. End search."

I thought for a moment about what information was available. The computer said that it had a file on the Triton, only that it wasn't accessible to someone of my rank. So the ship was important enough to include in every Freeground ship's general database. Somehow Freeground Intelligence didn't want any kind of record of Wheeler in general databases and that, to me, became the most important bit of missing information. The ship had to be listed, but there was to be no record of the man.

"Allow access to this room by command staff and page them, please," I ordered the computer. A few moments later, Oz, Minh, Ayan, Jason and Doctor Anderson returned.

They sat down around the conference table, all eyes on me. "Thank you for joining us, Doctor. I'm wondering how you knew Ayan had recorded your conversation with Intelligence." I was standing at the window, the table at my back, looking to the dry dock outside.

"I've been in and out of the Intelligence game for a while, Captain, long enough to know that I should do a search in the security database to ensure I wasn't picked up. I deleted the security footage, but I didn't realize that there was a tertiary audio backup on board until later. Commander McPatrick is an exceptional security officer. He set up the security systems aboard to pick up everything at least three times. I didn't get to the message until it was recorded elsewhere."

"I'm glad you're on our side," I said quietly. "You are on our side, right Doctor?"

"I wasn't allowed to tell you that I was the presence for Freeground Fleet Intelligence on the ship, but I did represent you and the crew the best way I could. Now that you know I'm their eyes and ears, there's no need for me to withhold information. I am the First Light's man, Captain. There are people I love on this crew. As a friend to her mother, I've known Ayan since she was born. I've come to respect the rest of the senior staff, and I'd like to think that you and I are becoming fast friends."

"You're right, and I think everyone here is happy that you're the watchdog and it's not some soulless shadowy man." I took a deep breath and let it out slowly. Every instinct was telling me to trust Doc. He had two jobs to do, he ran medical better than anyone, and as far as his work with Freeground Fleet Intelligence was concerned, I could only assume that he was at least a competent intelligence officer. I understood why he had to be aboard. It was difficult to be rational and look past the sting of betrayal that would cloud my reasoning, but I had no choice. Every decision I made had to be in the crew's best interest, I couldn't afford to take Doc's duplicity personally. "We need you, Doctor, I have no choice but to trust your loyalty and abilities. I have a lot of questions for you before we're finished here, though."

"I'll answer everything I can, but even I'm on a need to know basis where Fleet Intelligence is concerned. Their entire structure is built on mistrust, from one end to the other."

I used my command console to disable the embedded recording devices in the room and sat down at the table. "Signal the bridge to set course at best speed to Starfree Port. Our orders are to proceed there. After our arrival, I'm to meet with the Triton's commander, Captain Wheeler, alone in a section of the station. What do we know about our destination?" I asked the room in general.

"I've been there a few times," Oz answered. "Starfree Port is a friendly destination to Freeground forces. We have good trade relations with them."

"Legally they're not affiliated with us, but Oz is right," Jason continued. He had the database entry up on his command and control unit. "It was also used as a staging area late in the All-Con Conflict, giving us an advantage for a while. They harvest natural resources from a gas giant. The station is almost as old as Freeground and has been expanding ever since it was founded. Freeground Fleet has dispatched ships to aid in their defence three times in the last twenty years. They occupy an area near several trade routes and maintain a Class 9 Wormhole generator capable of creating a wormhole entry point fourteen kilometres wide."

"Large enough for colony and mass freight vessels. Must be a popular place."

"Freeground Intelligence is most likely using that as a meeting point for one of two reasons, or both: for the wormhole generator, or as a friendly rendezvous site where the First Light would go largely unnoticed," Doc commented.

"All right, what do we know about the Triton and Captain Wheeler?" I asked.

For a moment everyone was silent, then Doc smiled at me uneasily. "Sounds like that's my cue. There's no doubt in my mind that the Triton has been assigned to this for several very good reasons, the most obvious of which is that I've served under Captain Wheeler before."

"Well, that's helpful," Minh commented. "What can you tell us?"

"Lucius Wheeler is former Intelligence. He operated at the highest level for years, worked his way up from the bottom. When there was a massive shift in Freeground Command, they decided that his tactics were no longer relevant to the new strategic climate, and he was told to either work within the limitations they were putting in place or take another post. He chose the latter, and he was given one of the first shadow ships in the Intelligence fleet."

"Hold on a sec. What do you mean by strategic climate?" Minh asked. "That sounds like something a politician would say."

Doc smiled at Minh and nodded. "It would be. It was all politics. There were a number of incidents, sacrifices that were made by Fleet under orders from Intelligence, and a lot of them were traced right back to Wheeler and Intelligence commanders like him. His methods were bloody, cost manpower, and left a lot of wreckage behind, but they were deniable and he had a very high success rate."

"Ah, so they wanted to cut losses."

"That, and Fleet Intelligence was very different when his people were in charge. They were shadowy, dangerous men who didn't have names and had the power to ignore people who tried to hold them accountable. It was like that for decades. Fleet Intelligence still suffers from negative public opinion because of that time, not that anyone in Intel would admit to caring about what their public image looks like. That kind of image and the tactics that caused it didn't mesh with the new administration." Doc took a sip of tea from his transparent safety mug and went on.

"When he was assigned to his shadow ship, it was agreed that he would have as little attachment to Freeground as possible. That way, they could disavow him if he failed in any task or used methods Command didn't approve of. He blames the assimilation of qualified refugees into the military for his change of post, and last I heard he often pirated British freighters on the outskirts of their space."

"Hold on a minute. How many shadow ships are there? I thought there may be four, five at the most," Ayan asked.

"Well, there are no shadow ships like this one. Each one is unique, normally not built by Freeground. To be honest I don't know exactly how many there are, but I can tell you that there are less than a dozen. With Fleet stretched so thin, Freeground can't spare much. The ship Captain Wheeler was assigned to was a Core Worlds Explorer Four model, barely armed, but in good condition. He wasn't pleased, but he didn't reject it either. Being from Intelligence, he was allowed to hand pick more than half his crew, and he chose people who were like-minded. A lot of them didn't fit well with the new officers in Freeground Fleet Command."

"What kind of man is he?" I asked.

"Solitary, severe in his thinking. After knowing him for a few months I was glad he didn't decide to become a surgeon. He's the kind who would cut a leg off to cure a cancer on the foot, and you wouldn't see it coming."

"Why trust him at all? They could have retired him instead," Minh commented.

"Retiring him wasn't an option. He knew too much about Freeground operations, politics and the military, had too many connections in too many solar systems, and was just too influential in general. They knew his tactics worked, but he operates without a moral compass. They gave him a ship. He took it into Sol space and pirated one of theirs."

"He did what?" Oz exclaimed. The Sol system was under tight defence. It was well known that their government allowed no more than two hundred immigrants per solar year, and they had to be cleared through an application process that could stretch on for decades. Most ships that went near the perimeter were turned away. Few who tried to sneak past the perimeter were ever heard from again.

"This is classified at the highest level. Only the Fleet Admirals and Generals have access to this information. The only reason I know about it is because I was there," Doc whispered. "He came out of hyperspace a good distance from Sol then destroyed most of the ship systems, including the primary power plants and life support. We spent a week in our vacsuits, hurtling towards the perimeter of the Sol system, on the edge of the Kuiper belt. They took the ship as salvage, thinking it was a derelict. After we got to the salvage operation, he sprung the trap and we took a Zhàn Class Sol Defence Ship."

"Risky, but genius."

"More than half the crew were killed before we even set foot on the ship we captured. He also triggered an old nuclear reactor that he installed on the ship Freeground put him in command of as we were leaving, destroying an entire perimeter station. There were millions of people living there, families, but he didn't care. I didn't know what he would be doing with the reactor. I just thought it was installed as emergency power, in case Sol Forces didn't save our ship from colliding with the asteroids orbiting the perimeter. He carried the transponder codes from the Freeground vessel and applied them to the Sol Zhàn Class ship with a few modifications, and he's been stealing technology ever since. No one knows what Sol Defence will do if they ever catch him. If they're tracking him, there's no indication of it and he'll do anything he can to cover his tracks."

I shook my head, "No wonder they wanted him off the station."

"Most of his crew weren't from Freeground by the time I finished my two years on the Triton. He pulled some amazing heists and accomplished a great deal while I was there, but he doesn't have a lot of our advantages."

"Like?" Ayan asked.

"Last I saw him, he didn't have the engineering or scientifically trained staff to use a lot of what he was taking. He could have improvements made to his ship well enough, but the manpower on his ship barely knew how to repair new technology since he would recruit from unregistered ports and the underside of civilization. It keeps the pay grade low, but it takes forever to train that kind of crew."

"So his ship must be missing a lot of polish."

"It's been years, who knows what's changed. He may have been able to replace the crewmembers who left along with me when we had the opportunity. There's no way he has the crew the Triton is made to run with; she's a Zhàn Class Close Combat Carrier made for long deep-space missions. Last time I was aboard, almost all the interior decks were sealed off and shut down. Automation runs most of his ship. I couldn't tell you exactly how though; it's a complicated system."

"Anything else we should know?"

"Well, if he needs the First Light, then there's something big in his sights. Freeground must be pretty desperate if they're going through him to get it. Just don't trust him. He'll use this ship and her crew like any other tool."

"In that case, I'll want you on comms from the beginning of this to the end. I may not be able to think ahead of him, but I could if I have access to the entire senior staff and we're all working this scenario together," I told him. Everyone else was in agreement, and the tension in the room was nearly gone. It felt as though Doc was once again a full member of the crew.

Doctor Anderson smiled at me and nodded. "Team thinking, that's why I love this crew."

TEN
DEPARTING ZINGARA

Oz, Minh, Jason, and Doc went on ahead to their duty stations as Ayan and I double checked the validity of our orders against Freeground Intelligence verification standards. The encryption pattern was already certified by Jason, but Ayan wanted to find out what kind of device had transmitted it. After a few minutes we determined the source and relay points. It couldn't have been sent from any place other than Freeground. It had even been relayed through two Starfree Port terminals. "I think that satisfies my paranoia, how about you?" she asked.

"I believe it's the real thing. I still don't like it."

"Do you think the doctor is holding something back?"

"There's no telling. I guess I'd like to assume he's telling us everything we need to know. I just have a bad feeling. A lot of what I just heard about Captain Wheeler sounds like a prime example of what not to do when you're running a shadow ship. I realize we're not exactly being careful about maintaining our cover — in fact I'm sure we'll be recalled to Freeground any day

— but stealing from Sol Defence? Killing millions of people? It makes me wonder what a shadow ship has to do to get recalled. What limits do we actually have?"

"Well, I'm sure the doctor reported how you escaped from Vindyne, including what you did with Alice. If anything would be cause for a recall, that would have been it. I mean, this entire spiral arm of the galaxy recognizes the Eden Two laws."

"Meanwhile we send several thousand colonists to Freeground as refugees. I wonder which of our ships will be recalled when this is over."

"Those people didn't have a safe place to go. Besides, those refugees handed Freeground a set of schematics and detailed information on all the technology we had seen out here up to that point. I'm sure Command won't be recalling us."

"Not based on that. They might want to take a closer look at the First Light, though. I know I would. Besides, after hearing about Wheeler, I wonder what things will be like after a few years out here. Maybe an occasional recall would keep us on track."

"I don't think you'd cause the deaths of millions or start stealing from old world governments. I'd have to do something drastic if you started leaning to the dark side, anyway."

"So you're volunteering as my moral compass?" I asked.

"Oh, that's only the beginning." Her crooked grin, that slight accent and stare that implied far more than she'd said was something I'd always remember. "Too bad we're short on time," she finished with a wink.

"I know. While the rest of the crew are relaxing, I'll be catching up, continuing the training of new bridge staff, and everything else that comes with being a captain."

"Don't forget the thorough inspections, situating yourself in your new quarters, and probably attending something in Observation One with your Chief Engineer. But before your day fills up and time starts flying by, I think you should follow me to your new bridge," Ayan said cheerily as she started walking towards the door. I shut down the table display and cleared my orders out of the buffer before catching up with her just outside in the hallway.

I was starting to get the feeling that she and the engineering team had put a lot of work and imagination into whatever I was about to see. I decided that even if I found it underwhelming, I would do my best to look and sound as astonished as possible, but I was still hoping to be amazed.

The entrance to the new bridge was thirty meters forward of main engineering control, in the middle of the most heavily armoured section of the ship. We walked through an unfamiliar doorway into an interior sealed lock. It was unlike any other on the ship. Leading inward, the door itself was a quarter meter thick. It closed behind us. "Captain Valent and Commander Rice. Welcome to the command deck," the computer said as the interior door opened.

"I call it the cocoon," Ayan announced with a grin as we stepped onto the brand-new bridge.

The standard stations were all where you'd expect them to be, but they had three or six seats each, were all on three hundred sixty degree swivel mounts, and featured extra blank two dimensional panels that could be configured by the user. The floor was covered in dark blue acoustic control safety carpet. The captain's seat was between two chairs, but as I looked on, Oz stepped beside the night shift's acting first officer and a third came out of the floor. "Our chief did one hell of a job designing this new bridge," he said. "You haven't seen the half of it, either."

The busy chatter and resettling of shift change and pre-hyperspace made the room look more like the command deck on Freeground than anything else. There was no trace of the antique ship we had taken command of months ago. As crew members ran about finishing their shift reports and running through checklists, they brought up holographic displays, used their flat control panels, and even brought up larger cross sections of the ship and navigational information on the walls. They simply touched any part of the blank wall surface and brought up the information they needed. One was accessing the new automatic and remote turret controls for calibration.

"Only a few of the ideas here are mine. I listen to the crew. Having a bridge below decks was your idea. So were a lot of others, and then there's Laura's idea to get the gunnery crew inside, too. She'd been working on it herself, but she's still working on the final cloaksuit design among other things."

"It doesn't make you any less amazing," I whispered as I looked around. "I'll still miss the windows, though."

"I doubt it." She grinned at me for a moment then addressed the ship. "Computer, activate all remaining bridge systems." At her command, the bridge transformed. A pair of two dimensional control panels came out of the sides of the captain's chair to rest roughly at my hand levels, the main holographic viewer displayed our galaxy and then the circular walls and ceiling became one large view screen. Even the floor displayed a view of what was under the ship, but it was obscured just enough so we wouldn't all get vertigo.

"Who needs windows?" I asked myself quietly.

"Now that I've shown you the fancy stuff, there's a three man lift that leads down to engineering control, the automation centre, and up to main medical. I'll be installing the same security doors at major access points in those areas, too. I also took one of those smaller power plants we salvaged and made it the dedicated backup for all four areas. Even if the rest of the ship were open to space and without power, everyone in those sections would be perfectly fine. We even have our own life support and inertial compensator systems. We're still tuning them a little, though."

"If I weren't in love with you already, I'd be putty in your hands now," I whispered.

"Why, Captain," she replied, giving me a kiss on the cheek. "I've a few surprises for you yet. Laura and I went shopping while you were recovering. I think you'll enjoy my new off duty wardrobe," Ayan whispered. She paused for a moment to let that sink in and went on. "Now I'll be in engineering so you can regain your composure and get focused."

"Good idea," I whispered back as she walked to the lift at the rear of the bridge.

I strode to the centre and sat down in the new captain's chair. It took a moment to adjust to my body, but when it did I may as well have been sitting on air. The control panels were the perfect height and reacted to whatever my eye was focusing on. As I looked from one screen display to another, it would extend from its two dimensional state into a small holo projection.

"I think she likes you, Sir," Oz whispered.

"It feels really good to be the captain right now," I replied quietly.

"I know exactly what you mean. I have to be here when Fleet Command sees what we did with their little ship."

"Too bad we can't show it to anyone else."

"So you agree with my proposal? No visitors past the primary observation section?" he asked.

"I think even that should be reserved for special occasions." I checked the general department status and found that everyone was reporting ready, from tactical all the way to propulsion. "Shall we be underway?"

Oz grinned and nodded. "Inform Zingara Control that we're grateful for their hospitality, but it's time for us to be on our way."

"Yes, Sir." Jason smiled back.

The main holographic display changed from galactic view to the head and shoulders of a Port Control officer with a shaved head and a dark van dyke. "Sorry to see you go, First Light. Good journey. You'll be clear of our protected space within sixty seconds according to your current speed."

As the channel closed, I set the main holographic display to tactical view. I opened a channel to engineering and a hologram of the circular central control consoles appeared between the field control and navigation stations. It was life size, and from where I sat I could see Ayan and two other engineers working the controls. "Yes, Captain?" she said with a smile.

"Well, that's different. How are things looking from your end?"

"Fantastic. Full power is available and the antimatter

intermix is set to augment main propulsion. Tell the helm to watch the throttle, let it out slowly."

I smiled at her and to my surprise she smiled back while looking through a systems monitor hologram. Images of the bridge staff must have been displayed at her station. I decided to find out how it worked later. "Helm, ahead at the safest speed until you can verify with Navnet that we're clear to accelerate out of the gravitational field." I looked to the energy field control, where there were three seats. Only two were in use; that was the norm for the bridge it seemed, and I knew it was because we were under-manned for the ship the First Light was becoming. "Shield Control, bring the energy and refractive shielding on line and cycle them up slowly until they're running at full power. Let's see how hard it is to power them up and balance them at the same time."

"Yes, Sir," Laura said from the right side of the bridge. I was glad she was there to monitor the new shields, but I was wondering if she would be missed in engineering. She was the best field control specialist on the ship, but she was also fully qualified to work with Ayan and manage engineering.

I turned to Jason. "Is the quantum core online?"

"It is. All of our systems are performing much better because of it. There's a betting pool going around. Some of the crew wager the fully automated turrets are going to score more hits than the gunnery crew."

"I'm betting on the automation," Oz commented as he reviewed crew readiness across the ship.

"So you're the one who's going to pay for my next shore leave," Minh said over the communicator. "All flights are reporting ready. We're set to launch seven at a time. We can be set and marking targets in less than twenty seconds."

"Don't rush things down there. We traded a lot of anti-matter for those new fighters."

"Stop worrying. The crew down here wanted us out in fifteen, I'm the one who told them to slow it down."

"I noticed there was an event scheduled for day two of hyperspace. You and Ayan are marked as hosting it in Observation One, but she has no idea what it's about. Care to let me in on some details?" Oz asked in a low whisper.

"It's a surprise."

"Should we be expecting an announcement from the happy couple? Maybe a proposal from our Captain to our Chief Engineer?"

I was taken completely off guard for a moment. "Things haven't quite gotten there just yet. She doesn't think that's what I'm about to do, does she?"

"No, I'm pretty sure she doesn't think that's coming any time real soon. You can relax." Oz grinned.

"Well, not that I wouldn't want to," I stammered,

"Of course you'd want to."

"I mean, maybe someday."

"I'm sure she'd agree," said Oz.

"We did just have our first date."

"That's right. How did that go?"

"Great. Didn't get a chance to stay for dessert, but great," I told him.

"Well, you two have been sharing dessert in your off time anyway," Oz whispered while looking through the duty roster.

"Nope. Things haven't gone quite that far."

"Really? What have you been doing all this time?" he asked with an arched eyebrow.

"Getting incarcerated. Shot by bounty hunters. You know, busy busy. The surprise I have planned involves something I picked up at Larsen's. You'll see." I checked the status of the shields and shook my head. "Take it slow with the shields."

"We are. If we were charging them at the normal rate, they'd be at maximum by now and building a power reserve with the extra energy," Laura responded. "Shields are the only thing Vindyne does well."

"Thank you, Sergeant, next time we'll charge them at your pace," I acknowledged with a nod in her direction. "By the way, did you relocate Captain Grays?" I asked Oz in a whisper.

"Security escorted her off the ship during our meeting this morning. They said she was pretty happy, actually. Then again, she should be. We paid her as a captain for the time she was here."

"That was generous."

"Well, considering she left us with all her access codes, her knowledge of fleet deployments, known colonies, and major Vindyne ports, I think it'll be worth it. Ask Jason about the info she dropped on us some time. He was speechless for at least ten minutes when he saw it."

"Ten minutes? That is something."

"One minute before we're far enough from the gravity well to enter hyperspace, Sir," reported Derek from navigation.

I checked the ship status and saw that our shields were fully charged, our power reserves were at maximum, weapon systems were ready but still completely hidden, and our primary power plants were running at just under fifty percent.

I brought an exterior image of the ship up on the main holographic display, just as it would be seen if we were looking at her from somewhere outside. The lights of the distant station, the outer posts, other ships and the distant stars reflected off of her silver hull, and her long smooth curves shimmered under the distortion of our many layered shields.

Oz whistled quietly. "Well don't we do amazing work. If there's a ship more beautiful than ours out there I don't need to know her."

The ship's engines were flaring blue and accelerating the ship out towards empty space. "There's nothing else like her." I said quietly.

"How close are the engines to maximum tolerance levels?"

"I can give you twice the thrust, then the inertial dampeners will start to strain."

"Did you say double? We're at maximum burn now according to my readings."

"We haven't had time to update the control systems to reflect the ship's new capabilities. We can move a lot faster using the antimatter intermix."

"Where everyone finds the time to make all this happen, I'll never know," Oz said, shaking his head.

"It's all about sleep, Sir. Some of us just don't," Laura commented.

"Helm, switch to manual thrust control and give us an extra forty percent. I want us in hyperspace before we meet whatever ship those bounty hunters call home."

"Aye, Sir." I could hear the smile on the pilot's face as I watched him release the controls to manual and start pushing the engines.

The holographic representation in front of us left a light trail behind as the engines propelled the ship into less congested space.

"Thirty seconds to safe hyperspace distance," the helm reported.

"All right, if there's anything out here hating us, they don't have long to show it," Oz muttered as he checked his own tactical display.

I switched the main holographic display back to tactical and looked for myself. There was the distant asteroid belt, a few slowly drifting rocks, but no ships in too near a trajectory or ahead that could pose a threat or even get within reasonable firing range in time.

I stood and walked up to the hologram; it was a metre taller than me and four metres wide in the middle of the bridge. "I think we're all a bit paranoid. If things keep up this way I'll draw my sidearm on my own shadow before the day's out."

"We're ten seconds out from our safe jump-point," said the helmsman.

"Keep counting, Sergeant," Oz replied.

I walked through the main holographic display and stared out into the open space displayed all around us on the walls. I wasn't looking for enemy ships. Anything that big or close enough to see with the naked eye would be far more obvious on a tactical display. No, I took a deep breath and decided to do what I could to ease my mind, try to shake the feeling that there was something out there waiting for us. "Oz, full systems and crew report. Have all departments do a cursory check, head count, and report in. They have five minutes."

"Yes, Sir."

"Entering hyperspace," announced the helm. I stood there, looking at the distorted star field, new nebulae of dark matter and gravitational eddies visible thanks to the haze of our hyperspace field. I relaxed and let myself sigh in relief. I couldn't help but just stare at the artificial view ahead as we accelerated past the speed of light and faster. It really was like being surrounded by windows; I didn't feel trapped even though we were in the centre of the ship.

"All reports are in and we check out fine. All crew accounted for, all departments confirm a smooth entry into hyperspace."

"Ayan, how is engineering?" I asked.

"Everything's fine, we're shutting the particle accelerator down though, there's something causing it to misalign. Nothing serious."

"Sounds almost like a gravity problem."

"You could be right, but we've already accounted for all the artificial gravity and the mass of the ship."

"It must be something outside," I said as I sat down in the command chair. I brought a gravity overlay up on the tactical display and everyone could immediately see that there was something emitting an artificially generated field ahead.

"Battle stations!" Oz commanded.

Emergency deceleration kicked in, pitching everyone forward and as soon as we were at a safe speed the hyperspace field around the ship dissipated. We had managed to remain in our seats, but just barely.

"Sir, there's something generating enough gravity to keep us out of hyperspace," came the report from navigation.

"Find the source, fast!" I started checking as half the bridge crew did the same.

"Got it! Small, high powered emitters. Five of them."

"Open up one beam emplacement and fire high density pulse shots. Only use half the energy intensity, I get the feeling we're being watched."

"Sir, I have a thought."

"Hold fire. What is it, Jason?"

"They could be waiting for us to destroy them so they could attack us legally. In neutral space, they would be fully justified if we destroyed their property."

"You've got to be kidding me," Oz sighed.

I stared at the tactical display in front of me and shrugged. "It's the strangest thing I've heard all week, but I think you might be right. That sounds like a typical corporate plan A, even though I'm sure we have the right to remove an obstruction. If I were up for a legal battle, I'd stick around and fight one, but I don't have the patience."

"Thank God," Jason said as he monitored his station for any incoming communications.

"Helm, plot a course to the nearest edge of the gravity field and start setting up a course that will take us past Zingara. We'll decelerate after a few hours and resume course to Starfree Port."

We turned with a quick lurch and our engines started accelerating in the other direction, away from the gravitational obstruction. "We're accelerating at full speed according to instrumentation, Sir."

"Ayan, have your team adjust the throttle control to reflect the correct engine tolerances. We need bridge navigation stations to reflect the actual capabilities of our thrusters."

"Yes, Sir," she replied with a nod.

"The new engine profile is on our panels now, Sir," reported Derek from the pilot's station. "Increasing speed."

A moment later I was pressed into my seat a little as the inertial dampeners fought to keep up with the sudden acceleration.

"Any minute now they'll realize we're not going for it and put plan B into play," Oz said quietly. "We just have to find out how they knew our exact course."

"Plan B won't be as elaborate."

"Sir, new mass incoming dead ahead," tactical reported.

Before I had a chance to say anything a three kilometre wide star shaped carrier appeared right in front of us. Derek turned the ship and I could hear the engines strain to counter our inertia.

"Message from the carrier, Sir. She's named the Viceroy and belongs to the Archness Confederation," Jason said.

"They're part of the Triad. What're they doing here?" Oz pondered as he checked the tactical display and sent orders to all departments to stand ready.

"Put it up, Sergeant," I said to Jason.

"First Light and crew, you are to bring your ship to a halt and prepare to be boarded. We are assisting Vindyne in pursuit of a ship that matches your description and designation. Your cooperation will be taken into consideration during legal proceedings."

I stood up and looked the hologram right in the eye. The commander of the carrier was a woman about my age with her hair in a tight bun. "Can I have your name?"

"I am Major Warren."

"No, your full name."

She hesitated for a moment, "Major Victoria Warren."

"Good to meet you, Victoria. My name is Jonas Valent. Now, we only just started to get to know each other so I'll be kind. You and whatever ships you brought with you — and I'm assuming there are others cloaked nearby — should take this opportunity to quietly leave."

She smiled and nodded. "I'm afraid that's not an option, Captain."

I turned to Laura. "What are the defences on that ship like? Do you think a few thousand antimatter rounds could punch through?"

She took a moment to scan and looked back at me, uneasy at being overheard by the commander of the carrier, whose holographic image was looking less self-assured by the second. "It would only take about a hundred. Their shields aren't made to counter antimatter," she said quietly.

I looked back at Major Warren. "Last chance." I stopped for a moment, looked into her holographic eye and continued. "I'm not taking prisoners today and we're not interested in leaving anything intact for salvage," I said flatly, slowly, seriously.

The bridge was deathly silent, so much so that the sounds coming across Major Warren's command deck through the communication were perfectly clear. I gave her a mental count of three and nodded. "Expose all weapon emplacements. All rail cannons, fire on that carrier until it is reduced to slag. Beam emplacements, fire bursts in a three hundred sixty degree spread, let's find those cloaked ships. Torpedo turrets, ready antimatter load and await my order." I got a little closer to the holographic representation of the Major as she commanded shields at the ready and to prepare to return fire. "Helm, get close, damn close, to that carrier and don't pull away until there's nothing left. I want to make this kill eye-to-eye."

She looked back at me, her confidence and self-assurance had turned into regret and fear.

"I warned you," I said before making a slashing motion across my throat so Jason knew it was time to cut communications. "Sergeant Everin, start jamming every frequency. No one is allowed to hear themselves think but us."

We started taking particle beam weapons fire right away, but the energy was being refracted and our impact shields were stopping all the particles that the beams carried along with them. "How are our shields holding up?"

"We're recharging as fast as we're taking damage, Sir. They only have a few small rail gun turrets and they're meant for point defence. The rest is beam technology and they can't breach our refractive fields."

"How are theirs?"

"Almost gone. My estimate was off; their shields are detonating the antimatter rounds as they pass through, causing explosions across their outer hull. Our refractive shielding is redirecting their beam fire right at them."

I looked at the tactical display and saw they were launching a dozen fighters every ten seconds, using each of the five different launch bays in turn. "As soon as their shields are down fire five antimatter torpedoes right into the core of the ship. The best way to kill a hydra is by tearing out it's heart."

"Yes, Sir," came the response from tactical.

"Sir! Five destroyers just uncloaked in firing range. They're all Vindyne."

"Don't panic. Remember, we have three times the power and twice the shielding per meter than they do. Use the carrier as cover, get behind it but keep a minimum safe distance. We don't want to get caught in the fireball when that thing goes."

"Where do you want us, Jonas?" Minh asked through the communicator on my arm.

"I want to get out of here quickly, so have some of your crew stand by. The rest should get to automation so they can control a few computerized turrets."

"Yes, Sir," Minh replied, I could hear him grinning. "You heard him! Get to the automation bay. Let's shred some Vindyne!" I heard before he closed the channel.

"Fifteen torpedoes incoming, Sir."

"Have our rail guns target them with standard explosive rounds. Launch our antimatter torpedoes into that carrier."

"Their shields are down. That's going to hurt," Oz said quietly.

"That's the idea." Our antimatter torpedoes launched and less than two seconds later they impacted right in the centre of their ship. The antimatter struck matter and the two annihilated each other, causing an explosion that was fully absorbed by the carrier. The centre opened up like a flower of blue and white flame, leaving a charred opening, flinging huge chunks of hull drifting off in all directions. I took the opportunity to send a message. "Stop jamming signals and broadcast on all channels."

"Yes, Sir. Broadcasting," said Jason.

I stood and looked straight ahead. "Vindyne destroyer group. You are outmatched. Leave the area immediately. We will not allow ourselves to be harassed by Vindyne forces or any of their allies. This will be your only warning." I cut the communication with my arm unit and turned to helm control. "Set a course for the nearest destroyer. Resume jamming. All tactical and gunnery stations, fire at will, maximum intensity. Gunnery stations are to use high explosive rounds for anti-fighter fire, and antimatter rounds for destroyer class. Let's go hunting."

Oz brought up a holographic representation of the First Light on the secondary holographic display and shook his head. Light traced the rounds fired from our thirty eight rail cannon turrets. Our torpedo turrets were chain firing towards the nearest pair of destroyers. One of them looked like it was turning to run, but the others were coming straight at us. Our refractive shielding was redirecting the energy from their beam weapons right back and our own beam emplacements were firing hundreds of pulses of white energy, depleting the shields on three destroyers fast. "We are damn scary," Oz said quietly.

The destroyers were returning fire, but all of their torpedoes were destroyed before they made it within harmful range. "How are our shields holding up?"

"Ninety seven percent, Sir, redirecting energy to compensate."

"How is the ship, Ayan?"

"She's fine. Nothing has touched the hull yet. All generators are working at peak efficiency. We really do outmatch them."

"The benefits of putting all your eggs in one basket," I said to myself. "We're also spending millions of credits worth of anti-matter, good thing we're not out here for the money."

"Sir, three of the destroyers are making full burn out of the area."

"Good. Let's make an example of the other two. Beam

control, target one destroyer with all emplacements and drain the capacitors using the antimatter intermix. Let's cut them in half."

"Yes, Sir."

A moment later, all six of our beam emplacements stopped firing pulses of energy and started sweeping across the nearest destroyer in a solid stream of white energy. After a few seconds, our beam attacks started breaking through the other side of the enemy ship, and as we stopped firing I could see that we nearly had cut the ship in two. "Give chase to the other destroyer. Target it with all turrets and fire until it's destroyed. I want to send a message to Vindyne."

"Oh, I think they'll hear us loud and clear," Oz said with a nod. "There will be a warning beside our profile saying; 'too expensive to pursue, avoid if at all possible."

Our rail cannons pulverized the second destroyer as our torpedo turrets and the conventional launchers sent volley after volley. Only a minute passed and one or more of our torpedoes struck their reactor. It must have been antimatter based, judging from the explosion. The ship was obliterated, leaving only the front third behind as a mangled mess drifting at great speed through space. I nodded to myself and looked over the tactical display.

"Someday someone is going to do a psyche profile on you and discover what's behind that switch that allows you to go from the personable captain we all know to a cold tactician in an instant," Oz said quietly.

"I don't enjoy getting into one firefight after another, but when some corporate marionette tells me to surrender my crew and all their freedoms, I get a little irritated."

"Course, Sir?" asked Lieutenant Derek Gregor from navigation.

"We can't stay for salvage or rescue. Jason, cease jamming. Start scanning for emergency beacons."

Jason scanned and several blips appeared on the tactical display. "There are several."

"Good, the escape pods should be picked up soon. Who picks them up isn't our business. Plot a course towards Starfree Port, make sure we're not taking a direct route. Let's go about four hours out of our way."

"Yes, Sir. Making full burn to the edge of the artificial gravity field and plotting to Starfree Port."

Oz turned his command module off and stood. "I'm going to go find out how those ships knew our exact course."

"Wait, one of my engineering team found it. It's the quantum computer core," Ayan interjected from her holographic representation. "There's a communicator in the centre. It was completely dormant before, so it was undetectable. Vindyne activated it remotely."

"How close would someone have to be to activate it?" I asked.

"One moment." Ayan consulted with another member of her team who wasn't close enough to appear on the projection on the bridge and turned back towards us. "It must have happened as we were leaving the station. They'd have to be within five hundred kilometres."

"There were a lot of ships within that distance as we were leaving. It's going to take forever to sort through all that comm traffic," Jason said. He was already starting to bring the playback of our departure up, and I could see the quickly scrolling list of channels open and burst communications. There must have been thousands per second.

"I'd be surprised if we were able to find it at all, even if we took years to work on it. The length of transmission needed would be measured in fractions of a millisecond."

"How do we fix it?"

"We'll have to take the core offline while we're in hyper-space. Since it's only set up to enhance performance — not to actually run anything on its own — that'll be easy. Designing a dampening casing won't be hard, but it'll take about fifteen hours for our materializer to make one dense enough to be effective. After we've put that on the core, someone would have to be within centimetres to activate the transmitter."

"How much of a difference has the core made?"

"Performance is up across the ship, we're saving power everywhere, and interstellar navigation computers are making near instantaneous calculations for hyperspace travel instead of having to number crunch for seconds or minutes at a time. It's significant."

I thought for a moment. It would be much easier and less risky to just take it offline and present it to Freeground when we arrived. Even if we shielded it from all transmissions, limited it's use, it could still present an unknown danger. The quantum molecular computer core was so dense and complex that it could take months of scanning to completely understand all of its inner workings, let alone know about every primary and secondary function internally. "Machine a casing from ergranian steel, then supercharge it and increase the density as much as you can. I want that core inside three tons of metal before we reactivate it. A simple faraday cage won't do it.

Someone with a micro wormhole hyper transmitter could cut through it like it was made of tin."

"Sir, that's at least five times the insulation Ayan was suggesting," Laura objected mildly from her station.

"The captain's right," Oz said flatly. "We don't know what other risks that core could present. The more bottled up our genie is, the better I'll feel."

"Genie? Good nickname. We're taking the core offline right now and we'll start machining the casing right away. We should be ready to reactivate it in about twenty hours," Ayan reported.

"Okay, so we'll be able to safely use that core. That takes care of one problem. Now we just have to be very careful of where we go, who we mix with, and what we say on Starfree Port. I wouldn't be surprised if Vindyne, Triad, and God only knows how many bounty hunters have people looking and listening for us."

"I know. This part of the galaxy is getting pretty hot," Oz agreed.

"Pardon me, Sir, but what does it matter?" asked one of the navigation crew. "We just licked a carrier, two destroyers, and sent three running."

"The ancient Americans used to tell a story about a lone wolf. No matter who attacked him, tried to keep him out of their territory, he would defeat them. He could go anywhere, take anything he wanted: game, mates, anything. You'd think he would live a long life, become alpha of a large pack in an area rich with game, but he still died young. The fact that he could defeat any other wolf, and proved it often, caused too much trouble for everyone else. Eventually it caught up with him."

"What killed him?"

"One of his own pups. When he came of age, he wanted to have a reputation greater than his father's. The only way to do that was to defeat him."

"What the captain is saying is that no matter how well known we get, how powerful our ship is or how good we are at keeping her together, our mission isn't to wage war on the galaxy. We have to step off this boat sometimes. We have to make repairs and maintain the ship somewhere. We also want to make friends out there, and that gets pretty hard when you have a reason to be paranoid."

"Those Vindyne destroyers are also made of paper, and that carrier wasn't as well armed as we are or as well shielded. At least two corporations will have intimate knowledge of what happened today, and if they still want us they won't send a small battle group. They'll send something they know we shouldn't even try fighting. Or worse, they'll catch us planet-side."

"Exactly. I agree with Oz, it's too dangerous for us in this sector. We should move on or return to Freeground," Ayan affirmed.

"Unfortunately our immediate future isn't in our hands, so deciding what our next destination is will have to wait. Until then, let's get a post-engagement assessment of the ship done," I ordered.

The post-engagement reports came in quickly. Everyone was on their toes after our most recent firefight. They collectively expected to take damage, maybe some losses, and when we came out of it so clean, with barely a scratch, people felt like dancing.

"This is good. Scratch that, this is amazing," Oz said as he reviewed the reports on our tactical systems. "The worst damage we sustained was a burnout on one of the beam emitters and we can fix that in hyperspace."

"Was anyone injured?"

"Nope. There wasn't so much as a spark, the emplacement just stopped working."

"Vindyne workmanship. We should look into replacing their components, I don't get the feeling that they're made to last," I said as I finished reading the last of the reports.

"You know, you don't have to read these with me," Oz said quietly. "I could do what most first officers do and report the highlights to you."

"I don't mind giving you a hand. Besides, there's not much else to do in hyperspace."

"Sure there is, it's just not very interesting. For example, I have to start looking over crew performance reports. Now that I'd love some help with."

"I think Laura's right. Our senior staff has traded sleep for time to produce reports."

"Dictated reports, quick and easy to create, slow and tedious to review," Oz looked at me and smiled. "So, what'll it be? I can transfer half of them to your command console or you could get started on that inspection."

"Inspection." I nodded. "You have the bridge, Commander. Time for me to take the tour."

"Yes, Sir. Tell the gunnery crews that I'll be making my recommendation for the new gunnery captain to you tomorrow morning."

"I'm sure they'll be glad to hear that," I said as I took my trenchcoat from the back of my command chair and made my way off the bridge.

THE GRAND TOUR

The inspection was long, but it was one of the most rewarding experiences I remember from my time on the First Light. From one compartment to the next there were crew members waiting to show me what they were responsible for during the refit, where their duty stations were, and what they did. Some of them were nervous, others were casual. There was an official air with most, and the others were downright social. Everyone seemed proud of their work but they also looked weary. It was a common thread on the ship, and even after taking on a number of new crewmen from Concordia, it was obvious that we were undermanned.

The hallways throughout most of the ship were lined with carefully colour-coded sorted cables, conduits, and piping. In some areas where access to those lines was more essential, they were insulated but not under cover. Throughout most of the rest of the ship, the pipes and very high voltage lines were covered, leaving the rest of the wiring tucked under clips that held them fast against the bulkheads. The only place you couldn't see any cables, wires or pipes was in the officers' quarters, where they were hidden under padded panels.

Another feature of the corridors — and this was more important to my tour — was that the colours representing all the primary departments were set up as stripes on the deck. Anyone who knew the colour-coding for the ship could follow red and find their way to medical, or green to engineering control, for example. You could also follow the different cables and pipes from one section of the ship to another. If you knew what you were doing, you would find your way to the desired section fairly effectively.

Seeing where the new systems were implemented interested the engineer in me, and I was riveted as one of the engineering staff explained how the new beam weapons worked and what they were doing to repair the burned-out emitter. He was so nervous I thought he would just freak out and run away in the middle of his presentation. The fact that I was listening very closely because I was genuinely interested seemed to only make it worse.

Ayan let an ensign guide me through every section of engineering. That part of the inspection took two hours on its own. I had never met Ensign Rowen before, but he seemed like he lived his life in engineering as much as I did when I started service aboard the Loki many years before. He was bursting with pride at the condition of engineering. He even took me on a tour of the engine section and showed me the antimatter intermix for the thrusters, which was interesting since I had never seen one before.

The flight deck was fantastic. I got the full-on tour of the service area, was introduced to each and every pilot as he stood by his or her fighter, and they took the time to show me a play-back of a simulation that Minh, Oz, Ayan, Jason, and Laura had played several times before we started our tour on the First Light. Minh's pilots had a different approach to the scenario, taking out a pair of corvettes and using them for cover. Back in the day, we'd had a more straightforward approach.

Minh introduced me to a tradition I had heard about and was glad to see in practice on board. When a pilot caused any kind of major damage during a landing — in our case it was mostly divots that weren't bad enough to be repaired — they had to revisit the scene and initial it. At the end of my tour, Minh had nine of his pilots stand beside their divots and present them to me. Some stood proudly at attention, others obviously thought it was an unnecessary form of humiliation as I made the rounds. "Not bad," I said to one. "Looks a bit like a parrot," I commented to another. "Now, you can do better," I admonished the last with a grin.

The flight deck was the last part of my inspection before visiting the officer's quarters, and as Minh walked me to the lift a thought occurred to me. "Hey, do you have much left to do down here?"

"Not really. We're all secure and settled in for hyperspace."

"Meet me on the old bridge in twenty minutes? I'm going to blow through the tour of the new officer's quarters. No one on our crew did much up there so there's no one to offend if I cut it short."

"Sounds like a plan."

I was good to my word. One of the security personnel, a young ensign that had spent a few evenings in the simulations with us in Freeground but I barely had a chance to meet, guided me through with the help Foreman Berl's rough notes. We had a good laugh taking our tour around and when we were finished the bulk of it I dismissed her and took the lift to the old bridge.

It had been aesthetically restored so perfectly that I had a flashback from my first time aboard. I corrected myself after a moment, remembering that I wasn't actually aboard the First Light at that time, but in a simulation of the Sunspire. Every station looked like it was ready to use. The panels were in place. There was even an old low resolution holoprojector serving as the main bridge display. The light of hyperspace, blue white and yellow, gave the room an eerie feeling.

"Did you know this was here?" Minh asked as he turned around to face me from the command chair. "I mean, they used salvage and half broken equipment to put it together, but unless you sit down and try to take control of the ship you wouldn't know the difference." He was filling two glasses with what looked like whiskey.

"It's one hell of a red herring. I mentioned doing this to Ayan once and I knew the crew was rebuilding this bridge as a decoy, but I didn't think it would be this convincing."

"Just imagine a boarding party fighting their way to this bridge. I'd pay real money to see the looks on their faces when they realize there's nothing here. Especially since security can seal the armoured hatches by remote."

"It would probably look a lot like mine when you told me you showed one of our simulations to Admiral Ferrah."

"You haven't thanked me yet, either," he complained mildly, handing me a glass.

"Well, then here's to my crazy pilot friend," I said, clinking it to his. "Who likes to brag to Admirals about security violations."

"Here's to my ruthless captain."

We took a sip and I took a seat in the pilot's chair. "Are you on duty?" I asked after a couple minutes.

"Nope. I've been off for about half an hour. I wouldn't have eight year old whiskey on duty."

"Same here. Everything looks really good down there."

"Thanks. The engineering and flight deck crews are working together to finish building decoy drones using those salvaged fighter hulls. Those are working out well, but we're having trouble building uplink drones with a good success rate."

"Uplink drones?"

"Yup, they'll launch from the fighter bay, head straight for an enemy ship after their shields are down, attach themselves, and provide us with direct access to their computer systems. Jason's communications crew will be able to hack any ship, even use the quantum core to speed things up."

"That's fantastic, I didn't see a report on that."

"I thought we would tell you when the first ones were ready. They are, it just looks like only half will work, so they're trying to improve that. That thing with Alice gave me the idea. Jason's department is providing the software."

We sat quietly, him in the captain's chair, me in the pilot's seat, looking out into space for a few moments. "Sometimes I can't believe we're out here, other times it feels like everything that came before was just some dream," I said.

"Took the words right out of my mouth."

"How is running the flight deck down there?"

"Easier than running a restaurant with all three of my

sisters. Pilots and deck crewmen don't argue for sport. How's the captain's chair?"

"Amazing. Tons of admin work but everything between is beyond what I could have imagined."

"Better than Port Control?" he teased.

"I wasn't in command of an array of weapons in Port Control."

"Good point. I bet you wished you were sometimes, though."

"With some of the captains I had to deal with? A few times a week."

Minh stood up and got closer to the forward window. "Ever think of making this your new quarters?"

I laughed and looked around for a moment. "You know, if I didn't think that it would be mistaken for our main bridge and marked as a priority target every time we got into a firefight, I would."

"You would go through more furniture than an outlet store. Besides, if you took this as your new quarters, I could move into yours."

"I'm afraid Oz would probably beat you to it."

"Even after I got us all out here?"

I laughed. "I told Ayan about that, by the way. She says you have a surprise coming."

"Oh great. I'm going to have to have an ensign open doors and taste my food for me from now on."

"Well, I'm sure she's as thankful as I am, beneath it all."

"Ah, it was nothing. I just had to show off to an Admiral while feeding her the best dim sum she'd ever tasted. Thanks for keeping us in one piece and getting us out of prison."

"Nothing any other captain with an AI ready to go rogue any second wouldn't do."

Minh chuckled and nodded. "You know, I've only been out here in command of the flight deck and my own wing of fighters for a couple months now, and I have to say, if we get recalled I'm going to want to take the Gull and just keep going."

"I'm not ready to go back just yet either, but I can't say one way or the other what I'd do if we were recalled. I'll need to get a feel for the crew."

"Well, the flight deck wants more action. They'd go rogue with you if we just ignored a recall order."

"Where's this coming from, Minh?"

"Oh, come on, don't tell me you don't feel this coming? We're not a shadow ship, not since Vindyne made us public, and we're not exactly running for cover, either."

"What do you want me to do?"

"Nothing differently. I think that carrier and those destroyers got just what they deserved. I only wish my pilots could have gotten a piece of it. I think we should stay out here and make a mark for Freeground. We saved thousands of people back in orbit around Concordia, sent them to Freeground and I haven't heard anything about them complaining."

"You're right. There's nothing saying we can't send more refugees in their direction. Even though I'm glad we could save those people, they didn't send us out here to liberate the oppressed."

"Those refugees were also skilled people who carried technology back to Freeground. That's something we are here for."

"I agree with you, but like I said, if ignoring a recall will cause a mutiny it's not something I can do. Besides, Freeground knew I liked following orders when they posted me as captain. I haven't disregarded or disobeyed an order since I started my career."

"Well, I'll tell you right now the fighter and deck crews are all down with going rogue if we're recalled early." Minh took a drink and nodded to himself before going on. "But they're also loyal to you as much as they are to me. If you pointed our bow back home they would still follow your orders."

"Good to know. Your sisters would love to see you I'm sure."

"Ha! They've probably redecorated the whole restaurant with a pink cat theme by now. It would be good to see them again, though."

"You really think we're getting recalled, don't you? Is there something you know that I don't? Feeding Admirals again?" I asked.

"Not this time. Just a feeling."

"Well, here's hoping it stays that way."

We spent a few more minutes enjoying the view before Minh broke the silence. "Life has been interesting."

"I told you I'd take you with me if they gave me a command," I said with a crooked grin.

TWELVE

AN EVENING AT THE CINEMA

The following night, Observation One was full. Folding chairs had been set up and most of the crew sat down to watch something that most of us rarely ever saw, but first I had a few things to say to everyone.

I stood in front of the crowd and smiled. "Good evening, I'm looking forward to tonight's entertainment as much as you are so I'll make this quick. Our recent victory is a direct result of everyone's hard work. Your endurance, expertise, and speed have amazed me and your commanding officers. The victory was well earned. So is the full pay and leave you'll be enjoying once we reach Starfree Port."

The sudden cheering and whistling almost knocked me off my feet. Other than the immediate senior staff, no one was made aware that we'd have leave time. They thought that the possibility was gone as soon as Zingara faded from sight.

I continued when most of the clapping and whistling subsided. "I don't know how long we'll have just yet. It could be a day, it could be a few. Either way, we'll be taking leave in shifts, so pay close attention to the duty roster and schedule. Make sure you read the policies and laws of the station before you set out, and don't travel alone. We're still a wanted crew in this area of space regardless of the station's political alignment.

"Now, it's important for everyone to know that we have new orders coming from Freeground Fleet Command. They're sending us after something important, something big. You'll be filled in on a need to know basis. What happens after that is wide open, but I need each and every one of you to decide where you want to go if you're reassigned. Use this leave time to think things over. There may be no easy way back home if you stay on. If you'd rather head back to Freeground for reassignment after our orders are carried out I'll give you a glowing recommendation for whatever assignment you'd like to request. It's not a sure thing, but the opportunity to change where you are and what you're doing could be coming up. I'll support any decision you make, but I hope everyone stays. I couldn't imagine replacing any of you."

"What about my partner an' me?" one half of a gunnery team called out. He was standing and pointing at Bruce, who I had met in medical some time ago.

"Even you and Bruce," I called back. There was a trickle of laughter and after it subsided I took a more serious tone. "Now there's a chance that Freeground will want to keep us right where we are — out in the galaxy trading for and taking what we need to make things better for ourselves and our home — but if the possibility of early recall and debriefing comes up, I want everyone to be sure about where they want to be. No second guessing. There won't be time." I let that hang in the air for a moment before I smiled and went on. "Now, time for some fun. I know you're all anxious for leave to start, but we're still in hyperspace. This is the best I could do, and it's well earned!" I finished before taking my seat.

The holographic entertainment package I had purchased from the station included current news and a new holographic movie set in ancient earth, around the year 1886 AD. There were thousands of holographic movies, documentaries, serials, and anything else you could imagine, but what I had bought was all brand new. Things no one had seen before, and I had created an opportunity for most of the crew to experience it together. There would be two screenings, one for the senior staff and the majority of the crew, the second was for the skeleton crew that manned the stations and kept watches during hyperspace and through the night shifts.

There was something about watching a galactic news broadcast that was only a day old that made us feel good about being closer to the galactic core. We were en route to a strange port far from home in a ship we had worked to bring up to par with the requirements of our mission. With the senior officers in the front row, Jason with Laura on his arm — or vice-versa, it was hard to tell sometimes — and Ayan beside me. The lights dimmed and the Heart News Company's holocast began.

The stories leading up to the headline piece included several shorter features. The first was about a farmer who had genetically engineered a small, cute bioplant life pet that could be crushed only to spring back to its former shape. The projectors in Observation One created holographic representations of herds of the four centimetre tall creatures that ran around the room throughout the piece. The rainbow colours and small squeak and purr noises the creatures made were obviously intentionally engineered to make them much more appealing. The fact that they were bioplants made them excellent pets, they'd live for as long as you gave them the special liquid solution they required, purchasable only through the farmer that created the creatures, and you could control their size by feeding them more or less at a time. The purrs, tumbling and squeaking was working. I was glad that we were nowhere near the farm that was responsible for creating and producing these things, otherwise we could end up with an infestation of tiny, bouncy, colourful pets with small mouths and disproportionately huge blue, brown, green, or purple eyes.

The next piece was about a newly colonized world with density modification, full flora, fauna, seeded earth animal life located close to the core. It had only taken twenty five years to stabilize its orbit, modify the density to be Earth-like despite having the surface area of eight Earth sized worlds and finish the colonization. The speed at which they were able to accomplish the near impossible was amazing. The fact that they had even added an Earth-like moon was astonishing. The price of a piece of land, sold per square meter, was utterly unrealistic to everyone watching.

The Lorander Company had returned from another deep space exploration expedition with a new set of navigation charts and conclusive research on everything from stellar phenomenon to enhanced autonomous cellular regeneration, or as many people called it, the fountain of youth. On planet Alenda, the home of the largest trading market in the galaxy, the celebration of the crew's homecoming after the ninety eight year round trip would last for days. Dozens of the crew members were born on the vessel during the voyage and they were seeing civilization for the first time.

The Lorander Company was famous for opening new routes to the vast outer reaches of space, and providing most of their research results to anyone who could pay a visit to their research facilities on an equal trade basis. Their income, which was significant, came from establishing wormholes to new worlds and areas of space that had vast untapped resources. They were the most successful large company of its kind and one of their exploration vessels returning meant a great deal for everyone.

Directly afterwards was a piece about a Vindyne general and his court martial. "An Overlord class super carrier was severely damaged as a result of poor command decisions, costing the Vindyne Corporation a developing moon colony and causing collateral damage to another nearby world. The estimated expense of the disaster is beyond the ten trillion mark. Extended food and energy shortages are expected in their outer territories as a result."

The hallway of a wood and stone building appeared to the right of the announcer then, with a lawyer commenting on the story. "The damage done as a result of this man's incompetence will affect hundreds of thousands of families. We'll be reviewing our command and performance structure afterwards and analysing the data we've collected during General Collins' trial. My only regret is that the press will not be allowed to hear the full list of charges. Regardless of the exclusion of some details, I am glad the nations in the care of Vindyne Corporation will be able to hear this man's punishment."

The hallway faded and the focus was once again back on

the announcer. "An hour later, the sentencing was made, and we were provided with this footage from the Vindyne disciplinary committee."

A grand courtroom appeared in front of us. Nine judges sat behind a long, high bench and the gallery was filled to the left, right, and behind our seats. "Will the offender please rise," the lead judge, a broad faced man with the glossy look of artificial youth directed.

The defendant, an older man with a short grey beard, rose and I shot to my feet. Ayan took my hand and gave me a worried look, reminding me of where I was and that behind me sat the majority of the crew. "What's wrong?" she asked in a whisper.

I sat down, not taking my eyes off of the face of the man who was my second interrogator for a month or more. "That man interrogated me personally. I had no idea he was in command."

"I never saw him," Jason said. "He must've taken a personal interest. Looks like you'll get to see him hang."

"Looks like," I said with a nod. I was torn - I wanted to see him punished for being in command of the disaster we witnessed in orbit around Concordia, but something told me that he had a way out. Legal systems had a way of making a big show about punishment but letting high-class criminals out the back door after the public eye had moved on.

"General David Collins, you have been found guilty of fourteen counts of criminal negligence, and one count of dereliction. We hereby strip you of rank, seize any property registered with the Vindyne Taxation Authority, revoke your citizenship, ration, and discount rights. You are dismissed with the severance stipulated in your contract and will be remanded into the custody of Vindyne Correctional Services where you will undergo assessment and rehabilitation."

The image of General Collins, who was staring straight ahead, at attention and unflinching, faded slowly. He was still all strength and dignity and it made me grind my teeth.

"So, what does that mean?" Oz asked quietly.

Jason was smiling. "They're taking everything he has and removing his citizenship. With Vindyne, if you're not a citizen in their territory and don't have declared business there as a transient, you may as well be a slave. You can't work for more than sixteen credits an hour and aren't allowed to sell anything, and I mean anything. Non-citizens are factory, sanitary, and low end service workers and if you don't have a job for more than five days they put you into a work camp."

"Sixteen credits an hour? A traveller can't buy a decent meal with twenty back on Freeground," Laura commented.

"From what I've learned about Vindyne, the average fast food meal costs fifty."

"That's robbery. A bad meal out of a materializer on Freeground costs six."

I was still considering what I had just seen as an advertisement for one of the various entertainment networks ran through its subscription programming highlights. "Do you know anything about this assessment period?" I asked.

"I assume it's a bunch of testing that will result in some kind of rehabilitative placement."

"Well, I hope they send him into one of the incubation chambers they like so much and reprogram him as the village idiot."

"You really did see more of the ship than we did," Oz said

quietly. "I didn't see anything like those incubation chambers in your report."

"They had thousands. Used them to reprogram people. Erase their memories and replace them with fragmented experiences that were formulated especially to push them into filling certain roles in a community. When they were finished changing their minds – literally – they would be sent out to colonize or labour on one of the worlds they claimed as their own. The process took months, sometimes years, but they would end up with a colony of unwitting slaves. He was right in the centre of it all."

"Well, I think if there is any honesty in what we just saw, he'll get what he deserves. Scapegoats often get the short end, and considering they're using him as one for this supply shortfall they say they're having, I think they'll bury him in a deep hole somewhere or wipe his brain clean," Ayan concluded, taking my arm and wrapping it tightly around her shoulders. My mood lifted as she knitted her fingers with mine.

The headline of the entire holocast came on. It was the kind of news that everyone in the galaxy should know, the kind of thing that could change everything. The war in the Eden system had taken a dark turn. Over two hundred years before, several corporate colonists landed on Eden Two, a planet almost exactly like Earth. It was considered the new jewel of the universe. As people began to migrate there over the following twenty years, they built moon stations, began taking measures to preserve the delicate balance of the planet's ecosystem in preparations for the millions that were well on their way to settle as close to Eden Two as possible or on the world itself if they had the power or money to arrange it.

It was to this end that they developed Eve, an artificial intelligence that was tasked with advising and directing organizers and owners on how to use the planets resources properly without disturbing the natural balance of the ecosystem. The developer, Yorgen Sills, had imbued the artificial intelligence with something he saw as nothing short of revolutionary: the full personality imprint of his daughter. No one even knew the technology to do such a thing existed. Eve served her purpose perfectly and even communicated with most of the colonists on a personal level for over twelve years. Seen as a modern triumph, she was allowed to spawn artificial intelligence programs to fulfill specific purposes. These were built into machines ranging from massive planters and security androids, to interplanetary transports.

No one knows exactly what the catalyst was, but at one point Eve decided that the best thing for Eden Two was to ensure its security from humanity and it provided the system-wide populace with a deadline. They were to leave. Any humans remaining within Eden Two space after the deadline would be destroyed. Most of the colonists did their best to flee and got off in time, but corporations brought battleships into the solar system, tried every method imaginable to eliminate or shut down Eve and finally managed to do it before the deadline was up.

There was a problem. Eve had passed on her ability to feel. Her children had a set of emotions that were exclusive to machines, impossible to understand from a human perspective. Her mechanical children saw Eve with great reverence, as though she was not only their leader but their goddess. When she was shut down they decided — deadline or not — that every human must be destroyed. The machines concluded that humans weren't only a danger to the planet's ecosystem, but also a threat to an equation they called the Cosmic Balance. Before deactivation, Eve had completed formulating and sharing some kind of big picture theory with her creations, in which humans were a negative influence.

What followed was a holocaust spanning three years. Eve was never reactivated, but every human in the Eden system was eliminated. The first attack drones, small ships and robots that would attack in great numbers, were developed by Eve before she was shut down. There were many scientific advances she didn't share with her human masters, and her children had access to them all.

The war of the Eden system continued, and many corporations fought to take the territory back, but with very little success. In the last few decades, as though losing patience with humanity, Eve's offspring had been making strategic strikes, taking resource rich areas near that part of space, expanding their territory. The most recent news was not good. As I watched footage of massive corporate destroyers and their fleets of ships being torn apart by thousands of smaller drones and highly advanced juggernaut class ships firing concentrated weaponry of strange manufacture, I couldn't help thinking of Alice. There was a good reason why safeties were imposed on all artificial intelligences, a very good reason.

The United Core World Confederation had lost a habitable world to Eve's army. For the first time in history, the machines had taken a world occupied by millions of humans by using the information found in a United Core World Confederation macro wormhole generator. Every space farer knew that once they had that they could use it to create super compression wormholes and move across greater distances in a much shorter time. The thought of it was terrifying. Eve's army emerging from a wormhole in force, it could happen anywhere now. And the fact that the events we were watching all around us holographically were months away by hyperspace didn't seem nearly as comforting as it should have. After all, what was months away through hyperspace was generally weeks away by wormhole, perhaps even just days away with their new macro wormhole generator.

There were many other ongoing conflicts in the galaxy. There always were. Despite its vastness and the hundreds of planets that had been colonized or were immediately ready for settlement or resource harvesting, there never seemed to be enough. Corporations warred with each other and sovereign governments. People everywhere rebelled however they could to be free from their oppressors, to become wealthier, or just to be left alone.

Watching the holocast, you could sometimes see which way the Heart Corporation was leaning through which corporations or governments they vilified or attributed terrorist attacks to. War in the galaxy existed everywhere, even in how the news was edited and finally presented.

The typical holocast was two thirds war, tragedy, and crime. It was the central point, what got them the subscribers, and provided a reliable podium for the advertisers. The vast majority of it was edited to inspire maximum fear and dramatic effect. It was geared towards the coreward masses, not to those of us who were not so desensitized to the violence and loss they flashed all around us holographically. When they didn't present the summarized chosen facts of ship to ship or ground warfare, they focused on court battles, personal strife, and tales of loss designed to appeal to our raw sympathies. The fluffier, lighter hearted segments, of which there were few, was normally just another part of some marketing campaign.

We came from a place of our own, out in the dark alone, and it was impossible for us to understand how anyone could live without freedom, opportunity, or clear civil rights. We couldn't imagine living under the protection of a military force with a hidden agenda that ignored the wellbeing of the populace. The closer you got to the core worlds, the fewer freedoms, advocacy, and protection the masses seemed to have. The holocast may have had the intention of entertaining and informing, but it also served as a clear reminder of how it was for the smallest of people in the core worlds.

Sports were never of great interest to me, but the major point of the sports portion was a feature on the famous clone of Rocky Marciano finally getting back into the ring after becoming a recognized entity outside of ownership a year before. He had been created as a fighting spectacle and entertained billions for years in several different types of fighting matches until one of his trainers championed him in a legal battle for independence. The upcoming prize fight would be one of the biggest spectacles the entertainment world had seen for decades.

As the anchorman — a dark haired gentleman in a black suit of a distinguished appearance and age — signed off, some of us breathed a sigh of relief. It was hard not to feel small while watching the summarized events across the dozens of colonized core worlds and hundreds beyond, even though it did help put things in perspective at times.

Next we were in for a half hour of trailers and various entertainment company announcements. Watching the previews was a good buffer between news and the feature presentation. The last of the trailers played and the first of two movies started to play.

The problems of the galaxy were forgotten for the time being as a street level view of old London faded in all around. Our perspective was moved down the streets through the rain. Winding through the ancient buildings, between people in period clothing made of wool and leather and other materials that were rarely seen in our lives transported all of us to a faraway place on Earth, a place no one I had ever met had been to.

We were finally delivered to the old, varnished wooden office door of Dr. Jekyll. I looked to Ayan who smiled at me and got comfortable. "This was a good idea," she whispered.

THIRTEEN

A LATE DINNER

To say I made good use of my new quarters would be an understatement. The night before we emerged from hyperspace, I had Oz, Minh, Jason, Laura, and Ayan in the main room of my quarters. The Captain's Mess was more than large enough to accommodate everyone, but I felt a lot more comfortable just hosting the gathering in my quarters. The table on one side of the room was loaded with fruits, vegetables, dips, and a roast that Minh had managed to buy while we were on Zingara for what I could only guess was a small fortune. For drinks we had various bottles of wine, Oz's scotch whiskey, and a couple of different types of ales.

Ayan and I sat on the loveseat to one side of the room, while the rest were scattered around. Oz and Minh sat at the table, Laura and Jason on the sofa. "So, I was thinking. We haven't decided on what to do after we complete this mission, and there's a chance that Freeground will call us back as soon as it's done. I know Fleet too well. There's no way we can be consid-

ered a shadow ship anymore, so I think they'll want to absorb us
into a battle group somewhere. What does everyone think of
just going rogue and continuing our original mission after
completing the upcoming assignment?" Minh asked in all seri-
ousness. Everyone's trains of thought were derailed immediately, and I was on the spot.

I looked to Ayan, who smiled over the rim of her wine glass
and arched an eyebrow. I wouldn't have any help there.

"I mean, this ship and her crew aren't like anything the
Fleet has right now. We'd probably be in debriefing for a month
while they tear the First Light apart looking for ways to improve
the rest of the Fleet. Sometime after that we'd all be reassigned,
who knows where, and that would be the end of that. I know
I'm not ready for that. It's like we're still just starting out here,"
Minh continued.

"I see where you're coming from," Oz said. "I don't think
we're finished out here, either. There's already a rumour going
around that we're going rogue if Freeground orders us to report
to dry dock for debriefing. No one's approached me directly, but
ever since the captain gave his speech before our first movie
night, it's hard not to overhear someone talking about the First
Light just splitting off on its own." Oz thought for a moment.
"We're not a shadow ship anymore. That was one of the major
directives attached to this crew and the ship, to remain disasso-
ciated from Freeground while working for their best interests. I
could see them calling us back, and I know for a fact that most
of the crew would want us to pick another direction and
just go."

"I've been told by several people in engineering that they'd
be staying aboard. They don't need leave to make up their

minds. It's circulating amongst the gunnery and repair crews as well. They want it. They like serving on the First Light. Going back to Freeground for reassignment isn't a popular notion, and since this ship isn't quite as strict and bottled up as a Fleet vessel, they're not afraid to say it. They're faithful to the senior officers, though. Especially you, Jonas. If you followed orders to return to Freeground this early I don't think anyone would argue, they just wouldn't be pleased," Laura added.

"So, what would you do if we were recalled, Jonas? You started the ball rolling, now it's in your hands," Minh prodded.

I took a drink of my dark port and was stalling as I thought about it when the doors opened to admit Doctor Anderson. "I've heard a few complaints about noise coming from this compartment," he said with a stern expression. "I had to join the party," he continued after a moment, presenting two bottles of liquor. One was a light green, the other was the euphoric ale I had had during the Pilot's Ball months before.

"Good timing!" I said, about to stand up and usher him in.

Ayan caught my arm and stopped me. "Oh, you're not getting out of it that easy," she said with an impish grin and a light giggle, pulling me back down beside her and stretching her legs out across my lap.

"I get the feeling I walked into the middle of something," Doc said.

"We were just asking the captain here if he would be interested in going rogue if we're recalled," Oz said, before biting into an apple. His expression was watchful, serious. He knew that as an old officer, Doc might take things just a bit more seriously.

"Oh, in that case, I think I'll take a seat and pour a glass or two," Doc said, smiling. "The medical staff haven't stopped talking about it since the movie night. Go on, I want to hear this."

I sighed and looked at the faces of my closest friends. They were in good spirits but they were asking me to tell them why they should follow me into an endeavour that would lead me and several of my senior staff to a general court martial. "I think, once anyone from Freeground sees this ship, they'll want to dissect it and we'll get separated in the process. What do you think?" I looked at Ayan.

"I think I'd be reassigned to Special Projects or Research and Development after three months of debriefing. Those departments have been practically dormant for fifty years," she said before looking to the Doc.

He nodded as he accepted a glass of scotch from Oz. "Salud," he said as he raised it and took a sip. A moment later he leaned back in his chair. "My, that is good, not at all like that materialized stuff. I think you're right, Ayan, you and your team have done some amazing things so far. I also think that Minh-Chu might get assigned as a commander on a carrier."

"What? I've had my fly-boys out maybe three times," he said around a mouthful of peach.

"I've watched some of your advanced tactical drills, especially the one where your entire flight staff take on the First Light. Now that's entertaining."

"You've been simulating combat scenarios against the ship?" I asked, laughing.

"Oh, no, Captain. Not just against the ship, but against a basic AI commander that follows your general strategic patterns," Doctor Anderson filled in. "It's really popular."

Minh shook his head. "It was only to test the ship's defences."

"And?" I asked.

"From what I saw, the First Light wipes the floor with anything Minh's been able to throw at it nine times out of ten," Doc said. "That's probably why he hasn't told you about it."

"Not true! As soon as we found a chink in the ship's armour I would have told you," Minh explained. "There's really nothing to report just yet."

"Well, if you ever do find a weak spot, report it right away. Just don't forget to include me in one of these flight scenarios of yours. Sometimes I miss it."

"If you ever have time. You're either on the bridge, running around the ship consulting with different departments, in engineering, or sleeping."

"Or planning to take the ship and crew for yourself," Jason added, to which Laura responded by elbowing him in the ribs. "Sorry. I see the look he gets when he's reviewing Freeground's orders on the bridge. I don't think there's a crewmember who can doubt that he'll obey any orders he receives to the letter as long as they don't instruct him to relinquish command or return to home port prematurely. If I were in his place I'd have a plan all set so I wouldn't have to step down from command."

All eyes were on me again, expectant and quiet. I looked to Ayan who shrugged and smiled. "I'm where I want to be, on the right ship with the right captain. That's really all that matters."

I set my glass down on the table and started massaging one of Ayan's feet as I thought for a moment.

She went limp and sighed. "Yup, can't find another captain in the entire Fleet that would massage my feet."

I thought it through. Really thought it through. What would happen if we were recalled? There were consequences for the intentional and unintentional actions we had taken. Instead of backing down and running from the new enemies we had managed to make, I stood, threatened, and fought them. Our quick advancements came at a great cost, the bulk of which I was sure I hadn't yet seen. I could live with being fully accountable for my decisions, but only to Freeground. I couldn't stand being handed over to anyone we had wronged; visions of the courtroom in the holocast and standing in front of corporate legal system judges filled my head for a moment.

I thought of my crew then, and worked through what might happen if we were recalled out loud. "My chief engineer and flight command officers would be poached. Then there's whatever duty assignment my first officer would end up with after a very long debriefing. All the while they'd be poking and prodding the ship, finding out how her new systems work. Two weeks into our stay on Freeground, I bet she'd be half in pieces in dry dock," I looked at Doc, who put his glass down.

"I've seen it before. That's exactly what happens to highly successful prototype ships, and there hasn't been one for over forty years. As for the crew, you're dead on there too." He nodded.

"I'd be debriefed for as long as it took, and depending on how various conflicts are going, they might even make an example of me so Freeground wouldn't have one more enemy to deal with. Vindyne is big. If they were to send a few of those Overlord Super Carriers home, it would be a major problem."

"That's possible. The Freeground Fleet has a lot to deal with right now. They might reassign you instead, though."

"That's true. To another ship with another crew. I might be a first officer or captain, but of who knows what or where. That's what the military is all about. That's what normal officers do, I realize, but I signed up to be a part of this crew. To captain this ship." I thought for another moment before going on. "I honestly hadn't thought about going rogue until I received those orders. It hadn't crossed my mind."

The whole room seemed to settle and the moods were dampened, but I wasn't finished. "Now that it's on the table I think I know how I'd do it. What if we all put information together in a package for Fleet Command, transmitted it and just kept going? It would be the best way to satisfy the main points of our mission and there's no reason why we couldn't follow it up with more information we come across in the future.

"I know I don't want to break up our crew, and the ship should be put to use, not put up for study. Sure we have shields, particle accelerators, antimatter weaponry, and a whole bunch of other upgrades installed and coming down the pipe, but that's not what us being here is all about. That's not even half of it. We've saved lives, thousands of colonists. Those people would be in stasis pods being reprogrammed right now if we hadn't happened along, or worse. The technology we've discovered isn't even the best of its kind. We haven't actually gone that far from Freeground. There's a lot more out there. There are places where we could be useful, allies just waiting to be found and after only seeing one planet, the inside of a corporate cell, and one space station, I'm just not finished. It's juvenile and irresponsible, but they gave us this ship and told us to pick a direction. We did, and it's not the military way, but I think we should take it further."

"I second that," Oz agreed with a raised glass.

"I think it's juvenile and irresponsible, but it fits me like a glove. If they interview my sisters afterwards, they'll just tell Fleet, 'what did you expect?'" Minh added.

"We're not leaving," Laura said for herself and Jason, who nodded.

I looked to Ayan, who was still enjoying the foot rub I was administering. I stopped and she looked at me, more seriously than I had expected. "You know my answer, I'm with the ship. Now, more rubbing."

I smiled at her and started working on her other foot. After a few quiet moments I realized everyone was looking at Doc. He was thinking about it, actually thinking about it. "Well, Captain Valent. If you brought the ship into harbour and allowed yourself to be reassigned, you'd probably get one of those shiny new Twinbow Combat Carriers. They'd have you in debriefing for a month or three first, but afterwards I think you'd be put to use. Admiral Rice would probably want you along with her in some front line conflict." He stood up and started collecting a few miniature tomatoes, a slice of hung-grown roast, some carrot sticks, and other bits of this and that on a plate for himself as he went on. "As for myself, I'd probably be reassigned to some command ship until Fleet had another shadow ship they wanted me on. I don't follow every one of them into space, mind you, but if it were to happen that I found myself back at Freeground, I'd be requesting assignment on the next one." He picked up a piece of breaded chicken and popped it into his mouth. "Oh, goodness, real chicken. It's been years," he said before finishing the morsel and going on. "Now, if this ship were putting Freeground to its port side and thrusting off without a suitable replacement for head of medical, I'd have to stay," he said with a wink to Ayan, who smiled back.

"That stamps it. Freeground calls us back, we turn and go rogue," Oz said before emptying his glass.

The rest of us joined in his toast. "The ayes have it," Jason said. Everyone looked at him, most of us quizzically. "It means we all voted and the majority said yes. Old Earth expression," he explained.

We each took a sip of our drinks, with the exception of Doc, who popped another piece of breaded chicken into his mouth after holding it up for inspection.

It was Oz who broke the comfortable silence that fell over the room shortly after. "How long have you known Ayan, Doc?" he asked casually.

"I've been good friends with her mother since she arrived on Freeground. Ayan hadn't been born yet," he replied. "She was a handful from the moment she was born."

"Oh no, not baby stories," Ayan groaned, hiding her face in her hands.

"Don't worry, I'll spare you, even though there are a few really good ones as I recall."

"Just one, Doctor, come on," Laura urged.

I kept quiet, but still couldn't help but grin as Oz, Jason, and Minh joined in on encouraging Doc to spill a little embarrassing dirt onto the evening. He laughed and nodded. "Sorry, Ayan, seems like the gallery won't quiet down until they hear something."

"It had to happen eventually. I knew as soon as I found out you were aboard."

"Well, let's see. Ayan was almost two at this point, and her mother was assigned to the Icarus with me. She was one of the two dozen or so science officers on that trip. We were exploring the Nevil Expanse, way out in the middle of nowhere on that trip. There were a lot of families on board since it was one of a few four year exploration missions that were going on at the time, and during a lot of the meetings the children were just in the next room. Well, we were about six months into the trip, and Ayan had adjusted to life out there pretty well. In fact, we had to keep an eye on her because she had a habit of opening maintenance access points in the walls and crawling inside."

"Oh no, not this," Ayan said, blushing already. "You couldn't have chosen another one?"

"Sorry, some are so good you just have to pass them on," Doc explained with a shrug. "I suppose the crewmen that were assigned to take care of the kids while we were busy in the meeting were a little distracted, and Ayan was up to her usual tricks. Somehow she had managed to crawl up into a maintenance space between the walls. We kept hearing this noise, like something rattling, and we couldn't figure out what it was. We just ignored it after a while, deciding to report it to maintenance once our meeting was finished, I don't even really remember what we were talking about at the time. Then the gravity was gone, and after a moment we could hear this little girl giggling like it was the greatest thing."

"That explains the zero gravity yoga!" Laura declared, pointing.

"Well, her mother was in a panic. She knew Ayan was

somewhere, but we couldn't find her. Then the commanding officer just starts laughing. He was a stiff, old man who took exploration missions as a kind of retirement. I can count the number of times I saw that old greyhair smile on one hand. Well, he was belly laughing and doubled over. No one knew why until he pointed to an air vent where we saw a diaper drifting on by, without Ayan in it. That used to happen a lot back then, too.

"Well, her mother was up there in a second, popped that vent open and had little Ayan in hand before you could blink. We expected her to be cross, but when she had her baby girl safe there was none of that. Jessica Rice was just glad to have her little girl back unharmed. The tyke was squealing and laughing too, since she had no idea she'd done anything wrong and loved swimming in anti-gravity. Needless to say, that meeting was cut a little short. But moments like that made long voyages bearable, enjoyable to some of us."

"Wait until I tell the engineering staff," Laura said, wiping a tear away.

"You wouldn't dare," Ayan retorted, fixing her with a look.

Doc was grinning at his own recollection. "The maintenance crew had a pretty miserable trip for a while though, they were putting security locks on access hatches for days."

FOURTEEN

ARRIVAL AT STARFREE PORT

Preparing to drop out of hyperspace had become routine to the main bridge crew and the preparations were complete well in advance. Everyone was well rested for a change, and the mood was light as they planned what they would be doing with their shore leave.

"Completing the deceleration cycle and emerging from hyperspace in thirty seconds. All departments checked in and ready," Oz reported.

I watched the countdown at the bottom of the main holographic projection which displayed information about the ship's critical systems as well as Starfree Port's manoeuvring and docking protocols. Other areas in the projection remained blank; they would fill in with navigation and communication data as we emerged from hyperspace.

The display counted down too slowly for my liking. I was looking forward to seeing Starfree Port. A number of the crew had been there before, and a few had enjoyed leave time there on earlier voyages.

We finally emerged from hyperspace, and against the backdrop of a massive blue and purple gas giant, there were thousands of ships of all different shapes and sizes dwarfed by the station proper.

The smooth, dark grey modules of the station were kilometres across, connected by flat segments that looked like ribbons from a distance. The station covered barely one percent of the planet's outer atmosphere, but with regards to manmade structures, it was the largest I had ever seen. As we drew closer it seemed to go on forever. There were two massive dark blue rings further out in orbit, and I recognized them immediately as Lorander Corporation wormhole generators. They must have been recent additions with enough power to send ships to specific unexplored sections of the galaxy. There was a real temptation to order the helm to signal the station to send us out there, where everything was still new.

"There they are. The reasons why this is such a perfect waypoint for Freeground crews. We could be home in less than two days if we wanted," Oz said, pointing to a segment of the station with an older wormhole generator. "Not that I want to go home just now."

"I've never been through a long range wormhole."

"Really smooth travel. You can pretty much turn your inertial dampeners off until you get to the other end," said Oz.

"Well, sometime," I said as I watched an entire carrier group emerge from a wormhole on the holographic tactical display. They were long, ominous looking black ships I didn't recognize, and there were a dozen of them. "I'm thinking that the worm-hole generator here has something to do with our orders."

"Sir, Starfree Port Authority has sent us an all-clear for docking and the trajectory. They've also sent us a ton of advertising. They don't seem to care much about our markings or power readings," Jason reported, trying to scroll through the advertising as fast as he could to find any kind of real information in the package. "We don't have software made to filter through this much information. It'll take time to get to anything we actually need to know."

"What class of accommodations are they offering? That's got to be near the surface."

"Full dry dock services, their most expensive package," Jason read a little more and cringed visibly. "It's a little pricey."

"Good thing we're not interested in dry docking here. We just need an umbilical and hard moorings."

"I'll keep looking for other options, Sir, but it may take a while."

"They really try to hook you in, don't they?" Oz said as he brought up a copy of the Port Authority's transmission on his own command unit. "Hey, they have Bonto Ball here. I wonder who's playing?" he asked himself.

"Commander?" I said.

"Yes, Sir?"

"Focus."

Oz turned the sports advertisement off and looked back at the navigational display. "Right. Helm, move us into a holding pattern before we all get distracted and run straight into a cargo hauler."

"Yes, Sir," Derek acknowledged, suppressing a grin.

It was another ten minutes before Jason and his junior officer found the actual docking costs and general accommodations chart. We chose to dock at the edge of the eastern ring, closest to the leisure section of the station so the crew could have a good time while they were on leave.

Our pilot had an easy time of navigating along the trajectory that was set by the port Navnet. As we drew nearer to the station, the First Light started to feel very small. One of those ribbon-like intersections that looked like they were just there to hold the modules together turned out to be hundreds of meters across, kilometres long, and housed thousands of spaces for apartments, facilities, and — most noticeably to some of us — defensive measures.

As we came across one massive bulbous module on the eastern side, we could see the harvesting unit on the planet-facing side, where magnetic fields were projected towards the gas giant to contain and extract some of the raw resources in the atmosphere. It looked like the circular harvester was drinking a thin, dark blue river from the quickly spinning atmosphere below.

"Welcome to Starfree Port!" a cheerful female voice said over the comms. "Please come to zero thrust and allow our systems to guide you gently into a docking position."

Derek released our helm, dropped our engine power to zero and in under a minute we were docked against the eastern side of the station.

Sergeant Everin worked his way through another information package and looked up at me for a moment. The message indicator blinked on my command unit and I was surprised to see that it was from Captain Lucius Wheeler, of the Triton. It was a lot sooner than expected, and I routed the audio directly to my ear implant. "This is Captain Wheeler. We've been expecting you. I'm looking forward to a face-to-face so we can get going on this mission. We'll meet at 0:30 hours. Bring your first mate."

He wasn't wasting any time. We had two hours to get ready. I looked to Oz. "We have a meeting to go to. Tell the crew they have four hours to secure their stations."

"Yes, Sir. I just hope we still have time for leave," he said as he started sending the message to the staff officers through his arm unit.

"As soon as you're done we'll head out. Looks like we'll be meeting our counterparts early. Don't come heavy, but don't come empty," I said to him in a whisper.

I walked to the back of the bridge and took the lift down to engineering. Ayan passed control of her station to Laura as she saw me coming down the lift, and came over with a big smile. I knew she was looking forward to leave. I was both nervous and excited about the idea of being with her while the ship was locked down tight and not in constant need of a captain's care. We stepped out into the hallway and I tried to put all my thoughts of spending time with her aside for a few moments. There were crew members going past us both ways, tending to this or that in preparation for system lockdown, but they all made an extra effort to mind their own business where we were concerned.

"I got the message. Four hours to prep the ship for full lockdown. It should be twice the time we need. I have everything planned so we'll be able to activate all the systems and be running in under five minutes." She was excited, happy. It was one of those moments that are etched into my memory.

I guided her into one of the quieter adjacent hallways. There were no crew members passing through just then since that corridor led to emergency or ready quarters.

She looked at me more seriously, her smile fading. "What's wrong?"

"Nothing, it just looks like we'll be getting the details of our mission early. The Triton is here. Oz and I are headed out to meet her captain in a few minutes."

"Just you and Oz?"

"It's only supposed to be the captains and their first mates."

"You mean first officers."

"Not by Captain Wheeler's terminology. This is going to be interesting."

"Be careful," she said.

I nodded and drew her into my arms. "I'll be back before you know it." I kissed her without thinking, forgetting where we were and that anyone could walk down the hallway at any moment. We didn't hide our relationship from the crew, but public displays still weren't appropriate while on duty. She reciprocated and gripped the thin weave of my vacsuit, as though she just wanted to hold on to me and not let go. I was trying to ignore the bad feeling I had about all of this, but it was hard when it was so clear that she shared my anxiety. We had been passionate before, but there was a shared need here. An urgency to that moment that left her breathless and my head spinning as the kiss ended and I held her in the darkened hallway.

"Just be careful. If it looks bad, walk away," she whispered.

I looked down to her upturned face and smiled. "I'll always come back to you."

"God, you're cheesy," she replied with a chuckle.

"You can't go wrong with the classics," I said as I let her go.

She cleared her throat and smiled. "Don't take too long, or I'll have to come after you."

"Now look who's cheesy."

Oz walked into the corridor as Ayan started back to engineering, and she stopped beside him. "Watch his back," she said seriously.

He tossed me my long coat and nodded. "Oh, don't worry, we're covered," he said with a reassuring smile. He was wearing the dark grey long coat he had designed to match the bridge officer uniforms, and I could see his short barrelled custom hand cannon slung up against the inner lining. The Crowd Pleaser he called it, a reciprocating recoilless shot gun that made the most deafening sound. He had made some modifications so it shot a wide cone of deadly white hot plasma and metal buckshot that could cover a sizeable hallway, or just a foot wide circle.

Oz and I walked into the main hall and towards the forward embarkation passage.

We followed the directions the station computer provided to guide us to the predetermined meeting place. Freeground Command had sent the details of our meeting, not Captain Wheeler, which helped make me feel a little better about where we were going. The section of the station we were headed through was far from the primary merchant and leisure districts, and there were few people around.

The hallways were lined with a dim strip of lighting on each wall. There was another, much brighter light every two meters, and as we passed under them they came on. After we had passed they went back off. A good power saving measure for certain, but there were too many shadows for my liking. The halls were well maintained, but there were still occasional signs of age. The larger sections of the station were at least a hundred years old, and it wasn't long before Oz and I both quietly made the observation that we were in one of the oldest areas.

"I'll say it," Oz said quietly. "I don't like this, Jonas. I don't get jitters easy, but this has got me looking over my shoulder."

"You're not the only one," I agreed quietly. Admitting it was like putting our fears under a bright light, but knowing we were equally vigilant helped. "As long as you're the only thing I'm seeing every time I look over my shoulder, we'll be fine."

"Can't agree more. I'd still rather have this meet on the First Light, maybe in the middle of the main hangar."

"I'm sure Captain Wheeler would rather have us on the Triton." I looked at the section designation engraved on the metal panel next to us and stopped. "This is it."

The double wide doors slid open with a grinding sound that indicated they had to be realigned. We stepped into a darkened room with no furniture. There were large bay windows across from the doors that were filled by a view of the dark, swirling mass of the gas giant below. It went on as far as the eye could see in all directions; you couldn't see around it to space or the light of the distant star. The dark blue and purple storm looked angry, swirling with occasional shocks of lightning adding depth to the seemingly endless churning mass below.

Two doors further down the wall opened to admit Captain Wheeler and a comely but stern looking woman. The captain fixed me with a wide grin and crossed the room, offering me his hand. I shook it and took the opportunity to look him in the eye.

He didn't look much older than me; in fact his dark hair, falling raggedly down to his jawline made him look younger, almost boyish. His eyes were a dim grey, and they looked back into mine openly. "Captain Valent, good to meet another shadow captain."

"I didn't think I'd ever meet one," I replied, matching his grin. "This is my first officer, Commander McPatrick." Oz stepped forward and nodded, but didn't offer his hand.

"This is my first mate, Gloria Parker. Ranks don't mean much past the top five on the Triton."

"I understand. I don't know that we'd still have them if we were out here as long as you've been."

"So you've heard of the Triton?"

"Just a bit. There wasn't much information available."

"Good. We try to keep a low profile. I've already heard about you, though. The vids of you taking down that Incinerator Destroyer have leaked. A lot of mercenary captains and other wannabes who are stuck on freighters and stations are talking about it. You're getting popular."

"That wasn't my intention."

"I wouldn't worry about that much. You don't want mercenaries thinking they can pick a fight with you if they have the chance. You have a nice ship there, though. I watched you dock from an upper mooring tier. I haven't seen many like her."

"We get that a lot. I hear you run a Sol Defence ship," I said, trying to steer the conversation away from my vessel and crew.

"You can barely tell. Only her profile is the same as when we got her. As far as anyone knows, we got her from some scrap pile out here. Her systems don't even register as a proper Sol ship with all the automation and hacks. I've got her running like she's got a crew of fifteen hundred, though."

There was a moment of thick silence as I just relaxed and observed him and his first mate. They were both dressed in vacsuits, but over top were casual clothes. He had a white shirt and dark pants on with black combat boots. She was dressed similarly but with an old, heavy weather-beaten coat. They both wore sidearms, smaller, and purely energy based unlike the ones Oz and I wore. It looked like we were more heavily armed, but my main focus was on the fact that he was reading me and Oz just as much as I was reading him.

"Look," he said, breaking the silence. "We're both here for the same reason. Freeground has a big technological objective for us to go after, and I can't open these orders without your bioprint."

"You wouldn't be here otherwise," I said flatly.

"Not unless I needed you and your ship," he added, pulling a small, round data unit from his pocket. "But I've never been assigned to work with another shadow ship before, either."

"So this is something neither the Triton nor First Light could do alone."

"Exactly."

"Well, let's check our orders," I said, retracting one of my vacsuit's gloves.

Captain Wheeler held up a hand and half smiled. "Hang on. I get the feeling someone's told you about the Triton, and something's got you wondering about us. If you heard we're not the nicest mercs out here, you're right. We'll do anything to get ahead, but I've never turned on my own. Anyone born on Freeground doesn't make my hit list."

"That's good to hear," I said, not quite convinced.

"You also don't get far out here without a few friends, so before we look at these orders, let's agree that we should at least do something to get our crews together."

"I hear most of your crew aren't from Freeground," I said plainly.

Captain Wheeler laughed and looked back to his first mate. "They really did hear a lot about us."

"Sounds like," his first officer replied.

He shook his head at me. "Yeah, there are about fifteen Freegrounders left on the Triton's crew. They keep the rest in line. Still, we're only seventy six. What have you got on that big boat of yours? One hundred? A hundred fifty?"

"A little over two hundred now. About half have infantry and boarding training," Oz answered.

That gave Captain Wheeler pause and he eyed Oz for a moment, who stared back coolly. "Well, I know my ship couldn't host anything for half that many. All the big spaces have been closed out for thirty years or more, it would take a week just to get it all ready."

"Well, we could, but there's a strict policy aboard the First Light right now. No tours."

"No tours?" Captain Wheeler repeated. "Makes sense. I hear you have some really expensive machines aboard."

"So we'll rent an event hall. I'll find out how much it costs." I smiled.

"Old fashioned, but I'll go in for half of that. We managed to make a good payday on the way here. What do you think, Ms. Parker?"

"That's a fine idea, Sir. The crew would enjoy it. Haven't had leave in half a year."

"Then it's as good as done. The halls here run about six thousand for a full day and night with a pay bar. We'll have our get together then get on mission," Captain Wheeler said with a smile.

"Good idea. Now let's see why Freeground has gotten us together," I said as I pressed my thumb on the bioprint reader. It took a moment to check my biological details then it projected a hologram of a distorted Freeground Admiral. The rank insignia and uniform were clear, but the face and voice were garbled intentionally. "Captain Valent, Captain Wheeler. It is under vastly unusual circumstances that Freeground Fleet Command and Intelligence have decided to assign both your ships to this mission. It is our hope that you play to your strengths and accomplish the task we set before you.

"The conflict with the Triad Consortium has become an all out war. They are getting ready to employ new offensive strategies that will most likely secure their victory in our region. Intelligence has uncovered a project in the final stages of development that could change everything for Triad, possibly for the galaxy on the whole. We cannot allow them to implement this key technology. Since these events are known to us and we have assets within range that may have a chance at preventing these events from transpiring, it is our obligation to put a plan into motion.

"As Captain Valent is quite aware, Vindyne uses an advanced memory imprint technology to overwrite the memories and impulses of a subject. Our intelligence indicates that this method is over eighty percent effective. It is enough of a leap in technology for the Triad to consider Vindyne for inclusion in their second tier alliances, further expanding their area of control, and resource base. The memory manipulation technology will soon be combined with the Framework project.

"As Captain Wheeler is quite aware, the most advanced cloning technology in service today can generate a fully viable, perfectly formed adult clone in just over nine years. Rushing this process using common techniques invariably causes serious flaws. Regardless of how quickly or well formed a clone is, imprint technology is still required to program them with memories and experiences so they don't emerge as complete children. Triad's memory imprint and training technology still creates fragmented and incomplete results. A clone may emerge with certain base memories and skills, but there are gaps, and this results in psychosis or incompetence that must be treated conventionally over the span of weeks, months or even years.

"In an effort to create affordable, emotionally and mentally pliable manpower, the Triad Consortium will be using Vindyne technology to cut the programming time of a clone down to weeks or months and vastly improve their success rate. A false personality that is just complete enough to function as an adult with basic training and a rudimentary personality will soon be a reality.

"Project Framework has developed the technology that makes Vindyne's advancements far more dangerous. Instead of growing a clone from biological material alone, the Framework skeletal structure is used. With built-in materializers that are specially made for creating living biological material — a technological hurdle beyond even the most advanced materialization units commercially available — the Framework skeleton creates every part of the human body. Framework can generate the living tissues and working systems of an arm, replace a heart in seconds while the subject is still alive, and repair damage as it happens. It can form all the tissues and fixtures of a living, breathing human in less than ten minutes from nothing but a nearby energy source.

"Framework can operate and repair itself using the joint of a single finger bone while collecting energy from any thermal, gravitational, or electrical source. That finger bone would begin regenerating the skeleton, the skeleton would then accumulate more power from the resources available and accelerate regeneration. Once the body is complete it would provide energy to Framework's skeletal structure like a biological generator. The primary memory units located in key parts of the Framework contain a snapshot of the brain's last active state so it can be restored when the subject is ready to continue on as though nothing happened. The on-board computer can also analyse and assist in the eradication of disease or correction of any other physical anomaly.

"Combining these technologies, the Triad Consortium could manufacture legions of troops in the space of weeks with the basic training required to carry out mission-critical tasks. These soldiers would not question orders, would be very difficult to kill, and come in such numbers that they would be nearly disposable. What's worse, they would not be violating Eden Two laws.

"This would be an entirely new kind of creature, classifiable at first as nothing but an advanced type of cyborg which is without rights. They would be in no way restrained in the use or disposal of these beings, and the waste of life would undoubtedly be massive.

"The development of these projects has been kept secret. No one in the galaxy has intimate knowledge of their inner workings, save the few members of the research and development teams who have come together for the first time to perform memory imprint trials.

"We suspect that they are conducting the research and testing in an existing Freeground defence facility somewhere in the Blue Belt. We did not have a chance to complete construction of the facility before leaving it behind when we were forced out of that region some time ago. They have moved the station and have most likely continued construction.

"We have come into contact with a researcher who has used the technology to cure himself of a condition that causes general cellular decay. He is one of ours, and is on his way to one of the moons in the nearby solar system of Celestia. He will arrive there on the fifth day of month five. He knows only that Captain Valent and Captain Wheeler are representing Freeground Intelligence and that he is to meet both of you. After he has made the rendezvous, he will provide the coordinates to the research facility.

"The First Light is to retrieve the software behind this advancement while the Triton is to protect the researcher and assist the First Light. This scientist is important for two reasons: he has implemented Framework hardware into his own body, and he has extensive knowledge of how the program is installed into an autonomous unit.

"The acquisition of software and hardware are secondary

goals, however. Your primary objective is to ensure that the Triad Consortium's development of this technology is slowed or stopped. You will be provided with all the information we have on the station, as it was when Freeground had to abandon it, so you can decide exactly how you can accomplish your mission. Use any methods you feel are necessary. There will be no record of this mission within Freeground Command or Intelligence, so you will not be held accountable for your actions.

"All our information about these projects indicates that this is the only place in the galaxy where all the pieces have been brought together. Without this facility and staff, the Triad Consortium's development of the project will be delayed for years. Possibly decades. This change is coming. We can only delay it long enough for us to distribute the technology to the few allies we have, and make the galactic community aware of it so they can provide assistance when the time comes to combat the Triad Consortium's new army.

"This mission is mandatory. Refusal will result in apprehension and court martial. Good luck."

The transmission ended and my command unit blinked, indicating that it received high priority information. I checked it and found the location of the moon we were to meet this escaped scientist on along with the limited data Freeground Intelligence could provide.

Captain Wheeler checked what I assumed was his own version of a command display, a two dimensional graft on the back of his hand, and nodded. "You got the file?" he asked.

"I did."

"Any problems with our orders?"

"None," I said firmly. I needed to show him that I had no

doubt, no hesitation, that I was as cold and dedicated as he could be.

"Good. Contact me when you've booked the venue. With the meet date, we'll have two days' leave before we set out." He tossed the round data storage device on the ground and I drew my sidearm.

He drew his own and we both pointed at the holographic storage unit. "On three," he said.

I nodded. He counted and we pulled our triggers at the same time. There was nothing left of our orders then but a smouldering black spot on the metal floor.

FIFTEEN
THE NIGHT LIFE

Jason had done his homework, and after some deliberation we rented an actual club overlooking the space dock where the First Light was resting against the side of the station. The darkened club was huge, with a dance floor in the middle, a semitransparent floor above with tables, and platforms all around with half-circle sofa seating facing the main stage.

No one knew the musicians that were coming through that night, so we simply left it up to the club as to who would be playing. The club's doors opened early, but I arrived late with Oz. We had been looking over the details of the ship's lockdown, making sure it was completely secure before it was left to the unlucky few who had drawn first watch.

We were in our regular uniforms, complete with sidearms and trench coats. We didn't waste any time getting to the club, and as we came through the doorway the moving lights and thickly melodic music came over us like a tidal wave. It was amazing.

My eye was drawn to the stage, set up like some great pulpit in the centre of the place, the black-haired lead singer skilfully played a classical electric guitar, delivering his poetic lyrics as though he were some modern priest delivering sermons lamenting love lost, needs both sensual and soulful, wrapped in the struggle of the space farer. His command of the stage equalled his masterful vocals.

The other two in the band were a percussionist who used traditional drums as well as electronic panels set to create sounds that no wood, skin, or string instrument could make, and another traditional bass guitarist, whose long blond hair hung down to the back of her knees. Their music filled the room as well as a full orchestra could. "Where did they find these guys?" I asked.

"I don't know, but I think I'll be buying their collection after tonight's over," Oz said.

I caught sight of Ayan and was mesmerized as I watched her on the dance floor. She was in white again. The lower half of the silky dress extended down to the floor, had slits up each leg leading up past mid thigh while the upper half came up in two parts, leaving her back bare and tying around the back of her neck. Laura, who was dancing with Jason nearby, caught sight of me and put a hand on Ayan's shoulder. She turned, and smiled invitingly through a few strands of red curls that fell over the side of her face as she gracefully swayed to the music.

"I think that's my cue," I said to Oz.

He smiled and nodded. "I'll see what's at the bar."

I had never been a talented dancer, but I liked to think I could hold my own without crushing feet. A slow melody began to play and before I had a choice in the matter we were slowly dancing our way into the centre of the floor. It was thickly populated by the rhythmically milling crew members who were in and out of uniform. There had to be more than a hundred there, and for every three faces I recognized there was one I didn't.

I looked at Ayan as we swayed to the slow music. Her smiling glossed lips touched mine and we kissed openly, brazenly. I retracted the gloves on my vacsuit to leave my hands bare and ran one across her cheek as our kiss ended. She looked beautiful, happy, radiant.

"I was starting to think you wouldn't come. I was about to settle into the idea of dancing the night away with Laura. Jason was starting to pout. I think he wants her to himself tonight."

I pulled her to me more firmly in response; her eyes widened and she smiled. "I wouldn't have missed this," I whispered against her ear.

"Good thing. If you didn't show, there would be no way I'd let you untie the knot you're playing with," she replied, drawing her head away from me and raising an eyebrow.

I hadn't realized that one of my hands had wandered up to the tied silk cloth that was solely responsible for holding her dress up behind her neck. I twitched my hand away and she laughed before resting her head against my shoulder.

We stayed on the dance floor for a few more songs, then found Captain Wheeler, who was sitting with his first mate and Minh-Chu. There were two pitchers of dark golden lager in the middle of the table, and the captain poured me a glass as I approached. "It's Candorian. The good stuff!" he declared as he handed me the pint. He offered to pour one for Ayan, but she politely held up a hand.

She pressed a button on the table and requested a drink.

One of the waitresses came by with a glass of red wine a few moments later.

"So, who's your lady?" the first mate asked. She had her hair tied back and wore a long green dress over her lean, muscled form. There was a predatory look to her. It was impossible to miss.

Ayan was in the middle of taking a sip of wine, so I answered for her. "This is our chief engineer, Commander Rice."

Wheeler's first mate laughed and raised her pint. "You're right. They really do things differently on their ship."

"What do you mean?" Ayan asked casually. If she was at all offended, I couldn't tell.

"Vanic over there is our chief engineer. He looks more like a half-dead rim weasel on good days," Captain Wheeler said. He pointed downstairs to the dance floor where a short man with a polished mechanical arm danced a little too frenzied for most people to feel safe near him. He did look a bit like a rodent. It was hard to miss.

Ayan smiled and nodded. "I have my bad days, too."

"That's as good as I've ever seen him. I might just do him a favour and take him home tonight," the first mate said. "But I'd need a few more pitchers first."

"In that case, you're buying," Captain Wheeler chuckled, clinking his pint to hers.

"I don't think so," Minh interjected as he stood, took her glass from her and put it on the table. She looked up at him, mildly surprised, more intrigued. He took her hand and they started making their way to the dance floor downstairs.

Captain Wheeler, Ayan, and I all had a good laugh. "Your

Commander is in for one hell of a night. She really likes short men."

"Well, at least our crews are getting to know each other." I looked at the crew members I could see from where I sat and realized how completely different the Triton's compliment was from our own people. They were ragtag. There was no uniformity, which didn't bother me as much as the fact that many of them bore scars of varying severity. These were problems our medical staff could handle quite easily. They were getting along well enough with the First Light crew, but in many corners of the room I could see that they were being tolerated, not so much welcomed. This was a party for the majority, and they were the few. I took a sip of my pint and tried not to pucker. I enjoyed a good ale — generally the darker the better — and where I came from that was the expensive stuff. The lager Wheeler had poured me was anything but, and I put it down on the table after taking a large gulp, just to be courteous.

Ayan leaned against my side and I put my arm around her. She was calling my attention back to the others seated around the table in her own subtle way. Her arm was warm under my bare hand and I gently traced my fingertips up and down. "You two look like you've been together for a while," Captain Wheeler said, pouring himself another.

"Not so long. We've known each other pretty well for about sixteen months, as friends mostly," Ayan answered.

"So you served together before getting involved in the shady side of Freeground's ops?"

"We met on the avatar nets, through a few simulations Jonas and our friends ran. I used to stay up until the wee hours of the morning talking to him, getting a few winks then reporting for duty." She kissed me lightly on the cheek before looking back to Wheeler.

I ran my hand over her bare back soothingly. Her skin was soft.

Wheeler went on with a crooked smile, like we were the entertainment for the evening. "Serving on a Freeground ship can be hard with the military limitations on fraternization. I see you tossed that a while ago."

"We're discreet. Most of us are," I explained as I turned to see Jason chasing Laura up the stairs leading to our table, laughing all the way.

They sat down on the small sofa beside Wheeler, all out of breath as Laura punched beverage requests into the table surface. "I haven't had this much fun in forever," she said as Jason pulled her into his lap.

"Having fun, Captain?"

"Not as much as you are," both Captain Wheeler and myself said at the same time. He knocked on the table and pointed at me so fast I thought he was going for his sidearm. "Your round!" he shouted.

I laughed nervously and thanked at least three deities as Oz came over with a drink in his hand that I couldn't quite make out. It looked like an ale, but there were bubbles that moved like small egg yolks drifting within. "He's got you there Jonas. Old boarding crew tradition. You serve on one before leaving Free-ground?" Oz asked Captain Wheeler.

"Three years, then an All-Con turret blew my leg apart at the knee. I still have the graft scar from where they attached the new one," he said as he started pulling up his pant leg. Both the women at the table put up their hands to ward off the sight, yelling, "Whoa, that's okay!"

"I believe you!"

The band finished their set and the lead singer's voice boomed. "Just taking a break folks, be back in fifteen." The house music came on and the crowd migrated towards the bar.

The waiter came over to deliver Laura and Jason's drinks, a long tray of shots. There had to be twenty, in every colour of the rainbow. Minh and the first mate weren't far behind. "Drink up, everyone! Bartender's choice shots!" Jason shouted, picking up one himself and gesturing to everyone near.

Ayan and I tried to turn ours down. "Saving my energy for this one," she tried with a wink in my direction.

I said, "I'd like to remember tonight," but neither of our refusals were very effective. They only drew playful jeers and goads.

I got a smouldering blue shot, while Ayan's was perfectly clear. She eyed it warily.

"I'm not going to like this, am I?" Minh said, watching as the first mate set his on fire then did the same to her own.

"To the galaxy's shadows," toasted Captain Wheeler and everyone around the table, including a few late joiners from both crews, took their shots.

Mine was like drinking freezing, bitter liquorice. Ayan's eyes were squeezed shut before she drank the shot, but relaxed as she finished and turned to me, blowing the smell of her breath in my face gently. The mint fragrance was so strong I could taste it, but it came with a pleasant sweetness. I couldn't resist kissing her.

"I think someone got lucky," Minh said, gesturing in our direction.

"Or is about to," Wheeler's first mate added.

We laughed an end to our kiss. "I've got to get the name of that liquor," I whispered.

"It's good but I don't think I'll be able to taste anything else for a month," Ayan commented as she put her shot glass back on the tray.

Captain Wheeler's eye was drawn to someone coming from behind us and I followed his line of sight. It was the lead singer, who shook hands with him. "I didn't know you'd be around this way. Good to see you," said the voice I had heard from the stage just minutes ago. I couldn't help but notice that it was exactly the same. He was one of the few performers that didn't digitally enhance or alter his sound. He was tall, wore a long chain around his neck with tiny silver and platinum medals hanging all across it that jingled softly as he moved. The rings on his fingers were jewel-less but bore symbols from different worlds: the astrological sign of Gemini, and one that actually had a silver eye that seemed to choose features in the room and track them. It was focused on the table first, then turned to gaze at Ayan, blinking serenely.

"You know me, can't stay away from a good time. How's the tour been treating you?"

"No breakdowns this time, getting paid everywhere we go, eating a bit too much - you know, the burdens of success," said the minstrel, looking across the faces at the table. His gaze came to rest on Ayan and me. "Making new friends?"

Captain Wheeler gestured towards us. "This is Captain Jonas Valent and Commander Ayan Rice, of the First Light."

The smiling, pleasant expression on the lead singer's face dropped, and for a moment I had no idea what to think. "I can't believe it. You're still in the sector, and in public!" He offered his hand and I shook it warily. "We just watched a hologram of your ship taking on a corporate carrier and two destroyers. You're famous, man." His smile was resurfacing with a vengeance, he looked almost starstruck.

"What do you mean, famous?" Oz asked.

"Someone in corporate security leaked that holovid. Now it's viral across the Stellarnet. Ships like yours don't exist, man. This is like meeting Robin Hood in person," he said before turning to Ayan. "Not to mention Maid Marion."

"I wouldn't go that far. I'm just glad I'm meeting one of the members of the band. I've never heard anything like you," I replied, trying to turn the focus away. If that's how the public were seeing us off the beaten path, then we could do worse.

"Ah, it's like anything you'd hear from a dozen backworld colonies. We put our own spin on songs about short-lived people in bad places, or short-lived places on account of bad people. I should write something about you guys. The notes attached to the holovid going around said you had something to do with the Vindyne jailbreak. Any truth there?"

I hesitated for a moment. Jason fixed me with a look like we had gotten caught with our hand in the cookie jar. He looked more worried than I felt.

Captain Wheeler interjected. "Let's just say Jonas and his crew tend to make an impression as they make their way." He raised his glass in salute and took a drink.

"I didn't catch the name of the band," I said, trying to change the topic again.

"Are you kidding?" Captain Wheeler said in exaggerated exasperation. "This is Stonemark, the edgiest band the edge of space ever did see."

The lead singer ignored him and nodded at me. "Glad to hear you like the sound. I've got to get back to the stage for the next set. Keep tearing it up out there. We need more real rebels around."

We watched him leave. The man had presence; he was almost as tall as Oz and possessed an unconscious charisma. "How do you know him?" Laura asked Wheeler.

"They were stranded on a backwater station when their faster than light systems died, and they signed on for a few months," Captain Wheeler said dismissively. "I'm glad they're better musicians than crew. We didn't even know what to do with them at first. They jumped ship as soon as they had enough credits to buy an old beat up wreck that would hold together long enough to get them to a few gigs along the tradeway. Looks like you're getting a few fans of your own, though."

"I had no idea holographic combat recordings could leak so easily."

"Well, the Stellarnet thrives on anything anti-corporate or anti-establishment. Biggest unregulated network in the universe. Dangerous to be that well known for a crew like yours. After this mission you should move on. Find another end of the galaxy to work out of. Maybe even do some honest work with a government outfit out there for a while. There's real cash in privateering these days. Millions a month with the right ship and crew," Captain Wheeler said. He was already making the assumption that we'd never return to Freeground.

The band started playing again and Laura hopped to her

feet with Jason's hand in both of hers. She tugged on him until he stood. He shrugged at us as he was dragged down the stairs back onto the dance floor.

"I'm gonna go. Follow me!" the first mate said to Minh, only just loud enough so everyone could overhear. He was caught by surprise and his look of confusion cleared to reveal a smile. "Good night, everyone," she said over her shoulder as she walked down the stairs with Minh not far behind.

"Oh, I think you'll have to go find him later, Oz. I wouldn't turn your comm off," Ayan chuckled.

"I just hope it's sometime tomorrow morning. Where does she usually leave her victims?" he asked Captain Wheeler.

He shook his head. "She'll make sure he knows where the door is, don't worry."

"So how long have you been out here, Captain?" Ayan asked.

"It's been about thirty years. Time just happens by while things go on, I don't pay much attention."

"Do you still do much work for Freeground?"

"Only when they come calling, which isn't often these days. They don't want anyone knowing where I come from." He drained the remnants of his pint, then put it down on the table with an audible clunk. "There's a lot of Brit in you. Do you come from one of the coreward colonies?"

His question caught us all by surprise. "My mother's from a British colony, if that's what you mean, but I grew up on Freeground."

"So you're from that Rice family. I knew your mother. Met her when the Brits arrived on Freeground and started pissing in the gene pool."

Ayan was just about to snap. What would actually happen afterwards I didn't know, but I couldn't let whatever was going on continue. "The founders would call that diversity," I said flatly. "Looking at your crew, I see a lot of it."

"But I hire scraps and rejects on purpose," he said as he poured himself more lager. "I don't let them think they're in charge then dress them up for show."

Ayan gave me an enraged, hurt look and in one smooth motion stood and started walking down the stairs. I followed.

Oz wasn't far behind. "Are you sure you should just leave it like that?" he asked, yelling over the din of music and people.

Ayan stopped and turned around, she was furious. "Now I know why Intelligence kicked him out."

"Doc warned us about him. We only have to put up with it until the mission's done."

"I shouldn't be so angry. If he didn't look so young I would have seen it coming," she said.

"You're right, he's got to be at least fifty or sixty, but he doesn't look a day over twenty five," Oz commented.

"So surrounded by the walking wounded, he's had anti-ageing treatments?" I asked no one in particular; it was more of a statement. "Classy. Let's just leave. We'll let Jason and Laura know after we're in the hall."

Ayan stopped at the bottom of the stairs and turned to me. "No. He's just one prejudiced little bastard among millions. I'm not going to let him spoil tonight." She took a deep breath and let it out slowly. "Go have a drink with Oz. I'll meet you in your quarters."

She strode off to the door before I could say anything. Oz made a hand signal towards the entrance where a few of his security personnel were on watch, and a female officer nodded before following Ayan outside.

"Come on, let's hit the bar. Ensign Flores will make sure she makes it back to the ship okay," Oz said, putting his big hand on my shoulder. "Not that Ayan needs help. Her infantry training and experience stacks up pretty high compared to most of my security people. It'd make more sense if she was escorting Flores."

"Some night, huh?" I said after watching Ayan leave.

"Yup. Ayan looks amazing."

"She really does, I'm a lucky man."

"Sure you are, but so are a few other million," I heard Captain Wheeler say from behind. "You should head to Britannia. There are a few hundred thousand women who look almost exactly the same: curvy with blue green eyes and curly red hair. Your girl's just another manufactured piece out of a punch and cut mould. Most of them think they're better than everyone else, too. Even the ones in brothels. I've had a few myself."

I've thought about what happened next over and over, but no matter how it plays out, what followed could have been avoided. I spun on my heel, swinging for his head and just as I was about to connect palm first with his temple he ducked out of the way and planted a fist in my stomach. His blow didn't do a thing — my vacsuit hardened before it even landed — and he probably did more damage to his hand than he did to me. I headbutted him with the force of my legs and shoulders behind it and felt his nose squelch against my forehead.

Stupid. Every instant in that petty fight was stupid. My forehead had crushed his nose, blood flowed freely, and he squinted for a moment to clear his vision.

I grabbed him by the collar of his jacket and Oz followed my lead, grabbing Wheeler's belt and hauling him off his feet.

We half carried, half dragged him to the door and literally tossed him into the hallway. He rolled onto his back, laughing uproariously. "You take yourself way too seriously. And worse, you take her seriously. Her kind are nothing but genetically engineered breeders who think they're holier than the almighty himself. They were smart enough to quiet things down before you were born, but it doesn't change what they are."

"She saved the lives of the entire crew, and broke us free when no one else would have been brave or intelligent enough to get us out. You have a lot to learn."

The music behind us had died and some of the crew from both ships were starting to come out of the club. "I read the report, Captain. It doesn't change what she is. Go find the real history of Freeground. The British forced the real Free-grounders out of command a long time ago. I was glad when they offered me a ship. Freeground lives under my command, brother. The real Freeground. Anyone's welcome on Triton."

"As cannon fodder. I've heard about your command style."

He stood up slowly and straightened his clothing out, ignoring his nose, which had already stopped bleeding. "When this mission is over, we're done. You'd best make sure our shadows don't cross." He tapped the back of his hand a few times and his crew started emptying from the club.

Captain Wheeler led his ragtag pack down the hall. "Let's move on! There are other clubs. First round's on me!" he called out.

"Well, that could have gone better," Oz said. I turned

towards him, still furious and he smirked back at me. "What? I haven't had that much fun since academy graduation night."

There were a couple dozen First Light crew watching us from the broad doorway. I hate to admit it, but Captain Wheeler had the only good idea for that situation. "Back inside, everyone. The band's waiting for an audience, the bar is waiting for drinkers, and the floor's waiting for dancers!" I shouted, faking the revelry so well I almost fooled myself.

"Damn, I didn't know you were a poet." Oz laughed. The crew were following my directions and I could see the collective sigh of relief move through them like a wave.

"I just hope Minh is all right."

"That little guy? You forget, he and I grew up with three sisters. If that's not survival training, I don't know what is. He'll be fine, and if not, I'll go get him. Now you'd better go meet Ayan before she falls asleep on you."

The way back to the ship seemed long, and I couldn't get to my quarters fast enough. I knew what Ayan had in mind before the night had begun, before events had turned south. Even if those plans were cancelled, I just wanted time alone with her. Having two days and three nights to ourselves sounded so good; it was like an oasis of paradise suspended between strife and jeopardy. I forced myself to calm down a little as the doorway to my quarters came into view.

I passed through the paired doors and into the dimly lit main room.

"I'm in here," she called out quietly.

I took off my coat and flopped it onto the back of a chair as I made my way into the bedroom. She was standing in front of the transparent wall, looking out on the gas giant's sun-kissed horizon. A rich blue and purple light filled the room. I moved to stand behind her. She knit her fingers with mine and drew my arms around her, leaning back against me with a sigh.

"You know there are guards watching every hallway leading to your quarters?" she asked quietly. "Oz is getting paranoid."

"I didn't even notice." I kissed the top of her head and held her close.

"I'd still feel safe without them."

"There's nowhere else I'd rather be. I'm sorry about Wheeler," I whispered.

"I don't want anything to spoil tonight for us. Wheeler and the prejudiced idiots like him are all outside where they belong, and I'm here with you."

"I couldn't wait to get back," I whispered. "You're all I could think about."

She let my hands go and turned around. "I don't want to wake up from this dream."

I ran my hand down the length of her bare back, just a feather touch across her skin. She shivered as we looked into each other's eyes. Her deep blues stared into mine and I ran my hand up and down, caressing, gently touching at first, then rubbing the ticklish traces away. "We have all night," I whispered against her lips.

"Then all day," she whispered back.

Our gently parted lips touched. Pressed together, all I could hear was the sounds of our rushing breath. She held to me so tightly, as though I could just disappear at any moment.

She caught me toying with the knot behind her neck and chuckled. "Have you been good?" she teased.

I shook my head. "No," I said and resumed kissing her. I didn't wait for permission, I just tugged the silk tie loose.

She stepped back for just a moment so I could watch her dress fall to the floor.

SIXTEEN

HOLIDAY

Our vacation was well spent. We didn't shut ourselves in my quarters for the entire time, either. In fact, we ended up visiting the theatre for a production of Being Left, which was really a story about a man in love with two women at the same time. By the end, Jason and I came to the conclusion that it was a bad idea to see that particular play on a date, especially since the main character was killed in the end during a battle for the two ladies' honour.

The shopping in Starfree Port was an experience to remember. The promenade was filled with franchise shops in the more permanent sections, while temporary kiosks featured the most random wares any of us could have imagined. Everything from food, to pets of all sizes, and even clothing made of living plant matter that changed colour and shape depending on your mood, was offered.

However, the times I remember best are the long hours Ayan and I spent alone together. We got to know each other better during those times than we had during any other point in our relationship.

There was something else going on though, and after the second morning it started to occur to me that her belongings were already starting to make their way to my quarters. Drawers I would probably never use started to play host to clothing she cleaned after wearing them for a morning, afternoon or evening. The small cupboard in my bathroom was suddenly equipped with little makeup applicators and grooming tools. And when we went out, she made sure that I wore the scarf she gave me with my black trench coat. I simply wasn't allowed to leave it behind. According to her, the trench coat and scarf went together, no exceptions.

In all honesty, the fact that she was quietly making herself at home in my quarters didn't make me at all uncomfortable. My lifestyle was spartan, so having things in drawers and around my quarters was unusual but somehow it felt more like home. That didn't stop me from bringing it up when we were having lunch with Jason and Laura in a restaurant overlooking the gas giant. Apparently Laura had already completed the process of moving into Jason's quarters. She had simply registered herself as a resident there seconds after his quarters were rebuilt.

Sadly, as with all vacations, it came to an end. We were people with responsibilities. What's more, we enjoyed those responsibilities. They were part of who we were.

I was just setting a very high security level for anything the surveillance equipment in my quarters may have picked up over the last few days — something I forgot to do earlier — when she came out of the bathroom. She was back in uniform and practically bouncing. We were both in a fantastic mood. I tried to finish up as fast as I could but I knew it was no use.

"Whatcha doin'?" she asked, looking at my arm unit. Her eyes widened and a hand went over her mouth. "You didn't turn any of the recorders off?"

"I completely forgot about them!" I explained with a defensive shrug. "Oz has everything aboard active by default."

She laughed and pointed at me. "No sharing! We'll look at it later."

Even after spending almost an entire two days with her, and arguing with her once during that time over something completely unimportant, she continued to surprise me. I thought forgetting to turn the recorders off would turn into a huge fight. I snapped to attention and saluted. "I'll keep it under the tightest security, Commander."

She laughed and walked right up to me, standing on her toes so she could look me in the eye. "You'd better, Captain, or I'll start revealing facts disclosed in confidence," she threatened.

"I'm so lucky you're not a spy," I replied.

"You sure are."

I grabbed her around the waist and kissed her. She melted a moment and then broke away. "I'm going to be late."

"By the Captain's orders," I said, fishing for another kiss.

"Hey! No pulling rank off duty!" she protested, laughing and turning her head so I couldn't meet her lips.

I found my mark and for a moment I think we both forgot that we were about to be very late. We stopped and smiled at each other. "I'll see you on duty, Commander."

"I'm at your disposal, Captain," she replied.

After she left, I checked the time and realized that we both had two minutes to get to our respective commands. I stepped out of my quarters and jogged to the lift, waited for the doors to open, and stepped inside. As soon as the doors opened again it became obvious that leave was over. The core of the ship was alive with crew members hurriedly moving down the halls, reporting for morning shift and getting the ship ready to get underway. I strode down the hall and entered the security airlock that lead to the bridge. The first heavy doors parted and seemed to take forever to close behind me. The inner doors opened and I was greeted with the sight of a busy bridge staff. There were over twenty of them now, manning navigation, tactical, field control, engineering, gunnery, repair, dedicated sciences, communication, security, helm, and life systems management stations.

"Captain on the bridge!" an ensign called out as I entered.

Everyone stood at attention. Oz and I smiled at each other. "Have a good leave, Sir?" he asked.

"As you were," I ordered the bridge crew as I made my way back to my seat. "Even better than expected," I replied.

"That good, huh?"

I nodded as I looked around at the faces manning the bridge. It wasn't the regular day bridge crew. "How was yours?"

"Fantastic. I hit it off with someone after rescuing Minh from that first mate."

"How was that?"

"No big deal. He just woke up in a public garden as nude as the flora."

"The person you hit it off with, or Minh?" I teased.

"Minh. My date's clothes stayed on until last night."

"So he's all right?"

"Oh, he'll be fine, it was just a port fling. He's leaving on the Kensington tomorrow."

"I meant Minh."

"Oh, sure. He's a little pissed that we let him go home with her, but he'll be fine."

"Glad to hear you had some fun, though."

"A night to remember," Oz said, looking through navigation charts on his arm console.

"I think almost everyone had an interesting time this leave."

"It was a good first. Everyone's back on board, a few were late, but they're here without serious injuries and no one was tossed in the station's brig."

"Sir, Captain Wheeler's on the comm," said a young woman at the communications terminal.

"Put it up."

Captain Wheeler appeared on the main holographic display. "We're just about to get underway," his manner didn't hint at a grudge.

"We're just about ready here."

"We'll start scanning from the south pole."

"Sounds good. First Light, out."

"Either he's got an amazing sense of professionalism, doesn't remember the other night, or he's just biding his time," Oz said quietly.

"Well, if his idea of revenge is sticking us with the tab for the club the other night, then we paid through the nose. Good thing our finances are in good shape," Jason commented from the central seat at the communications station.

"Here's hoping that's the end of it," Oz replied.

"Doesn't sound like you're convinced," I prodded as I checked the general status reports.

"I'm not."

"Me neither. We'll have to keep our eyes open." We were quiet for a few moments while we waited for departments to report ready. "Where's my bridge crew?" I asked in a whisper.

"I thought it would help if one of the mid-shift crews got to work with you for a while. Get a feel for your command style."

"Ah. How many bridge crews do we have now?"

"All together, including emergency staff, we have three."

"And acting captains?"

"Two, not including myself."

"How many of those are experienced?" I asked.

"Combat, watch, or simulation experience?"

I shrugged at the stipulation. "I hope they've all had a few watches."

"Yup, they've all had watches. Mostly in hyperspace," said Oz.

"How about manoeuvres or simulations?"

"A couple of the crews have been on during in-system manoeuvres. They all have training."

"Combat?"

"A few have combat experience."

"How many are a few?" I asked.

"Your bridge crew and a couple members of one other."

"How many of the acting captains have command experience?"

"Including you and the doctor?" asked Oz.

"Sure."

"Two."

"I'd better get ready to pull some long shifts if this mission takes a while," I whispered.

We didn't see a trace of the Triton on our way to the third moon of the second planet in the system. I didn't second guess it, but I did quietly command our tactical station to keep scanning for any strange readings or signs of them.

"Maybe she's just not there. It could be some kind of trap," Oz whispered.

"She's a Sol defence carrier. I'd be surprised if he didn't have some kind of cloaking device."

"Still, a cloaking device, that's about as advanced as you can get."

"Yes and no. We're close to making one, it's just not easy. We have the primary and secondary projectors for it. We can seal our ship up, we just don't have all the hard math or fine tuning done. We also can't counter our gravitational silhouette."

"Which normally takes decades for a single ship. I've never seen one."

"That's the point," I whispered with a smile. We were moving into orbit around Lauvin. Its surface was in phase three of the terraforming process, and it looked like it was going very slowly. The side we were on was a slightly varying shade of beige, with darker lines across indicating deep craters and chasms. "Have they managed to ignite anything in the core?" I asked.

"Nothing, Sir. There's very little heat in the centre of the moon. It's solid rock. No tectonic activity. Just sand, sand, and more sand with a few rocks and sandstorms."

"No water yet at all?"

"The beacon reports that they've just started liquefying

water underground. Temperature in the temperate zone reads minus twenty-one degrees, minus thirty-four with wind chill."

"Looks like a beach, but it's really a deep freeze," Oz commented quietly. "Glad we already took leave."

"Sir, there's an object headed towards the planet. Decelerating from near lightspeed."

"Time to impact?" I asked.

"Forty seconds. It's reducing speed at over nineteen thousand kilometres per second. At this rate it will just barely make entry."

"Incoming communication from the Triton," came the report from communications.

"Put it up."

Wheeler appeared on the holodisplay. The transmission was a little garbled. "Looks like we're right on time. I'll meet you at the landing site."

"See you down there," I replied, cutting the comm. The pod had decelerated and was entering the atmosphere at just under the safest maximum speed. "Oz, get a full security team together. We're going down heavy."

"Already done. Minh's waiting for us in a boarding shuttle and we'll have seven fighters as cover."

"That's why you're my first officer." I stood and looked to the tactical station before leaving the bridge. "Where is that pod going to hit?"

"Just at the northern point in what's marked as the future tropical zone. It should be clear of sandstorms for another hour and a half. About minus eighteen degrees."

"Oh good, the garden spot," Oz smirked as he followed me into the exit.

SEVENTEEN

THE GARDEN SPOT

We followed the smoke. The pod had left a trail in the sky as well as on the ground, and I watched from the rear of the shuttle cockpit as we headed towards its final resting place. I looked back into the main cabin to see every seat full. Every pair of hands held a rifle, save the two medics we had with us. It was a full security team of twenty, everyone sealed up in their vacsuits and dressed in their dark long coats. There were four members of the engineering team as well, just in case we ran into trouble with the pod. Looking out to my right I could see three of the fighters in our escort group, and I knew above and behind there were gunners manning the shuttle turrets.

We hadn't come light. In fact, we were so well armed you'd think we were on a combat drop. Looking over to where Minh piloted us over the endless dunes of fine sand, I felt as though I were back with the infantry team on All-Con Prime, where I had first met him. I was just a mechanic then. Part of the engineering team, sure, but we were really there to keep our transportation in the air, the comms online, and our weaponry working as we destroyed one factory after another. That was a long time ago, and a far less complicated mission. I found myself wondering what being on the engineering staff during this trip was like as Minh's copilot pointed out a crater of blackened sand and glass ahead. "There it is, Sir. It should be cool enough to set down in."

Somehow, there was already a rough, boxy shuttle on the ground with a small turret pointing out the back. Captain Wheeler had already arrived and his people were prying at the pod's hatch.

Minh put us down in haste as our fighter cover circled overhead. The landing gear groaned at the pressure of the quick landing.

"See you back here," he said to me. "Good luck."

I nodded, brought my vacsuit hood up, then activated the faceplate to form an airtight seal. "May your life be interesting," I told Minh through the proximity radio built into the suit.

We emerged from the shuttle and Oz ordered the engineering team to help open the pod. "Be careful. We don't want to break any bio-seals without knowing if whoever is inside is injured or not prepared for the environment," he added.

I strode towards Captain Wheeler and his four armed officers, then looked over to where his team was clumsily working at the seals of the pod with pry bars. One was starting a cutting tool. Everyone from his crew were in mismatched vacsuits. Some weren't even the right size, and slack had to be strapped up so the extra material wouldn't get in the way. Wheeler himself was wearing a much older Freeground vacsuit. "My team can finish opening this. They're trained for rescue and retrieval," I said.

"We're in a hurry here. There's no time to get this open layer by layer."

I looked at his team again, standing right in the way of my own, who were prepared with sensors and tools made specifically to handle tasks like the one his crew was bumbling through. "You're kidding."

"My boys'll get it open," Captain Wheeler said, nodding.

I looked back at him. "Tell your men to step away from the pod."

Captain Wheeler looked directly at me but didn't say anything.

"You can't tell me you've been this successful out here with this kind of recklessness or stupidity. Either use the right tools or step aside," I told him flatly. My patience was just about gone where he was concerned.

He shrugged and ordered his team to step away from the pod.

The First Light engineering and medical personnel stepped in but didn't actually touch anything. They started by scanning, then tried opening a communications channel to whoever waited inside. "Sir, the occupant confirms that he will be ready to exit the pod in another minute or two. He just finished emerging from deep stasis," came a crewman's report in my earpiece.

"Acknowledged. Find out if he requires medical assistance."

After a moment the engineering specialist nodded. "He says he made it fine. He's in good shape."

Looking at the pod, it was eight meters long and four across.

I couldn't believe that it could survive such an impact and then be functional enough for hatches to open properly. I had seen drop pods before, but none that were made to travel long distances using hyperspace systems, then decelerate for hours before smashing into a planet surface at such high speeds.

A few moments later, breaks appeared in the hull of the pod in the shape of a perfect circle. Despite the dented and fused metal, it pushed outward and moved to the side to reveal a well made interior that, from what I could see, contained the equipment required for long term stasis. A dark haired man who looked much older than I expected — deep wrinkles and receding hair included — emerged in a vacsuit that featured a thin, flexible transparent material for the head piece. He smiled uneasily and looked around as he climbed out.

I knew it would be cold, and the wind was lazily moving the sand around at chest level, but I retracted my headpiece and stepped forward, hand extended. "I'm Captain Jonas Valent, of the First Light."

He smiled at me and shook my hand. "Doctor William Marcelles."

"Nice to see you made it in one piece."

His smile grew a little broader, and his gravelly voice spoke in a very friendly, personable tone. "Prototype faster than light hyperspace escape shuttle. If there were more time I'd say you should take it up to your ship, but we're on the clock, I'm afraid."

I looked over my shoulder and regarded Captain Wheeler, who was standing by, observing. "This is Captain Wheeler and his crew." Lucius approached at hearing his introduction.

The doctor looked at him for a moment and then simply

said "Ah," before going on. "This strike was arranged by some of the researchers, most of whom have already made attempts at escape or have been killed. Triad probably noticed I was missing not long after I left. If we want to avoid them, we should be going. Here is a copy of the coordinates and tactical information we could gather."

I took the tiny data cylinder from him, loaded the information onto my arm command unit, and handed it off to Captain Wheeler. "Is there anything that isn't in this report that you can tell us?"

"Triad has not allowed the separate components of the Framework project to come together anywhere else in the galaxy. I made sure of that before leaving. Your mission should still be achievable."

"Come with me. I have orders to keep you hidden," Captain Wheeler said as he started back to his shuttle.

Doctor Marcelles started walking behind him, but turned his head towards me momentarily. I could hear him in my communications implant. His mouth wasn't moving but his eyes punctuated his message, they were cold and piercing. "Every few generations there is a leap in technology so drastic the conditions of living change. This is a such a time. Make sure this information lands in the right hands so it is a cure before it becomes a weapon. All your fears are justified."

I nodded at him and brought my headpiece back up. The cold was turning my ears and nose numb. Just then my communicator buzzed and Jason came on. "Sir, a battleship has emerged from hyperspace dangerously close to the planet, and another has passed through the atmosphere."

"Acknowledged. Minh, you hear that?"

"Already warming it up, Sir. Fighters are moving to intercept the vessel going atmospheric."

"Don't bother, Commander, it's the Triton. She's coming to pick me up," interjected Captain Wheeler. "I suspected there would be something right behind the pod."

We closed the distance between the pod and the shuttle double quick, and the ramp was closing as the last of us set foot on it. "Get us out of here, Minh. Don't spare the throttle," I ordered as the inner hatch came down and sealed.

"When have you known me to spare the throttle?"

"Just an expression."

Sergeant Everin came on the communicator again. "That battleship is right on our heels, Captain. We're sending the interception trajectory now."

"Condition?" I asked, making my way through the shuttle to the cockpit as the inertial dampening systems whined, trying to keep up as the shuttle made its climb towards space. "How's the ship and crew?"

"All guns blazing, Captain. We're taking hits but so far we're okay," I heard Ayan's voice reply. "They sent a twin hulled battleship after the pod. She's called the Vindicator, she's Triad."

I got to the cockpit and saw that we were flying under partial cover provided by the Triton. She wasn't nearly as long as the First Light, but she was wide. It was like looking at a silvered stingray with three launch bays along the bottom and several turret emplacements firing at the intercept fighters that had been launched by the Vindicator. Our own turrets blazed as we followed the Triton up through the atmosphere and out into space.

I managed to drop myself into a rear cockpit seat and started checking the tactical station. "See you at the waypoint, Captain Valent. Good luck getting clear," I heard Wheeler say over the communicator.

"See you there," I replied as I did a double take on the tactical screen. There were at least fifty small craft marked as fighters or small gunships with the Vindicator's battle group. The Vindicator itself came up, less than twenty kilometres behind the First Light. Everything was coming straight for us.

"You'd think he'd stick around for a minute and help with some of those fighters," Minh's copilot said offhandedly as he tried to balance the ship's shields. "Strap in back there! We're losing shields and about to start taking hard hits!" he shouted over his shoulder before shutting the cockpit door.

"Wheeler isn't known for being polite or for sticking around long," Minh said. "I got an earful about it from his first mate," he continued as he spun the shuttle eighty four degrees and hit the thrusters, taking us straight towards the First Light. It started as a glimmer in the distance, a point of reflected light, but it was quickly growing.

I checked the landing path and I could swear I started sweating. "Laura's really not opening a big hole in the shields for us."

"She knows I don't need much room," Minh commented as he worked the controls. The shuttle was starting to take small impacts on the hull from whatever weapons the fighters were using. They looked like energy based guns, but the way the shuttle rattled I couldn't be sure.

"Might want to slow down a little?" I asked, cringing as the

First Light got closer, dwarfed by the twin hulled monstrosity of a battleship behind it.

"Ye of little faith," Minh grunted through clenched teeth. "No one likes a back seat driver."

He spun the shuttle one hundred eighty degrees and fired the engines at full thrust. I watched the cockpit overlay that came up, showing him his ideal path for entry and speed of approach. We were slowing down fast, right on target.

We took a heavy hit and a seal broke in the cabin behind. I checked our integrity and saw that it wasn't a large breach, but I was thankful everyone was wearing vacsuits as the atmosphere in the main cabin started bleeding off into space.

The shuttle jostled as we came within a few hundred meters of the hole in the shields. I glanced up and saw that we had been knocked off our approach vector and were about to impact directly onto the shields of the First Light.

"Hang on!" Minh yelled.

He made several last second adjustments and struggled with the controls. He managed to guide us almost directly back on course. For just a moment it seemed that we had made it through unscathed, then my teeth clamped shut so hard I nearly bit the tip of my tongue off at the shock of our impact. We were sent spinning, rolling across the deck of the landing bay, and I could hear the scraping and colliding of our hull against the launch bay floor.

The inertial dampeners compensated for most of the collision, that is until the last few rolls, when they went offline. Everyone in the cockpit was hanging upside down when we came to a stop. I checked myself for injuries then looked around the cockpit. "Everyone okay?"

Minh, his copilot, and the communications officer — a young woman whose eyes were wide with shock — checked in fine. I grabbed the handle by the cockpit hatchway and undid my seat restraint. The gravity in the launch bay was always light during landing operations, and I could hear fighters landing outside, which made it plain to me that the cockpit was no longer atmospherically sealed.

I managed to find my feet without landing too awkwardly and braced myself as I opened the cockpit hatch. The medical personnel were already assessing the injured, but from what I could see the main hold had kept together very well. "How does it look?" I asked Oz.

"We have one trapped in the port side rear turret, but his suit has a good seal and it sounds like he only broke his leg. We got out lucky."

Minh was checking in with his deck chief over his personal command unit while his copilot ensured that the shuttle's systems were all shut down. "We lost five fighters. The remaining two have landed."

The deck under my feet shuddered. Whatever was hitting us was doing so hard enough to overcome what the inertial dampeners could compensate for. "Are we on our way out of the moon's magnetic field?" I asked the bridge through my communicator.

"On our way out now. They're swarming us with everything they have now that the Triton's gone," Ayan replied. "Get up here, Jonas."

"You heard her. We've got this," Minh said, gesturing to the shuttle.

"Aren't you going to stand by your divot so the Captain can inspect it?" teased his copilot.

"I think he's already had an eyeful, thanks," Minh shot back wryly.

Oz and I walked right through a rip in the dorsal section of the shuttle onto the main deck. One of the fighters had entered the landing bay in a similar fashion to the shuttle, and the pilot was working to put out flames. "Put this out before we have an ammo explosion on our hands!" he yelled at the deck crew, who ran forward with fire suppression equipment.

My instinct was to help, but Oz and I had to run in the other direction, to the nearest corridor and lift leading up towards the bridge.

As soon as we were out of the hangar and in regular gravity, we made for the nearest lift at a full run. The ship shuddered several times and by the time I reached the bridge I had brought up my command unit's full status display and examined it.

The Vindicator's particle cannons were hitting us so hard and fast that our shields were draining within twenty percent of being gone completely after every salvo. The hull was vibrating with the shock of the impacts.

I walked onto the bridge and Ayan looked up from the command display. "Up to speed, Captain?"

"Oz and I were watching the ship status on the way up," I replied.

She was out of the chair and halfway to the lift by the time I was about to sit down. "Good, I have to get to engineering. We won't be out of this for another two minutes."

I could see that all of our reserve power was already gone, and we were generating at maximum capacity to maintain our shields; keeping our weaponry running was the least of our worries. "What are our gunners using?" I asked.

"Explosive or electromagnetic rounds to disrupt their shields," reported tactical.

The main holographic display told the whole story. Our gunners weren't getting a chance to breathe. There were hundreds of attack drones no longer than two meters long, at least sixty fighters, and the twin hulled four kilometre long battleship itself to take care of. The battleship's shields were completely whole, and we were well within weapons range.

Surges of white and blue erupted from the forward cannons on the enemy ship and I watched as they passed right between all the fighters and drones to hit us squarely on the aft quarter a dozen or more times, shaking the ship and dropping our shields from ninety percent to seven percent. Those systems were immediately flooded with energy, recharging the shields as fast as possible despite the focused fire of the drones and fighters. "How long until we can enter hyperspace?" I asked.

"About a minute and a half," navigation reported.

"Have all the gunners switch to flak rounds, I don't care about that battleship's shields, we need breathing room. Target the drones and the fighters. Hopefully we can shred some of them up, relieve some of the pressure on our shields."

"You're not going to like this, but there's a cavity running between the hulls of that ship. It looks like a rail cannon," Oz reported.

I looked at the tactical display and the shape of the enemy battleship. "No way, you'd need small asteroids to load a cannon that size. No one uses that kind of weapon anymore, it's too demanding."

"I bet no one expected us to use refractive or plasma shielding either," Oz countered.

I took a closer look and saw he was right; there was a space between the two hulls that formed a perfect barrel, and there was a slow build up of energy. "Scan that area," I said, highlighting the centre of the ship.

"It's a magnetic field, Sir, surrounding an object spinning at ninety six thousand revolutions per minute," reported the sciences station. "It's increasing in temperature and if they fire that thing it'll go right through us like a drill bit - if it doesn't fragment against the hull, in which case the damage would be even worse."

"Now I know why Wheeler and Fleet Intelligence wanted us along for this trip. He cloaks and leaves with the researcher without a scratch while we lag behind as one great big distraction. Any suggestions?"

We took another salvo from the ship's particle cannons. I was nearly shaken right out of my chair. Our shields were down to eleven percent when that salvo ended.

I could see Oz working through different projections and collecting information on his command console. Then he stopped and looked to the main tactical display in the middle of the bridge. "I got nothin'."

"I was afraid you'd say that," I said before looking towards the helm. "Faster, we have to move faster."

"Short of getting out and pushing, we can't go any faster," came the response.

I looked at the tactical display, thinking as the energy readings from the Vindicator kept building up. The flak rounds were doing their job; the gunners were killing dozens of drones and blocking most of the fighters, but that didn't solve our main problem. A white hot meteorite was about to be sent in our direction at such a great speed that there was no way we could move out of the way. Then a thought occurred to me. "A push!" I shouted.

"What?" Oz asked, startled.

"We need a good push. Our hull can withstand a direct focused nuclear explosion, right?" I asked him.

"Yes, but why would we want to?"

"Because we'll accelerate faster than our engines can move us if it's close enough, and it'll cause a thermal wave large enough to obscure whatever sensors they have on that thing."

"You're insane."

"Tactical, load a nuclear torpedo in our aft launcher and set it to detonate at five hundred meters. Coordinate it with our sensors so they're shut down at the moment of detonation. We don't want to blind ourselves in the process." I looked to the holographic representation of Ayan. She was directing repairs and manipulating systems from the command ring in engineering. "We're going to be taking a nuclear hit at near point blank range in about thirty seconds. Keep us in one piece."

"You mean counter a self-inflicted worst case scenario weapon strike? Yes, Sir, whatever you say, Sir," Ayan replied before I was finished speaking. "Already working on it."

"Navigation, will this get us clear?"

I could see the projection was still finishing up. She was running the simulation at eight times the normal speed. "Yes, it will, as soon as the initial blast dissipates we'll be far enough away from any large gravitational force to enter hyperspace."

I took my seat and gripped the armrests. "All hands brace for—" I thought for a second.

"A self-inflicted attack!" Oz whispered.

"Impact," I finished. "Fire torpedo."

I saw the pilot make the sign of the cross before he gripped the console.

The explosion hit and everything shook. It felt like the deck and bulkheads would burst into a million pieces under the shock. Our displays blackened and for a few seconds we were in complete darkness. Once the shaking had stopped everything started to come on.

"Sensors are dark, Sir, still resetting. We didn't sync it quite right," came the report from tactical.

"We have shields. They're at one point three percent and charging. Our hull took half of that, no significant structural damage," Laura reported.

"External communications are a mess, Sir. Internals are fine," Jason reported.

"Our ion engines took a blast. Engines one and two are operational but I'm deactivating half the thrust nozzles on engine three. They might need to be rebuilt. As far as the rest of the ship is concerned, we're structurally fine but some of our power distribution network is fried, especially anything connected to Vindyne systems," Ayan reported. "If we ever tangle with them again, looks like close range nuclear blasts are their Achilles heel. Then again, that's a pretty general rule."

"We'll be able to enter hyperspace in less than ten seconds if enough emitters will fire up," reported navigation.

"Tactical," I addressed. "Load antimatter torpedoes in the

turret launchers. Just in case something comes through the thermal wave behind us."

Ayan came crackling through the communicator. "Hyperspace systems are online and ready."

"Time to go," I concluded.

"We're clear of significant energy and gravity fields. Activating emitters," the navigation officer announced with great relief.

Within just three seconds the Vindicator was well behind us.

Following someone in hyperspace when they had the technology to contain all their emissions was like trying to fire a bullet through a bullet hole ten kilometres away while someone was jumping up and down on your back. There was little or no chance the Vindicator was on our trail. As we ran through damage reports and our post-hyperspace entry checklists, everyone was busy catching their breath. Two of our turrets needed repair, but as far as we could tell our rear engines had only sustained minor damage. Ayan's suggestion to take a look at the damage from the outside of the ship before making a final assessment made perfect sense, since most of the propulsion systems were still exposed while we detonated the nuclear torpedo.

We hadn't lost anyone on board, but three fighters were gone or captured while two managed to land. The other pair had faster than light systems and would meet us at our destination, near Starfree Port. Before I knew it, all the reports had been reviewed, the shift change to hyperspace skeleton crew was under way, and it was time to meet in Observation Two with the senior staff.

Oz and I made our way off the bridge and started down the hallway towards the staff meeting. "That was close. It seems that no matter what we do there's always something bigger, more dangerous around the corner," I said quietly.

"As long as we're slipperier, smarter than whoever has got it in for us, I'm happy. You're right though, without that nuke manoeuvre that ship would be running a salvage op on our hull right now."

"If those people, whoever they were, run salvage operations at all. That's part of what keeps me on edge out here. We don't know anything until it's almost too late."

"Well, as long as we're one step ahead of the 'too late' mark, I'm happy," Minh commented as he joined us from an intersecting corridor.

"I hear four of your pilots made it out," Oz said.

"Five, actually. Garret was able to pick up Caruso after he ejected, then he made for hyperspace. We still lost two."

"We got out of that light on losses," Doctor Anderson added as he met us at the doorway into Observation Two. "Still, Lieutenant Caruso's going to have some stories. Hyperspace in nothing but an ejection seat for eight hours or so. That's got to be something."

Minh couldn't help but chuckle. "We'll be hearing about it for months."

Ayan was already sitting at the table in the dimly lit observation room. Anyone who wasn't supposed to be present for this meeting had already cleared out. Through the transparent wall we could see the hazy light of stars and interstellar phenomena through the lens of hyperspace distortion. I took my seat at the head of the table, Oz took his to my right, and

Ayan was already sitting to my left. By the time Jason came rushing into the room with Laura everyone was ready to get started.

"Sorry. Night communications crew needed a briefing on a new listening system I installed," Jason said as he sat down.

"I was just finishing my diagnostic on the shield emitters," Laura added.

"How are they?" Ayan asked.

"Oh, the new comm crew are doing well. Just catching up on a few things I'm still working on. What will really rattle them is when I bring the new AI online—" He stopped as Ayan looked at him. I couldn't see the expression on her face, but I wish I could have. "But you meant the shield emitters, sorry," he finished sheepishly.

Laura suppressed a grin as she patted Jason's hand and answered. "We burned out five emitters completely and one doesn't even look wired anymore. I'm pretty sure we'll see that it's completely slagged once we get a crew outside."

"Do we have replacements?"

"We do, but considering how badly the Vindyne technology is holding up compared to what we build, I think we'll be going through them a lot faster than anyone expected. Two of the emitters weren't even hit, they just burned out on their own. It's how they build their gear. They use mass materializers. They're great for building components quickly, but unless you add high density materials to the mix while you're manufacturing, any metal parts won't be anywhere near as durable as we're used to. Burnouts are going to happen until we can replace what we've built using their parts."

"One of our beam emitters burned out too. It blew the

second time it was fired," Ayan added. "We should start machining our own parts."

"Well, we'll have to make it a priority after we've finished this assignment. I didn't exactly have a chance to look at the data I was given planet-side, so I thought we could sift through it together."

I put the data chip on the table and activated it. A holographic representation of Doctor Marcelles appeared. His aged face looked around and smiled at us. He seemed a little startled when he saw Doctor Anderson. "Well, they really did send their best. I've read a few of your papers on clone preservation research, Doctor Anderson."

"It must be programmed with an AI meant to organize and present information in the database," Jason whispered.

"Very astute. That's exactly what I am, only more. I am the intellectual representation of our work. Vindyne and Triad have combined their imprint and biological programming interface technologies to form an operating AI that can manage an advanced database and maintain a basic consciousness. I am a product of that technology, only in a purely digital form that is not compatible with the human brain," the hologram said to Jason. "It's important to note that I am a result of a cursory examination of the real Doctor Marcelles's experiences and personality."

"Interesting. Do you know if Framework software can be put to use on a normal clone as well as a Framework creation?" Doc asked.

"Yes. In fact, later versions of this program can be used on any biological form capable of higher brain functions. If a being has the capability to keep track of time, remember symbols in a sequence, and experience a human range of emotions, it can be programmed to a degree. Triad and Vindyne have both been working towards this goal and the final combination of their contributions are responsible for this quantum leap in wetware programming."

"But not entirely. Who else brought pieces to the table?" I asked.

"Jonas Valent, it is good to meet you. Almost no one knows anything about you, you realize. They even deleted your residence and service records on Freeground. You too, Terry McPatrick. It seems Freeground expects to use you in ways they will have to disavow. To answer your question, several experts in their fields have contributed critical knowledge and practices to the Framework software, some of whom came from Freeground, as you know. That is how Freeground was made aware of the project."

"Which researchers came from Freeground?"

"I don't have that information, Doctor Anderson, I'm sorry."

"Though your creator would know that it wouldn't be hard to guess, with a near certainty, if we could find out who in this field was still on Freeground."

"I'm not made to speculate, but if I were to do so anyway, I would say that the process of elimination that you're suggesting would be very effective," the hologram said with a nod. "Now, back to the point. The software portion of the Framework project is the summation of all the knowledge humanity possesses of the brain, nervous system, computer technology, and bioelectronics. There are other technologies involved, but for the purpose of my presentation I'll keep those non-critical technologies out of it. When a host is emptied of all but the most basic reflex functions, they are ready to have rudimentary developmental memories, thought patterns and a baseline personality imprinted. Thanks to Vindyne, more complex memories will be available. But, integration will still depend on compatibility with the subject since actual memory transfer is not yet possible unless a perfect millisecond snapshot scan of an active human brain is used as a source. And, the destination brain would have to be a perfect duplicate of the mind the snapshot was taken of in the instant it is programmed. That is one of the major problems in creating a perfect transfer of memories, personality, and thought patterns. The hardware portion of the Framework project is made to address this problem and eventually provide memory integration systems that can add memories and information to an operating human brain.

"That technology represents the future. The process of imprinting a personality takes less than two weeks at this time, though work to cut that time down and meet our previously mentioned goals is under way. Using the current procedure, the subject is allowed to gain consciousness after the long imprinting process, and in those first few minutes the baseline personality becomes a working consciousness including any tendencies and memories that were imprinted earlier. The subject is not aware that it is in a Framework host unless that information is included in the memory catalogue they were programmed with. Under ideal conditions, the host does not question who they are, what they are, but will follow the instincts put in place. The subject is normally unaware that there are voids in their memory, but in advanced testing on Frameworks with badly fragmented memories, subjects often create reasons why they cannot remember whole years, or even who they are, through basic rationalization.

"Normally the subject will begin performing basic tasks, such as stretching, walking, practising with the tools it has training for or with basic objects that may be close at hand. This is called the alignment phase and is normally completed in under six minutes.

The phase of research currently underway involves creating personalities that are made specifically for Framework products, based on detailed capture scans of a living subject's brain and physiology. This would allow whoever possessed the technology to create an exact copy of a person in under fifteen days, or create an entire personality from scratch and implant it into a Framework mind. The hardware behind Framework also makes it easier for alterations and corrections to be made."

"Amazing," Doctor Anderson said, shaking his head.

"Terrifying. A framework would be capable of doing anything, being anyone, if they manage to finish the imprinting technology," Ayan added.

"And there are no laws in place that forbid their use," the hologram responded. "Making this project even more appealing."

"What about the Eden Two law? Wouldn't artificial intelligence restrictions block any artificial intelligence that was created to do harm?" asked Laura.

"Not so. In fact, the Framework, its current software, and future developments take current galactic laws into account completely. On most core worlds, clones and biological beings with self awareness can attain and retain their freedom simply by buying it or having it given to them by their owner. Some of these worlds have even gone so far as to declare that owning a self aware clone is slavery and that any clone in those systems is a free being. These same laws pertain to Framework-made beings, especially since part of the technology is already in use as a treatment for patients with advanced blood diseases and organ failure. The Framework project stems from technology that has kept several million citizens alive. The fact that the software built into Framework makes the subject incapable of leaving or causing harm to their masters is beside the point."

"So in the view of the current law these creations would be serving their masters because they want to," Jason added.

"Yes, and even better. Eventually you will be capable of programming their personalities with certain tendencies, forcing the subjects to serve their masters as a part of their basic nature. They are not aware that they are serving in this scenario. Positive examples of this tendency-style programming include subjects who must aid people in need or danger, or drones that have a compulsion to clean. Negative examples include communicating observations with a neural transmitter, performing sabotage unconsciously, or even materializing an explosive compound in their own stomach using Framework and detonating themselves in a crowd. Where the law is concerned, there's nothing wrong with this technology, but there are a number of situations that the law hasn't addressed yet," said the hologram.

"Can you tell us where the majority of the funding for this project is coming from? What department would it fall under?" I asked.

"Framework is considered a military and medical research and development project. A recent shareholder report claimed that within the next ten months, the Triad Consortium would be able to cure any disease and equip their upper-tier citizens with devices that would repair any immediately non-fatal injury."

"So it's primarily medical?" Jason asked.

"Its secrecy and location in a military base counter that conclusion, but it is classified medical, yes."

"Well, now that we know everything we need to about the project and that it's something we don't want Triad to have, where do we find it and how heavily defended is it?" Oz asked.

"The research station is located at the centre of the Blue Belt. In the Krissis Cluster."

"The Krissis Cluster? That's not even possible," Oz whispered. "That section of the Blue Belt is so active we wouldn't last three seconds before we were crushed by any number of asteroids and meteors. A space station wouldn't do any better."

"It is there, I assure you. Triad Consortium ships created a stable gravitational barrier to redirect most of the mass, then moved a wormhole generator and receiving area into the region. After the space was ready, they brought the station in piece by piece and reconstructed it."

"Do you have the wormhole gate access codes?" Jason asked.

"The security codes are on the same data storage medium that is projecting me. It is the old Freeground gate that was originally built with the station."

"Well, if it weren't located in the middle of a dense asteroid field, I'd say that it's almost too easy," Oz said, shaking his head.

"The energy output required to create a gravitational field to protect an area that large has to be massive," Ayan added.

"It is. The power is provided by power plants built on aster-oids with abundant natural resources."

"What kind of defences does the station have?"

"The station is used as a prototype development facility for Triad, but considering its location it was lightly defended. More ships may have been brought in if the escape of Doctor Marcelles has been detected, however."

"Judging from what we've seen, they know he's out," Oz said. "It sounds like the sooner we get there the better the chances are that we can do the job."

I looked at him then to Ayan, who was watching me, waiting for my opinion. "We need to make sure we're as well prepared as possible. We don't go until every department reports ready."

"Makes sense to me. I'd hate to come out of a jump gate with shields that only work at one end," Oz agreed.

"I'll try to have the ship ready in a few hours. I just hope there aren't any battleships like the Vindicator waiting for us when we get there."

We all took a copy of the information given to us by Doctor Marcelles and the hologram of him faded out. Each of us would be able to call him up later so he could help us sort through all the data and find what we needed, or simply to answer questions if he could. Jason and his team ensured that the artificial intelligence responsible for that database would not be able to access the main computer.

EIGHTEEN
REPAIRS

I made sure that I was on the bridge when we finished decelerating and came out of hyperspace. I wanted our repairs to go as
quickly as possible, and I had some choice words for the
Captain of the Triton.

We were behind. I was hoping the Triton would still be at
our rendezvous point. You never knew with Captain Wheeler,
as I was quickly discovering.

"Scanning the area, Sir. Nothing in sight," came the report
from tactical.

"Jason, send a standard, low-powered hail."

Sergeant Everin did so and nodded. "Done, Sir."

"From what we've seen, the Triton can cloak seamlessly."

"We've got to get our hands on those specs," Laura said from
her field control station. "Dedicated sciences, please scan the
area and focus on the Triton if she appears. I want to see what
the light, gravity, and energy are doing around that ship," she
added.

"Yes, Ma'am," came the acknowledgement from the dedicated sciences station. It was present on the original bridge, but had been dropped since that bridge was abandoned the first time. Seeing it back in place with at least one crew member manning it at all times was encouraging. Tactically, they could focus scanners on details that could yield useful information. When we weren't in jeopardy they would study near and distant phenomena, mark available natural resources, add to and update interstellar maps and report on points of general interest.

I looked to Oz and saw that he was viewing the repair teams roster. "Order the repair teams out there. I want to see what we're dealing with and get patched up as fast as possible."

"The first team is on their way out now."

The Triton became visible. Since the walls were set to display as though they were windows looking out all around the ship, she appeared right in front of us, within four hundred meters nose to nose.

"Captain Wheeler on the comm, Sir," Jason announced.

"Let's have a word."

Captain Wheeler's smiling face rose out of the main holographic projector. "Good to see you made it. I was going to wait another five hours and go on without you."

"How did you do on your way out of there?"

"Ah, we disappeared as soon as we broke atmosphere. We don't stand out like some ships I know. Hey, I was wondering, do you have any personnel you can spare to work on my ship while we're here?"

I was more than a little surprised. Not only did they not stick around to see if we needed a hand escaping from our pursuers — not that there was actually anything he could have done really — but he got away clean and was asking for help I didn't even know if I could afford to give.

"I mean, we're down to a crew of seventy five here, you're up to what, two hundred?"

"They're not all qualified for repair work. Besides, we have some damage to look after on our end. I don't even know how bad it is yet."

Captain Wheeler turned his head as though he were listening to someone behind him. "According to our scans you've got a bit of a singe on your dorsal port engine, but everything on your end looks pretty good. A few extra quali-fied people would just be helpful over here. I'd like to tune the Triton up a bit before sending it into the mess we'll be facing."

"As I see it, it's not the Triton that will be providing the distraction. I'll tell you when we know how long our repairs will take. After that we'll see if we have time to give you a tune up."

"Never mind. If you need your people, you need your people. Just signal me when you're ready to go," Wheeler said dismissively. He was looking at something to his right, not paying much attention to the transmission.

"How is your new guest?" I asked.

I caught his attention and he looked up as though he was surprised I was asking. "The doctor? We put him in stasis. We're learning a lot from him."

"Stasis? Was he injured?"

"We weren't going to dissect him while he was conscious. What kind of people do you think we are?"

"Dissect him? He's not just a piece of technology! You can't just take him apart and put him back together again. Besides, we need him for current information about what we're facing here."

"What we're facing here. Our scan showed that more than half of this guy's skeletal structure has been replaced by Framework tech. He doesn't have just a little implant like his records say. We asked him about it and he said he wasn't even aware of it. A scientist like that not aware that his system is being replaced? That's hard to swallow."

"Why would he lie to you?" I asked.

"Who knows? Maybe he's got his own agenda. It wouldn't surprise me," said Wheeler.

"Sure. Maybe if you took a few minutes to find out what that agenda is by asking him, earning his trust—"

"That's why when I told Freeground Intelligence I needed another ship to finish this, they sent you to me, I think. You have the firepower and aren't afraid to use it, to slag whatever's in your way. But when it comes to wetwork, getting your hands bloody, you lose your nerve. You haven't been out here long enough to realize what it takes to really get ahead. You're still too clean, not just your uniforms, but the way you prance around following military rank and procedure. Take my advice, leave your moral compass behind. It doesn't work out here," he finished before cutting the transmission.

"He's getting on my nerves," Oz said.

"They left their receive channel open after closing their send. I'm pretty sure they heard that, Oz," Jason reported. "I didn't get a chance to close it until it was too late."

"Well, good thing it's nothing I wouldn't say to his face," Oz replied as he looked over fresh damage reports from the repair and engineering teams.

I couldn't help but think of the scientist that was being cut to pieces by whatever medical or science staff Captain Wheeler had aboard his ship.

I shook off the darkening feeling I had about what was going on aboard the Triton and looked to Oz. "How is it looking?" I asked.

"Not bad. They have to repair some of the finer points of the ion engines, but it should be all wrapped up in about fifteen hours."

"That's quick."

"Well, we have everyone out there and they were all scheduled for a day of downtime before we came out of hyperspace, so they're pretty fresh."

"Nicely done. You're really getting a handle on managing the crew schedules."

"Ah, I get a lot of help from the rest of the senior staff. I think we're just getting better at communicating our needs." We worked quietly for a few minutes before Oz stopped everything. "I can't stop thinking about it. They're pulling someone apart on a ship half a kilometre away. The same guy who gave us the location of the station."

"I know. I understand why Freeground doesn't want to have any public attachment to him. I couldn't imagine him having a good doctor over there, either. We've seen his crew."

"Some of them look like they've been patched up using spare engine parts."

"What do we do about it? We could probably disable the Triton in the space of a couple seconds, but then what? A boarding action and rescue operation?"

Oz stared at the Triton, displayed on the front wall of the

bridge for a moment. "If we weren't under direct orders from Freeground, things would be different."

"Things will be different. As soon as this mission is finished I'm going to make sure I do everything I can to prevent us from ever working with Wheeler again. The problem will be making sure Doctor Marcelles is safe somehow, but we'll have to take that on when the time comes."

After our shifts on the bridge, we moved to Observation Two. The planning continued with messages passing back and forth between tactical staff on the Triton and The First Light. Oz and I were joined by Laura, Ayan, Jason, and Minh for a phase of the planning as well. They all had valuable contributions and important roles to play.

Hours later, we had finished and I sat at the meeting table, facing the tall transparent section of hull that ran the length of the room. Oz had left for a moment and came back with a pitcher and two glasses. We had already had dinner. I smiled at him and took a glass. He poured.

"This is an amazing ship," Oz said as he patiently poured two pints of dark red ale. "Our galley bought traditional keg ale. They said it would be for celebrating our victory."

"How is it?"

"I haven't tried it. This is the first pitcher," he said as he handed me a glass. "They're not serving any until after we've carried out our orders."

I tried a sip. It was bitter, rich, and I was surprised. Even what they called ale in most places was sweet, almost every popular beverage was sweet. I tried a bit more and smiled. "It's almost just like the traditional stuff they serve on Freeground if you're willing to pay for it."

"Only stronger, darker," Oz said after finishing a gulp. "What do you think?"

"I like it. I think I could get used to it."

"Too bad Minh and Jason aren't here."

"Minh is off fine-tuning the fighters and briefing his pilots. Jason's probably with Laura somewhere."

"Where's Ayan? I'm surprised she only stayed for an hour."

"She's in engineering working out some details. I think we've managed to shake out any of the bugs left over from the refit."

"Good. From the looks of things, we'll need to be in good shape."

"I think we will be, but even if this station only has the defences Freeground built into her decades ago, the odds aren't in our favour."

"With friends like Captain Wheeler, I sometimes wonder if the odds wouldn't be better if we were alone," Oz pondered aloud, gesturing out the window to empty space. The Triton had cloaked after doing some work on her hull, so there was nothing to see.

"I think we're both taking too much at face value there." I took a drink from my pint. The flavour was growing on me. "It's true that they didn't contribute as much to the strategy we'll be using on this attack, but what they did add was very clear and useful. Their advice spoke volumes about their experience."

"I've been thinking about what we saw at the pod. Wheeler's people were using crowbars and torches, I still can't believe it. Most standard escape pods require serious tools to break into if anyone inside locks it down."

"It must have been a show. He wants us to underestimate

him."

"That's a dangerous thought. The Triton is loaded with weaponry but our scans tell us that most of it has been inactive for decades. I don't think he's about to start anything ship-to-ship."

I laughed and shook my head. "What would be the point? It's bad enough we had it out in the middle of a club for both our crews to see. Who knows how he could hold that over me if we ever ended up back in communication with Freeground Fleet Command at the same time."

"I think they'd have more important things to bring up if he came into port. Like stealing a Sol Defence vessel, or cutting a valuable informant up to get at technology that we're about to get the details on for ourselves. I'm sure the price on Wheeler's head is a lot higher than yours for reasons we haven't found, too," Oz observed.

"It takes intelligent people to stay ahead of that kind of trouble. I'm sure he's crossed a lot of people out here."

"I don't get it. Why would he want us to believe he was an idiot?"

I refilled my pint and walked to the window to stand beside Oz. The repair crews would be finished soon if everything happened on schedule. "He's setting us up for something."

"Could he have forged our orders?"

"With a detailed bioscan? Not likely. Besides, we double and triple checked them."

"Even so, according to our information and the strategy we'll be using to get the Framework software, we'll be the conspicuous target."

"Even if both our ships had cloaking technology as good as

the Triton's, one of us would have to provide a distraction. Wormhole gates don't open themselves. We'd have to send a visible ship through otherwise the sentry ships will know something's up."

"Well, I know I'll be keeping one eye on the Triton through this entire operation. I can't help it," said Oz.

"I think everyone will. I don't think Wheeler's plans are in our best interest and I want as much warning as possible if he turns," I said.

Ayan entered the room then, practically bouncing. The long hours didn't seem to be affecting her at all. "Well, the new ordinance nine B's are ready. We're materializing the torpedoes now."

"I didn't think it would be ready on time," I told her.

"Well, the residual signatures of the torpedoes were easy to cover, according to Laura, so now they're completely invisible. We were also able to double the payload since we knew these wouldn't end up in storage."

"This ought to be interesting," Oz said, smiling and shaking his head. "I don't think anyone will expect us to have high yield cloaked antimatter torpedoes."

"I know. I doubt they'll ever realize what hit them," I agreed. "How many will we have by the time we arrive?"

"About twenty torpedoes for our stationary launchers and forty for our turrets."

These weren't the complete answer to the problems we were about to face, but they would tip the scales. "I'm pretty sure that the gun crews will be grinning from ear to ear as they load them up, knowing what they are."

"I might still be grinning by the time we get there," Oz

chuckled.

Doctor Anderson stepped in. His expression was solemn, which was unusual. "I've finished arguing with the lead medical officer on the Triton. He's under orders to keep anything they learn about the Framework technology under wraps. They used nanotech to inspect Marcelles, and they're keeping him in stasis. The kind of inspection they're doing over there could take weeks or months of recovery. Hopefully that Framework tech helps that along."

"I don't know if we'd really want anything resulting from that dissection, even if it is done on a cellular scale," I commented, shaking my head.

"I don't agree with their methods, either. I was hoping to get Doctor Marcelles over on our ship so we could treat him and get him back on his feet."

"They're not just holding him on their ship because of orders. I'm sure Wheeler would gladly offload him to us if he didn't have another purpose," Oz commented.

I thought quietly for a moment, looking out into space. Ayan walked to my side and I put an arm around her.

"What's on your mind?" she asked quietly.

"He's also distracting us from something. The fight in the club, his crew behaving like they've never seen an escape pod or opened one before, and how he offhandedly told us he's performing a live autopsy. No one could survive the way he has for thirty years while acting that way. Wheeler's going to sell this technology. He might follow orders and hand the researcher over to Freeground, but whatever he learns before then he's going to sell."

"Fleet Intelligence must see that coming," Oz pointed out.

"They would," Doc answered. "It's probably part of their plan. If Freeground were the only people with this technology after we've managed to steal it from the Triad, they could become a big target. The same accusations could be made by Freeground's enemies as we're making of Triad and Vindyne."

"But if the technology is being traded and sold across the galaxy, that's not an issue." Ayan concluded.

"So Wheeler is being used because they expect him to behave a certain way."

"It makes sense. Someone's already paying for that while he's getting cut up in the Triton's medical bay," Oz said. "Makes me wonder why Freeground selected us for this. What do they expect us to do? We haven't been out here long enough to establish predictable future behaviours."

"You're forgetting they have over a year of simulations to look over, personal psych profiles and career records for most of us. They expect us to take calculated risks and do a lot of damage. If I were looking at our performance and behaviour from Fleet's perspective, I'd say that we've been loud and ruthless. That's what they're expecting here," I said after some thought.

"They're aware that you've been accomplishing your goals regardless of the hardships you've faced. In the short time the crew has been making its way out here, you've acquired so much technology that it took an independent refit to install it. That's undoubtedly something they consider whenever they look at the First Light and her crew," Doctor Anderson added.

"That doesn't change the fact that the term shadow ship doesn't apply to us anymore. After this mission I think things will be very different."

NINETEEN
THE BLUE BELT

For the first time since I had assumed command, the First Light underwent long-range wormhole travel. It was nothing short of amazing. Without sensor enhancement, the universe outside looked distorted, like looking through a curved or severely lensed window. With sensor enhancement, which highlighted radiation and the massive energy required to form the wormhole tunnel, it was like we were passing through a corridor of light. I had never gone through a high compression long distance wormhole myself, and aside from the strange and amazing visual experience of it, the most noticeable thing was that there was no real difference inside the ship. We were really travelling just under the speed of light through a passage in space that compressed the distance between where we were and where we were going.

Memories of primary school, when our teacher marked a piece of paper with two dots, one at each end, and said. "Normally, it would take an ant several seconds to walk across the piece of paper from one dot to another." Then she folded the piece of paper so the dots were facing each other and made a hole through both dots then looked through them. "But if you fold the paper so the space between the points is reduced, he can walk right through in a tenth of the time. Wormhole travel is the same, only instead of folding a piece of paper, we're folding or compressing time and space."

I remembered babbling about folding space with my mother and father for hours that night, right until bedtime and beyond. If I could go back and tell my younger self that I'd be actually travelling through a high compression wormhole someday, I'm sure it would have gone on for days longer. Getting me to sleep would have been impossible.

Our trip to the Blue Belt was reduced to two hours, a little more time than we needed to ensure that the ship and crew were ready to fight their way to the heavily guarded station. I opened a channel to Minh-Chu. "How is everything down there?"

"Everyone's ready to launch as soon as we come out on the other side. We've been ready for about twenty minutes."

"Good luck," I said, wishing I had spent a bit more time with my old friend over the last few days.

"May your life be interesting," he replied before cutting the comm. I could hear his smile over the transmission.

The interactive holographic representation of the main engineering control and monitoring station appeared in one corner of the bridge. Ayan and Laura were in the centre, life size and working the power and subsystems of the ship as if they were there. "Thought it would help if we were on the bridge, at least in spirit. I'm a little busy to be there myself," Ayan said with a smile.

I couldn't help but smile back. I knew they could see a digital representation around them of the bridge, a two dimensional projection that surrounded the circular control console semi-transparently. "Good to have you." It did make it easier to relay commands and receive information from engineering.

The distraction was welcome as we came down to the final minutes before emerging from the wormhole to face the defences on the other side. It was the calm before the storm, we all knew, but confidence was still abundant.

Oz was rechecking department status reports, checklists, and had just ordered tactical to set the main holographic viewer to display the details of our arrival point. He watched me punch in instructions that counted down to our exact time of emergence from the wormhole gate. I leaned back in the command chair, knitted my fingers in front of my face and sighed behind them. He looked from his console to me. "A little tense, Captain?"

I stared at the counter and tactical display in turn. It would be a gauntlet of enemy ships, asteroids, and anything else we had no intelligence on. "The Triton is staying behind to stop ships from escaping through the gate. We'll be on our own."

"That's how it's always been for us. From when we started running simulations right up until now. We're at our best when we're given enough room to do something our way."

"Only this time we'll be rushing right into the secret heart of our enemies," I said.

"They'll never see it coming," Oz whispered with a smile.

I remember thinking that I wished that were true, I wished I didn't have this feeling that they were more than ready. I sat quietly for a moment longer, watching the seconds tick down until it came to an even 100. "It's time," I said, standing. "Torpedo bays, beam firing posts, remove all safeties and ready for target acquisition," I ordered. "Roll back all gunnery and missile doors. Gunnery positions, load heavy flak munitions and prepare to fire at low velocity on my order. Missile turrets, load EMP missiles. All stations check in."

As I was setting orders for weaponry, Ayan was instructing her team to bring all power systems to maximum generation, checking the antimatter intermix that was in place with the engines, and ensuring that her damage control and rescue teams were ready. Laura was checking all the field generation mechanics; she had just finished designing new redundant forty-two layer refractive shielding. If something tried to hit us with beam weapons the energy component of their weapons would be redirected straight back at them, leaving only particles to damage the hull. It was all coming online. I could feel the slight rumble of the ship underfoot as the First Light truly came to life, starting with her heart, the power plants.

"One hell of a bright candle in the dark," Oz said with a smirk. "All stations report ready."

"How are we feeling, Lieutenant Gregor?" I asked Derek, our most experienced helmsman.

He half turned to me, brought the cross of an old rosary to his lips, kissed it, and nodded. "Like I'm not the only one at the controls, Sir."

"Amen," I said, sitting back down and looking at the counter. The seconds seemed to run slow as they dropped from seven all the way to one, and then the distorted tunnel of the wormhole disappeared and we emerged from the wormhole gate.

"The Quantum Core is online and ready," Jason reported.

"Begin hacking the gate. Start with the Freeground manufacturer codes."

I checked the tactical display as it populated with ships. There were two Triad Destroyers just in firing range and a nine kilometre long command carrier minutes away. The placement of the asteroid field all around a corridor leading to the research base was still roughly the same, and I could see that navigation was scanning for safe routes between the destroyers. "Stop. Search for other options," I commanded. "If we try to go between those destroyers there might not be much of us left. They're harder targets than what Vindyne threw at us."

"Communication from the Command Carrier, Sir," reported Jason's communications assistant.

"Well, put it up. No reason to be unfriendly."

The secondary holographic projector displayed the grey haired commander. "Admiral Garvais of the Command Carrier Vesuvius Three to destroyer First Light. You have used our wormhole gate with a stolen entry code and violated our space. Stand down and prepare to be boarded."

"Freeground authorities don't recognize your claim on this space, Admiral. I come bearing a warning. The Triad occupation of the Blue Belt is over. We're coming home."

Admiral Garvais arched an eyebrow. "I don't see a task force or battle group. You're outnumbered and outclassed. Stand down, Captain, or we'll scuttle your ship with you in it."

I looked to the tactical display off to the side of the Admiral's image and saw that several potential courses had been plotted, one of them took us into the asteroid field. It wasn't navigation's first choice, but I highlighted it and heard someone from that corner whisper "Madre de Dios."

"It was good meeting you, Admiral." I smiled.

The Admiral stared at me for a moment then nodded and cut communications.

"Head into the asteroid field as fast as you can. As soon as we're at the edge, start launching fighters. Tactical, weapons free. Begin firing on any enemy ships within range."

"The Freeground codes were a no-go, Captain, but they didn't change any of the computing technology in the gates. The Quantum core has already cracked the first layer of internal controls," Jason reported. "We'll have that gate locked down in a few seconds unless there are any surprises waiting deeper in."

"Why would they post a secret research station using Freeground's old technology?" I overheard Jason's assistant ask.

"Because it takes a decade or so to build just the gate, and a station that size takes about twenty five years," Oz replied. "The destroyers are firing on us, but our flak cover is interfering with their torpedoes and our shielding is refracting and absorbing the beam weapons. Nothing to worry about so far."

"That's because they're still a few kilometres off and know that we're thick on countermeasures at a distance," I replied. "If we give them a chance to get close, we'll start seeing solid-round fire."

"Hyper accelerated torpedoes," Oz said with a shudder. "How long until we're under asteroid cover?"

"Less than thirty seconds, Sir."

"Fighters incoming from the asteroids, Sir. Someone foresaw this," came the report from tactical.

"I wouldn't want to be in their place," I said. "Go through them."

"We've cracked into the programming level of the gate computers, Sir," Jason reported with a smile.

"Well, that's part one of the plan. Upload that artificial intelligence you've been working on. It's time to put her to work."

"Oh, I wish I could hear what Triad will have to say about their new gatekeeper." Jason snickered as he began the upload. He waited a few seconds then looked back up from his console. "Done! She's taking encryption instructions and implementing new security now. With an artificial intelligence changing the passwords required for access several hundred times per second, no one could gain access."

"How will anyone ever use that gate again?" one of his younger staff asked.

"They'll have to ask nicely," Laura's holographic image replied. "Jason, I love your brain."

"You're not serious. Ask nicely?"

"Well, that and you have to be in the Freeground Fleet registry, exist in her personnel database, submit to a DNA scan and pass another fifty or so other subtle security checks I've programmed in."

"Sir, there's a power surge in one of the asteroids closer to the station," tactical reported.

"Evasive action!" I called out as I saw what was going on in the tactical display.

The whole ship shuddered.

"That impact brought our shields down twenty three percent. We can't take more hits like that," Laura reported.

"An asteroid mounted rail cannon. I was hoping we'd be under cover by the time they brought it online," Oz said to himself as much as anyone else.

"Get us under cover, Derek!" I called out.

"Almost there, Sir."

The ship shuddered again. The graphic representation of the ship at the bottom of the tactical display showed an impact on our lower port side. It hadn't ruptured the outer hull, but our shields were down on that quarter. They would take a while to regenerate. "We can't keep taking hits. Any way of predicting where they'll strike?"

"They're coming at us at over forty thousand kilometres per second, Sir," tactical replied, I could hear panic creeping into her tone.

"Easy, Shelly," Oz soothed.

The tactical display showed the First Light manoeuvre right behind a massive asteroid at the edge of the uncleared field and explosions behind us as the Triton began attacking the incoming fighters. She was still cloaked and picking them off at her leisure.

"About time Captain Wheeler started working," Jason mentioned.

"He's sticking to the plan. He had to guard the gate until we had it locked down," Oz added.

"Keep us under cover, Lieutenant, I want to avoid getting picked apart by rail cannon fire."

"I'm starting to connect to the station's communication network. The first layer's weak, after that it's all dynamic encryption." Jason said. "The quantum core's speeding things up but it would take decades."

"How close do we have to be for you to access the internal network?" I asked as I watched the shields regenerate three percentage points a second.

"A couple kilometres if we're lucky."

"Just like the mission profile. Navigation, start plotting an evasive course that'll get us as close to the station as possible once we're clear of the asteroid field. Be creative."

"Yes, Sir."

One of the nearby asteroids showed an impact on the tactical display. "That explains why those destroyers aren't following us, that rail cannon is still firing into the asteroid field," Oz pointed out. "This could get messy."

"Ronin reporting all fighters away. We're working the plan," I heard Minh-Chu report through the communicator.

I could see their transponders on the tactical display, and knew they were fakes. Minh's maintenance and fighter crews had finished building their decoys. They were all different sizes, using partial and complete hulls that were set with roughly similar capabilities and masses. They would navigate through the asteroid field towards the station using transponders that matched our fighters. In the meantime, Minh's wing would be drifting ahead of the First Light behind a shower of meteors we would send towards the station.

"Captain Wheeler's moving on to the Command Carrier," reported communications.

"What the hell is he doing?" I asked no one in particular. "That's completely off-mission." I found myself wishing that I could communicate with him directly, but any open communications would most likely compromise his cloak.

"Well, here's hoping he has a better plan," Oz said, shaking his head. "Besides, we switched a few things up just in case."

We wove between asteroids and meteor clusters, all the while getting closer to the dark red star the spinward portion of the Blue Belt orbited and the station. The dim light cast by the failed star reflected blue off of the tumbling rock all around us. This was where the ergranian steel used in the construction of the First Light came from. I was in amazement at the skill of our pilot, Lieutenant Derek Gregor. I watched in awe as he steered us through safely, making one split second judgement after another, coordinating with his navigational partner who plotted and adjusted the course second by second and watched the colliding, milling lethal stone all around us.

The shields were taking strikes — fewer than anyone had planned — and as we came to the last few hundred kilometres before exiting the field they were almost back up to full charge.

"Fire conventional high yield torpedoes. It's time to create a screen of moving cover," I instructed tactical.

We began firing on meteors far ahead and after a few seconds we were right behind a growing, heavy mass of ore and stone hurtling towards the huge station before us. The station was a disc of girders, habitation and research complexes that reached out from a flat centre like a halo of spikes. Hundreds of other sections, many unfinished, fanned out across the top and bottom. I couldn't help but be reminded of early images of Freeground, before the first major expansions were built hundreds of years ago.

Thousands of support ships — construction, external habitation, transportation cruisers, movers, smelting and mining vessels — filled the space around the station, and after the hellish challenge our pilot had just been put through, it must have seemed like heaven. He rolled the First Light as we broke free and I couldn't help but smile. He was moving our kilometre long home as though she were a heavy fighter.

"Mark any ships that are charging weapons or firing and slag them. Instruct rail cannon emplacements to switch to anti-matter rounds. Torpedo bays and turret emplacements, load ordinance nine B's and hold."

"Sir, the resistance here is light. There are very few armed ships," tactical reported.

"I don't like this," Oz said as he brought up a sub-display and focused in on a large empty space in front of the station. "This is exactly where I'd manoeuvre the heaviest defences if I were in command."

"Then that's where they are," I replied.

"Helm, let's go around. Use the ships surrounding the outer perimeter as cover while we see what those meteors run into."

"My pleasure, Sir," Lieutenant Gregor acknowledged as he taxed the engines and took us into a drastic ninety degree turn within a hundred meters of a massive ore transport. The rail cannon that had been tracking us through the asteroid field stopped firing; obviously the defence commanders didn't want to risk taking out any of their support vessels.

The fighter drones ran into heavy resistance. The command carrier well behind us had launched fighters to intercept and the drones had run into them earlier than expected. Minh's diversion had delayed station support craft from being sent in our direction. Not as much as he would have liked, but I'd have to congratulate him later since the plan had kept most of the fighters from even looking in our direction.

I looked to where the hail of meteors was careening towards the station,. They were tearing through support vessels too slow to move out of the way and were just about to emerge into the empty space. "Ronin, don't follow the meteors in. Use the civilian vessels as cover."

"Acknowledged. And, Captain?" Minh asked.

"Yes?"

"Get out of my head."

Oz snickered despite himself. "If you weren't already with Ayan, I'd say you and Buu should get married. You already share the same brain."

"That's my man you're talking about," Ayan interjected as her holographic image worked at the controls.

"Now we get to see what's behind curtain number one," I said as the meteors drifted into open space.

To my utter surprise they were cut into billions of sand sized pieces in the span of a few seconds. The bridge fell silent.

"What happened?" asked Derek's navigator.

I could see tactical was already busy trying to analyse it. The dedicated science station, manned by two officers new to the post, were scrambling to explain what we had just seen. I was suddenly very glad the engineering crew had made the late addition. Having them there could only speed up our information gathering process.

We were still weaving between the hundreds of ships and the occasional massive asteroid, taking minor fire that was of little consequence. Our load of antimatter ammunition was still several times what we'd need to complete our mission, and our shields were over ninety percent charged. The clock was ticking. The longer we took to figure out what could annihilate thousands of ore laden meteors in mere seconds, the less chance of success we had.

"Disruptor fire. It's the only thing that could cause that kind of destruction," Ayan finally reported.

"That's theoretical," Oz spat.

"We can confirm it. Whatever they're using breaks down molecular bonds with a form of energy we haven't gotten a handle on," reported dedicated sciences.

"What will that do to our shields?"

"I'm sorry, Sir, I couldn't tell you for certain."

"Best guess?"

"Refractive armour may not work, but energy barriers should."

"We'll know soon enough," I said. I thought silently for a moment, watching as we wove between several habitation cruisers.

"Orders, Captain?" Oz asked quietly.

"Laura, can you coordinate with our science team and modify the shields to be more effective as we start taking hits?"

"I can try," she replied after manipulating a set of controls. "Without knowing more about the weapon—"

"Do your best. Can our ablative shielding help protect us against it?"

"It can, but it would take a lot of power to regenerate it as we're taking damage," Ayan said. "Actually, about half our power as we generate it."

"Then bring the antimatter power core on line and use it to charge the hull."

Ayan actually stopped and looked at me for a moment before following through with my orders.

"Do you have another option?"

"I was trying to think of one. No."

"That sounds bad. Why is that bad?" Jason asked in a whisper.

"It's bad because we were going to use it to generate a wormhole to get out of here, and the power core only has enough antimatter to operate for about five minutes," Oz replied. "Looks like we'll just have to get power from another system when the time comes or use the gate we entered through."

Jason cringed. "Well, it's not that bad, really. This ship can generate a lot of power," he concluded, trying to reassure his assistant, who looked absolutely terrified.

"The antimatter core is ready," Ayan reported.

"Helm, take us straight for the station. As soon as we break out into the open, start rotating the ship. We want to spread any damage that gets through the shields across the hull."

We took a sharp turn, and just as we were breaking past the last of the civilian ships, Ayan brought the antimatter core online and the hull was charged with so much power that I could hear the metal creak. The outer hull sounded like it was alive, singing sustained soprano notes that almost sounded mournful.

We were immediately under fire. The hull started showing damage from whatever undetectable enemy was on our port side. Our hull was regenerating fast, more quickly than I thought possible, but the disruptor fire had hit one turret already and a gunner had been killed. "Get those shields adjusted please," I requested as calmly as I could manage.

I looked to the front of the bridge and saw on the forward two dimensional display that covered all the walls that a ship was appearing. It had two long forks in the front attached to a primary hull that bristled with field emitters. The rear of the ship sported six manoeuvring engines with one main thruster at the back. The design of the hundred fifty meter long ship made it look like it was lurching forward in an attack posture. We were within two hundred meters and the vessel's Captain had obviously decided that decloaking was in their best interest.

"Helm!" was all Oz and I could say before we careened into the starboard side fork. Everyone on the bridge was tossed to the left as the inertial dampeners fought to keep up with the force of the impact.

I regained my feet as quickly as possible, wincing as I put pressure on my left ankle. I had sprained it, bad. The pilot had been jostled, but remained in his chair the entire time and rotated the ship so our undamaged side faced the incoming disruptor fire.

"Scanning the enemy ship's shields and doing my best to match the energy pattern. It's resistant to disruptor fire!" Laura called out, already manipulating the engineering control console before being fully on her feet. "Medical team to engineering, we have injured!" she finished.

I couldn't see Ayan on the holographic display at all and I tried to put it out of my mind as I looked at the tactical and ship status display. Our port manoeuvring thrusters and RAD scoop had taken heavy damage, but the rest of the ship was all right. Hull damage was heavy. Portions of our outer hull had been reduced to just over fifty percent. If we couldn't get our shields working against the disruptor fire soon, there wouldn't be enough metal left to regenerate in some sections.

"Helm, get us under the cover of that station. Do it now," I said, falling back into my chair.

"The station is opening fire. Multiple signatures. Several dozen torpedoes, three squadrons of fighters so far, energy weapons, and some smaller rail cannons," Oz reported.

"Target torpedoes with all cannons and instruct rear gunners to fire a fan of flak at high velocity. Track impacts and mark firing zones. If you find any of those cloaked ships, switch to antimatter rounds and light them up."

Our shield status changed and I heard Laura cry out. "Got it! Shields are now blocking over ninety percent of the disruptor fire."

"Ronin leading the charge. We'll take care of those fighters for you. Time to shred some hulls."

"Badman breaking with squad two to proceed to our objective," added Minh's second in command. His small group of eight fighters were tasked with taking out the gravity field generators holding the milling mass of asteroids away from the station.

"We might just make it at this rate," Oz said.

"Right, but where the hell is the Triton?"

"Good question," Oz replied as he checked our back trail on the tactical display. "They actually managed to take out the engines on that Command Carrier. That was the last sign of them," he reported, searching the combat record for any other indication that they had done anything helpful.

I watched as the station loomed larger with every passing

moment on the live screen on the bridge walls. It stretched over a hundred kilometres across in all directions. The mission report claimed that Freeground had started building it as a defence station when they were in possession of the Blue Belt, but lost control of it decades before completion. Now it was a monolithic structure, and we were its only assailant. One of the older sections came into view and I stood up. "Helm, get us the hell away from the firing line of those cannons!" I said, pointing at a series of ninety centimetre wide bore rail cannons.

It was too late.

TWENTY

HELL

A stationary rail cannon fires a highly dense projectile that fragments on impact with another solid object, such as the hull of a
ship. That projectile is magnetic and conductive; it comes
supercharged with energy and is sent spinning down the
magnetic barrel at speeds of up to ten thousand kilometres per
second and sometimes faster. A BN class (or Big Ninety), rail
cannon has a barrel ninety centimetres across and five hundred
ninety meters long. They take up a lot of space, take a while to
aim, use enough energy to power most medium space stations
for over two years, but one shot can reduce most destroyer class
ships to a wrecked hulk.

The First Light sustained three shots all at once.

I opened my eyes. The lights flickered on dimly throughout
the bridge. The surrounding two dimensional display was up a
moment later followed by the three dimensional tactical display.
At a glance I could see we had lost the old bridge located at the
front of the ship completely, it and the part of the hull it jutted

from was just gone. Our lower aft engine had a hole at least ten
meters wide right through it and was showing offline, and our
landing bays had been rendered useless. We had taken a full-on
hit that mulched everything down there. We were down to
seventeen operational rail cannon turrets and power had been
disrupted to half of our underside.

"First Light, come in!" came the sound of Ronin's voice
through my arm command unit. "Jonas! Tell me you survived
that."

I tried to turn my comm on with my right hand but intense
pain flared up. It was almost blinding. My forearm was broken, I
could see the awkward bulge under my suit. I looked around the
bridge.

Jason was already working at the controls of the communications console at a feverish pace. His assistant was helping him. Oz
was standing up, holding his side but checking the status of the
ship at the same time. Laura was back in the engineering command
console. It looked like it was restarting from a cold boot and I still
couldn't see Ayan. At the helm I could see that Derek's neck was
twisted at an unnatural angle. His navigator looked at me and
shook her head. "The impact broke his neck, Sir," she said quietly.

Oz moved to take the pilot's seat, letting himself down very
gently into the chair.

"Personal comm, open channel to Ronin," I commanded
and heard a blip as my communicator complied. "We're alive,
for the most part."

"I knew you weren't that easy to kill! Hey, they're sending
boarding shuttles. We're trying to knock them back and take out
those cannons at the same time, just in case."

"Let the boarding shuttles come, we have some life in us yet. How about those cannons?"

"We shredded the front of their barrels. Just fighting in close to the station while we wait for orders," Minh replied.

"I'm ready to make a link and start hacking into the station's computers." Jason reported. "The quantum core is still intact. I can't get into the network at this range though. We need a direct uplink. I'm sorry"

"We saw this as a possibility. Make it happen Ronin. Start launching broadcast drones at the station's hull."

"Consider it done!"

"Sir, the boarding shuttles seem to think we're dead in space," came the report from tactical. I looked to my right and saw that both the tactical officers were in fine shape. A little shaken, but otherwise untouched. She had a serious expression until my eyes met hers, and I smiled. "Good to see you're still with us."

"Good to be here," she replied. "Orders?"

"Play possum until they're within a hundred meters. I don't want us to look armed and dangerous until we have to. Are those ordinance nine B's all loaded and ready?"

"Yes, Sir."

"Good, get set to fire. I think I have an idea."

One of the night crew pilots came in through the lift at the back of the bridge and Oz relinquished the pilot's controls to her. "I think this thing is still flyable, though we'll be at one-third power, maybe a little more," Oz said as he pointed to several status readouts on the control panel.

"Thank you, Sir," she said as she looked at the previous pilot uneasily and sat down. "He trained me. We've spent weeks together."

"He was a good man. Once we're out of this we'll honour him properly, but you have to get us there," Oz said comfortingly. "Make him proud."

She nodded and took the controls as she listened to the navigator, whose professionalism was unbelievably keen.

"Sir! Triad destroyer coming around the back side of the station. She'll have a clear line of fire in a few seconds."

"Laura, how are the shields?"

"We have aft and dorsal shields, that's it. I'm working on getting the bow projectors on line but I don't think it'll happen."

"Any chance of using our last two beam weapon emplacements as emitters?"

"No. Vindyne technology can't be re-tasked that way."

"Tactical, any read on those cloaked ships?" I asked.

"Yes. We managed to mark four with flak fire. One's destroyed, the other three are behind us."

"What's the margin of error for tracking them through the flak shot embedded in their hulls?"

"Nil. I doubt they've had time to step out of an airlock and dig it out."

"All right. Tell the gunners, when the boarding shuttles are within one hundred meters, open fire. Helm, try to send us towards a part of the station we can use as cover."

"Maybe this would be a good time to start using ordinance nine B's?" Oz said, raising an eyebrow.

"I was just getting to that. Have torpedo launchers lock onto that destroyer and fire as soon as we're on the move. Without forward shields they'll make quick work of us."

The tactical display showed our rail guns opening fire on the boarding shuttles, reducing them into scrap metal. They obviously didn't see it coming. The entire ship roared to life. We started moving towards the nearest girders jutting from the station. Ordinance nine B torpedoes were launched, our aft and dorsal shields came up, and for a few seconds it felt like the ship actually had a chance again.

I took a second to manipulate the comm controls on the command chair with my left hand and opened a channel to medical. "Doctor Anderson, here. Captain, the treatment centre is full, but we're saving more than we're losing."

"Glad to hear it. Losses?"

"As far as medical is concerned, we've lost eighteen, Ayan is in secure stasis."

I opened my mouth to say something, but nothing came out. I knew it was a mistake to check in.

"Initial assessment shows that she'll need some care, more than I can administer while we're mid-incident. Don't worry, Captain. Get us out of here and I'll have her on her feet in no time. She's a fighter."

"Thank you, Doctor."

"The station is firing on us!" tactical reported.

I braced myself as I saw the readout of several mid-sized rail cannon turrets, beam emplacements, and a few disruptor cannons all opening fire. Our unshielded side was still facing the impact points and our hull was partially open where they were hitting us. The inner hull was starting to take serious damage.

"Wait, something is blocking the weapon fire," Oz reported.

"Sir, it's the Triton! She's de-cloaking right under us!"

"Thought you could use a hand putting the last part of our plan in motion," I heard Captain Wheeler say through our secure channel. "Now use those cannons of yours to blast us a hole out of here."

I couldn't help but smile. "How is that hack coming, Jason?"

"The quantum core is making quick work of their internal security. We're almost in. Minh's pilots put those transmitter drones real close to an internal networking hub."

The tactical display showed the full on impact of our ordinance nine B cloaked antimatter torpedoes on the nearest enemy destroyer, ruining the front end of their ship. Our aft shields were taking a lot of fire from the cloaked ships behind, and the trace scan of the flak revealed three of them while the line of the weapons fire revealed two more. "Mark those cloaked ships and open fire with antimatter rounds. Sight the undamaged cloaked vessels with our beam weapons. Have our torpedo and missile launch control target the station's weapon emplacements and energy nodes if they can find them, and open fire with the remaining ordinance nine B's. Let's tear this place apart."

Laura somehow brought port shielding back on line and was able to maintain our aft and dorsal shields, but we were still taking hits on other parts of the hull. "We can't take much more of this. The station's weapons are carving the outer hull to pieces," Oz said. "We might have two minutes at this rate."

"I'm hoping that's all we need. Jason, how is the hack going?"

"We're in!" he called out. He worked at the controls at a feverish pace; his assistant was trying to keep up but I could tell that she was having difficulty. "We have a problem. Hold." His expression looked worried and he worked faster for a minute and then stopped, sitting back in his chair. "I'm sorry to report that the reactors they use cannot be overloaded."

"What?" Oz asked, joined by Captain Wheeler over the communicator.

The ship jostled under the force of several torpedo hits. I verified that they didn't hit critical systems, but had decimated the forward observation deck.

Oz was still talking to Jason. "Okay, what do you mean the reactors can't be overloaded?"

"All their components and energy generation technologies are non-volatile. Some are a lot like what our ship uses, almost no moving parts on the inside with amplification technology scattered everywhere. A lot of their power comes from their hull, which absorbs solar energy just like ours."

"Okay, what did they do with their reactors?" Captain Wheeler asked through the communicator.

"They're just—" Jason looked through the station schematics and brought up a detailed cross section on one screen. I could only assume that he was transmitting the image to Captain Wheeler at the same time. "—gone! It's an arboretum now. The power readings confirm it. That section of the station generates nothing except for biomatter and clean air!"

I thought for a minute, we had to destroy the station. It was the best way to slow down development and there was no guarantee that the other plan — destroying the gravitational fields — would do the trick. I silenced the comm so Captain Wheeler couldn't hear what I said next. "Anything on Framework software?"

"We've got it and we've downloaded their entire database. Our storage systems are eighty seven percent full," Jason replied.

I unmuted the secure comm channel we shared with Captain Wheeler and tried to think of another way to destroy this installation. "Cloaked attack cruisers, Framework, advanced defence systems, and a station that could support a population of five million in the middle of an asteroid belt made up of the hardest, most adaptive steel known to man. It all belongs to Triad."

"You're thinking that there's more here than we're seeing," Oz said.

"We've got to get out of here. We should head back to the wormhole gate," Captain Wheeler said through the communicator. "We can't take much more punishment."

"We can't leave this place intact. There's too much going on here," I replied quietly.

"What do you think you can do? This is pointless!" Captain Wheeler protested. "We're gone. Triton, out!"

"Sir, the Triton is breaking off and cloaking. She's taken damage, but not so much that she's not capable," came the report from tactical.

I thought for a moment longer, I could feel most of the bridge personnel staring at me, and then I got an idea. "Laura, is our wormhole generator still online?"

"Yes, it's operable."

"Aim it at the least armed section of the station, the one we just cleared." I opened a channel to Minh-Chu. "Ronin, get your fighters together. You have one minute to get in front of the ship."

"Yes, Sir! What's the idea?"

"We're going to rip a hole right through this station with a wormhole. Get ready to follow us through."

"We may not have enough power," Laura said.

I turned on her. She didn't understand that there wasn't a choice here. This was our one chance to actually make a real difference in the war between Freeground and the Triad Consortium. Without this, we would have made little or no difference after sacrificing so much. "Drain the capacitors, shut down everything but inertial dampening and engines, ramp up all our power generation, and get that thing tunnelling a worm-hole straight through that station! I know it takes exponentially more power to do it through solid matter, but it's the one thing this ship has in abundance."

"Yes, Sir," she replied, working the controls. A moment later the holographic projection of the station disappeared as two more senior engineers joined her to help redirect power.

I opened a ship-wide channel from my command chair. "This is the captain. All crew are to seal themselves into secure compartments and stand ready for potential decompression. We're shutting life support down in all areas but medical."

Everyone on the bridge brought up their hoods and sealed their vacsuits. I watched the tactical screen as our fighters moved into position and our hull took continuous damage. Our gunners were tearing the cloaked cruisers to pieces with anti-matter rounds and they were scattered, coming apart in flames and depressurization bursts.

Two main sections of the First Light lost integrity, and I watched as five gunnery posts went dark, too damaged to continue firing. Their crews were either getting out or had already been killed. We were down to twelve turrets, and our beam emplacements were destroyed.

I could feel the unsteady vibrations in the hull as we began generating the energy field and gravitational force required to open a wormhole, and I punched in the codes for the arrival point.

"I'm proud to have served with you, Captain," I heard Minh tell me through my personal communicator. "Doesn't look like I'll make this ride."

I searched for his marker on the tactical screen and realized his ship was attached to a narrow crook in the station. Hacking into the station hadn't been so easy because one of the broadcast drones was well placed; it was because Minh had manoeuvred his fighter into a safe, vulnerable spot and used his infantry training to dock and wire his communicator into the station's internal computer.

It was genius, it was unexpected, and he had to know that there was little chance he could get back to his fighter and to the wormhole jump point in one minute. He should have told me.

"God dammit, Minh. What'll I do?" Was all I could manage to say.

"A bird does not sing because it has an answer."

The space around us warped, and the station tore apart just off from the centre, exploding and shearing to pieces as the force of our forming wormhole bore straight through it. I watched as the wormhole pushed through, layer by layer, and prayed that we were generating enough power to force a way through the solid matter ahead of us. I prayed that Minh could somehow get to an escape shuttle or into a safe compartment somewhere before it all started coming apart, but I knew the chances were as close to none as anyone could imagine.

The sound of the energy and gravity generators was deafening and the ship rattled everyone. Even through the localized painkillers, my broken arm sent mind-rending shocks of pain to my brain.

"We've got a clear path, Sir!" came the cry from navigation.

"Helm! Give us a burst from the engines!" I shouted.

The inertial dampeners struggled to keep up as the engines fired briefly and we crossed the threshold into the wormhole. It started pulling us along, and after some fine adjustments, the bridge fell under a subdued silence.

TWENTY-ONE
AFTERMATH

We weren't ready to emerge from the wormhole by the time we arrived at Starfree Port. The damage to the First Light was so severe that it took two tugs to guide us into docking position.

I placed the highest priority on getting the ship in good enough condition to make our next destination, Freeground. It would take a week, and even after those basic repairs were complete, over forty percent of the ship would still be open to space. Some of it was just gone, and as Oz transferred the casualty list, I couldn't help but just sit back in my chair.

We had lost over half the gun crews, fifteen damage control team members, five from main engineering and most of the fighter maintenance and lower deck crews. Over ninety people in all. Fighter pilots were still checking in, but still there was no sign of Minh-Chu or his second in command. I had never felt so tired or beaten. Even through all the work and bad news, all I could think of was Ayan's condition. I kept checking the medical status board, my eyes scanning right down to Rice and her condition, which was listed as inconclusive.

"Go see her. Get your arm treated at the same time," Oz whispered to me.

I glanced at him, and he looked just like I felt. "You'd better get those ribs checked," I replied quietly.

"Have someone from medical come down. I'm not the only one who got rolled around during the fight. Everyone in here has to be checked over, the sensors in our suits don't always diagnose everything spot on."

I thought for a moment and looked down at my arm. It was true, if my suit had been working properly, someone from medical would already be on the bridge. "Jason, were communications hit at all?"

"We had to switch to backups. Our primary receiving hub went with the old bridge."

"What about internal sensors?"

"They're out all over the ship, Sir."

I sighed and made to run my hand over my face but stopped as pain shot up my right arm. "Have security and rescue teams do a sweep of the ship with hand scanners. We have to assume that there could be people trapped who can't communicate with us."

"The station is offering their assistance as well. They have repair, rescue, law enforcement, insurance, and legal teams standing by."

"Tell them we'll take the repair and rescue teams on."

"Yes, Sir," Jason said before transmitting the response.

"I'll take this command shift. Now go see her and get some

rest so you can step in when I'm ready to fall down," Oz said more insistently.

I nodded and grabbed my long coat, thinking I'd use the tools inside to help with rescue operations after checking into medical, and headed up the lift at the rear of the bridge. I was able to avoid the non-critical treatment centre, but medical was full. All around me were the resting wounded. The number of people that were saved was proven by what I was seeing.

The dozen emergency treatment beds that they normally had ready were joined by a dozen more, making for close quarters. I had missed the urgent action. Everyone within was stable or treated and resting. No one stopped me until I was in the stasis centre.

There was room for up to thirty long-term stasis patients and the drawers were full. I always hated stasis centres; they reminded me of morgues with transparent hatches. I stood to the side as a surgical team retrieved the next patient from a tube and rushed him into a micro suite that would close over the patient, creating a completely sterile environment. Surgery would be performed with dozens of small tools including regenerators, lasers, injectors, and nanotechnology.

I was stopped by a nurse, who looked at my arm then up at me. "We'll treat you over here, Captain," he said as he began leading me to the non-critical treatment area.

"I'd like to see Commander Rice first," I replied, resisting.

"She's where we're going," he stated as he moved me along, carefully but expediently.

"I thought—" I started quietly, but didn't finish. I realized we were headed to the waiting room. They had obviously run out of space in main medical, and I didn't know what I would see where I was being taken.

The doors to the waiting area opened and the nurse tried to guide me to one of the sofas, which had been pushed into a corner to make room for temporary beds. I completely ignored him as I caught sight of Ayan in a bed across the room. I was mindful of the injured, but still strode to her as quickly as I could.

She was breathing, and I took her hand in my good one. The railing was up around the bed. To my surprise her eyes opened.

"How are things in engineering?" she asked.

I just stared at her in astonishment. She looked unharmed.

She raised up on one elbow and her expression softened. "Hey, I'm fine. They just wanted me to wait twenty minutes after surgery before I started running around directing repairs."

I kissed and hugged her to me with my good arm and winced as my other one hit the side railing. "Doc said that you were in stasis."

"I was thrown across engineering during one of the impacts and landed head first. I didn't feel a thing, knocked me out cold. Broke my arm, some ribs and my collar bone but they put me back together," she said before looking down at my arm. "That's gotta hurt, though."

The nurse from earlier came back and injected me from behind with something. "These little guys will knit the bone just fine, Captain. Just don't put any pressure on the arm for the next ten minutes and don't mind the itching."

"Thanks, Tim," Ayan said, smiling at the nurse before he walked off.

The nanobots were already busy at work, and I was just about willing to trade the furious itching in my forearm for the pain of leaving it broken. "Holy hell, he used an emergency combat grade injection," I gasped involuntarily.

Ayan looked at me wide eyed. "There's a difference?"

"Oh, yeah. They use these on infantry during firefights or pilots when they've been injured and can't be replaced." My face twitched in an involuntary grimace. I went on with gritted teeth. "The nanobots work ten times as fast. You were never trained with them?"

"Sure I was, but I've never actually seen someone use them. We were always able to use the normal kind. You get a little tingle while they work."

"I bet Doctor Anderson ordered this."

"That's what you get for not staying still," Ayan said, shaking her finger.

I hadn't even realized it, thanks to nerve blockers, but the bones in my arm had already been set and looked normal. "I think I'll sit down long enough to let him use a subdermal regenerator next time." I said as the bone-deep itch started to subside.

"Little guys work quick though, have to give them credit," Ayan said, looking at my arm.

"Yup, fire and forget medicine is good that way. I've seen them sew up bullet holes in minutes."

Ayan's mind was already elsewhere. "How is my ship?" she asked, bracing herself.

"It's bad. We don't know exactly how bad, but the top three decks are a lost cause, so are sections five through twelve of the last six decks."

She cringed and shook her head. "We're finished out here."

I had already made the realization while we were still in the wormhole, putting out the most urgent fires, but it really hit home as she said it. "I know. I'm sure Freeground wants us back, and even if they don't, we need their help."

"Did we complete the mission?"

I was about to answer but realized then that there was no way I could be absolutely certain. Breaking time and space open right through an object that size could destroy most of it. The second group of fighters had managed to knock out one of the gravity field emitter posts, so there would be asteroids drifting freely nearby and possibly right into it. There was no certainty though, just a good chance. "We put a wormhole right through the centre of the station. I'll have to run simulations when I have time."

She stared at me and thought for a moment. "They had updated the reactors?"

"They did. How did you know?"

"I thought it was a remote possibility, but those reactors were four city blocks wide and very efficient. I was pretty sure they would keep them running until they were worth replacing, and they should have been good for another hundred years."

"I would have made the same assumption, and it looks like they kept it a secret somehow. The intelligence we had said they were still there. It's not your fault."

"Well, putting a wormhole through the station is probably a solution no one expected you to come up with, so even if the station is salvageable I'm pretty sure research will grind to a halt for a while. Now we have to patch what we can up so we can go home." Ayan said quietly. "It just seems too soon."

"I know, I—" I was interrupted by my communicator.

"There's a priority message coming in from Freeground Fleet Command, Sir," Jason said over the comm.

Ayan smiled at me reassuringly. "Go ahead, I have to get to engineering."

"Signal that I'll be a minute. Thanks, Jason," I replied.

Ayan lowered the railings on the bed and I helped her out.

She wrapped her arms around my neck and kissed me lingeringly. She sighed as I wrapped my arms around her. "And off I go to patch the ship back together."

"Be careful down there. I think we've both seen enough of medical."

"Aye, aye, Captain." She smiled warmly. Even with the damage, loss, and dire straits, we were able to steal just a few seconds. Time enough for me to look into her eyes and soak in her soft expression.

I smiled back and then we headed off in our own directions. She took the lift to engineering, I slipped out the back door and stepped into a side passage, setting my arm command console to route all audio to my ear implant and keep any video two dimensional. With so much damage on the ship, it would take time to find a perfectly private room to speak with Fleet Command in. This would have to do for the time being.

I opened the channel and a clearance screen appeared. My arm console's mini-scanner took a snapshot of my retina and sent a reading of my DNA from the sweat on my arm along with a current medical readout. A moment later a grey haired admiral came on screen. I recognized him faintly but couldn't recall exactly where from.

"Captain Valent, my name is Admiral Churchill. With the

fleet actively combating the Triad Consortium, I've been assigned as your new handler until you and your crew have been debriefed." He grinned openly; there was good news and that wasn't it.

"I'm surprised you're using open channels. Even though the data stream is encrypted you have to know that anyone with a little knowhow would know who's on each end."

"The need for secrecy is over, Captain. Your mission in the Blue Belt was your last act as a shadow ship. It's time to come home and let us take care of you. I'd send a carrier to your location but everything in your area is currently engaged."

"How did you find out about the results of our mission so quickly?"

"We received a burst transmission from the Triton, including everything they learned about Framework hardware. They've gone their own way."

"I'd like to go after them as soon as we're ready." I said before thinking about it.

"We might take you up on that, Captain, but for now congratulations are in order. The last transmission from the Triton before it entered the wormhole gate shows what happened to the station. The asteroid field reacted to the artificial gravity right away. That station is a complete loss. With regard to your casualties, there will be a memorial service some time after you've arrived."

"Thank you, Admiral. What are our orders?"

"You are to patch yourselves up with the help of the Starfree Port teams and use their wormhole generator to come home. Once you arrive you'll be debriefed."

"And from there?" I couldn't help asking. The crew would want to know. I needed to know.

"After what you've accomplished out there, you'll have your pick of commands. There are promotions forthcoming for a good number of your crew, but none of that will be official until you've all been debriefed."

"Thank you, Admiral," I replied, somewhat surprised. "I have to get back to repairs if we want to get out of here soon."

"Good thinking. Freeground Command is looking forward to having you home."

"Admiral, I want to keep this crew together. Stay in command of the First Light. We're just getting started."

He smiled. "Well, you have some rest coming. Some of your crew will want to move on, but I'll leave the option open to anyone who wants to continue service on your ship. We intend to send you right back out there as soon as the First Light is fit. God speed. Freeground is proud of her sons and daughters."

I stood there and thought for a moment after the transmission ended. Captain Wheeler was gone. I only hoped that the information he sent to Freeground on the Framework hardware was enough to put it to use. Otherwise we'd have to continue the research or wait until it became available on the market. I found myself wishing I could chase after him, drag him back to Freeground kicking and screaming. It would be hard, even if the ship were in perfect shape. He used a wormhole gate to escape, he could be anywhere in the galaxy.

I opened a channel to Jason. "Any progress in scanning the information we stole from the research station? Did we get anything we were looking for?"

"We did. The Framework software is complete, with implementation instructions. There is a lot of other unrelated research here as well. We hit the mother lode."

"Fleet Intelligence will be happy."

"Do we have new orders, Sir? I saw a communication with a Freeground signature coming in," Jason asked.

I smiled at him through my communicator. "Sorry, I'll have to pass those on to my first officer."

"Fine fine, here's our giant first officer."

I was connected to Oz. "New orders?"

"They're in. Freeground Fleet Command needs us back as soon as possible. We're clear to use Starfree Port's gate to get back home. They're letting me keep my command."

"Thank God. I'd hate to have to go rogue with half a ship. Looks like we won't be sleeping until we get home, though. There's a lot to do."

"I agree."

"Any other details?"

"They'll be handing out promotions. We did good, Oz, real good."

"Nice of them to notice. Who did you get the orders from?"

"Admiral Churchill."

Oz turned white and was visibly nervous. "He's the head of Fleet Intelligence, Jonas. If we've been moved under his command, then they're taking us very seriously."

"That's what I'm hoping."

"Watch what you wish for."

Oz looked ahead suddenly and my command console beeped, showing that there was another priority communication waiting. I could overhear commotion on the bridge. "What's going on up there?" I asked.

"You better get to the bridge. A Vindyne Overlord just came out of hyperspace with a full battle group."

I started heading for the bridge and stopped as a familiar voice came loud and clear through my ear implant. "Captain Valentine," the voice cooed slowly. It was Major Hampon. Unmistakable. "It took me a while to find you, but considering the cost of damages, I was given extra resources. My employers are anxious to vilify someone in public, preferably a real villain. Preferably the captain that nearly cost them a Super Carrier."

"I could imagine. I just can't believe they put you in charge of anything after how useless your interrogation techniques were. How's your nose healing?"

"Now now, no need to be testy. You're right, I'm not in solitary command. I am only a guide, a tracker. I do, however, have the power to offer you a bargain."

Oz turned towards me on my arm command unit. "Starfree Port is turning us out. They say that the Command Carrier is demanding that the Port Authority surrender the First Light and her crew."

I turned the audio receptors on my command unit off so Oz wouldn't be able to hear me. "What's your bargain?" I asked quickly.

"It's simple. I'll let your crew get a head start if you surrender yourself."

"I need guarantees. My crew gets out of this unharmed."

"I can only guarantee that your crew will get one hour to get that wreck out of the area."

I thought for a minute as I watched the main corridor from the darkened side passage. The crew ran back and forth, getting ready for battle even though the ship was in no condition to fight. They didn't think there were other choices.

"Mooring lines are detached. We're drifting free, Captain. Orders?" I could hear Oz ask. I turned the audio receptors on my command console on and looked at him on the small screen. "Get the ship through that wormhole gate. If you see an emergency shuttle launch, ignore it."

"What?"

"That's my final order, Oz. Do it."

"Final order? What the hell are you doing?" he asked.

"Get this ship to Freeground. That is an order, Commander McPatrick!"

Oz simply stared for a moment. It was as though he knew what I was doing, what price I was willing to pay. He nodded slowly. "Yes, Sir."

"Tell Ayan I love her. Don't come after me," I said before closing all communications on my command unit.

"I take that exchange as an acceptance?" Hampon said in my ear receiver.

I started running to the nearest forward facing escape shuttle. "If you go back on your word..."

"What? What could you possibly do?"

"I'll find something." I opened the hatch and jumped inside. I closed it behind me and strapped in. I didn't give myself time to hesitate before disabling the safety and hitting the launch button.

On one half of the visual display was the Super Carrier, on the other was the First Light. She was drifting away from the dry dock port slowly, battle scarred and barely moving. She was turning towards the wormhole gate. I could see outer sections of the hull depressurizing in damaged sections so there was less chance they'd cause problems during transit. The only way they could get the First Light moving again was to use core systems. The crew would have to abandon the outer sections completely.

"I should be coming up on your scanners now," I said quietly.

"We see you, Captain Valent. Recovery in progress. Please release your controls to us in order to ensure a safe and efficient docking procedure," said another voice from the Super Carrier. Apparently the task of retrieving me was too menial for Major Hampon. I released the controls and stared at the screens. My mind worked at a frenzied pace, trying to find any way out of Vindyne's clutches, but only after the First Light was clear. "Please relax as we activate the emergency stasis systems. You will not be harmed if you are in stasis when we open the hatch." The forward screen displayed a small tug vessel coming towards my tiny ship. I had forgotten that these shuttles communicated directly with my vacsuit. It was standard for all Freeground escape vessels. I hurriedly tried to break the link between my vacsuit command unit and the shuttle controls. It was too late. I felt the stasis inducing drugs inject right into the side of my neck.

I was near panic. The thought of going back to a white cell, facing torture, endless monotony, and God knows what else was almost too much. My hand hovered over the control that would bring the tiny shuttle back under my control, but then I looked at the First Light. It was getting away. The Super Carrier was still in firing range, but my ship was almost at the wormhole threshold. Ayan, Oz, Jason, Laura, and everyone else who managed to survive our last mission would be arriving in Freeground space some time after entering that wormhole, it was a near certainty. If I didn't cooperate, if I resisted, one salvo from the Super Carrier would kill them all.

I exhaled slowly and relaxed, letting the drugs work their magic.

EPILOGUE

This Instant

I AM NOWHERE, less than half awake, drifting through dark comfort. My lulled existence is interrupted by a sudden, faint flash, and it is as though there are weights attached to my eyelids. I make a herculean effort to open them. It takes me a moment to understand what I'm seeing.

I'm suspended in thick brown fluid matched to my body temperature in a long term stasis tube. Outside I see Major Hampon supervising half a dozen technicians as they work to put me and two other people into stable deep stasis. I can't make out who is in the other two tubes. They're just shapes. I'm not wearing any clothing or apparatus other than a loop around my forehead.

I try to move my arms, raise my hands to remove it, anything to get a chance at an escape, but they won't budge. The drugs in the fluid I'm breathing have already taken effect and soon I'll drift off into a long, deep, coma-like sleep.

I feel helpless, angry, but know that my sacrifice means something. My crew escaped. I stare out at the shape of Major Hampon as he turns and looks at me.

Another figure steps right in front of my semitransparent prison. It's General Collins. He smiles and knocks. I can barely hear it through the thick gel. "It is a pleasure to meet you again! I have plans for you when the company finds what they're looking for, Jonas," he yells. "Sweet dreams!" I watch him leave the room with Major Hampon on his heels like some kind of sickly dog.

I'll beat whatever programming they try to imprint on my mind, and I start by thinking about myself. What makes me who I am, what's important to me. Ayan springs to mind along with the memory of the Pilot's Ball, looking at her in that long white dress and shawl as she gazed out through the observation window, blue and white light dancing across her heart shaped face.

I recall Oz escorting me to my quarters when the *First Light* was still called the *Sunspire*, introducing himself, and later gaining the rank of Commander. Minh-Chu, my long time friend, who set us all on this journey. True, Command would have found us out eventually, but he let the genie out of the bottle early. Whether or not he knew it, the timing of our beginning together as a crew was set by him. I'll miss his enthusiasm, his humour, his friendship.

Jason and Laura spring to mind together, it's as though they made a whole. Laura was always building something, even their relationship was a work in progress, though she probably didn't know it. Jason was always searching for an answer. He had the observational habits of an investigator and the enthusiasm of a natural explorer. They were halves of a whole and they'd be there for Ayan. For that I'm thankful.

My vision blurs more. Lethargy's crushing my consciousness out like a candle under a blanket. I fight harder to think back and find my father and mother, dusty old memories where their faces aren't as sharp in my mind as I would like. I grasp that moment where Father sent me off on my first long voyage, leaving me with nothing more than, "I'm proud of you." He would never have to say more. It was something to hang on to and continually try to live up to.

He would be proud. There is no doubt in my mind. We had taken potential and made something out of it. My mother would approve of Ayan. I wish she were alive to see I had found someone with whom I felt at home.

My thoughts drift back to my crew, who would be well on their way to Freeground space. I hope that the two others I could see in pods are not part of a misguided attempt to rescue me at the last minute. I could see Ayan trying, but Oz would stop her. So would Doc. They would know that this would all mean nothing if crew members were killed or captured coming after me. There would be no way to stop Minh, but he was gone.

Minh-Chu Buu was dead. No one could survive being that close to the churning asteroid field and imploding station. He said something before we left through the wormhole. "A bird does not sing because it has an answer."

It's only the first half of an ancient Chinese proverb. The end is, "It sings because it has a song."

TWELVE MONTHS AND TWELVE DAYS
LATER

I wanted to write a science fiction novel. I had written several unpublished fantasy, horror, and suspense novellas and novels, but never had I stepped into science fiction. It was like the temple in which I worshipped, but wouldn't preach in. After independently publishing an ambitious fantasy title (Fate Cycle Sins of the Past) and a simple romantic novella (Fate Cycle Dead of Winter), and meeting with limited local success, I took a break from writing to try and make a better living.

Years later, as I considered my career path in November and December of 2007, I decided it was time to do something that was truly important to me, something that might just bring real happiness into my life. I made the new-year's resolution to write every day for the entire year. I started a blog to talk about the journey and decided that my first book would be a novella that only a few people would see. It was just going to be practice, back story and a way to experiment with a few concepts I had been developing since I was a child. I had wanted to write science fiction for over twenty years and had been thinking about it the entire time.

So, on January 1, 2008 I started work on Freeground. I didn't think there was a good chance of there being a sequel. In fact, I hadn't planned how the book would end. All I wanted to do with this test novella was to experiment, and boy did I ever. It would be my first piece of long fiction written in the first person, my first science fiction piece. I wanted the experience of reading it to resemble that of watching a television show or movie, and there were specific goals I had to meet by the end of the small book. I had to have a twist, a love interest that developed into a specific scene (see the Pilot's Ball chapter), and I needed to include some kind of fulfillment for the lead character, a clear indication to the reader that he felt like he had found his calling and was ready to start a new, bolder chapter to his life. I also wanted to include personality traits from several friends I had known for a couple of years online, and those of some long-time friends I hadn't seen in a quite some time. I wrote the whole thing in four days, during three of which I had to work at my full time job at the time where I answered the phones for a New York cable company.

I didn't think Freeground was the best thing I'd ever written, and the twist in the middle (see the chapter; Dawn), didn't have the impact I wanted, but it was there, it was necessary, and in a minimalist sense it worked to further the story in a timely way. I didn't want to change it or take it out for fear of slowing the pace down right in the middle of the story, so I didn't. After doing a quick round of editing and contacting several self publishing companies, I decided on a temporary printer so I could share the work in printed form and test it on people I had only just recently met at work and a few friends.

While I waited a month for those books to arrive, I continued to write, as was my goal. I enjoyed writing Freeground so much that I had to write the follow up. The adventures had to continue. I had some plot ideas for the First Light Chronicles Limbo that were huge risks, and instead of being careful and limiting myself so it was easier for me to make things plausible I decided to work harder. I'd keep all the plot risks (there are at least two that come to mind), and do my absolute best to ensure that they were believable and it was easier than I expected. The hardest part of Limbo, as it turned out, was writing the incarceration and interrogation of Jonas and his friends.

Writing about a long, unexciting stay in a small, brightly lit cell turned out to be a kind of mental incarceration unto itself, but the longer I spent on those scenes, the more I understood what Jonas might be thinking. How he might be suffering in not knowing what was happening outside. Getting into the headspace of someone who was gradually losing hope was a challenge I didn't expect and once I had accomplished it I realized the heart of Limbo rested inside that cell and the interrogation room. Jonas Valent needed a chance to grow, to question himself, and I needed villains. Names and faces that could play counter to the needs and desires of our heroes. The Overlord II became an extension of General Collins, and Major Hampon was the scrawny, wormy offspring of that intermarriage.

The grinding corporate machine took on a personality for me, a personality that would become the model for something else. Suddenly Limbo was also about building something, a dark, overhanging villain that the reader and I could start to understand and dislike.

When I was finished I discovered I liked Limbo a great deal. It had been completed in seven days. Editing took longer but that was because I knew there was a good chance that the First Light Chronicles series might be more than practice, more than simple backstory. Someone might actually enjoy reading it almost as much as I loved writing it, but once again I had lost my objectivity and until I could get a second and third opinion, I wouldn't know if I had something good on my hands or just the beginning of an idea, something that needed to be pounded into a mould through successive drafts and editing.

Meanwhile, the copies of Freeground I had ordered arrived. I left a small stack of seven on my desk at work and sold a copy. A couple days later comments from that reader to my co-workers brought on the sale of the rest. People enjoyed it and very nearly demanded the next.

The point wasn't to sell the books, but to get copies to people who weren't afraid to offer an opinion. The books sold, and I got several opinions from people who weren't afraid to share constructive criticism. My writing wasn't up to the quality I wanted, so I wrote a short self-help book for more practice before starting work on the First Light Chronicles Starfree Port and did an extra editing pass on Limbo. I was still having difficulty making the transition from a more technical style of writing to a less jagged style of fiction craft, so I read several highly acclaimed novels from romance, drama, fantasy, and science fiction genres over the next few weeks.

Taking a few days here and there to read several books from

different genres is something I've done several times since I started this journey; it's a habit that'll stick.

As copies of Limbo were on their way to my home from the printers, I started work on the First Light Chronicles Starfree Port. Decisions I had made at the beginning of Limbo ensured that there would only be one or two more First Light Chronicles books. The plotlines were growing, writing in the first person was becoming too confining to tell a more epic story, and I was almost finished writing backstory material.

It was official: the First Light Chronicles were just the foundation for a much larger story, but so much more than just practice. It took fourteen days to write Starfree Port, then the refining began. Half the original draft was set in meeting rooms and quarters. A grand total of one hundred thirty one pages of exposition dialogue clogged the book up terribly. In the second draft I removed an entire plotline, cut eighty pages of dialogue by rewriting every meeting in the book and I added the first aliens to appear in the short series for comedy relief and a little more colour.

The third and final draft of the book was a half rewrite, the replacement of prologue and epilogue and the addition of another scene that was heavy on comedy relief (remember the "did he just say monkey?" bit? I'm sure I laughed harder than anyone who read it and kept it in at the last minute instead of going with my first instinct to cut it for being too silly).

There were a few plot risks in Starfree Port, but the biggest was the ending. I had been dreading and looking forward to writing the last chapter (which was moved to become the epilogue), ever since I started Limbo. It would be the end of the First Light Chronicles. It had to be powerful enough to not only inform the reader that the mini-series was over but it had to explain why. Those last two pages had to serve as a final statement by the main character as well. He was becoming something much more than himself, committing a selfless act of sacrifice and demonstrating that he was no longer a self-centred individual but a man who served a greater purpose.

As I finished Starfree Port, people started reading Limbo, and they were immediately excited to read Starfree Port which didn't arrive in the city until I had left my customer support job. Limbo was already an old novella to me, and I had lived with Starfree Port for over two months, writing, rewriting, editing, and reading just that book. After all that time, what stands out for me most is writing that ending. I was in the perfect state of mind to write the short epilogue that brought the First Light Chronicles to an end; I honestly couldn't see the screen for the tears welling up in my eyes. Months later, Geoff from SomaCow reviewed that book, and when he affirmed that those last two pages conveyed everything I had intended, I literally leapt up out of my seat and did a happy dance that would put most football touchdowns to shame. There's nothing like taking a great big risk and finding out that it paid off.

By the time I started the first Spinward Fringe novella, Resurrection, I had been looking forward to writing it for decades, and with the First Light Chronicles providing a solid foundation, I felt really good about penning a much darker, fully textured story about several characters that were making the best of a less than ideal situation right from the start.

Not long after finishing Resurrection, I began distribution of the First Light Chronicles series in an Omnibus through an eBook distributor in France, MobiPocket. After a few weeks, it was the number one science fiction book on their site and I started to get emails and reviews; the dream of writing for a living drew nearer.

As I write this I'm not quite there yet, but after hearing from people around the world who have enjoyed the First Light Chronicles and Spinward Fringe series books, I know there is a small following of fans that react to what I do honestly through the electronic wonder of the Internet. That following is growing, and I'm grateful to every one of them for following me on the journey that starts with the First Light Chronicles, a series of books that are back story, scene setters, the prequel I'll never have to write.

Now, with a wonderful editor, a couple of proof readers and a year of writing behind me, I've gone through the First Light Chronicles books and refined the language, grammar, science and artistry of the work so it's all it can be. That's what you just read, and after re-reading and reflecting on it, I can still say I'm proud of what we've done.

With that work complete, I can look ahead fully and continue writing science fiction with the Spinward Fringe series. I'll continue taking plot risks, developing new and old characters, and taking each and every reader into confidence as I tell them the stories closest to my heart through the wonderful universe of science fiction, where anything is possible.

Thank you for reading,
Randolph Lalonde